The Red Staircase

*Novels by Gwendoline Butler*

THE RED STAIRCASE
MEADOWSWEET
THE VESEY INHERITANCE
SARSEN PLACE

# The Red Staircase

## Gwendoline Butler

Coward, McCann & Geoghegan

New York

Copyright ©1979 by Gwendoline Butler

**Library of Congress Cataloging in Publication Data**

Butler, Gwendoline.
  The red staircase.

  I. Title.
PZ4.B9856Re     1979     [PR6052.U813]     823'.9'14     78-3166

ISBN 0-698-10981-3

Printed in the United States of America

# Chapter One

The wind was blowing in my face, a cold wind blowing across the water of the Baltic, to where I stood on the deck of the *John Evelyn*. The wind seemed to go right through my clothes. Ahead I could see the docks and quays of St. Petersburg. It was May, we were the first ship into the Gulf of Finland since the winter ice had melted. The wind was cold but the long, light summer days of the north were approaching. Soon there would be no night, only endless, pale day. I knew all about it from my reading, although I had never been to Russia before, hardly ever out of my native Scotland. The prospect frightened me a little more than I had admitted. But it was upon me now. Even now the trunks were being piled on deck ready for arrival, and I could see my own box, black leather with my name on it in white: The Honble. Rose Gowrie.

Tentatively I looked up at the man standing beside me, Edward Lacey, late of His Majesty's Scots Guards. We were already on strained terms. I knew what lay between us: the shattered, bloody body of a boy lay between. I had seen the look in his face as I knelt beside the boy on the Surrey docks and knew what it meant. I had summoned up such looks before. Edward Lacey neither liked nor trusted me, but his task was nearly over. Soon he would hand me over to the Countess Denisov, and could then bow out of my life.

I hated men, anyway. *"Pour cause,"* as my French governess used to say. Edward Lacey's cool English voice irritated me. Not his fault. I dare say my own had a Scottish burr. Years and years later, across a crowded room, I heard Prince Serge Obolensky say that as a result of having learnt English from a much loved Scots governess, he and his brothers spoke like "some Russian branch of a Highland clan, if you can imagine such a thing," and I wanted to shout out "But there is, there is, and we Gowries are it."

Edward Lacey looked at me. "Nearly there." Polite as always, but stiff, he seemed to me colder than the wind itself.

We had boarded the small cargo ship, the *John Evelyn*, at London docks, going out on the evening tide.

The captain bowed as he passed us on the deck. I was a passenger of special quality on the *John Evelyn* because I had been seen off by no less a person than Prince Michael Melikov. To my surprise he was waiting at the Surrey docks as I arrived in a cab from the railway station after my long overnight journey from Scotland. He was wearing a deep violet velvet overcoat. I never saw a man wear coloured velvet before, but on him it looked sombre and rich and yet correct.

He had bowed to us and spoken in his deep, sweet voice: "Here I am to see you off, Miss Gowrie. You did not think you had said good-bye to me? No, I could never excuse myself to those good ladies, your cousins, when we next met in St. Petersburg, if I did not see you safely aboard."

Behind his friendly brown eyes was nothing, he had no real feeling for me. I sensed it without knowing why.

"I'm looking forward to meeting them. I never have, you know. I believe they came once to see us at Jordansjoy, but it was years ago, when my parents were not long married and I was only just born. They were old then." And must be older now by my twenty years. It was now 1912. "Our Russian cousins, we call them, but they are as Scots as I am in *blood*, although four generations of Gowries have lived in St. Petersburg now." I was talking nervously, but there was something about Prince Michael's empty eyes that alarmed me. He knew it, too.

Edward Lacey arrived in a cab at that point. The two men nodded to each other, from which I concluded they knew each other slightly, as was possible in London society then which, although in size growing every year, was still small enough for everyone in it to know everyone else. Even I, small and insignificant in it as I was, could be "placed," to use the idiom then current. If you couldn't be "placed," then socially you did not exist. I could be "placed" because my family, impoverished as it was, had an ancient pedigree and a heraldry recognized by the Lord Lyon King of Arms in Edinburgh. None of which gave me even a dress allowance.

As I attended to my luggage, I saw Prince Michael Melikov look at my skirt, made at home, I may say, by my own hands and with the help of Tibby, my old nurse. The skirt *was* short, you could almost see my ankle, but although I am a Scot and have not lived in London, I have an eye for fashion, and we took all the fashion papers back in Jordansjoy. Skirts that year were short and straight and very tight, quite difficult to walk in, and I approached the gangway of the *John Evelyn* with circumspection. It's a knack, I dare say, to walk well when it feels as though your knees are bound together, and I shall master it in the end.

The two men were standing side by side. How different they looked: the Prince tall and elegant, but with the withdrawn, inward expression of a man used to books and libraries, and Edward Lacey, almost as tall but broader of shoulder, with the look of the open air about him, active and energetic; the one as unmistakably Russian as the other was English.

They were both watching me. The notion struck me and

would not be dismissed. I felt as if they were *studying* me. Politely, of course, but with intent. And not for my looks, either. I know what that sort of look is like: I know what it is to be admired. At the memory of some special glances I had once treasured, my spirits plummeted. I gritted my teeth, and pushed emotion away; I would not be bitter.

The dockside was very busy, many craft were taking advantage of the high tide to load. A string of lighters and barges was passing down the river towards the estuary. Its tug gave a melancholy hoot as it went, and another ship answered, part of the perpetual conversation of the river. It was evening, a fine night in early summer. The smells of the summer mingled with the smells of oil and dust in the Surrey docks, and with the strong odour of horse. A dray horse, which had brought a load of packing-cases to the side of the *John Evelyn* to be hauled aboard, was pawing the cobbles. There was a young lad sitting on the dray, ostensibly minding the horse, watching the scene and calling out jokes and ribaldry to the stevedores and dockers labouring around him. He had a tin whistle stuck in his waist and presently he started to play a tune. A gay little rag-tune: I shall never forget it. I think it was called "Irene," a name itself which was to mean much to me. Strange that name coming then; what an uncanny trick life has of striking a note that it means to repeat.

The boy leapt down from his seat on the dray, and began to dance as he whistled, scuffling his shoes about in the dust. His mates began to sing a few words, not tunefully but with great enjoyment. A man bearing a great box on his back began to move his hips to the tune, others took up the movement.

"Oh, these Cockneys," said Prince Michael, "they know how to enjoy themselves. Great is their poverty, and yet they can sing. Our peasants are the same."

His comment was heard and picked up, the pity in it resented.

"Here, you mind your words, old Russki," called one. "We

get a day's pay. It's beef we 'as for our dinner. And we don't fear the lash."

"Oh, the bull-dog breed," I heard Edward Lacey mutter. "They look poor enough to me."

I thought they looked grubby, but by no means under-nourished; I believed it about the beef. "I am enjoying the dancing. I should quite like to join in. Will you rag-time with me, Major Lacey? I know how."

Someone had introduced a mouth-organ and the gaiety was infectious. "Come on, miss," called the whistler. " 'Ave a go."

I saw Major Lacey begin to stretch out his hand towards me as if he meant to take me at my word and move me into the dance. He did not hate me then at all events.

The loading of the *John Evelyn* had continued all this while, the crew not quite drawn into the scene on the docks, but not untouched by it either, calling out and whistling in tune as they passed close.

The last two of the great boxes, full of machinery as far as I could judge, were being hoisted from dockside to ship, swung up and aloft. Then between my holding out my hand to Major Lacey and his motion of acceptance, something went wrong with the hoist, a great crate swung out, slipped from its hook and fell. It landed upon the whistler.

One moment all had been life, movement and music, the next we were all frozen into a fresco of horror. Then the scene broke, hands pulled the crate away, and dragged the boy out. The same hands turned him tenderly upon his back, so that he lay there, face staring up at the sky. There was blood on the dust. He was moaning; I could hear him from where I stood.

I hurried below to him. Behind me I was conscious of men hurrying off to get a doctor and to summon an ambulance.

"Oh, God, why isn't he unconscious? Why didn't it knock him out?" It was Major Lacey's voice. Another voice was threaded through his: the Prince muttering in Russian.

I knelt by the boy. Great beads of sweat were rolling from

his forehead; I took a handkerchief and gently wiped them away. His eyes moved to look at me, but with every tortured breath a groan ripped through his mouth.

Someone took my arm, I think it was Major Lacey, and tried to draw me away; I took no notice. All my attention was focussed on the boy. If I could help him, I would know it. I closed my eyes. His chest was crushed, the rib cage had fractured, puncturing the lungs.

"Please come away, Miss Gowrie." It was the Major still. "There's nothing you can do. Help is coming."

"I always try," I said dreamily. "I have to."

"Of course, of course, but come away."

I took the boy's hands in mine; his were deadly cold and very heavy. My own, as usual, felt weightless as if they no longer were attached to me. Then his hands became light and mine heavy. He stopped moaning.

I smiled at him and after a moment he gave a faint smile back. We did not speak.

Slowly I withdrew my hands and stood up.

"Better now," said the boy.

"Yes." The whistle, miraculously uncrushed, was by his side. I picked it up and put it in his hand. As I turned round I saw Edward Lacey's expression.

An ambulance arrived then, and a young doctor jumped out. He gave the injured boy a quick, surprised look, and then occupied himself with a swift examination before supervising his transfer to the ambulance. "Brave boy," he said, in a puzzled way.

At last I went aboard the *John Evelyn*. The light was fading fast. I was unsurprised to find that over an hour had passed. I remember Prince Michael's smile as he finally went away, which accentuated rather than took away the emptiness of his eyes. He smiled, not for me or with me, but because of me; I was quite sure of it.

After I had unpacked, I went on deck again to watch the Thames-side slipping past. We had sailed almost immediately on our coming aboard. My cabin was small, but I had it to myself. I arranged my clothes, put out my silver-backed hair-brushes that had belonged to my mother, and around them placed the photographs of Grizel and young Alec, old Tibby Mackenzie, and my brother Robin, gone from us five years past. My pantheon, as naughty Alec calls them. Four faces where there had once been five. One god had gone from my pantheon. Again, I tried to repress bitterness, but the taste of it remained in my mouth even as I stood on deck and watched the lights of London and her satellite suburbs, Greenwich, Woolwich, disappear into the dark. The water was growing rougher as we felt the pull of the open sea.

I had made myself a hooded cloak of thick plaid and lined the hood with fur from an old tippet handed down in my family for generations and at last consigned to me. "Bring warm clothes," my old Russian cousins had advised. I pushed back the hood and let the soft fur fall across my shoulders in unaccustomed opulence, and I wondered what the future held in store for me. I suppose every girl wonders this, but I had special cause.

Edward Lacey came up behind me. I recognized him by the smell of Turkish tobacco and Harris tweed that I had already identified as peculiarly his own. Then he moved to my side. He took out his pipe.

"Do you mind if I light up, Miss Gowrie?"

"Oh, no, please do. I enjoy the smell." I had smoked a cigarette myself once, but I did not tell him; he found me shocking and puzzling enough already.

He struck a Swan Vesta, and the tobacco smouldered fragrantly. He took a puff or two, then the pipe went out. Pipes always do. But he did not relight it. Instead he stood there looking into the murky river.

"It was bad about that boy: a great pity." He made show of lighting up his pipe. "I was puzzled by what he said: better, that's what he said. But how on earth could he be with that great wound in his chest?"

"He will die, I think," I said slowly. "He may be dead now."

"But he said he felt better."

I shrugged.

"As you held his hands, he felt better; I myself saw the muscles of his face relax. I have seen wounded men before and know how they look in their agony. The pain was gone."

"I think perhaps when you are as close to death as he was the pain ceases," I said carefully. "I believe that must be how it was."

"You cannot explain it otherwise?"

"I can't explain it any other way," I said awkwardly.

"Is that all you have to say? It was a strange moment, you know."

"It was nature," I said. "It can be merciful."

"And it can also be cruel," he said with abruptness. "It is much more usual for it to be cruel in my experience."

Well, I knew all about natural cruelty, having had an experience of my own in that line. I thought I knew as much as he did about that.

I kept silent; I was aware he was studying my face. "So it is true what I had heard," he said at last. "I would never have believed it. Tell me, did you arrange that episode on the dock, or did the gods conspire to support you? The Prince was convinced, you know."

"I don't know what you mean."

"I must warn you that you have a sceptic in me."

"Major Lacey!"

"I hope you know what you are doing, that's all."

"Indeed I do, Major Lacey," I spoke with dignity, I hoped, but my cheeks burned. "I am going out to St. Petersburg to be a companion to a young lady of noble family."

"Yes."

"My cousins, the Misses Gowrie, got me the post. The pay is good. I am poor, Major Lacey, something you probably know nothing about, and I need the money." I needed desperately to get away from my home, but no need to tell him that fact. It was my own private wound.

"I think you are a dangerous young lady, Miss Gowrie," said Edward Lacey. "Good or bad, I can hardly tell." He seemed shaken out of his usual calm.

Angry tears were in my eyes, I struggled to control myself, but my voice shook.

"I don't know why I should be insulted in this way," I said.

"If you don't, then I do not. Good night, Miss Gowrie, good night to you."

With tears of fury blinding me, I hammered on the iron deck rails till my hands ached. "Beastly, beastly man!" I cried. "Stupid and obtuse like all of them. I hate him. I hate all men."

In Jordansjoy, the archaic, crumbling home of my ancestors, they would have understood my rage.

Till yesterday there were three of us at home still: I, Rose Gowrie, the eldest child, my sister Grizel and young Alec. Robin, our brother, our pride, went to India with his regiment five years ago. He was the bravest and best of us all. And then he died, killed in a small incident on the border with Afghanistan that no one ever heard of again but was the death of him.

Jordansjoy has seen many tragedies in its many hundreds of years of history, but Robin's was one of the sharpest.

The neighbours were tactful and left us alone. Grizel and Alec and I drew in on ourselves, alone with old Tibby, who has been nurse, housekeeper and governess all rolled into one to us since our parents died. She was our great support, unsentimental and forthright, quite devoid of self-pity (although Robin had been her nursling) and not allowing us to repine either.

"Forbye, you're young," she said stoutly, "with your lives all before you."

Jordansjoy was the shell of a once great house. The castle was in ruins, a romantic and beautiful wreck which had inspired Sir Walter Scott to a well known effusion. The grand mansion erected by an early Gowrie in 1790 and decorated in the finest neo-Hellenistic taste of the period had proved impossible to heat or live in, especially as the family fortunes fell away. For the last generation the Gowries had lived in

eight or nine rooms in the stable wing, which was in fact a remarkably beautiful quadrangle of stone buildings, our ancestor having demanded a high standard of living for his
horses. We, of course, kept none. Behind the shuttered windows of the mansion lay rooms of mouldering hangings and
worm-eaten furniture, anything of any value having been
sold long since.

"Poor, but proud, that's the Gowries," announced Grizel,
"but we shall marry well, because we are pretty and have
pleasant voices."

"Ach, the vanity of you," said Tibby. "Pride goes before a
fall, you know. Stay still, will you, while I mend this great
rent in your skirt; you're a sight to see. How came you to do
it?"

"Climbing over a hedge after Bothwell." Bothwell was our
dog, a rangy great beast of mixed ancestry, but ferocious
fighting powers, hence his name. "Dear Bothy then," and she
threw her arms round his powerful neck, he giving her lol-
loping great licks, for he was a sentimental beast. "He was
stuck in a snare."

"He shouldn't go hunting then," said Tibby sharply. "Nor
you go climbing after him, a great girl of seventeen. Is that
the way to get a fine husband?"

"It might be," rejoined Grizel with a giggle. "I saw Kitty
Murray jump over a fence after Lord Mornington and she
married him a month later."

"She was on a horse, Grizel," I said sharply. "Naturally she
jumped."

"Ach, you've got no sense of humour since you got engaged," said Grizel. "I suppose Patrick doesn't like you to
laugh."

"Patrick Graham's a fine young man," said Tibby, "and a
good soldier, everyone says so."

"He's awfu' dull," said Alec.

"That's just because he won't talk to you," I said sharply.
"Why should he talk to a little boy? I don't find him dull."

"And if he's not dull, he's mad then," said Alec. "He's got

an awfu' temper on him. What a wax he was in the other day
when Bothwell and I . . ."

"Ah, leave her be," interrupted Grizel. "She's in love with
him."

"Just as well I am, since I'm to be married to him in a
month."

The Grahams were our neighbours at Jordansjoy, living in
the economical, frugal way that a large family and an army
pension impose on a widow of good family and small income.

I had known Patrick as a boy, but then he had been away
for years with his regiment, first abroad and latterly in London. When the regiment came home to Edinburgh there was
a ball given at Holyrood House. Old Lady Macmaster introduced Patrick: we had the supper dance together, and then
all the dances after, and by the end of the evening I, at least,
was in love. With Patrick it took a little longer. Or so I
thought.

But he told me otherwise one day, early in our engagement, on the occasion of one happy visit to Jordansjoy.

"I loved you the minute I saw you."

"Oh?" I raised my eyebrows sceptically. "At the dance? If
you were not going away to London this minute I would call
you a liar." I held his hand tight. "It's been a lovely visit," I
sighed, "but hardly ever alone."

We were walking together to the railway station. The
countryside was very quiet and still in the blue dusk. Patrick
began to hum quietly to himself as he did when he was happy. I recognized the song; a poem of Robert Burns set to music: "My love is like a red, red rose."

"We're alone now." He stopped and drew me to him and
kissed me. It was a kiss of a different quality from any we had
ever before exchanged, and yet I had not thought us unlov-
ing. I found myself breathless, gasping, with my heart
thumping.

"I shall remember this time," I said.

"I'll see you do," and he bent to kiss me again.

It was our first such moment.

"I'll be back next month for a brief visit," he promised.

And he did come back, and it was a lovely, memorable visit.

Now I was waiting for him again.

My wedding-clothes were almost ready, my wedding-gown being made in Edinburgh and the rest at home by me. I had sold my mother's pearls to pay for my trousseau, using half the proceeds and giving half to Grizel, because, after all, she too would have a wedding one day.

"He's coming this evening, isn't he?" asked Tibby.

I nodded: she had asked me twice already, an unusual sign of anxiety in Tibby. "Yes, we are going to see the house he has taken in George Street." It was in one of the finest parts of Edinburgh, and while his regiment was stationed there we would live in it.

For answer she drummed on the table with her fingers.

"George Street?" This was from Grizel. "Very smart. How elegant you will be."

"Patrick has to think of his future," I said, and I said it with a sigh. The appearance of things, the admiration of his neighbours counted with Patrick. His extravagance worried me. I knew he spent more than he had, and I suspected he had gambling debts. But he had promised me to forswear cards. The Gowries had particular reason to fear the card-table since a succession of gambling, drinking generations had impoverished us.

"So his mother says every time I see her," observed Tibby dryly. "Ach, she's a *thin*, wee woman, is Mrs. Graham, with a miserable way to her. I'm sorry to say it of your mother-in-law-to-be, Rose."

"I know what she's like," I said, and indeed I did, having had more than one brush of my own with that cheerless lady.

"Mother sent her love and all that," said Patrick that evening, as he let us into the empty house in George Street.

I nodded in acceptance. She didn't quite like to throw me over. The Honourable Rose Gowrie still counted for something, with her brother Alec a very young but undeniable peer.

Together we made a low-spirited tour of our future home; the house seemed chill and unwelcoming. "Of course, it will be better when we are living in it," I cried, trying to drive away the cold.

But the cold seemed to have crept into Patrick too; he seemed preoccupied and quiet. In every relationship they say there is one who loves and one who allows himself to be loved. I knew I loved Patrick more than he loved me. I wished that I did not love him so much; I could see the dangers. But there it was, he had only to turn his head or move his hand in a particular way he had for me to feel a pang of love. I did my best to hide it, but I expect he knew; he was not unworldly, my Patrick.

I prattled on through our tour of the house, ignoring Patrick's unease, and giving a good imitation of a young woman happily in love and soon to be married.

"Good-bye," Patrick kissed my cheek. "I'll be on leave next week. And will come over to Jordansjoy."

For a moment I let myself hold on to his hand. "Till next week: I shall have my wedding gown then. Not that you are to see it, of course, but it will be delivered. And I shall have all sorts of last-minute questions you must settle about the wedding party, and our wedding trip. So mind you are ready."

"Yes, we must discuss the wedding." Another brief embrace and he was gone.

I went home to a headache, bed and a sleepless night. Grizel was awake and called out to me: "Come and gossip with me, love." But I pretended I was tired and did not go in. I dared not face her sharp eyes.

But they all of them knew about it soon. At our next meeting, which was in our parlour, I saw Patrick had something in his hand when he arrived: a little packet, neatly done up in fresh, brown paper. I thought it might be a little present for me. Patrick did sometimes give me presents, a good book or a leather note-book for my accounts, that sort of thing, and now was the time for presents if there ever was, these weeks before our marriage. I couldn't expect much after we were married. A brooch with a white river pearl from Perth, perhaps, if I had the good luck to bear him a son.

He did not look in a present-giving mood; he was wearing his dark town suit and carrying lavender gloves. In fact, the wicked Alec, as he passed him in the door, was heard to mutter, "The mute at the funeral." There had never been any love lost between Patrick and Alec, since Patrick had recommended that Alec, that freedom-lover, be sent away to Eton since "only a top flight public school could whip him into shape."

Our parlour at Jordansjoy had one long window which we keep filled with sweet geraniums. Patrick stood with his back to it, so that he was in silhouette and I could hardly see his face.

He could see mine, though, and I suppose it looked foolishly young and gay.

"The wedding flowers are chosen," I began. "Do you want to know about them? Heather and roses for my bouquet, of course."

But he interrupted me, saying, his voice a tone higher than usual and abrupt, "Look here, Rose, the wedding will have to be put off. Postponed."

I stared, perhaps I said something, I don't remember, it can have been nothing coherent.

"It can't go ahead next week. You can put what explanation about you like. Blame it all on me. It *is* my fault."

"I don't understand."

"I'm transferring to the part of the regiment that's going off to India. It's no place for a woman. It's a bachelor's job."

"I wouldn't mind India. I'd like it."

"No, it's no good, it wouldn't do, not for me, nor for you. It would be a wretched business, Rosie. Besides, I'm off within the week."

"*Already?*" I remember that cry. Then I stopped. "But why? What have I done? That you don't love me is clear, but why treat me in this abominable way?" I choked back my tears.

"I'm not the right husband for you. Our marriage would be a mistake." He handed me the parcel. "Here are your letters, and the book you gave me."

I threw them on the floor in a fury, and for the first time in the interview felt bitter.

"Please, Rose," he said, "I have thought about it very carefully. It is in your interest and mine."

"I suppose it's your mother," I said bitterly.

"No, not Mother, although she has been worried."

"Oh, *has* she?"

I sat down; my fury ebbing away had left my legs curiously weak. I suppose he thought I was coming round.

"Well, you know, Rose, there are things  . . ." He didn't finish.

"So there has been talk about me?"

"No, not exactly talk, everyone knows you are a thoroughly good girl, but it seems you have the capacity, that is, you have the power, I mean you can  . . ." He had come to a miserable stop.

"And that is why?" I knew what he must mean.

"No, not exactly." He quailed before the fury of my eyes, but he stood his ground—I give him that. When he had made up his mind to do a thing, Patrick did it. And after all, he had his mother behind him. "No, no, the fault is all mine: I'm not good enough for you." He looked at me. "Forgive me, Rosie?"

He had given me an antique rose diamond ring, and I suppose he took it with him, for I never saw it again. I remember nothing of the circumstances of its handing over.

Tibby says she came in and saw me standing staring out of the window, and that I turned to her with tearless eyes and said, "He's gone, Tibby. Gone for good."

I don't remember this either, but I remember crying with

my head in Tibby's lap, with Grizel raging in the background.

Then I raised my head. "And you know, Tibby, I think it is partly because of —" I swallowed hard. "You know what I mean? He has heard about the child at Moriston Grange, and perhaps about the dog."

"Oh, the wretch," muttered Tibby, smoothing my hair.

"And it's not my fault, Tibby. I don't understand, don't even know how it happens. No one does."

"Poor love, poor love."

When I was thirteen, I held a bird in my hand that the cat had clawed at; it was torn and bleeding. "It will die, poor thing." But presently it moved its wings and flew away. "The warmth of my hands took the pain away," I said to Tibby. I was much gratified.

Tibby gave me a strange look, but said nothing. That was the first time that I remember. Only then, later, there was the stray dog with the broken leg. I thought nothing of it, but the child from Moriston Grange was brought to me, so I suppose there had been talk. I tried to send the child away.

"I'm embarrassed, Tibby. I would rather not. Please ask them to go away." I hung my head, not even wanting to meet her eyes.

"Poor love, you shouldn't be pushed. But he has such a lump on his knee, and the doctors can do nothing till the fever goes down. It's the pain, you see." In spite of herself, her eyes were pleading. "Just one little touch, love, maybe not even that." And I heard her mutter, "God forgive me" under her breath.

After that episode I didn't struggle so much inside myself. But I never admitted anything to the outside world. It was tacit that I had this gift, which I neither liked nor understood. I was a freak. Who wants to be a freak?

We glossed over the breaking off of my engagement to Alec: I don't think he fully understood what had happened. In any case, he was still young enough for the adult world to be inexplicable to him and its motives something he need not bother to comprehend. Since he'd never liked Patrick he was quite glad to see him go, and with him all threat of banishment to a "foreign" school. ("Foreign" for Alec began at the Border.)

So that when he came home with the tale he told, the impact was all the harder.

In all innocence, he came in from play, sat himself down at the tea table and announced with satisfaction: "Well, he's away, then."

I was pouring the tea, Tibby was cutting bread. "Who?" I asked, not really attending.

"That Patrick." He took a slice of bread and butter and devoured it rapidly. "Him."

"Don't talk with your mouth full, Master Alec." He was only Master Alec to Tibby when she was cross. "Mind your manners, please. And where has he gone?"

"I *must* talk with my mouth full if you ask questions," said Alec, continuing his eating. "I must answer: that is manners. He's away to India," and his hand reached out for another slice. "You never told me that." He looked at me accusingly.

I was silent.

"It was none of your business," said Tibby.

"And he's not off before time, his sister Jeannie says, for there were bills falling around him like snow. We were playing marbles."

"And has he left the bills behind him then?" said Grizel in an acid tone.

"Every penny cleared, Jeannie says." Alec turned his attention to the scones and honey. "Praise be to God."

"Money from heaven then, I suppose," observed Grizel. "For I never knew the Grahams had a rich uncle."

"Ach, no, he was paid." Alec was all man of the world.

There was a moment of complete silence.

"Paid?" It was my voice I heard.

"Yes, to go away," continued Alec, through his tea.

"Well, that's an odd thing," observed Tibby in a temperate voice. "And how much did they pay him?"

"Three thousand pounds, Jeannie says," went on Alec, quite oblivious of the effect he was having. "Or it might have been more, she's not quite sure. She couldn't hear very well."

"Why not? How was she hearing them?"

"Through the crack in the door. You do not suppose they were telling her?" asked Alec with fine scorn. He looked up, and for the first time he seemed to take in the audience he had. "What are you all staring at me like that for?"

"You may be jumping to the wrong conclusion," said Tibby, giving me a straight took over Alec's head. "It may not be at all what it seems."

"I'm sure of it. Don't look at me like that, Tibby, I know I was right: it was worth three thousands to Patrick to break his engagement with me. So now I know my price. Three thousand pounds, give or take a few more pounds that Jeannie could not precisely hear."

"But whoever was it that paid him? And why?" asked Grizel wonderingly.


Events then followed with a naturalness that made acceptance of them inevitable.

I was wretched at Jordansjoy, an object of interest to all the neighbourhood as the girl who had been jilted. Very nearly on the steps of the altar, too. Former generations of Gowries had been the focus for gossip and hints of scandal, and now I had revived the fire with my shame. For it was shame of a sort. Even those who took my part assumed it was my own fault that "put off" Patrick Graham, although he had, of course, "behaved disgracefully." I kept my head high, but it was a bad time.

When the letter came from our Russian connections, it seemed to contain an answer to prayer.

About eighty years earlier a Gowrie had gone to St. Petersburg as a merchant and banker, had prospered and settled there. His family stayed on, and the next generation, until by now they were as much Russian as Scottish, except in blood, because they always married among the large Anglo-Scottish community in the capital. Not all of them were rich and the elderly Misses Gowrie, whom we called our cousins, supplemented their income by teaching English to the sons and daughters of wealthy Russian families. They also acted as a sort of unofficial employment bureau for governesses. English governesses were greatly esteemed and well paid in Russia.

Through Miss Emma Gowrie came the invitation for me to go to St. Petersburg to act as companion to the young daughter of the Countess Dolly Denisov. Young Russian girls of nobility are never allowed to go anywhere without a companion, it seemed.

"It's a good offer," said Tibby, raising her eyes from the letter. "They don't ask much from you except English conversation and companionship, and they pay well."

"Of course the girl may be a horror."

"She sounds nice; sixteen, speaks a bit of English already, likes animals. And what a pretty face!"

I picked up the photograph that had come with the letter.

"Yes, charming little face, isn't it? I don't suppose she's as innocent as she looks. Oh, yes, I'll go, Tibby. I think I'd go anywhere to get away."

"You'd be rash to turn it down, I'll say that." She pursed up her lips. "The letter says that if you take passage on the *John Evelyn,* leaving the Surrey docks on May second, you may have the support of a Major Lacey who is travelling out to see his sister. They have Russian friends in London, too, whom they name." She shook her head. "They have planned ahead. You are much wanted to go."

"But you'd rather I didn't?"

"No, I don't say that."

Grizel threw her arms round me. "Oh, Tibby's an old cautious puss, you know she is. Go, Rose, go. It's the door to your future, I know it is."

A door to my future? It was very nearly the door to my death.


I came back to the present to hear Edward Lacey's voice again.

"Peter the Great built St. Petersburg because he wanted a door on the world," he was saying.

"Hadn't he got one, then?"

"The Western world. Moscow was in many ways an Oriental capital. He wanted to change all that. He did, too. But I think Russia has been paying the price for it ever since. What a country."

"You have been here before, of course?"

"Yes, I have interests here. And then my sister is married to a Russian. She expects a child this autumn. I shall hope to introduce you, Miss Gowrie, when she's out and about again."

"Oh, thank you." Perhaps he didn't dislike me as much as I had thought. "Yes, I should like that. I shall know so few people apart from my cousins and the Denisovs."

"That will soon change," he predicted briskly. "The Russians are an endlessly sociable people. The Denisovs will take you around. Dolly Denisov lives for the world."

"Ariadne is only sixteen," I said.

"Never mind, you won't be cloistered." He had his eyes screwed up, staring at the quay. "There's the Denisov motor car already waiting for you, I see."

"A motor car?"

"Yes." He sounded amused. "Did you expect a sledge? It is summer and there are very few motor cars in St. Petersburg, but of course Dolly Denisov has one." He held out his hand. "Good-bye for the time being, Miss Gowrie."

He hadn't spoken to me often on the voyage, and then only with formal politeness. An irritable imp inside me made me determined to make him speak out. Nor were my motives entirely frivolous. Except for my cousins he was my only bridge with home things. I must make it as solid as I could. Make him like me, or if I couldn't do that, make sure I liked him.

"I wonder if I shall be happy in Russia," I said with a sigh, looking up at him from under my lashes. If he had a heart in him at all he must reassure me, I thought.

He put out a hand towards me. For a moment I thought that, after all, he was the sort of man who will try to get a woman alone. I had already met one of that sort on board: the Captain, who had tried to fondle me under the guise of tracing out our route on the map. Then I saw that he was just drawing me away from an open trap-door in the deck, through which seamen were transporting great wooden boxes, marked Made in Birmingham.

"That depends on you," he said, thus turning the problem neatly back towards me. Not a dash of sentiment, I thought, and more than a suspicion of cleverness.

"On me?" I raised my eyebrows.

"Yes. If you are the sort of girl who can accept it for what it is, a country entirely itself, and not be continually comparing it with what you know at home, then you will be happy. Or on the way to it."

"I think I can manage that."

"And learn the language. The real Russia is hidden, otherwise."

"I already know a little Russian," I said thoughtfully. "Our local schoolmaster used to read Chekhov and Turgenev with me. He had learnt the language from his mother, who went out as a governess."

"And you must manage not to fall in love," he said.

"I shall not fall in love. I can promise you that."

He gave a half-smile. "Then you are the first woman I have ever met who could give that promise."

I cannot fall in love, I thought, because I am in love now. In love and hating at the same time. With Patrick.

"But then, after all, what does it matter?" he said. "You might be the better for it. I've been in love many a time and got over it."

"I don't believe in *that* sort of love," I said, somewhat primly, I suppose. "I don't call it love."

"Oh, you believe in the undying, eternal sort of love, do you? Well, I don't." But he said it with a forthright good humour that I could not but like.

Well, I've learnt something about you, I thought. You are no romantic.

"Are you going to be in Russia long?" I asked.

"I have a year's leave from my regiment to visit my sister and travel about the world. After that," and he shrugged.

"Will you ever go back to the Army after that?" I wondered if he knew Patrick. He might know his name, I thought, or have heard of him.

"Who knows? It depends what happens in the world. There are many ways of serving one's country."

"Being a soldier must be one of the noblest," I said.

"Oh, you think so, do you? But war is war you know, and is very often not noble at all. No, not a modern war," he said, looking seawards and away from the fast approaching city of St. Petersburg. "No, not noble at all. Say, rather, squalid and terrible."

"Oh, but surely," I began, "does not war purify?"

"I shall quarrel with you if you start on those lines," he said sharply. "And I do not wish to quarrel with you. I have spent most of this journey *not* quarrelling with you."

"What?" I stepped back in amazement. "You have hardly spoken to me."

"And that's why. Had I spoken, I would have said, 'Go home at once, young woman, go back to where you came from.' "

"Then we should have quarrelled."

"Exactly."

"And now you *have* said it."

"So I have, and if we are not quarrelling, we are close to it.

But I won't do it." He held out his hand. "We shall meet later in St. Petersburg, I'm sure."

I stood there, puzzled and disconcerted. In the end I decided that it was what he had seen of my gift in operation on the London docks that made him dislike me. And yet he did not seem like a man whom unconventionality would bother. But he had shown me something of himself. I had got a great impression of integrity.

I ought to have run after him and said, Why, why do you feel like this just because I tried to help an injured boy? But I didn't move; I could not bear to speak about it.

I watched his tall, erect figure disappear down the gangway. I had not found Edward Lacey easy to know, but with his going went my last link with home.

Now I was Rose Gowrie, alone, ready for her great adventure. With a beating heart, I turned my face to meet the Denisovs. The Denisovs and Russia.


No one had told me about the May nights, how white they were, and how intense, and how they would affect me. I kept thinking of Patrick; I had come to Russia to forget him, and he was all I could think about. These long, sleepless nights were one of the phenomena of my first weeks in St. Petersburg. There were others. One was the cold. Heaven knows Scotland in May is often cold enough, but I was not prepared for the cold wind of Russia that made me huddle in my clothes. But they told me it would be warm enough soon, and then I should see. Everyone in the Denisov household seemed to take a delight in offering me the contradictions of St. Petersburg, as if it had all been specially constructed to amuse me. It was my first introduction to one aspect of the Russian character: its capacity to charm. At the beginning (and indeed for a long time after) Dolly Denisov seemed to me charm personified. Partly it was her voice, delicate, light and sweet.

"You speak such excellent English yourself, madame, that

I wonder you need me to speak to your daughter." I turned away from the window from which I was studying the St. Petersburg street scene, which never ceased to fascinate me.

"Ah, but poor Ariadne, she needs your company. She must be gay, happy. I love her to be happy. Besides, I cannot be with her all the time." A slight pout here, as of one sacrificed already too much to maternal duty.

But I knew already that Dolly Denisov had other amusements besides motherhood: her appearance, for one thing. Never had I seen such dresses and such a profusion of jewels. Perhaps she saw my smile. "Ah, it's no joke, Miss Gowrie, being a wife at eighteen and a widow with a daughter at twenty."

"And such a daughter," said Ariadne, giving her mother a loving pat. "Sixteen years you have had of it, Mamma."

"But luckily the English nation has been specially created to provide us poor Russians with the governesses we need," laughed Madame Denisov, "and thus to lighten my burden."

English or Scottish, it was all one to her.

A joke, of course, but partly meant. You got a new slant on the Anglo-Saxon people and the great British Empire in Russia: we were not, as I had supposed, the nation of shopkeepers and diplomats and colonizers, but a race of trustworthy governesses.

The Denisov motor car had duly met me off the *John Evelyn,* as Edward Lacey's sharp eyes had observed it would do. The motor car showed me the Denisovs' mettle: it was of surpassing elegance, the body-work of maroon with a sort of basket-work corset enclosing it; the metal-work looked like well-polished silver and the upholstery was lavender-blue watered silk. Did I forget to say that it was perfumed? As I stepped inside, a sweet waft of rose and iris floated towards me, nicely mixed with the smell of Russian cigarette smoke. I discovered afterwards Dolly Denisov smoked incessantly, a long, diamond-studded cigarette holder always between her fingers. Not that Madame Denisov was there herself at the quay, of course. She was out at one of her numerous engagements and, indeed, I did not see my employer for the first twenty-four hours after my arrival. But Ariadne, my dear pupil, was there. A spoilt face, I thought quickly, but when I took in her friendly bright eyes and her gentle smile, I saw she had her own beauty.

She held out her hands in welcome. "I am so glad to see you, Miss Gowrie. I have been excitedly looking forward to today." Already she spoke excellent English. I should have little to do on that score. At once she sensed my thought, demonstrating that quick intelligence I was to know so well.

"I speak English all the time with Mamma. Naturally."

"Naturally?"

"Here one speaks either French or English, and Mamma says she likes French clothes and English conversation."

It was a fair introduction to Dolly Denisov and, in its calm, good-humoured presentation of the fact, of Ariadne also.

While I was talking to her, I was trying to take in all that I could see of St. Petersburg as we drove. It was a city of bridges and canals. Water was everywhere. I could believe the stories of how the city had risen out of the marshes at the command of Peter the Great. It was early afternoon and the sun sought out and flashed on gilded domes and spires.

"That is the dome of St. Isaac's Cathedral," said my companion, observing my intent look. She pointed. "And that is the spire of the Fortress Cathedral."

The streets were wide but crowded with people. Many of the men seemed to be in uniform, of all varieties and colours, so far as my excited eyes could see. I supposed that later I would learn to recognize what each meant, and to appreciate the significance of this green uniform, and that red livery; this astrakhan hat and that peaked hat. At the moment I could only see that they must mean something. Our motor car wove its way in and out of a great variety of traffic: private carriages, carts, and oddly shaped open carriages whose iron wheels rattled across the cobbles. At one junction an electric tram clattered across our track, motor and tram so narrowly missing a collision that I caught my breath. But

Ariadne remained calm, as if such near misses were an every-day occurrence. At intervals, a majestic figure wearing a shaggy hat of white sheepskin and a long dark jacket would stride through the traffic, oblivious of all danger, and forcing all to give way before him: a Turcoman, living reminder of Oriental Russia.

Now we had turned along a water-front, passing a great honey-coloured building, and then a lush, dark green stretch of gardens. There was what looked like a row of government buildings of severe, grey stone; these were succeeded by a row of shops and some private houses.

A few more minutes of driving and then we had arrived at the Moyka Quay. The motor car stopped outside a house of beautiful, pale grey stone, with a curving flight of steps leading to an elegant front door.

As we drove up, the door opened. I suppose someone had been watching. But this was always the way it was in Russia: there it never seemed necessary to ring a bell or ask for a service; every want was unobtrusively satisfied before the need for it was even formulated. The servants were so many and so skilful.

I was taken up to my room by a trio of servants and a laughing Ariadne. With a flourish, the girl showed me round what was to be my domain. Domain it was: I had two lofty rooms with an antechamber, and my own servant. I almost said serf, but of course the serfs had been freed in 1861 by Alexander, the Tsar Liberator. Nevertheless, the servant who bowed low before me was old enough to have been born into servility, and I felt you could see it in his face where the smile was painted on and guarded by watchful eyes.

"Ivan will stand at your door, and anything you wish, he will do. You have only to say."

"I shall have to learn more Russian."

"Ivan understands a little English; that is why he was cho-sen. On our estate a few peasants are always taught a little English. Also French and German. It is so convenient." She held out her hand and said sweetly, "Come down when you are ready. We have English tea at five o'clock."

Somewhat to my surprise, and in spite of his Russian name, Ivan was a negro.

When Ariadne had gone, leaving only Ivan standing by the outer door, I explored my rooms, which were furnished with a mixture of Russian luxury and Western comfort. Carpets, tapestries and furniture were expensive and exotic. Great bowls of flowers stood everywhere. The bed in the bedroom was newly imported from Waring and Gillow of London, by the look of it.

I unpacked a few things, stood my photograph of the family at Jordansjoy by my bed where I could see it when I went to sleep and proceeded to tidy myself to go down to the Denisovs' "five-o'clock." I washed my hands. I found that the rose-scented soap in the china dish was English.

It may very well be that young Russian noblewomen never go anywhere without a companion, but otherwise it seemed to me that Ariadne Denisov had a good deal of freedom. For the first evening she entertained me on her own, presiding over dinner and then playing the piano to me afterwards.

On my way up to bed I saw a small, dark-gowned figure moving along the corridor a short distance ahead of us. Not a servant, obviously, from the sharp dignity with which she observed, "Good night, Ariadne," disappearing round the corner without waiting for an answer.

"Mademoiselle Laure, the French governess," explained Ariadne. *"The* French governess," I noticed, not *"my* French governess." Thus Ariadne dismissed Mademoiselle as a piece of furniture of the house, necessary, no doubt, to its proper equipment, but of no importance. Her attitude contrasted strangely with the welcome to me.

Sitting up in bed, plaiting my hair, I considered the scene again. No doubt I had imagined the flash of malevolence from Mademoiselle Laure's eyes. Yet she had spoken in English when French would have been more natural to her. No, emotion was there, and I would do well to heed it.

I mused quietly and considered where I had landed myself. The house was furnished with a mixture of luxury and primitiveness. For instance, I had noticed beautiful carpets and fine pictures, jasper and lapis lazuli were used to decorate the walls of the salon, but there was absolutely no sign of piped water. No water-closet seemed to exist, and I had an antique-looking commode in my room. Private and convenient no doubt, but even Jordansjoy did better. And there was dust under the bed.

But all the same, I liked it here. Magnificence suited me, never mind the dirt.

I had been told that only the very rich had their own houses, called *osobniak,* and that even the well-to-do chose to live in flats. But the whole of this great house seemed given over to the Denisovs. The servants were to tell me stories that the house was haunted; I wonder now if houses can be haunted by ghosts from the future as well as the past, and that Dolly and Peter and I were the spirits that moved around the house and are still there now. How strange if I should have met my own ghost.

Madame Denisov was a widow with one child, Ariadne. But Ariadne had spoken of her "Uncle Peter," so that I knew there was someone else living in the house. She had pointed out his photograph to me, showing me the face of a neat boned, dark haired young man, her mother's younger brother, with a look of Ariadne herself, the features which seemed sweet on the girl possessing elegance on the young man.

The next day, somewhat later than I might have expected, I met Dolly Denisov.

She was sitting curled up on one end of a great sofa, a bright silk bandeau round her head, a pink spot of rouge on each cheek and something dark about her eyes, puffing away at a cigarette, and chattering at a great rate to Ariadne in her high-pitched, lilting voice. She leapt to her feet when she saw me and came forward holding out a delicate, jewelled hand.

I don't remember her opening words, I was too absorbed by her physical impact; I was swimming in a strange sea, excited and exhilarated. Then we were sitting down, side by side on the sofa, talking as if she was really interested in me.

"And did you sleep? Visitors sometimes find our summer nights trying."

"I *did* find it difficult to sleep."

"And you dreamed? We always say that there's nothing like a St. Petersburg summer's night dream."

"Yes, I dreamed." I had dreamt of Patrick. She knew all about Patrick, of course. Everything of my sad little history had been explained to her by the Misses Gowrie, those useful go-betweens.

"Everyone dreams here in the summer. When they can sleep at all. I can *never* sleep. All the time I am exhausted." She didn't look it, though. Energy crackled from her. "But then we go to our estate in the country and there I rest." She added: "You will enjoy it there. It will be most interesting to you."

"Oh." I considered. No one had told me about the country estate, but I was certainly prepared to enjoy it.

"Foreigners are always interested in our country estates because in them is the heart of Russia. We know what we owe to our peasants, Miss Gowrie. You must never doubt that. Between the landed proprietor and his peasants is a bond that only God can break. Outside Russia people do not understand this."

"No," I observed, thinking of the comfortable farmers around Jordansjoy and the sturdy small holders in the hills who certainly did not regard themselves as having any mystical union with impoverished gentry like the Gowries. "But perhaps we don't want to." It would after all be an awkward fact to handle. I was sceptical of it myself, but I saw that Dolly Denisov believed.

"Well said. A good remark," she said.

All the time she had been talking to me I had been conscious of her eyes upon me; she seemed to like what she saw, because I saw her give a tiny little nod. I had passed some sort of test.

Well, I had always supposed there would be one. It had never occurred to me that Madame Denisov would entrust her treasured daughter to an almost unknown girl without scrutiny. Whatever she had been looking for in me she had now found.

Our conversation was broken into by a procession of servants carrying salvers laden with food and wines which they proceeded to lay out upon a series of small tables before bowing and retiring. I watched, frankly enjoying the scene: it was as good as being at a play.

No sooner had they departed than a stream of guests began arriving, almost all the men in uniform of one sort or another. (I discovered very soon that in Russia there was a uniform for everyone from university professors to roadsweepers, even wet-nurses having one with blue ribbons for a boy and pink for a girl.) The ladies, for the most part, were as richly decked out as Dolly Denisov, with one or two poorer-looking figures dressed in dingy dark clothes, and including the elderly lady who speedily helped herself to a plate of assorted delicacies and retired to a corner to eat it as if she had not seen food as good as this for some time and would not do so soon again.

Last to arrive was a trio of musicians who came in quietly, settled themselves in a corner and struck up. No one took the slightest notice, although by all accounts the Russians rated themselves very highly as music-lovers.

Ariadne skipped around, sometimes bringing guests up to me to be introduced, sometimes leading me up to them. Madame Soltikov, Count Gouriev, Professor Klin, Prince Tatischev, the Princess Valmiyera, she was named with especial respect, and it was the little old lady sitting eating her plate of delicacies.

It was all done by Ariadne with apparent spontaneity, but I noticed that in fact there was always careful reference to Madame Denisov.

"Count Paul Suvorov, Lieutenant Woyna, Dr. Doratt."

Smiles, bows, friendly words, interested faces, everyone anxious to put me at my ease. Once again Ariadne danced away. Only the old lady was heard by me to mutter under her breath: "Too pretty, too pretty, not spirited enough. *Moi, je suis sceptique.*"

If I didn't know better, I thought, I'd believe *they* were being presented to me.

I scratched my forearm idly. Another scratch and I remembered what Lady Londonderry said to my grandmother: "All Russians have fleas," she had written. "The only difference between the nobility and the lower classes is that the lower classes have lice and fleas, whereas the nobility only have fleas."

I was pondering this thought when I saw that Dolly Denisov was standing near me. I gave another gentle scratch; I suppose it *was* imagination.

"You look thoughtful, sad. You are lovesick, you are thinking of him you loved, the one you were to marry."

"No," I said. How could I say I was wondering about fleas?

"Yes, yes, I see it. And it is natural. But it will pass, I promise you it will pass. And for you, it is better not . . ."

"Since he didn't love me, I suppose it is."

"For you, anyway. Believe me, I know." She sat down on a nearby sofa and patted the seat beside her. "What would you do if he were to come back to you?"

Oh, Zeus, I thought, now she wants to dig into things.

"Do? Nothing."

"But you still love him?" A sly, humorous look was turned on me. Not so much fun for me, though.

I shook my head. Better to deny it. It would be true one day.

"Russia shall be your cure-all," said Dolly.

Ariadne came dancing up. "Mamma, Mamma, the Princess is going."

"Oh, they are all going." Dolly got up.

A small, dark-clad figure crossed the room diagonally, walking towards the door. I recognized Mademoiselle Laure. So she had been here all the time.

An irrational vexation possessed me. We were two of a kind in this household, Mademoiselle and I, and yet she seemed to avoid me, whereas I had made tentative explorations to see if I could find her room.

"There goes Mademoiselle Laure." I pointed her out to Ariadne. "I didn't know she was here."

"Oh, she came to listen to the music, I suppose," said Ariadne. "She is very fond of music."

If she had listened, then she was the only one who had done. The musicians had played sadly, as if they never expected an audience. Now they had packed up their instruments and were filing out, one after the other like the Three Blind Mice.

"I suppose she has a room somewhere near mine?" I asked.

"Mademoiselle Laure? Oh, I think she is in a room somewhere on the next floor," said Ariadne vaguely, as if she did not know and did not care. It was all very unlike the treatment of me.

The next day Dolly Denisov clapped her hands and announced that Ariadne would be taking me on a tour of the city. Was I rested? Was I comfortable? Good. To be introduced to St. Petersburg was a necessary preliminary to my duties.

Duties, I thought. There seemed to be no duties, only pleasures.

We duly set off in their large motor car, with Ariadne pointing out the sights. We had passed this way yesterday.

"There is the Rouminantiev Garden—so beautiful. One day we must walk there. Oh, all those buildings are part of the university, but that one over there covered with mosaics is the Academy of Arts. Mamma says it is unsightly, but I rather like it. Oh, and that's the Stock Exchange—looks as if it were hewn out of solid rock, doesn't it?" She spoke through the speaking-tube to the footman who then spoke to the chauffeur. "Go on to the Peter and Paul Fortress, then the cathedral, and then down to the Nevsky Prospect." She turned to me. "That way we'll go past the Vladimir Palace and the Winter Palace. You'll like the Nevsky Prospect, the shops are gorgeous," and she giggled. She and her mother had the same sort of delightful, rumbling little laugh.

Ariadne had her orders, I decided, and the tour, which looked so artless, had been carefully thought out. The city was laid out before us in its great beauty, with everywhere trees and water and buildings either of rich, red brick or stone, apricot-coloured in the sunlight. The sombre bulk of the Fortress of Saints Peter and Paul, the Kazan Cathedral, the Winter Palace itself, I saw them all. And at the centre of all was the Nevsky Prospect.

"It is the longest and widest street in the world," said Ariadne proudly.

"How long is it?" I asked.

"Five miles from the Alexander Garden to the Moscow Gate."

"It is immensely broad." I was struck by the width of the street; the pavements seemed so wide that a dozen people could have marched side by side up them. As we drove slowly along, I could see that on either side were shops. Very soon Ariadne stopped the car.

"Now we will walk," she said, and took my hand tightly in hers and led me along. "This is the glittering world, Miss Rose. Perhaps I shall have to renounce it one day; who knows what may happen? But while it is here, let us enjoy it. Look, here is Alexandre's." She drew in a deep breath. "Oh, I adore Alexandre's."

Together we stared at the window full of expensive and elegant objects—jade boxes, scarves of Persian silk, chains of gold and ivory, a delicate parasol of white lace with a diamond-studded handle. Never had I seen anything like it. By comparison Jenners in Prince's Street did not exist.

"Do you have anything like this?"

I shook my head. "In London, perhaps. Not in Edinburgh."

Past Alexandre's was Druce's, the "English Shop," where were sold English soap and tooth-paste and lavender water (which was much used by the men). After that we went into Wolff's, the great bookshop, where Ariadne lavishly bought me several books about Russia and a copy of the *London Times.*

"Across the road," she said in a low voice, "is Fabergé's

shop. Even I hardly dare look in there, it is so expensive. Old Madame Narishkim spent the whole of her husband's salary there in one day, just buying two presents for his birthday. Or that's the story, anyway." She gave that giggle, so like her mother's. "The old goose is silly enough for it."

A golden voiced clock somewhere chimed the hour, and it reminded Ariadne of something. "Let's go to Yeliseyeff's," she said. "I have to order some *ryabchik* for Mamma—tomorrow she gives a dinner party, and she loves those delicious little game birds."

Yeliseyeff's, as I was to discover, was a large provision store filled with exotic delicacies from all over the world. Great jars of crystallized apricots and plums, drums of mysterious marrons glacés, bowls of strawberries and peaches, sacks of dark brown nuts. Season had no place in Yeliseyeff's calendar; any fruit could be had at any time. They had another branch in Moscow but the St. Petersburg shop was said to be the finest.

Ariadne ordered the little game birds for her mother from a smiling assistant, added to it the request for a box of pralined almonds for herself and then led me to the grand treat of the morning.

"Coffee and ices at Berrin's," she announced.

Berrin's was the French *confiserie* on the Ulitza Gogolyn around the corner from Morskaya Street, just off the great Nevsky Avenue, and thither we were driven in the car which had all this time been following us at a discreet distance.

There, at a round mahogany table in the window, we ate tiny sponge-cakes and ice-cream, served to us by a tall French woman, dressed in brown and black, a colour combination I had never seen before (and it would certainly have looked dowdy enough at Jordansjoy) but which I now saw was of great elegance.

If this is to be my life in St. Petersburg, I thought, I am on easy street.

But I suppose even then the question was slowly forming itself in my mind as to why the Denisovs really wanted me in St. Petersburg.

An incident with Mademoiselle Laure sharpened the process. I had seen her several times and tried to catch her eye, but she always turned away. On purpose, I thought.

I was right, she was avoiding me, and when I went up to her one day in the Denisovs' library and tried to talk to her, she turned away angrily. I suppose I had been in Russia then for three weeks.

I had inadvertently put my hand on hers, a personal touch I should have avoided, and she wrenched it away.

"I am sorry: your hand is cold," she excused herself.

But I refused to be put off. "We ought to understand each other, you and I: we take the same place in the household."

"Hardly."

"I have been here three weeks," I said on a note of surprise, "and not spoken to you at all."

"Three weeks? I have been here three hundred times as long." Her vehemence had more than a touch of bitterness in it.

"Come and sit in my room with me," I said. "I expect you know it—it is so beautiful."

"I know it!" She gave a short laugh.

A strange and terrible thought struck me. "Was it your room once?"

"My room? I have that room? No, it would be strange if it was. Between the French governess and the English governess there is a gulf fixed." There was an unmistakable edge of mockery in her voice.

"Scottish," I corrected absently. Without anyone telling me, I had already grasped that a hierarchy existed, and that English governesses stood at the top, with French and German ladies well down in social esteem and salary. Russian governesses, if they existed, and I had not yet met with any, were no doubt at the bottom. It was one strange aspect of Russian society. "Still," I said, "we do the same sort of job."

She laughed, an incredulous, bitter hoot. "You think so? You really think so? How innocent. How terrible to be so innocent. And dangerous. Well, Russia will soon teach you."

"What do you mean?"

"Oh, Russia will teach you. Not I. I excuse myself." And giving me a stiff little nod, full of suppressed emotion, she departed.

I told myself uneasily that she was nothing but a spiteful, jealous woman, but still I wondered.

I had no one to ask; my kinswomen, the Misses Gowrie, were in Moscow and not expected back for some weeks. Dolly Denisov, although apparently approachable, seemed never to say anything I could settle on. She seemed content for me to drift away my days with Ariadne in conversation, visits to other splendid houses and walks. I had instituted the Scottish "afternoon walk" and Ariadne, although at first doubtful, now enjoyed the habit as much as I did. But we seemed to have no purpose and no direction in our life. I told myself that it was all very Russian, and that this was how I must expect it all to be.

Only, there was Mademoiselle Laure's observation, and then, once or twice, I caught Dolly Denisov looking at me with a strange, appraising scrutiny.

I had plenty of time at my own disposal when Ariadne was taking her music lessons, or singing, or learning dancing with the French dancing-master, or taking drawing lessons; she did all of these things, one or two of them brilliantly, none of them regularly. Madame Denisov had waved a vague hand when I asked permission to explore the library and the picture gallery.

The library was a lofty, dark room, filled with ancient volumes in Russian, French and German, as well as a smaller library of Greek and Latin. Of these books no volume seemed later in date than 1840. English literature had a section all its own and was mainly made up of novels. Dolly Denisov had a very representative collection of English light fiction, and I spent quite a lot of my free time there, gratefully reading my way through a number of delightful authors like E.F. Benson and Elizabeth whom poverty had hitherto kept from me.

The picture gallery was a long, tunnel-like room filled with dark portraits of fierce-looking soldiers and ladies dressed with an air of fashion and expense that suggested Dolly Denisov was running true to form. They were a dull lot, and except for certain slight differences of dress, could have been found, perfectly at home, at Jordansjoy. But at the end of the gallery were three or four strange pictures that exploded with colour and light. A scene of water-lilies in a pond, a plump woman sitting at her dressing-table brushing her hair, these were two of them. Another was a country scene, but so angular, bold and bright that I had never seen anything like it. Yet another was of a girl dancer, resting on a chair, her face in repose, plain and spent, and yet she was an object of great beauty.

Just beyond this group of pictures was a door. One day out of curiosity I opened it. Behind the door was a small hall and leading out of it a heavily carpeted staircase going straight up into the wall.

I went to the foot of it and stared up; I could see nothing because the staircase curved sharply. A scented, murky, musky smell hung over the stairwell as if fresh air never reached it.

I wondered where it led, but on that day something unwelcoming, even slightly sinister, about the stairs kept me back.

But the place fascinated me and I kept thinking about it. The next time I was in the gallery I went again into the small, red-carpeted foyer that led to the stairs.

This time as I stood there, I heard a movement behind me. One of the servants came through the door bearing a heavy silver tray on which were covered dishes.

I was beginning to speak a little Russian by now; at any rate I could ask a simple question and more or less make out what the answer was. "Where does the staircase go?"

The servant, he was old and grey, stared without answering. Then he said, "Ah, the sacred staircase," and crossed himself as if he meant cursed rather than sacred. Later I came to observe that the servants, like many an oppressed minority, often used a word in the exact opposite sense to the way they really meant it. In secretiveness they found both protection and defiance "To the tower."

He said no more, but went on up the stairs, and out of sight. On that thick carpet his feet made no sound.

I knew now that someone lived up at the top of the staircase.

The silence of the household about this unmentioned inhabitant began to oppress me. The mystery worried me. I thought about it at night, those pale nights, and when I was not dreaming about Patrick, I dreamt about the staircase.

One quiet afternoon while Ariadne was at her singing lesson and Dolly Denisov out upon her own concerns, I entered the foyer from the picture gallery and crept quietly up the stairs.

The staircase wound up and up in three curving flights. No wonder no sound had floated down to me at the bottom.

Ahead of me was a solid oak door with a polished bronze handle. I opened it.

I was on the threshold of a large, dark room, curtained and lit by lamps although the afternoon was bright. In the middle of the room was a great state bed of gilded wood, heavily decorated with swags and carved fruits and little crowns, and hung with rich tapestries.

In the bed, propped on cushions was an old lady, before her a bed table spread with playing cards. She raised her head from her cards at my entrance and stared. Then a radiant smile spread across her face, and eagerly she held out her hands. She said in English, "At last you have come. I always knew you would."

# Chapter Two

I had never been in such a room before. It was so shut in and artificial that I felt the outside air could never penetrate at all. Over the window were heavy, plush curtains of deep red, and over these were layers of muslin, draped and pleated in elaborate folds. On the floor was an ancient Turkey carpet whose very redness seemed to suck up what air was left in the room after the endlessly burning lamps and the great stove had taken their share.

I stood on the threshold, shaken by my reception and not understanding it.

The old woman in the bed and I stared at each other. Then she gave a cackle of laughter. "Come in, girl, and don't stand there staring."

Slowly I advanced into the room, vaguely conscious of great, gilt mirrors on the wall, uncannily reflecting everything in the room, making every image smaller and clearer than in life: gilt furniture, the old lady in the bed, the lamps, and the girl at the door who was myself, a girl in blue and white spotted silk, her face pale.

"Come on, come on." The voice was imperious. "Come right up close and let me have a look."

Obediently, as if mesmerized, I came right up to the bed and let her look at me. Her hand came forward—dry and cold it was on mine, glittering with diamonds. Age had shrunk it and discoloured it, until it looked like a little brown animal's paw.

Her face was old, older than anyone's I had ever seen. At Jordansjoy we thought of Tibby as old, but she was not old like this. This woman looked as if she and the last century had grown old together. I saw a thin, lined, wrinkled face, cheeks bright rouged and neck and forehead powdered white. Diamond earrings sparkled at the ears, and a great pearl necklace dangled from her throat. Out of this painted, ancient face stared a pair of dark, keen eyes. But every so often heavy lids fell over the eyes, turning the eye-sockets into dark pits which made her look dead already. It was a disconcerting trick, due, I suppose, to a weakness of the muscle beyond her control. Yet I came to suspect that she used her weakness to intimidate.

"Good," she said again; her voice was almost a whisper, a ghost of what it must once have been. "I am pleased with you. You have the right look. Genuine. I knew I should be able to tell. At my age a skin peels from the spirit and one senses things at once. But you kept me waiting. I even began to think you had not come."

"I didn't mean to," I said, flummoxed.

"And how long have you been here?" There was a hint of imperious displeasure in her voice.

"I've been in Russia three weeks, and more."

"Ah, so long? Well, I cannot rely on being told the truth. I have to allow for it." Her eyelids fell, revealing the bruised, violet-coloured eye-pits.

I didn't know what on earth she was talking about.

"I am Rose Gowrie," I said. She opened her eyes; now their blackness seemed opaque, then light and life gleamed in them.

"So indeed you are: Rose Gowrie come from Scotland," she said with satisfaction. "And I am Irene Drutsko."

The name, as even I knew, was one of the oldest in Russian history. They looked down on the Romanovs as parvenus.

"Yes, I am a Drutsko, by birth as well as marriage. We have a lot of the old Rurik blood in us. They say by the time we are five and twenty we are all either saints or mad; I leave you to discover which I am." Again the eyelids drooped, but were raised quickly (although with an effort, I thought). "No, you need not kiss my hand," she went on. "Your own birth is noble. Besides your grandfather was my lover when he was an attaché here. It was a short but most enjoyable relationship."

"That must have been my great-grandfather," I said. "He *was* here. I've seen his portrait in Russian dress—very romantic."

"So? One confuses the generations at my age. Yes, he was very beautiful. He loved me to distraction. When he was called back to London he said he would *se suicider*."

"He was eighty-two when he died," I said. He had also had eight children and two wives, both married and all begotten after his sojourn in St. Petersburg. I wondered what he had said to her. He had gone down in our family sagas as a tremendous old liar. A great beauty, though, as she had said. We all got our looks from him.

She ignored my remark as, later, she was to ignore what did not fit in with the picture of her world as she saw it. Instead she said, "How strange that the blood of that worldly man should run in your veins. Truly the ways of God are beyond us." She took my hand caressingly. "Ah, my little miracle, my little treasure from God."

"Am I?" I said doubtfully, withdrawing my hand as gently as I could; dry and cold as her hand was. it seemed to take warmth from mine. It was hard to get my hand away. For her age she had a firm grip. "I'm here to be companion to Ariadne and to talk English to her."

"Ah?" Her eyes lit up with mockery. "Is that what you think?"

"Of course. Madame Denisov (is she your niece?) engaged me." I spoke up stoutly in my own defence. It seemed to me that I was obscurely defending myself, although I couldn't tell why. A little trickle of alarm moved inside me.

There was a moment of silence and during it I became more aware of my surroundings. I was standing by her bed. Behind me was the door through which I had come in. Now I noticed that in the wall behind the bed was yet another door. I wondered where it led.

"You think so?" Her question seemed to give her satisfaction. She shook her head. "No, Ariadne is not so important. You have come to *me*. You will . . ."

Behind her the door opened an inch or two, then halted. I saw it. She saw it, too, reflected in the mirror; she stopped in mid-sentence. Behind the wrinkles and the rouge and the powder her expression changed, with amusement and satisfaction draining away and blankness taking their place.

I looked at the door. It was still open; I hadn't imagined the first movement. Someone must be standing behind it, waiting to come in.

"Please go now," she said, leaning back on her pillows and closing her eyes. Pretending to close them, I thought, because I could see a glimmer through those painted lashes. "After all, I am greatly fatigued. Good-bye, my dear, your arrival is my great joy. Come again soon. I will arrange it."

"But Madame Denisov—" I began.

She interrupted me: "I find it best to make my own dispositions. Good-bye for the moment."

Did the door move a fraction as I went away? In the mirror I thought it did.

I was half-way down the red staircase when it struck me that from where she lay in her bed the old lady could watch both the doors. More, anyone opening either door could see who was in the room, reflected in the mirror, before entering. What a room for conspirators.

At the bottom of the staircase, hurrying to get into the picture gallery, unwilling that anyone should see where I had come from, I ran into the English-speaking negro servant appointed to my use. On a silver salver was a decanter of wine, ruby red, and a red Venetian glass goblet.

I think we were both surprised to see each other, he the more so, perhaps, since from his flushed face I suspected that some of the wine had found its way down his own throat before he set off on his errand.

Guilt and the wine pushed him into speech. "You've been up there, miss? Is she on her own?" He made a gesture as if crossing himself. "I don't like her on her own. She's worse then."

"Who?" I asked.

"Princess Irene, the old witch." He muttered the last few words, but I heard them. He started to hurry past me; he was a big man but light on his feet.

"I think she's not on her own now," I said.

What I said seemed to mean something to him.


I didn't mention anything of this to Dolly Denisov or Ariadne. I wasn't proud of myself, either of my original inquisitiveness or of the secrecy it led to. It was Russia; I see that now, and in particular the way it manifested itself in the Denisov household. Without my knowing it the atmosphere of the house was affecting me.

But the next day Dolly Denisov raised the subject herself. In her own way, and obliquely.

We met over the tea-cups while Dolly smoked and Ariadne nibbled macaroons.

"You have settled down so well, Miss Gowrie." Dolly smoothed her glossy hair, which today was pinned back with a tortoise-shell-and-diamond comb, shaped like a fan. "I am so happy."

"I love it all," I said with honesty.

"And soon letters from home will start arriving, and that sad little look I see at the back of the eyes will have gone."

"Yes," I said. But none from Patrick. No letters, ever

again, from Patrick. I don't think Dolly Denisov can ever have been truly in love or she would not have said what she did. But perhaps she didn't believe it. Hard to tell with Dolly.

"You miss your family, of course you do. We Russians understand about families. That is why we live in such huge houses, so we can all live together." She reached out for a cigarette and the dark silk of her flowing tea-gown slid away from her arm to show half a dozen barbaric-looking gold bracelets. "Even in this house we have an old aunt living. She is too old and frail for you to meet; she sees no one," said Dolly easily.

I said nothing. Old, Princess Irene certainly was, I thought, frail, too, no doubt, but it wasn't true she saw no one.

"One day, perhaps, I will take you up to see her. She is history personified. Do you know, as a girl she danced with Prince Metternich? She was a great flirt, I am afraid. So many scandals." Dolly laughed indulgently. "Never really beautiful, but she knew how to attract. Oh, she was worldly, Tante Irene, and now look what she has come to: a recluse, quite cut off, seeing no one. The sadness!"

I kept quiet.

Dolly clapped her hands, bracelets jangling, rings flashing. "But soon my good friend Miss Gowrie and her sister Alice will be back in St. Petersburg from Moscow. I have news of it, so Rose, you shall see *some* of your family."

And so it proved. Dolly Denisov was well informed. Perhaps she always was: it was a thought for me to ponder. Within the next few days a letter came to me from Emma Gowrie, asking me to "a tea" in their flat, near the Marinsky Theatre. "Dear Rose," wrote Miss Emma, "we quite long to see you and hear all the news of our dear Scotland." Where they had been but once, I knew. "We are 'at home' every Wednesday, but this coming one will be a special day in your honour. You will see we keep Scottish ways here. Do bring darling Ariadne with you. Such a charming girl."

I showed the letter to my employer and her daughter.

Ariadne danced with pleasure at the invitation, and said she should love to go, she adored her dear Misses Gowrie.

"But perhaps our Rose would prefer to see her relations on her own," suggested her mother.

"Oh, no, not at all," I protested. But then Dolly and Ariadne put their heads together and decided I should go on my own; Ariadne would go for her singing lesson with her best friend Julia, and call for me afterwards in the carriage. It was charmingly done: they were full of feminine wiles and contrivances. Dolly Denisov was the practised exponent of the art at which Ariadne was still a prentice hand.

My kinswomen had a very small apartment in Zakhariev-skaya Street, which was not quite as near the Marinsky Theatre as I had imagined. The truth was that nowhere in St. Petersburg was very near anywhere else, so huge were the streets and so many and various the canals. Moreover, the Misses Gowrie had succumbed to a Russianness in their description of places and events; it was often so diffuse and romanticized as to baffle someone brought up to the precise ways of my Edinburgh-bred Tibby, to whom a vagueness was as bad as a lie. After a while I got to allow for this characteristic of the country and even enjoyed it, seeing that it added an extra dimension to life.

Emma Gowrie opened the door to me herself, taking my hand and pumping it up and down in welcome. She was a stout lady in a short dark linen skirt and a masculine-looking shirt with a stiff collar. "Rose, my dear girl, it's a pleasure to see you. You're a sonsy lassie, my dear, a sight for sore eyes." She gave me a hearty kiss. "Ach, you've a look of your grandmother, hasn't she, Ally dear?"

Over the years and through the generations of absence from Fife, the St. Petersburg Gowries had clung to their Scottish accent, but upon it rested the shadow of the Russian tongue they spoke so often.

"She has indeed, sister," said Miss Alice gently. She was a softer, greyer version of her sister, her clothes less stiff. Emma Gowrie remained resolutely Anglo-Scottish in appearance; the Russianization of Miss Alice had proceeded further.

Their apartment, crowded with possessions, was a mixture of both their worlds. Plaid and tartan on the furniture, Landseer landscapes on the walls and a samovar on the table. The furniture itself looked of Russian manufacture, with a good deal of dark, almost black wood, yet with decorations of the beautiful green of malachite. It was a Scottish "five-o'clock" but with Russian tea. The scones and the apple jelly and the honey were thoroughly Scottish, however. The tea service was Worcester, but the teaspoons were of heavy Russian silver.

"We get the honey at Yeliseyeff's," said Miss Alice. "You can taste the heather in it. But those little buns, do try one, come from Filippov's." The little buns were as Russian as the tea; I took one; it was light but chewy, sweet and yet spicy. I thought it delicious.

I was getting used to Russian tea, too: pale, fragrant and very hot. I would never get used to the little saucers of jam that appeared with it, though.

For a little while I sat on the sofa alone (except for a great red tabby cat) and was the only guest. Then other people started crowding in. But they still had time for me.

"Our At Homes are famous," whispered Miss Alice. "All due to Emma. She is so intellectual, so respected."

Feared, too, I thought, perhaps, as I listened to the smart crack of her conversation, sometimes conducted in Russian, sometimes in English and occasionally in French.

Emma came and sat beside me on the sofa. "Now you must think of us as another home," she said. "Come here whenever you like."

"Oh, I will."

"I expect Dolly keeps you pretty busy?"

"In a way," I admitted. "Ariadne goes about a good deal, and where she goes I go. But there's time to myself."

"And you write home regularly?"

"Oh, yes. Almost every day I write something—a sort of journal letter."

She patted my hand. "That's right, my dear. Keep in touch. Do you know, never a week passes without me getting or sending a family letter? It's the only way, otherwise one becomes *déracinée*, foreign, and that would never do." And she looked around her, comfortably certain she was irreversibly British.

"Oh, but I shall go home after my year with Ariadne."

She looked away. "One never knows. People always say that. But they come back."

"It's a very good post, I admit. And I love it in a way I never expected: it's all so grand."

"Ah, I dare say. And what about Ariadne and Madame Denisov? Get on, do you?"

"Charming," I declared.

"Dolly's a good sort." It was almost grudgingly said, as if there might be other things to be said about Dolly that could not be encompassed in that simple phrase; I suspected there were.

"Met the brother yet?"

"No."

"You will. He's always around his sister. Ten years younger than Dolly, yet she mothers him. He lets her. But he is like all those Russian men: one day he will throw off the hand that seems to lead him."

"He sounds interesting."

She threw up her hands. "Russian family relationships: I will leave you to find your own way about that murky pool."

"I've met Princess Irene," I said, thinking that this might well be one of the constituents of the murky pool.

She jerked in surprise. "Have you, indeed? I did not think Dolly would do that."

"She didn't. We met . . . by accident." It had been a kind of accident, I told myself.

"I've never met her myself. Only heard about her. I could have met her when we were both younger, but our paths never crossed."

"She's a good deal older than you," I said. "Older than anyone I've ever met. She said something rather curious. . . . She said I'd been brought over from Scotland for *her*."

"Oh, nonsense."

"That's what I thought. But she doesn't seem like a woman who talks nonsense."

"You're here to be a companion to Ariadne Denisov and talk English with her."

"She talks English beautifully," I observed.

She shrugged. "It's the custom for Russian girls of good family to be accompanied wherever they go. And as for the English, well at one time the nobility spoke French among themselves. They still do, but as the usage of French spread lower and lower in the social scale, English became more 'snob.' German," she said with satisfaction, "has never been fashionable."

"I suppose that's why I'm so well paid," I said. "And why I live so differently from Mademoiselle Laure. It made me uneasy at first."

Emma Gowrie did not answer. Then she said awkwardly, "It was a bad business about your young man. I'm sorry."

"I suppose it was better to find out he did not love me before we were married rather than afterwards," I murmured, although, as a matter of fact, I did not believe it. Once married, Patrick would have been happy enough, but perhaps I might not have been.

"You would have been wasted," said Miss Emma with conviction.

Her sister Alice heard. "Marriage can never be said to waste a girl," she ventured.

"Speak of what you know," rapped Emma Gowrie, in her eyes a fanatical, suffragist's gleam.

"I may not have been married, Emma, but I *was* once engaged to be. Only *his* death prevented it. I know your views, but not all girls throw themselves away," and she drew herself up with a gentle, ruffled dignity.

"For some women there is a vocation, a calling," began Emma, speaking almost angrily.

Am I such a one? I thought. Are generations of Ariadnes really my destiny?

She saw my disconcerted face. "Dear Rose, do you not feel it yourself?" Then she shook her head and said, half to herself, "But I forget . . . so young, so young."

More guests arrived, taking my hostesses' attention away. I relaxed and enjoyed the occasion. Most of the guests were eager, determined women like Emma Gowrie, earning their own living, making their own way in the world. Then Ariadne skipped in, eager to take me away, gay as ever.

"Now, you have had her long enough, Miss Gowrie. She's not all yours, you know. She is *my* Rose, and no one else's."

"Yes, yes, I concede your claim." Emma was good-humoured; she always indulged Ariadne. We all did, she was everyone's pet. "But remember she is my blood relation."

"I admit it freely, for without your efforts, dear Miss Gowrie, how should I have got my Rose?"

We went home in a *likhachy,* the better sort of cab, almost like a private carriage, with carpet, padded seats and a sleek horse. More ordinary people travelled in a *droshky,* a much less comfortable contraption on iron wheels.

It was nice to be so much wanted and sought after, but a little puzzling, too.

There was a budget of letters from home waiting for me when we got back to the Denisov mansion; I longed to carry them straight up to my room and read them, but Ariadne said no, there was a special visitor in the drawing-room and I must come in and meet him.

"Oh, who?"

She screwed her face up in a wry grimace. "Oh, I suppose you would call him a suitor."

"A suitor? For you?" I was surprised. She seemed so young.

"Oh, don't worry, Miss Rose, these things take years and years in Russia." She smiled. "I'm not supposed to know. But, of course, I do know. Goodness, my nurse told me of the arrangement when I was five. But I pretend I don't know. My mother understands I know, but she pretends that I don't." Then she sighed. "I shall have to make up my mind soon or it will be too late."

"You can choose, then?"

"Oh, I expect so," she said cheerfully. "Mamma would never force me to anything, but why should it be no? He's rich, gentle, and quite pretty, I think."

"We say handsome with a man," I said.

"Handsome, then," accepted Ariadne blithely.

In the drawing-room were two men. One, tall and slender and young, bore a marked resemblance to Dolly Denisov, and the other—yes, seeing him suddenly through Ariadne's eyes, he was handsome.

"My Uncle Peter," introduced Ariadne. The tall young man bowed. "And this . . ." no doubt from her voice and manner of amused archness that *this* was her suitor . . . "Major Lacey."

"But of course we know each other." I held out my hand. "I am very glad to see you, Major Lacey."

And it was true. I was surprised how happy I was to see him. He had thought me a charlatan and a poseuse, and had let me see it, and yet I was pleased at the sight of him.

He also seemed pleased and shook my hand with real vigour. To Ariadne he behaved with amused good humour, taking her little flirtatious onslaughts on him with calm, as if he was perfectly used to managing her. If they did marry, the relationship would be a happy one. He had brought Ariadne a box of bon-bons.

"Ah, from Aux Gourmets," she said with greedy joy, opening the box at once. "Let's all eat one."

Both the men took a chocolate.

"Men always eat chocolates," observed Ariadne. "They drink brandy, they smoke cigars, they gamble, they ride their horses too hard and on top of it, they eat sweets."

"Yes, we're a dreadful lot," agreed Edward Lacey.

I liked him better now that I saw him on Russian soil, and I felt more relaxed with him than I had done on the journey. I suppose I believed I understood him better now I saw him with Ariadne. Everyone thinks that they understand a lover. Courting Ariadne as well as seeing his sister provided an adequate motive for his stay in Russia, which he seemed disposed to make a long one.

"I am not idle," he said to me. "I can see that stern, puritanical look on your face that all fellow-countrymen of John Knox get when they contemplate a man not working hard for his living. Russia interests me endlessly. I find plenty to observe and think about. And I have a cousin at the embassy. I brought over some letters and papers that the regular King's Messenger had no place for. That took some talking over."

"Oh, ages, I should think," I said sardonically.

"Oh, diplomatic business goes at its own pace, you know, and usually takes longer than you expect. And then they wanted to find out from me how things go on at home—politics and so on—the sort of detail they can't get from correspondence in the London *Times*. Oh, I'm a useful fellow." He smiled. "In my way."

Peter Alexandrov said nothing, but continued to watch us with the air of gentle detachment that seemed natural to him. I supposed that as the women in his family were such talkative creatures as Dolly and Ariadne, it behooved the men to be quiet.

I wondered why Dolly Denisov wanted Edward Lacey as a husband for her daughter; I supposed he was rich. Looking at him I saw that there was a sort of gleam on all his appurtenances, from the shining leather of his shoes to the thin, flat gold of his watch and the fine linen of his shirt; over all was a lustre that betokened wealth. I wondered I hadn't seen it on the ship, but I supposed I had been too wretched, too sunk in my own depression. Money would matter to Dolly. And then, of course, he had a sister married here, and "interests" in Russia, so that, once married, he might well settle here.

What Edward Lacey could see in Ariadne I did not have to ask myself: he would be getting a charming, lively, playful wife. If that was what he wanted, of course. I was conscious, inside myself, of a faint surprise. He seemed too much of a man for such a girl. But then, I had every reason not to trust my understanding of men. I gave him and Ariadne a sceptical look, which he, at least, saw.

"And how are my old friends, the Misses Gowrie?"

"Very well. Arguing a little between themselves," I said.

"They always do. But when one thinks of what their life has been. After having so much and now so little."

"I know they lost a great deal of money," I said. It was the way in our family: if one generation had money, then the next lost it.

"Their father built up a great fortune as a merchant; everything he touched turned to gold. As girls they knew every luxury, and that means something in Russia, I can tell you. And then their only brother, years older than they, gambled and dissipated the lot. The two women were left with precious little—not much more than the furniture and china of the home in which they had lived. But they turned to and supported themselves by this job and that, teaching English, acting as companions, arranging posts for others like themselves in rich Russian families." Edward Lacey spoke with respect.

"They seem to know everyone," I said. "But a lot of what you have told me is new to me. Family history that has gotten buried."

"Yes, they have a host of friends," he agreed. "But their brother—I knew him myself before he died—he was one of those whom Russia ruins. Saving your presence, Peter."

"Oh, no one is a harsher critic of my beloved country than I am," observed Peter equably. "Although I agree about Jim Gowrie: he adopted the worst vices of our society, and, not being a Russian, they destroyed him."

"They destroy some Russians, too," observed Edward Lacey.

"Oh, yes. I do not deny it. But it is like a disease: being natural to us, we have some hidden resources of strength against it. Many are maimed, but not all die."

"What happened to James Gowrie, then?" I asked. His fate had been kept secret from the child I had been.

There was a moment of silence.

"He killed himself," said Peter Alexandrov. "Shot himself through the mouth. Oh, there is a sickness in our society, all right, and where can it all end?"

"It is part of your sickness to have no answer," said Edward Lacey.

"Possibly. Or too many answers."

"Oh, politics, politics, they can never touch *us*." Ariadne interrupted their conversation with gaiety. "Let us ignore unpleasantness and have a good time."

"Wretched little butterfly," said Edward, but he seemed to enjoy her prattle. Presently they went over to the piano where he turned the pages and Ariadne played and sang. I suppose it was a courtship, in the Russian style.

Under cover of the music Peter and I were left looking at each other.

Then Peter gave a short laugh. "Ariadne knows nothing, and yet she knows everything. She is like an animal that knows instinctively how to lead a happy life. But give her time. She will grow up. The women in our family mature late. But Ariadne will still be happy, it is her gift."

Perhaps that was what Edward Lacey liked, and perhaps it was the gift I lacked.

"Lucky Ariadne," I said.

Peter smiled. "Ah, but you have your own gifts."

I kept my face expressionless. It might be that Edward Lacey had told him about the episode with the injured boy on the London docks. They seemed on easy terms; he might have mentioned it. I hoped not. I hated any hint, any mention of that gift I did not understand.

But Peter said nothing more, and soon the others came back from the piano and suggested that we go out to see the new horse that Edward Lacey had just bought and which was "a regular winner."

After seeing the horse (which introduced me to the idea that Edward Lacey kept a stable in St. Petersburg) I went back to my room.

There, I sat down by the window and opened my letters from home. My sister Grizel's was the longest and the least well spelt and Alec's was the shortest, produced in his best copper-plate hand, and containing one brief sentence about seeing a fox.

Grizel produced a string of home news, such as the state of her Sunday hat, the sad disappearance of our best laying hen (a fox was suspected) and the fact that she was invited to a house-party at Glamis and had "absolutely nothing to wear and no way to get there except by walking."

I raised my head and smiled. I knew that Grizel would get to her house-party (some hopeful suitor would constrain his mother or his sister or his aunt to drive her over) and she would look delightful in her old clothes.

Tibby's letter was more down to earth; she, too, mentioned the hen, which was obviously a sore point with the whole family, but blamed the local tinkers and not the fox. She concentrated on health. She told me how the minister was, how his wife was, how the postie's rheumatism had made him "terrible slow" with his letters lately, and finally she told me how she, Grizel and my brother were. I was delighted to hear that they all seemed in rude health.

But as I turned the last page of her letter I saw a frantic postscript which seemed to have been jointly written by her and Grizel.

"My dear Rose," wrote Tibby, "we have just heard that a terrible trouble has fallen upon the Grahams; Patrick has disgraced himself in India and must leave his regiment in dishonour. We don't know the details as yet; I dare say we *never* shall, but I *feel* for his poor mother."

In Grizel's hand, I read: "Rose darling, Patrick is accused of mutiny, who would have believed it of him? And he has fled. No one knows his whereabouts, not even his mother. Well, thank goodness you are not married to him, my love, that's what *I* say."

But I thought: poor Patrick, poor Patrick. And I also thought how little I knew him after all.

That night, instead of dreaming about Patrick, I dreamt about myself. Troubled, restless dreams in which my own identity seemed lost, and I wandered like a ghost through an unknown countryside.

I woke in the pale dawn and lay looking as the sunlight began to colour the room. I held my hands up in front of me and looked at them. Ordinary, quite pretty hands, with long fingers and the narrow nails inherited by all the Gowries. Why was it my hands could do the things they did?

At first my own powers had seemed so natural to me that I thought nothing of them at all. Only as I took in the way other people reacted to them, especially the look on Tibby's face, the silence with which she met any manifestation of it, did I grasp that I was abnormal.

And I did not understand it; I could no more explain it than I could explain why my eyes were blue.

So I kept silence; I used my gift spontaneously, I could not help myself, it happened, but I never spoke of it. It must be the reason why Patrick had left me. He couldn't marry a girl like me. I had never spoken to him of my "gift." Once I had tried but I had stopped, silenced by his pale, uncomprehending stare. But he had obviously learnt, somehow, and been frightened away. The notion that he had been paid to go now struck me as ridiculous. Still, he had gone, and terrible disaster had struck him in India.

Breakfast was a late meal in the Denisov household. Indeed, as often as not, Dolly did not appear at all, and Ariadne and I breakfasted alone. Because of this lateness, some hot chocolate was always brought to me in my sitting-room.

I could hear Ivan's arrival now, hear his heavy tread, and the chink of cup upon saucer, as he arranged the tray on the round marble table in the window. Presently I heard him draw back the curtains.

I put on my morning wrapper and went in. "Good morning."

Ivan bowed, then poured the chocolate from silver pot into Sèvres cup. A rusklike biscuit, dry but quite palatable, was always served with this little meal.

I drank some chocolate and crumbled a rusk in my fingers.

"How's Princess Irene?" I asked.

"Bad-tempered. She is always cross."

"She's very old," I said thoughtfully.

He didn't answer, and poured me some more chocolate, but I saw his left hand make a tiny gesture.

"What's that you did?"

He was silent, staring at me with great, velvet-soft eyes, blank of expression as a cushion. I was beginning to realize that though Russian servants were invariably good-mannered, they had brought silence to a fine art.

"You made a shape with your forefinger." I recalled that the first time I had stood looking up the red staircase he had crossed himself. "Come on: what did it mean? It meant something."

Reluctantly, he said, "It's to ward off the evil eye."

"*My* evil eye?"

"No." He had lowered his eyes. "Hers. The Princess's."

"Ah, I see." I could understand that she might be feared: almost I feared her myself.

"She's sold her soul to the devil, and will never die," he said solemnly. "We think she entertains the devil in there, up the red staircase, and that's why we dislike to go."

"She entertains someone up there," I said thoughtfully.

"No. Not living souls. Dead men."

"You don't believe such things, Ivan."

"Dead souls," he repeated. Then he gave a deep laugh.

"But they eat and drink wine, these dead souls; they have good appetites."

And, giving a series of deep, satisfied chuckles, as if he had said something that amused him very much, he picked up the tray and pot of chocolate and left the room.

If he had been a Scottish servant, I would have stopped him, but I already knew enough about Russians to know that all I would get from Ivan would be silence.

That day I got my first taste of the other Russia. So far I had been cocooned in a world of luxury and security: now I was to see the dark side. I buttoned myself into a cool, white linen shirt, for St. Petersburg was beginning to be hot, and went downstairs where Ariadne was waiting for me.

She was waiting for me to go with her to church. Like many Russian girls of her class and generation, Ariadne had strongly developed religious feelings, although of a somewhat dreamy and simplistic sort. Religiosity rather than religion, my old Tibby would have called it. It was a matter of duty that I should go with her, but, in fact, I was entranced by the richness and beauty of the service and music.

I had instituted the habit of walking there: Ariadne fell in with the idea to humour me.

We were turning in to the street which led to the church when we saw a line of police drawn up across the road and we were stopped. Beyond them we could see a small group of people being questioned by two policemen, and in the distance right down at the end of the road was a glimpse of the Nevsky Prospect where a large number of people seemed to be milling about.

"What's going on?"

The police officers were eyeing us, and one man stepped forward. "You may not go that way, Excellencies," he said politely.

"What is it?" asked Ariadne.

He bowed. "A bomb in the Imperial Library, Excellency."

"Oh, the anarchists again, I suppose. Was anyone hurt?"

"I believe so." He was clearly reluctant to add more.

Adriadne turned back to me. "The police must think the criminals are still in the neighborhood; you can see they have the area cordoned off and are searching."

I had my eyes on the little group already under investigation; I saw a girl, quite young and neatly dressed in dark clothes, a young man in the characteristic suit and narrow cap of the student and two older men, both working-class.

"Perhaps they have them, or think they have," I said. Even as I looked, the four were led away by the police.

"The girl was very young," said Ariadne. "Younger than me. It frightens me a bit."

There was much to frighten one in Russia, and I was only just beginning to realize it.

"Let's go home," I said, and I took Ariadne's arm as we turned our backs on the scene and walked home.

At the door Ariadne excused herself. "I'll have some tea and bread in my room. I won't come in to breakfast. I think I would like to be alone for a little while. You know, if we had been a little further on on our walk, we might have been near that bomb. The Imperial Library is not so far away from the church. We might have been hurt."

"And the girl?" I said. "If she's guilty, what will happen to her?"

"The Fortress of Saints Peter and Paul first," said Ariadne. "That's where they take political prisoners. And then," she shrugged, "Siberia, I suppose. It is terrible, isn't it? However you look at it. Terrible what she did, and terrible what will happen to her. Russia is a terrible country. And today I have to go shopping for clothes with my mama!"

And she ran away upstairs.

Thoughtfully, I went into the breakfast parlour. So now Ariadne knew that politics could reach out and touch her.

I found Mademoiselle Laure there, for once, coolly drinking tea. Her appearances on occasion were as puzzling as her disappearances. No rule seemed to account for them. But this morning, I learnt, Ariadne was to go to her mother's

French dress-maker, and Mademoiselle Laure was to go along, too. Presumably to see fair play.

I was to be left to my own devices. Mademoiselle Laure inclined her head to me over the tea-cup, as if it gave her some satisfaction to pass on the information. She was wearing a tight black dress with a small miniature, set with seed-pearls and plaited hair, at her throat: I was in white even to my shoes. We made a strange pair, I all white and Mademoiselle Laure all black. There was something total in that blackness. Almost as if she were in mourning.

She saw me looking at the miniature and laid her hand protectively across it. "It is the anniversary of his death, and on that day I always wear his likeness, and dress," she indicated with her hand, "as you see."

"His death?"

"Georges. Georges Leskov, my betrothed. He died of a fever before we could be married."

"Oh, I'm sorry. I had no idea."

"No matter. He loved me, and to the end. I have that consolation," and she gave me a meaning look.

I flushed. Bitch, I thought. "I wouldn't have let him die," I said.

"I, too, would have saved him, Miss Gowrie, if I could." She looked at me: there were tears in her eyes. "I nursed him day and night, did all the unpleasant duties a nurse must do, never flinched at inflicting pain. Could you do that, Miss Gowrie?" She lowered her eyes. "But you would not have had to, one touch of your hand . . ."

"What do you mean?" I said sharply.

"You know what I refer to, Miss Gowrie. Do you suppose Madame Denisov did not get a nice little character sketch of you before she engaged you?"

I flushed again. "I suppose she did."

"Oh, you have no need to worry. She doesn't hold it against you. No, indeed. It is I who ought to do that. I tell you frankly, I am a sceptic, not one of these sensation-hungry, superstitious Russians. I do not believe in miracles."

"Nor I." I bent towards her, anxious to show my sympathy. "I'm so sorry, truly sorry. What you did was nobler and finer than anything I have ever done. What I do . . . well, it just happens, spontaneously, almost without my willing it." I frowned, trying to be honest. "I think there *is* an element of my willing it; that is, I must desire to help, but that desire is called out of me, willy-nilly."

She didn't drag her hand away as she had done before, but her face softened a little. "Then you are truly unfortunate," she remarked.

As this chilling comment was uttered, we both heard the voice of Madame Denisov outside. Quickly Mademoiselle Laure said, "Take a word of advice from me, if you are not too proud."

"I'm not proud at all."

She gave me a sweeping look. "Oh, you have pride. I can see it in the way you hold your head and in the stare of your eyes. Well, you've come to the right place to take a fall." She buttered a slice of bread and divided it into four equal segments, one of which she put into her mouth and ate carefully. "You have been with the Princess Drutsko." I made a quick movement of alarm. "Oh, don't worry; I have said nothing to Madame Denisov."

"How do you know?"

"I saw you come down the staircase. I have taken that walk myself, and know where it leads. Oh, yes, the Princess was my friend before she was yours. Don't trust to her loyalty, will you? It does not exist."

There was no mistaking the bitterness in her voice, nor of my failing to understand what lay behind it. "You have no need to fear me," I said slowly, "I am not your rival."

She gave a short, incredulous laugh. At this moment, Dolly Denisov, accompanied by her brother Peter and followed by Ariadne, swept into the room. Behind, fussing and chattering in various tongues, came the little suite of attendants who seemed needed to get Dolly off on any major expedition: French maid, Russian assistant and German secretary.

"Come, come, we must be off, we're late already. Peter, you must come in the motor car with us. After the dress-maker I am going to Fabergé's, and I must have a masculine opinion. Only a man knows about diamonds. Pearls, now, I could have managed on my own." One never knew if she was serious or not, and although Peter protested that he wanted to stay and read in the library, I knew he was doomed to go. "Get your hat on, mademoiselle. You should have been waiting for me. Am I to wait for you, then?" She caught sight of herself in the mirror. "Upon my word, I look a fright this morning. Now, where are my gloves? I can't find my gloves. I know they were in my hand. Things are always missing here. No wonder the servants say there is a black spirit in the house."

"Do they?" I was startled.

"Oh, yes. They think I don't know what they say. Of course I do. Ridiculous, superstitious nonsense. Still, I'm bound to say things do seem to go wrong here, somehow."

"Here are your gloves, Mamma," said Ariadne, handing over a long pair of pale violet gloves, "where you laid them, on the table. It's Aunt Irene who's the black spirit, I think. It's her they mean."

"Now, that *is* rubbish, Ariadne, and I will not have it. Remember, *we* must always be above foolish superstition. We can only be dragged down by it. Ready now, Mademoiselle Laure?" And she swept them all out. Peter did not want to go, I could see it in his face, but she made him, all the same.

I was left alone to amuse or bore myself as I chose. Not that one was ever alone in that house, for a servant was always within call. Watching, too, I supposed, knew indeed. They anticipated one's wants so finely that they must be keeping a very sharp eye on all that went on. One of the little modernizations put in by Madame Denisov's father had been an arrangement of speaking-tubes, through which you were meant to hiss a request to a servant waiting in a room below. They were never used, for, as Dolly Denisov said: "You have only to clap your hands here and a servant appears. I *did* use one once," she had said with a peal of laughter, "and then the silly creature only shouted back." She added: "My father would have had him flogged for it, but one doesn't do that sort of thing now, of course."

There was one of these speaking-tubes just before me now, in the library, a beautifully designed mouthpiece of ivory and bronze, protruding from the wall. Dolly Denisov had told me that all the work had been done by one of her father's servants, an ex-serf, who was a skilled craftsman. Much of the furniture in the house had been built by the carpenters and *ciseleurs* on their estate. It gave one a new idea of what the serfs had been, not all peasants by any means. Our dominie in the village near Jordansjoy, dear old Dr. Rathmore, had been a fine Greek scholar in his day, with a degree in the humanities from St. Andrews University, and he had instructed us in classical history, so that I saw one might draw a parallel between the serfs of Imperial Russia and the slaves of Greece and Rome, where not all the servile had been illiterate labourers, but some had been men of infinite skill. One does not like to think that the Parthenon was built by slaves, but it might have been so. It was certainly true that many of the beautiful pieces of furniture and bronzes that I had already seen in the great houses in St. Petersburg had been made by unfree hands.

I picked up the speaking-tube and blew down it. I heard my whistle go travelling through its length.

Then distantly, distantly, a tiny little voice spoke back. It spoke in Russian, but I knew enough Russian to understand what it said:

"The time is not yet. But I shall come to you. You must not come to me."

The voice, so remote, yet so clear, startled me. I gave a gasp, and the exhalation of my breath travelled down the tube again.

Again the voice said, "The time is not yet. But I shall come to you. You must not come to me."

"Who is that?" I said. "Who is talking?"

This time I didn't get an answer. There was only dead silence. After waiting a minute more I replaced the plug that stopped the mouth of the tube; I saw that it was decorated with a lion cut in low relief in bronze and bore the initials of the Alexandrov family.

The shuffle of felt-covered feet, a noise I had come to associate with the arrival of a servant (for in the Denisov household all the servants were obliged to wear their soft, almost silent footwear), made me turn round. My own black Ivan was in the room. His eyes were on the speaking-tube.

"Who could have been talking to me down there?" I asked. "Such a strange way of talking. And I think I frightened away whoever it was."

"There is no one at the other end, my lady," he said politely. "The tubes are not used. No one attends to them."

"I tell you someone answered me."

He was silent, pursing his lips.

"A man answered," I persisted. "And he told me that the time was not right, and that I was not to come to him but that he would come to me."

Ivan's answer was to cross himself and say, "Those are accursed things, those tubes, and should not be used."

"Oh, there's no harm in them, Ivan; they are useful devices in their way. Perhaps not necessary in a house like this, but in other establishments I should call them very helpful. You have certainly no need to be afraid."

I spoke cheerfully, a little incredulous that so intelligent a man (and Ivan was that) could be fearful of a harmless contraption like a speaking-tube. But I supposed, underneath, he was a superstitious peasant at heart.

An opaque, blank look, an expression which I had to learn to interpret but with which I was already familiar, settled on his features. I had seen facsimiles of it at times on the faces of the other servants when Dolly or Ariadne spoke sharply. It could hardly be called insolence since they were, perforce, always so polite, but I noted a quality of stubborn resistance in it.

"Yes, I see you don't believe me, Ivan," I said, "but I assure you I did hear a voice. But I won't go on. What is it you want?"

He bowed. "I am to conduct you up the red staircase to the Princess Irene."

When I had least expected it, the summons had come. How convenient, I remember thinking innocently, that I should be free and Ariadne out with her mother.

The staircase to what I had begun to call the Red Tower seemed stuffier, the air more scented and dead than ever, and the Princess's room, when I got there, was full of cigarette smoke.

The room, overhot as before, and artificially lit, although it was full daylight outside, was a sight in itself. I was taking in the details more fully on this second visit. I saw now that not only was it full of furniture, but that every piece of furniture was covered with objects, several low tables bore burdens of silver-framed photographs, flowering plants (there were always so many flowers in Russia), enamelled boxes and porcelain figures. Even at a glance I could see that many of the objects were valuable, for instance, an intricately worked egg of silver and tortoise-shell on a stand of lapis lazuli, but others, like a papier mâché bowl of hideous red and a paper fan with a nasty bead handle, were rubbish. As I looked round I realized that the clutter and muddle reminded me of something: then I saw what it was: our old nursery at Jordansjoy. This was a playroom for an old child.

Princess Irene was sitting up in her bed, wearing a brocade and fur jacket, a little matching turban, and smoking a small black cigarette. At my appearance, she held out a regal hand. "Ah, so there you are. Gratified you came so promptly, most gratified." She didn't sound it; more as if she had taken my appearance for granted.

"Oh, I wanted to," I said honestly. "And fortunately Ariadne is out with her mother, so I was free."

"Naturally I know where my niece is." She had a bed-table in front of her on which she was laying out a pack of cards, in

some elaborate-looking game. "She has gone to her dress-
maker and taken her daughter with her. Peter has gone, too,
and much may he enjoy it. Dolly choosing a dress is a pen-
ance I would not wish on any man." She turned over a card.
"Ah, the queen, a good sign." She puffed at her cigarette.
"Not that I believe the cards can really tell the future, at my
age it is a little difficult to take *that,* but," and here she gave an
elegant shrug, "a little wink from the Fates is very accept-
able." She gave a cough, a deep, rolling cough that shook her
whole body and left her gasping. Another wink from the
Fates, I thought, and not such an agreeable one.

The cigarette rolled from her fingers; I picked it up and
put it on a silver saucer, which was half full of the cigarettes
she had smoked already.

"And have you told my niece that you have visited me
here?" Her dark eyes gave me a sharp look.

"I think you know the answer to that question," I said
slowly. "You who know everything that goes on in this house.
No, I have not."

"Good. Good. Of course, she will discover and perhaps be
quite cross. She has a temper, you know." Another sharp
look here.

"I can imagine."

"Not that it matters. I rather like to annoy Dolly." She gave
a deep chuckle. "And it improves her complexion. She's
rather sallow, isn't she? Don't you find her sallow?"

Bemused and fascinated, I did not answer. It was true that
by the standards of the vivid red mantling of Princess Irene's
cheeks, Dolly was indeed lacking in colour.

"You don't answer. Very wise. I like a girl who knows when
to keep a still tongue in her head. It's a sign of good breeding."

She was a wicked old thing, and needed to be taken down a
peg or two, I thought. "I wouldn't speak about my employer,
in any case," I said. "It's good sense as much as good breeding."

"Dolly's not your employer. I am. Aha, that startled you,

didn't it?" And she leaned back on her pillows in triumph, only to burst out into one of those deep coughs again, so that I had to lean forward and retrieve another cigarette.

So the money that supported this luxurious household was hers? I was surprised, but I could accept it as the truth. "Perhaps you pay my salary," I began hesitantly, "but it is to be with Ariadne that I am here."

"Pay you, do I?" She gave me an amused look. "No, Dolly is rich enough to pay for anything she chooses to indulge herself with. No, but it was on my instructions she sent for you. And not for Ariadne."

"On your instructions?" I echoed. Yes, I could see her issuing her orders to Dolly Denisov. What I couldn't quite see was Dolly accepting them.

"And Dolly was pleased to oblige me. She likes to forget I am here, but once reminded, she knows better than to be too difficult." The diamonds on her fingers flashed as she moved the cards again. "I knew all about you. Your old cousins, the Misses Gowrie, visit regularly below. I hear all their gossip. I find them very entertaining. In my own manner, of course. So I told Dolly to get you." The diamonds flashed again. "She took her time, she likes to tease me a bit, but you came at last. To me."

"But I came here to be with Ariadne. Madame Denisov invited me. Her letters were quite specific."

"So Dolly thinks. Or perhaps just pretends to think." The Princess flashed me a smile as bright as her diamonds. "But the fact is that you came here for me."

"I don't understand." But I did. Reluctantly, I did begin to understand, a little. I had not forgotten how that dry, cold hand had warmed itself in mine.

"I did not explain to Dolly *all* that I knew of you. I told her what a splendid companion you would be for Ariadne. She agreed, she was very willing. Dolly does not need my money, but she would like my emeralds when I die." She paused, then said grimly, "She will have a long wait. I don't intend to die." Her ancient hand, loaded with jewels whose antique cut made them look older than she was herself, took my own. "I do not want to die, and with your help, I will not."

Now that her face was so close, I could see the seams and cracks into which her fine old skin had crumbled: the rouge and powder accentuated rather than dimmed the damage the years had done. She was wearing a thick, heavy, musky scent that was like the smell of another century.

I knew now what she was asking me to do. I didn't know exactly how she had heard of my gift that shamed and perplexed me, but somehow, probably through the Misses Gowrie, she had. She didn't look mad, but there must be a trace of madness about her, somewhere. I felt immensely sorry for her, and weighed down by a great fatigue, as if she was already draining away my strength.

I withdrew my hand and stepped backwards from the bed.

"No one can stop death. Not when it's ready to come. Certainly not I."

A spark of humour showed in those black eyes. "But one can procrastinate. Do you know how old I am? In one month I shall be ninety years old; I have procrastinated thus far, so why should I not postpone death for another ten years and for ten after that? It's the pain when it comes that will kill me. You can stop the pain." Her voice was rising. "When it comes, it comes here, over my heart. It's coming now. Take it away from me."

Through the door behind her bed appeared the small, squat figure of an elderly woman wearing a long, dark blue dress and white apron. Her hair was braided all over her head in tiny little plaits and on top of them she wore a white cap like a little scarf.

With a hostile look at me and a "Go away, *baryshyna*," she hurried over to the bed. "Mistress, mistress, speak to your Anna. You will make yourself ill." *Baryshyna* was "miss," and not spoken in a very polite tone, either.

"I *am* ill, you fool. Go away, I tell you. Rose, Rose Gowrie, come here."

I did not move; not one step would I take.

"Do what Her Excellency says, *baryshyna*," ordered Anna sullenly.

"She's not ill," I said. "She's just pretending."

The old lady stopped her moans and lay back on the pillows, staring at me.

"You can't deceive me," I said. "I know whether you are in pain or not. And the pain, when it comes, is not in your heart, but deeper down in your guts."

Anna gave a shocked little cluck at my bluntness.

The Princess coughed, her shoulders heaving.

"Yes, there is the pain now."

"Then help me."

"No, it's not bad enough. I cannot help you until it is much worse." I could hear my voice speaking, but I seemed to stand outside my own body and listen to what it said as if another person spoke.

"Oh, the wickedness," muttered Anna. "She should be beaten. I'd beat her!"

"Be quiet, you are an illiterate old woman and know nothing about it," commanded her mistress. "A greater pain? Is that what I must wait for then? More pain?"

"Yes," I said stonily.

A faint smile curved the lips of that enigmatic old face. "Very well: we shall see. Anna, lift me up on the pillows and light me another cigarette."

"The last thing you should be doing," I said.

"Ah, but with you to save me," she said, giving me a flash of the smile which, I suppose, must have enchanted my grandfather, "I shall be quite safe."

"Don't count on that."

"Oh, but I do. It's very comforting to think you needn't die till you want to."

Outside on the staircase the air seemed hot and dead. I found myself swaying; I sank down and closed my eyes. I was spent; she had taken more from me than she knew. Instinctively, I understood it would never do to let her guess. While she was ignorant I retained free will. I sat there, leaning against the wall, and waited for the darkness that surrounded me to recede.

When I opened my eyes I found Ivan standing there, looking at me with a worried face. I realized he must have been outside all the time, waiting for me.

"Are you ill, Miss Rose?"

Only Ivan called me by name; the other servants called me by any gracious term that popped into their mouth at that moment: the fact that I was a Scots girl seemed to free their tongues; they called me Excellency, my lady, and sometimes *baryshyna,* just as it suited them, but it was all done with such good humour that I could not mind.

I stood up. "No, no I'm not ill. Were you waiting for me? Yes, I can see you were. But why?" Ivan, even if within earshot, was usually invisible. "Was it because I was *there?* Because I've been up the red staircase?"

He shrugged. "It's a place," he said, meaning, of course, it's a bad place, or perhaps just a queer place, or even just a place he was unsure of, one always had to read between the lines.

"She's only an old lady. What could happen?"

"They keep company with the devil up there," he murmured, looking at the wall and not at me.

"Oh, Ivan," I said, half laughing. I almost stumbled; I put out a hand and he helped me down the stairs. Together we got to the bottom.

"But of course a clever young lady like you doesn't believe me," he grumbled.

It was true that a door had opened in the wall behind the Princess on the day I had first seen her, and I remembered, too, my thought that she had a mirror carefully placed so that she could watch the door. The door had moved, and as soon as it had moved, she had got me out of the room. Or so I had thought.

A question occurred to me. "How many rooms are there in the tower where Princess Irene lives?"

"I have never seen. My duties do not take me in them. Only to the door where Anna meets me."

"But you know?"

"I have been told: three rooms leading into each other, one very small in which the woman Anna sleeps." His tone indicated that she could die there, too, for all he cared. "And a staircase leading down to the street, with its own entrance on to Moyka Street." A back door to the Denisov *osobniak,* in fact.

So Irene Drutsko could entertain whom she wished, with everyone coming and going unnoticed by the rest of the household.

"St. Michael and all his angels could come trooping up the stairs," said Ivan, accurately reading my thoughts, "or the devil and all his."

"And just as likely to," I said sceptically. "You don't really believe all that rubbish?"

He shrugged. No, he didn't believe the devil came visiting, it was just a handy phrase, covering a morass of distrust and fear. There it was again, I thought, the secret language of the oppressed. "The devil must be a gentleman compared to some I've met," was all he said.

Downstairs it was at once apparent that Dolly Denisov and her retinue were in the process of returning. Home at least two hours before anyone expected them. I could tell by the flustered way the servants were running about.

Ariadne came hurrying in first and went straight up the stairs, passing me where I stood at the door of the great drawing-room without a look.

Dolly Denisov followed, slowly drawing off her gloves and talking over her shoulder to her brother as she did so.

"I blame you entirely, Peter. I have wasted my morning taking Ariadne to choose clothes and she has chosen nothing. All because of you. How could the child like the silks and lace when you were being so critical? I have never before known you like it; you almost had the poor woman who was showing the dresses in tears. She was doing her best, you know, Peter. I shall never be able to show my face there again."

"Oh, come now, Dolly," protested Peter. He had followed her through the door, and behind him came Mademoiselle Laure; he looked flushed and she was deadly pale.

"You might almost have been doing it to get us home again, Peter," said Dolly. She caught sight of me then. "I would have been better advised to take *you* with me, Rose, than Mademoiselle."

"I do not regret getting us home early when Mademoiselle has such a migraine," said Peter gently.

Dolly gave an exasperated sigh, and looked, in no very sympathetic manner, at her daughter's French governess.

"It's the motor car," murmured Mademoiselle Laure apologetically. "The smell of the petrol and the way the car rolls about always bring on one of my headaches."

"Then I wish you had said so before we set out." But of course she wouldn't speak, I thought, glad as she was to be the one taken on an excursion, with me the one left behind. Dolly went on: "Altogether it has been the most vexatious morning! And then the police were so tiresome, stopping all the cars and carriages in the Nevsky Prospect and staring into them, on account of the bomb at the Imperial Library. Far too late, of course; the criminals are probably miles away."

"I'll go up to Ariadne," I said. "We saw *some* arrests this morning. you know. I think it distressed Ariadne. I'll just run up to her."

"No, I will go." Dolly started up the stairs in a decisive manner. "I want to have a word with that young woman."

"If Miss Gowrie would assist Mademoiselle?" suggested Peter Alexandrov mildly.

"Oh, yes, indeed I will," and I hurried forward. To my surprise she did not resist me, and seemed glad to have me help her.

So at last I saw her room, which, although not so splendid as the rooms I inhabited, was by no means the dreary attic she had implied. She had a comfortably furnished room, decorated with English chintz.

When I had got her undressed and lying on her bed, she seemed easier.

"Madame *does* know the motor car makes me ill, but she only chooses to remember what she wants to remember," she said weakly.

"Of course," I said, agreeing, to soothe her. "Can I get you a drink of water?"

"No." She moved her head restlessly on the pillow.

"What do you usually do to relieve the pain?"

"Nothing. There is nothing I can do but lie here and endure. Later, when the sickness goes, I sometimes take a long warm bath."

I put my hand on her forehead. I could feel an angry pulse throbbing under my fingers. "Does it still hurt?"

"Much less."

"Try to sleep."

"Yes, I believe I will be able to sleep now. You have been very kind, and I have been shrewish and ill-tempered to you. Unfair as well. But I will make it up to you. I will tell you why you have been brought here. I *know*. I should have told you before, but I was evil and stupid and wanted to see you in trouble."

"Oh, but I know it all."

"Do you? You really know? How do you know?" There was surprise in her voice. "Then surely you see the danger?" She struggled to sit up.

"I saw Princess Irene, poor old thing."

"Princess Irene?" She seemed genuinely surprised. "It's nothing to do with her. No, no, they'll use you, turn you inside out and then, if it suits them, abandon you. If all goes wrong, you will either be shipped back home, or at worse, who knows what could happen to you?"

A wave of nausea swept over her and she retched. I

pushed her gently back on the pillows, thinking her more than a little mad. "You can't talk now, you must rest. Presumably you think me in no danger today?"

"No, not today," she muttered. "Not today."

"Very well, then: tomorrow, tomorrow we shall talk."

I waited till her eyelids closed and then walked quietly to the door. When I turned round for a last look, her eyes were open again and she was looking towards me. Yet I don't think that it was I she saw.

"At last I believe I am free," she said softly. "I have tried so often to leave Russia, once I even got as far as Poland, but I always came back. Now I am free. I'll start a little school in my own town of Blois. It's what I've always wanted to do."

Her eyelids closed again and she was asleep.

# Chapter Three

Peter Alexandrov was waiting for me downstairs.

"How is she?" he asked.

"More comfortable," I replied thoughtfully.

"I was concerned about her. She is not a happy woman."

"No." I was still thoughtful. "But then, she has had a sad life: losing her lover just before they were married." Of course, I had lost my lover just before we were to marry, but it came to me suddenly that I did not intend to have a sad life.

"I'm sure Dolly means her to have a peaceful, contented life here with her, but Mademoiselle Laure is a woman of a jealous, suspicious temperament, and Dolly is sometimes very happy. They rub against each other, I have noticed. Now *you* deal excellently with everyone, Miss Rose."

"I don't think Mademoiselle Laure likes me," I said frankly. "Or she didn't—" I broke off.

"And now she does?" Peter was half smiling at me.

"She trusts me now, and yes, I think she is half-way to liking me. Give me a little more time. Tomorrow we are going

to have a long conversation and then at the end of it we shall
be friends," I said gaily.

Peter became serious. "Did she tell you how her betrothed
died?"

I was surprised by the question. "She talked about a fever,
and told me how she nursed him until he died."

"Yes, there was a fever, but that was not the first cause of
his illness." I stared at Peter, waiting. "A gun-shot wound,"
he went on bluntly, "in the head."

I hesitated, then: "Do you mean suicide?"

"Yes, self-inflicted, I fear."

"Oh, how terrible. But why? Was it known?"

Peter shrugged. "He was a man afraid of life, I think. You
find that strange, no doubt, Miss Rose. *You* will never be
afraid of life. Perhaps you have never yet seen anything in it
to fear."

I wondered what sort of life he thought I had at Jordansjoy. What about the time there was cholera in the village,
brought back by a sailor home from an Eastern voyage? We
were all under sentence of death then, and the infection
crept to our very door and lapped at it. My young brother
caught it and Tibby and I had nursed him together. Grizel
we sent away. What about the poverty and death I had seen
on every side of me in the cottages? And then I was a woman,
and what woman, rich or poor, did not face death in child-
birth? Only last year my cousin Charlotte Fairlie had died of
her first baby.

"All girls have fears," I said. "Some secret ones, too."

"Yes, I had forgotten that." He gave me a smile, uncannily
echoing old Princess Irene's. "And I should know with all the
experience of women I have in this house." The smile widened. "Still, I freely admit that they frequently defeat me.
Witness this morning."

"I'm afraid you did upset them."

"The clothes were frightful, Miss Rose; to a man's eyes,
quite frightful. Now I like a girl to look either graceful or

business-like." (Briefly I wondered which I looked like.) "But these were—well, I can only call them boyish—a flat look, with short skirts and great pockets."

I laughed. "I expect they were very smart. I am sure I would have liked them."

"I refuse to believe it. But at all events, my comments got us home (as Dolly did not fail to point out), and for Mademoiselle Laure's sake I was glad enough. Of course it was not only the Rolls that upset her," he said abruptly.

"It was not?"

"No, she was upset before we started out by the story of the explosions. And then on the way we saw the shattered glass still lying about. They might have cleared it up, I think. Then coming away, we saw a girl being marched away between two policemen."

"I saw a girl, too. Earlier, when we tried to go to church, Ariadne saw several people arrested, one of whom was a girl."

"The police arrest so many, often on mere suspicion." He shook his head sadly. "I believe the girl students are often the most dedicated among the revolutionaries," he said. "Little black cloth boots she had on. She was a poor girl. And you know, I suddenly had such a vivid picture of those little boots dangling from the gallows."

"Could it come to that?"

He shrugged. "If the government wanted to make an example, yes. I didn't say anything to Mademoiselle, of course, but perhaps she saw it, too."

"She never mentioned it," I said.

"Ah, but she would not."

He sounded as if he admired her. A tiny little pang of some emotion (surely it could not be jealousy?) moved in me. But then he went on:

"Women like Mademoiselle Laure never admit things: they turn them inward and feed upon them."

He had her remarkably well summed up, I thought.

"And you say you do not understand women," I said.

"One guesses. One unhappy soul is much like another. It is the rich and pampered beauties like my sister who bewilder me."

"But not Ariadne," I said defensively. I was becoming attached to that happy creature.

I got a glance from a pair of remarkably intelligent eyes, dark blue where Dolly's and Ariadne's were almost black. "No, not Ariadne. But who is Ariadne? Does she know herself yet? What is her identity? She is a blank page on which much may be written."

At this moment, Ariadne herself came into the room. "You are talking about me. I am sure I heard my name."

A blank page and who would write on it? I thought. But as I looked at that pink-cheeked, happy face, with its hint of sensuality, I knew that with Ariadne it would be a man. It generally is a man.

"Listeners hear no good of themselves, isn't that what they say in your country, Miss Rose?"

"Oh, I know I am safe with my two friends," said Ariadne cheerfully. "However, I am still in disgrace with Mamma," she added with a giggle. "Oh, she'll come round."

"You are a treasure," said Peter. A look passed between them: I saw the endearment meant something to them.

"But not her treasure," responded Ariadne. "Or not at the moment. Miss Rose, how is Mademoiselle?"

"Resting and recovering, I hope."

"Poor Mademoiselle, she hates us here sometimes, I think."

"She's planning to return home to France and open a girls' school, so she says."

"Goodness! Is she? Poor Mademoiselle." Ariadne went over and studied her face in a wall mirror. There was a spot that seemed to trouble her. Peter shook his head at her vanity. "I'm afraid she won't go. She always says that when she's particularly cross with us. But she never goes." She turned away from the mirror. "However, to punish me for my sins this morning, Mamma forbids me to ride with Major Lacey this afternoon. Instead I have a whole, great dull list of shopping you and I are to do, Rose. Poor us."

"It won't punish me; I love the Russian shops." I adored idling through the luxurious interiors of Alexandre's and Fabergé, enjoying watching Ariadne and her mother buy the expensive trifles that would never come my way.

"And as for you, Uncle, you are to go up to Mamma's sitting-room now. And wear armour, for she is very fierce." She watched her uncle get up and go to the door, then she said, "She has old General Rahl with her, and you know how disagreeable that always makes her."

Peter made a grimace.

"Who is General Rahl?" I asked.

"He's a friend of an aged relative we have living in the house. A retired soldier. Forcibly retired; he was bad at the job. Oh, he's not a bad old boy, but he's a policeman now of a rather special sort. He is a deputy head of the Third Bureau. You've heard of that institution, I suppose? It keeps an eye on us all. Well, I'd better join Dolly, or she'll be asking him to dinner for want of anything better to say. Good-bye for the present, Miss Rose."

When he had gone, I said to Ariadne, "So you did not mean it when you said, 'How could such things touch us?'"

Ariadne hesitated. "I did. I meant it with part of my mind. When I see us here so happy and contented, with everything about us so nice, I feel this is one world and all the bad things are in another."

"But surely General Rahl does not come here to inspect you?"

"Oh, no: he comes here as a friend. But of course one is bound to think of what he knows about one's friends, and even about oneself. I believe that the Third Bureau has dossiers on ever so many people."

"But surely not on *you*, Ariadne?"

"Oh, no, I suppose I am of no significance to them, but my mother and Peter have hosts of friends and go everywhere, and some of those friends would be bound to have 'doubtful' opinions. My mother has many close friends high in Court circles, of course, so her own position is irreproachable."

"I understand," and in a way I did, but I only understood in the limited way a girl of my background could; she spoke of a world still alien to me. I saw all that later.

"Ariadne," I said, suddenly remembering what I wanted to ask, "something strange happened while you were out. I spoke down one of those speaking-tubes you have in most of the rooms: I called down it and a man's voice answered. He told me that it wasn't the right time and I must wait or something like that. It was troubling."

"Oh, I shouldn't worry. I expect it was one of the servants playing a silly joke. They like to play the fool sometimes. After all, *you* were playing a kind of joke yourself in calling down it in the first place."

"That's true."

"Well, then. So you are not to worry." She smiled at me. "But I'll tell Uncle Peter."

She had spoken as merrily as ever, but I thought I noticed another note in her voice, a colder, harder note, perhaps even one of correction. I should not have used the speaking-tubes. It was not for me to play tricks. I was, after all, her paid companion. I had to learn my place. Did I read too much into the inflexion of her voice? Perhaps I did. I was getting as sensitive as Mademoiselle Laure. But I understood why: overdue sensitivity is one of the less advertised burdens of subordination.

A little later that day Ariadne went shopping to perform her mother's errands. It was the usual magnificent shopping list: an order for English biscuits and English marmalade at Yeliseyeff's. "Tiptree's, please," said Ariadne politely to the black-coated assistant, and smiled at me; then on to Brocard's to choose and purchase soap. I helped her choose tablets of pale heliotrope soap that smelt like a late summer garden, concentrated and made powdery. Ariadne bought and presented to me a box of three square tablets of pink soap smelling of roses. "For you: your name soap."

Then we went on to Watkin's, the English book-shop. I suspected the trip there was entirely to please me, because Ariadne took little interest in books herself, but she pretended she had to order some new English novels for her mother. "There is a new book by E. M. Hull whom she likes very much," said Ariadne.

There were some copies of the book already on display, so I examined one idly, while Ariadne transacted another piece of business about writing-paper. It was not the sort of book that found its way to Jordansjoy, where Tibby exercised something of a censorship. Still, Grizel and I had our own ways of keeping in touch with the world, and there was a copy of one of Elinor Glyn's works that was about the house for several weeks, masquerading as a novel of Sir Walter Scott's (an author after Tibby's own heart), without Tibby being any the wiser. E. M. Hull looked as if she wrote in the same vein as Elinor Glyn—I took it for granted E. M. Hull was a woman.

Raising my eyes from the book, I saw that although Ariadne appeared to be examining two different qualities of paper, she really had her eyes fixed on a distant corner of the shop. I followed her gaze.

I saw a group of four people: an elderly woman, soberly but expensively dressed, a girl of about Ariadne's age, a small boy and, oddly, a burly man in the uniform of a Russian naval rating. Two shop assistants were hovering around them, and a personage who looked like Mr. Watkin himself (if he existed) was also on hand. The boy was choosing a toy.

Watkin's had a whole corner of the shop devoted to English toys of one sort or another, the names of which I recognized from my brother Alec's conversation: Meccano, Bassett, and Hornby, magic names to toy railway enthusiasts. Behind the group a shelf was stacked with jig-saw puzzles and English children's annuals. The boy was choosing a railway engine. I saw him studying the one he held with close care, running one finger delicately over its outline. The boy was dressed in sailor's uniform, too; it was fashionable for boys then and for girls also, for that matter. But I did not fall into any confusion about the relationship between the boy and the man, which was clearly that of master and servant; there was a great social gulf set between them.

Ariadne put her hand on my arm as if to make sure my attention was directed to them. "It's the Tsarevich and one of his sisters," she whispered.

I looked with interest. "Which Grand Duchess?"

"I'm not sure; the next to eldest, I think, Tatiana. They all have the family face and look alike."

"The boy's different," I said.

"Yes." She hesitated. "There's been a lot of—well—talk. They say there's something wrong with him, that he's lame or something."

"He looks delicate, but normal enough," I said. "He's not a cripple."

"Still he often does not walk, the sailor carries him."

"He's walking now." And indeed as we watched, the boy ran along the display of toys, eagerly pointing something out to his sister.

"Yes, I think that must be the Grand Duchess Tatiana," observed Ariadne appraisingly. The girl was, after all, her contemporary; she was forming a judgement of her. "Not pretty, really, in spite of what they say, but has a nice expression. Olga, the eldest, she's called a beauty, but, of course, one has to say that of Grand Duchesses; the other two are just little girls."

The brother and sister were studying a book together, the boy pointing something out in an eager way.

To me there was something touching about his lively fragility, as if boyishness and enthusiasm *would* prevail against a frail body. He had a small dog with him, a liver and white King Charles's spaniel, and as I watched, I saw him lean down and give it an affectionate pat. When the dog leapt up eagerly, banging against his young master, the sister ordered the sailor to pick the animal up and carry it. "None of your animals are trained, Alexei," I heard.

The little group moved down the shop, with the other customers politely standing aside. There was no great fuss and no curtseys, although those gentlemen closest to the party took off their hats, but the shop was very quiet as if noise would somehow have been lèse-majesté.

They came close enough to me to see that the girl was wearing a little bunch of lily of the valley pinned to her jacket and to smell their scent. She held her brother's hand and stared straight ahead, almost too shy to acknowledge the weight of all the attention focussed on her. Her brother, on the other hand, smiled cheerfully all around. To him, at that moment, the world was good. But he was very slender and fine drawn, compared with the robust solidity of my Alec.

"My mother says he is all that stands between us and revolution," said Ariadne.

I was surprised; political judgements did not seem at all in Dolly's line. "Why does she say that?"

Ariadne thought for a moment. "I suppose because one can think about him hopefully. He is still so young that everyone can see him as representing what they desire, and he may become it. Who can tell? I think that must be what my mother means."

"I liked him," I said. "That is, I liked the way he looked, and the way he behaved to his sister."

"And he is fond of animals, too," murmured Ariadne. Surely without irony?

She finished her purchases and we went outside. We met Major Lacey just coming out of Cabasue's. He alleged he had been buying a tie. Ariadne greeted him joyfully.

"Hello, Miss Rose," he said cheerfully to me. "Settling in happily? There's plenty to keep one amused in St. Petersburg, isn't there?"

"I am never bored for one moment."

"Nor I. And I tell this young woman here when she talks of

boredom and ennui that she ought to know what English girls have to put up with. Not a tenth of the fun she gets. Ask my sister."

Ariadne giggled. "I am never bored with you, Edward. I don't know why, but I never am."

"It's because I'm a good boy, and lay my plans and think what will amuse the young ladies I escort. Tea at the Hotel Lausanne where they have a *thé dansant* going on? Ready and willing?"

"Well, I don't know if Madame Denisov would," I began doubtfully.

"She would want you both to enjoy yourselves. I swear it."

"Oh, yes," said Ariadne eagerly. "I *almost* asked her. Besides, she might be there herself."

All the more reason for not wanting us there, I thought, but did not say so.

"It'll be all right," said Edward Lacey quietly to me. On the ship I had thought him serious and even stiff, but seen here in St. Petersburg a cheerful, boyish side had emerged.

As we walked to the Hotel Lausanne, the two of them were talking away hard. I was silent. I felt very tired. A lot had happened today, since Ariadne and I had tried to go to church and had been stopped: the visit to Princess Irene up the red staircase; the sickness of Mademoiselle Laure; and now seeing the young boy, Alexei, in the book-shop among the toys.

Ariadne seemed very happy walking with Major Lacey. Presumably it was a coincidence meeting him. As they talked and I listened, I began to wonder if the whole shopping expedition had not been arranged by Ariadne to end in such a meeting. Now that I thought about it, there was a contrived air to the whole expedition.

The next morning, although I looked expectantly for Laure, she was nowhere to be seen. Apparently her promise (or threat) to talk to me and explain her vague warnings of danger had not been important enough to keep her from her favourite habit of disappearing.

I gave Ariadne her English lesson as usual. We were reading *The Idylls of the King* by Alfred, Lord Tennyson. Not my choice, I would have chosen something far simpler, but selected by Ariadne's mother, because she said she wanted Ariadne to understand English poetry. Emma Gowrie had privately advised me to alternate Tennyson with something livelier in case Ariadne got bored. Ariadne already was bored, judging by her yawns.

"You can close the Tennyson now," I said. "We'll start on *Pride and Prejudice.* Sit up, though."

"Oh, good. I fear I am not a poetic person." Ariadne straightened her back. "What is *Pride and Prejudice* about?"

I hesitated, wondering how to sum up the subtle complexities of the plot. What was it about, really? "Oh, several families living in a country village: two girls, Jane and Elizabeth, the eldest of a family of girls; a clergyman, a landowner, two love affairs and an elopement."

"Sounds like Russia," said Ariadne, yawning again. "You haven't seen our country home, have you? As long as it's not boring."

"It's a very amusing book."

"Delightful. The novels I read with Mademoiselle Laure were so dull. Goodness, they bored me! All about beautiful girls of noble birth thinking virtuous thoughts. Not like any of the girls I knew at school." She giggled.

"Did you go to school?" I was surprised.

"Oh, yes. I had one year at the Smolny Institute; that's the Imperial school for girls from the nobility. But I left," said Ariadne. "Back to poor Mademoiselle Laure."

"She was here then?"

"She's been here all the time. I can't even remember when she came. When I was in the nursery, I think." Yawns overcame her again.

"Have *you* seen Mademoiselle Laure this morning?"

"No." Ariadne paused in mid-yawn. She sounded surprised I should ask. "But then one never does. One never notices her."

"That's true."

"She does it on purpose, of course. Years and years ago when she was just starting out in the world, some preceptress said to her, 'Laure, always stay in the background.' And so she does. But it gives her pleasure. Of a kind."

"Yes," I said, "I think it does. And how sad that is, poor Mademoiselle. And you are a very clever girl to have noticed it. Yes, you are." And I looked at my pupil with some respect for her acuteness.

"Sad?" Ariadne laughed. "She likes power, does Mademoiselle; I've noticed that also."

At that moment there was a scream, then a short pause, followed by the sound of running feet. Ariadne and I looked at each other. I went to the door.

One of the maidservants was standing outside sobbing, her face was white and she was wet from her throat to her waist. She clung to the banister, swaying.

"What is it?" I hurried to her. Immediately she leant against me, resting her head on my shoulder, murmuring something.

"Make her speak," urged Ariadne.

The girl whispered something to me. I became aware that other servants were hurrying up, but all my attention was concentrated on the girl. I had caught her whisper and thought I knew what she was trying to say. "Speak up," I said urgently. "Repeat what you said about Mademoiselle Laure. You must speak clearly. I can't hear."

The girl raised her head from my shoulder, and said something that only I could hear, and I only with difficulty.

"What does she say?" cried Ariadne.

"What is it? What's the girl crying about?" The elderly woman who was the housekeeper had appeared. Mechanically, I handed the weeping maidservant over to her. I felt sick.

"She says that Mademoiselle Laure is lying upstairs, dead."

The girl gave a hysterical wail as if to confirm what I had said.

"Dear God," said the housekeeper, and crossed herself. "Be quiet, girl."

"She's mad. It can't be so," declared Ariadne. "Mademoiselle can't be dead."

"I'm sure she is," I said; I was already mounting the stairs.

"Come back," wailed Ariadne.

"Get help," I said. "Order two of the servants to come with me. No," as Ariadne made a move, "don't come yourself. Go to tell your mother. And then send for a doctor."

Resolutely I mounted the stairs.

The door to Laure's room stood open. The curtains were drawn and the blinds were down, but enough light was seeping through to see by.

In the middle of the room, surrounded by a nest of towels, was a flat tin bath. In it lay the figure of Laure, her head falling backwards, with her dark hair streaming to the floor; I could see her features foreshortened and distorted.

I walked over to one window, wrenched the curtains back and drew up the blind. Then I looked again in the full light.

She was lying in a bath of water, wearing a white shift. The water seemed stained with blood. The shift was unbuttoned and I could see her small breasts. Instinctively, I leant forward and buttoned it.

I knelt by the bath. "Oh, Laure, Laure, what have you done?" I could see that she had cut her wrists to the bone and then let her life-blood drain out in a bath of warm water. I could see the knife by my right hand as I knelt facing her. She had let it drop on a towel. "Why did you do it?"

The strangely posed and artificial death scene gave me an answer of a sort: it said that life had been to her such an ennui that she must end it the best way she could.

I picked up the knife and held it in my hand: it was an ordinary penknife, such as any woman might have in her writing-desk, but its blade was wickedly sharp and pointed. When she had wanted it, Laure would have had her weapon ready to hand. On the table by the bed was a dark blue medicine glass.

I got up from where I was crouching and looked into it: a little sediment remained; I supposed she might have taken some sedative to see that she became sleepy and died easily. Or perhaps she wanted to make sure she was too tranquil to draw back. I supposed I must have been the last person to speak to her, except the servants who had brought the bath and water.

There was the end of a dream in this room. I could feel it: Laure's dream which had kept her, sad and secretive, in Russia. You could sense it in the shut-in and cloistered atmosphere of the room, full of brooding and the stale scent of clothes and papers, but I couldn't tell what the dream had been about. "I feel free now," she had said. I could only suppose that she had woken up to find that freedom meant emptiness. Poor Laure, Russia had beaten her in the end.

I stood at the door, no longer able to bear looking at Laure, and almost at the same moment Madame Denisov, accompanied by the housekeeper and another maid, came hurrying up.

Dolly took a long look, then closed the door. "Go downstairs now, please, Rose, and stay with Ariadne. On no account is she to come up."

"But can't I help?" I began.

"No. Go downstairs. Leave me. I shall arrange everything that has to be arranged."

I went down to the big drawing-room to face Ariadne. She was sitting at a table with an open book before her which she was making no attempt to read.

She turned to look at me as I came into the room. "Well?"

"Yes." I sat down, facing her. "She is dead," I went on.

"How? What happened?"

I hesitated.

"Yes, tell us, please, Miss Rose." Peter's long length uncoiled itself from the big chair where he had been sitting. "I too am listening."

"I didn't know you were here," I said mechanically, my thoughts far away. I glanced again at Ariadne; I was unsure how much to say in front of her. "Mademoiselle Laure died in her bath," I began. "I know, that is, she told me, that she was in the habit of taking a prolonged warm bath after an attack of migraine. I suppose it was soothing and helped recovery. She must have been taking such a bath when she died."

"But how did she die?" asked Ariadne. "Come now, Rose, I shall find out, you know."

"Yes, you must tell us, Miss Rose," said Peter gently.

"She did not die from her bath, that is certain," said Ariadne.

"In a way, she did," I said sadly. "That is, I think it must have given her the idea. Wasn't it Marat who was stabbed in a bath?"

Ariadne gave a little hiss of alarm. "Stabbed?"

"Yes. You asked for the truth, and this is it: Mademoiselle Laure severed the arteries in both wrists with her penknife and then sat in the warm bath to die."

My news was received with shocked silence. Then Peter said, "The Roman way to die."

"Yes, I had the same thought."

"It's terrible," said Ariadne. She was very white, her cheerful ebullience doused. "Much worse than I thought. Poor Mademoiselle." She stood up. "I grieve for her."

"Had you any idea this was likely to happen, Miss Rose?" asked Peter Alexandrov.

"No. How could I have? I hardly knew her." I was even startled that he should ask me.

"But you were with her last night."

"I didn't think she was going to kill herself," I said sadly. "No, I got a totally different idea. She *did* say that at last she felt *free*."

"Ah," said Peter.

"But I did not interpret freedom as death."

"To the sick mind it may seem so."

"I suppose it couldn't be—no," I stopped short.

"What? What couldn't it be?" he asked sharply.

"I was wondering if it couldn't be an accident. But no, I see it couldn't have been. It's just impossible."

"What will happen now, Uncle Peter?" asked Ariadne nervously.

He shrugged. "We will leave the arrangements to your mother. She will know how to smooth things over."

"Here she is," said Ariadne. "Oh, Mother, tell us what you been doing."

Dolly Denisov came into the room. She sank into a chair with a sigh. For her, she looked dishevelled, even untidy, with flushed cheeks and a shiny nose. "Oh, the sadness of it, the utter, utter sadness. Give me a cigarette, please, Peter." Her hand trembled slightly. "Do you know, I could have sworn that I had not a tear in me for Laure Le Brun, but I have been crying for her: Dolly Denisov has been crying." Ariadne went across and took her hand and kissed her cheek.

"Yes, that poor, poor woman. But she was out of her mind." She got up and started to walk round the room, gesturing with her cigarette so that the band of diamonds around the holder glittered in the sunlight. "Mad, mad of self-love, poor thing, and I never knew. That was it, was it not, Peter?"

He nodded gravely. "I think so."

"Yes, yes, we must not blame ourselves. Ariadne, it was not your fault, never think so. Nor was it mine. Still I am sad, atrociously sad." She took a few deep puffs at her cigarette. "Oh, by the by, Peter, Dr. Burman has been most kind, and says he will arrange everything. All the formalities, you know. He feels sorry for us, says it has been extremely unfortunate for me. So kind of him, because, really, I was feeling a little *ruined* by this morning."

Peter stood up, and after a look at him, Ariadne stood up,

too. "I think we owe Mademoiselle Laure a little more than that," he said with determination. "I shall go myself."

"Not Ariadne," said Dolly at once.

"No, certainly not Ariadne." The girl sat down again. "I shall arrange the funeral service—her own church, of course. Fortunately, I know Monsignor LaRoche. I will order flowers, and choose a headstone with a suitable inscription. You may leave all that to me. And I will have a word with the servants—see they don't gossip too much. Nothing can stop their mouths altogether, as we know, but we owe it to Mademoiselle that they say the right things." Dolly nodded. "You and Ariadne will both of you have letters to write to Mademoiselle's family. She has one?"

"Yes," said Dolly, who plainly had forgotten about letters.

"A brother, I believe, in France." As Peter prepared to leave the room, she said, "Are you still staying with us, Peter?"

He paused at the door. "No, I am back at my apartment round the corner on Kinsky Street; my old servant is over his illness and back on the job. But I shall be here to luncheon, if you will have me."

"Delighted," said Dolly mechanically.

Dolly caused an especially fine wine to be served with our lunch, because, she said, "we need bucking up." She herself drank it with enjoyment, but very quietly, as if she were an invalid.

Dolly was distressed by Mademoiselle's death and *did* mourn her, but she was rendering the emotion bearable by making herself the chief victim, a victim who could be comforted by fine wines, cigarettes and soothing talk from her friends.

After lunch, Ariadne brought me her letter. "Will this do, Miss Rose?" She laid her letter on the table before me. "I addressed it to her brother. Have I said the right sort of thing? And is my grammar correct?"

"Your French is better than my own, I suspect." I was scanning the letter: she had done her task beautifully, in a few lucid and sympathetic sentences.

"In speech, perhaps, but I do not write it so well. Will it do, then?"

"Yes, admirably."

Ariadne gave a sigh of relief, and put down her pen.

The luxury and ease of life in the great house was already closing the hole over Mademoiselle's head. The letters had been written, the funeral arranged, soon she would be buried, then forgotten. A terrible tragedy: but of not much consequence to anyone. The police would have notes of it in the records, I supposed, and the French Consul would have made a note of it, and that would be it.

"Shall we go to church, Miss Rose? There will be a nice service there this afternoon. And it seems the right thing to do."

And it will close the hole over Mademoiselle's head even quicker, I thought. "If your mother approves," I said.

Dolly's reaction confirmed my thoughts. She was lying on a sofa in her own sitting-room, wearing a beautiful apricot-coloured crêpe-de-chine peignoir and apparently engaged in counting the pleats in her sleeve.

"Yes, of course. Very suitable."

"And Madame Titov will be there."

"Oh, so she will. I heard her say so at dinner yesterday." A quick look at me. "A very nice woman. Not a close friend, but someone I have known a long time." To Ariadne: "Perhaps it would be better not to ride with Major Lacey."

"He asked me: he was going to mount Miss Rose, too, if she wanted. You didn't know that, did you?" I shook my head. "But Uncle Peter saw him this morning and told him about Mademoiselle Laure. We could send him a message and ask him to meet us at the church and then we could all go to drink tea at Berrin's afterwards. Major Lacey is interested in the Church: he says he likes the music." She added, half proudly, "He says he is interested in everything in Russia."

"And I suppose you think it's because of you, little monkey?" said Dolly. "Off with you, then. And if Major Lacey should arrive at the church, I shall have to countenance it."

She was not making much secret of her promotion of the relationship between Ariadne and Edward Lacey, I thought.

"You look sad, Miss Rose," said Ariadne. "Still thinking of Mademoiselle Laure?"

"Yes, still thinking, and still perplexed." Why *had* she done it when I would have been ready to swear she was reaching out for happiness?

"Life does not always answer our questions," said Dolly. "Many are left unanswered, and there are always mysteries. Especially in Russia." And she stood up.

Walking beside Ariadne, I was still thinking of the scene in that shuttered bedroom. There were certain features about it that had begun to puzzle me. Her shift, I thought, unbuttoned. The knife, where it had fallen.

"Now you look thoughtful, Miss Rose," said Ariadne, breaking into my considerations. "But you often do. There is a certain sort of serious, quiet look you sometimes have. I have noticed it. Is it because you are thinking of home things? Have you perhaps had bad news?"

"No, not exactly bad news, but unexpected," I said, remembering the letter about Patrick's trouble in India.

"About your—?" She paused delicately, seeking for a suitable word.

"About the man I was going to marry? Yes." So Ariadne knew about Patrick. I suppose I should have guessed it. Whether told directly to her or not, it was the sort of information she would pick up.

"What was he like, Miss Rose? To look at, and as a person?"

Could I still remember what Patrick looked like? Faces, even beloved ones, fade so fast. "He was tall, fair-haired, with blue eyes, not a bit good-looking really."

"But you thought he *was,* all the same."

"I suppose so."

"And what was it like loving him? Forgive me asking, it's the sort of thing I am interested in!"

"I had noticed, Ariadne," I said. And not only in the discussion of it. I had noticed the eager way her body curved towards Major Lacey. *Now* she curled her arms happily and innocently around me, or her Uncle Peter, but soon she would be ready to entangle herself with other bodies. "But I don't know that I can speak about it; you see it had an unhappy ending, or no ending at all. I can say that while it lasted I knew what it was to be both happy and unhappy at the same time."

This kept Ariadne quiet for a while, as we walked along, side by side. The afternoon was now very hot, the sun striking off the stone in a dazzling way. Dolly had intimated that we would be leaving St. Petersburg soon for the country. Before we did that I wanted to see my cousins, the Misses Gowrie, again.

But she wasn't silenced. "Did he kiss you? Did you kiss him?" she asked suddenly.

"Oh, Ariadne," I demurred.

For a few more yards of our walk she was again silent, her profile pensive under her white parasol. Then she said, "I thought you might tell me. You see, I'm supposed to know so very much, and I know so terribly little."

"But hasn't your mother said anything to you? I mean on this sort of subject?"

She shrugged. Yes, kind, nice woman as she was, I could just see Dolly sliding away from any difficult discussion. Putting it off, in that procrastinating Russian fashion, till tomorrow. "I believe she thinks any true woman knows instinctively."

"And don't you?" I asked bluntly.

Ariadne's eyes opened wide. For a second she seemed to be staring past me at a picture only she saw, her expression rapt. "Yes, I believe I do," she said between parted lips.

"I should think Edward Lacey might be a gentle instructor," I said. And a skillful one, too, I admitted to myself. What a conversation, I thought, wondering what my employer would think of it. The truth was, that in spite of my brave front to Ariadne, I was very nearly as ignorant as she was.

Would Patrick have been "a gentle instructor"? I didn't know, but I doubted it.

"You're getting that look again," said Ariadne. "You are either thinking of your lost lover or poor Mademoiselle."

"Both," I said. "Both." And it was true. Ever since Laure had told me about her own broken love affair, there had been a link between them in my mind. Strike a note of pain and disappointment, and I saw them both.

"And there is Major Lacey," said Ariadne, suddenly demure. She pointed to where he stood outside the Church of St. Andrew. He came to meet us, smiling.

"Your uncle told me where to find you, and I was truly grateful for the chance to join you here."

We were very close to the open church door, and a wave of incense, Russian incense, stronger than anything I ever knew, blew towards us.

"Are you thinking of being received into the Orthodox Church?" I asked the Major.

"No, I come for the singing." Impossible to tell if he was serious or not. "I am sorry about Mademoiselle Laure. Poor woman. I hardly knew her, but I brought some tea back from France for her once. She didn't care for Russian tea and wanted some peppermint brew of her own. A tisane, she called it." He spoke with the amusement of a healthy Englishman who drank great cups full of strong Ceylon tea at breakfast and tiny cups of black coffee after dinner. I heard him say once: "I never take luncheon. Only a lamb chop and a glass of sherry," which I, raised in the careful style of Jordansjoy, thought a very adequate luncheon indeed.

As always, the church was crowded with people of all ages and conditions, rich, poor, sick and the fashionable healthy like Ariadne and Major Lacey. The smell of humanity mixed with incense was overwhelming. It usually took me a few minutes to get used to, although Ariadne seemed not to notice it. But I saw Major Lacey's nose wrinkle slightly. "By Jove," I heard him murmur under his breath, "rich."

Inside the church, the darkness was lightened only by candles. I stood still while my eyes adjusted to the light. Then I slipped into a seat beside Ariadne whose head was bent; she was murmuring reverently. Now that my eyes were used to the gloom I could take in the great splendour of the building. Everywhere that the light of the candles penetrated I could see the glint of gold. It shone from the golden candelabra, from the crosses and from the gold leaf used in the paintings which decorated the walls. The other colour which shone through the darkness was the blue of lapis lazuli, which I could see on walls, pillars and roof. Here and there were the deep green of malachite and the yellow of onyx. I felt as though I were inside a great jewelled box, but inside this box I felt stifled, not free and at peace as in the kirk at Jordansjoy. I was pressed down by the weight of too many centuries, and too much emotion expended in too much wealth of decoration.

The choir began to sing, emerging in procession from behind the great carved screen which concealed the tabernacle and the host. With them came the priests in their splendid robes of velvet and stiff silk, embroidered with gold and silver. In colours of mulberry and purple and deep blue, they walked, one after another, men with pale faces, dominated by their vestments. Incense was being thrown about lavishly in great clouds. The host was carried round and the people pressed close. A woman close to me knelt down to kiss the ground: Ariadne crossed herself continually. I sat with my hands folded, feeling a little apart; I was not drawn into the emotion spilling out all round me. I felt sad that I wasn't more touched; I felt reverence and respect for the ritual of the great tradition unfolding itself before me, but a little hard knot of reserve remained within. I wanted to give way, but I could not. I had been like this with Patrick, when I had wanted to show him some special mark of affection, had longed, really, to let my love overflow towards him, but something held me back, and I remained constrained and still. But within me, as I well knew, was a contradiction, because this coldness could as suddenly melt and turn me from shyness into someone burning and passionate. How difficult I was and puzzling to a lover, and how hard for him to handle. Perhaps it was this, in the end, which separated him from me—I think this contradiction would have gone with marriage, but I never got a chance to show him. Poor Patrick. I had been so angry with him at first, so full of injured pride and resentment. Now I only grieved for him. I hadn't thought of myself as to blame in the breaking-off between Patrick and me, but I saw now that I might have been. To a man under stress I had been an added problem and it hadn't been enough: he could not confide in me, and perhaps he had thought I did not love him in the way I should have done. He may have thought I loved him back too much and too little.

So as I knelt beside Ariadne, I was really thinking of Patrick.

"Time to go, Miss Rose," whispered Ariadne. "We must rise from our places. We are keeping the people behind us from getting out." She looked at me with pleasure. "You were far, far away."

"Yes, I was."

"You were quite carried away. Oh, it was the music, I know, it affects everyone, no one can resist it."

"Yes, it was very fine."

"Interesting counter-tenor they have in the choir," said Edward Lacey.

"Oh, yes, he is a genuine castrato," said Ariadne, with enthusiasm.

Edward Lacey looked a little disconcerted at her frankness. Possibly he thought that well brought up young girls should not be too familiar with the term "castrato," although anyone who has seriously studied music must know it.

"I thought he might be," he said. "Strange noise he makes. Vibrant but odd. One could hardly call it beautiful."

The crowd was pressing close against us, hemming us in on either side, making it difficult to move. We did slowly edge an inch or so forward. I was struck once again by the variety of people that made up the mass. A richly dressed woman was shoulder to shoulder to an old man in his working clothes, a fragile old creature in tatters and rags stood before a burly man carrying a silk hat. Behind them came a trio of schoolgirls in charge of a sister in flowing robes, and behind them the tall figure of a bearded monk. The girls were giggling amongst themselves, and I saw the monk give them a hard stare. I noticed his eyes particularly, as they had a keenly alive and searching glance. He turned his head towards me with a penetratingly clear look. I blinked.

Once, when I was walking in the woods around Jordansjoy, I came upon a young fox. He appeared on the path above me: the ground sloped, so we met eye to eye, and he stared at me boldly, unafraid. Now, to my surprise, I saw that free, questing animal stare again in this man's eyes. Strange eyes for a monk, I thought.

"We can move now, Miss Gowrie," prompted Edward Lacey politely.

The crowd was much thinner and it was easy now to make our way to the great door, where groups of people still stood about talking and settling their hats and gloves preparatory to departure. As we went forward, I could see that Ariadne had her eyes on a woman, soberly dressed in plain, dark clothes, who was drawing on a pair of white kid gloves and opening a parasol.

"Madame Titov," she said. "I want you to meet her."

"Oh, yes, I remember you mentioned her."

"She is a person it is very good to know," Ariadne assured me earnestly. "Nice in herself, and *important.*"

She didn't look important, rather she looked a shy, quiet woman, with a dowdy taste in hats, and yet with an air of being completely at ease in the world.

"And she's very *holy,*" went on Ariadne. "That is, devoted to the Church, you know."

"Pious," I said. "And what makes her important?"

"Hush, she'll hear. It's the Empress, of course. They are very close. She looks after the Heir. In the schoolroom and so on."

Ah, I thought, a governess, even if of a very superior sort. A sister to me beneath the skin.

"So that's why you want me to meet her? We are two of a kind."

"Not exactly," Ariadne smiled. "She is not a bit like you. Nor are your duties the same. But she wanted to meet you."

Inwardly I raised my eyebrows; so now it was she who wished to meet *me*. That hadn't been the story the first time round.

"I think the lady knows you are here," murmured Edward Lacey under his breath.

It was true, now I took another glance, Madame Titov was unobtrusively studying me as she fiddled with the buttons on her gloves. Clearly, she was waiting for us to come up to her. Nor did we keep her waiting long. Ariadne piloted me towards her deftly, towing Edward Lacey behind us like a small tug guiding a liner. Except that even out of his uniform there was something military in Edward's bearing, so perhaps I should have likened him to a man-o'-war.

"This is Miss Gowrie," said Ariadne breathlessly. "Madame, may I present Miss Gowrie: Rose, this is Madame Titov."

"Delighted," murmured Madame, extending a soft hand; her fingers seemed to melt into mine as I took them, and to give no palpable pressure back. Her expression was friendly enough, although I judged she was not a lady who ever allowed strong emotions to show. Perhaps she felt none. However, she allowed a little curiosity to creep into her expression as she saw Edward Lacey.

"Oh, Major Lacey," presented Ariadne quickly.

"Ah, I know your sister. Her husband's estate marches with my father's in the country, so they are neighbours. That counts with us in Russia, I can tell you; neighbours count for something when there might not be another family one can visit for another two hundred miles. I have known your brother-in-law all my life. Not that I am there much myself now, you understand? Your sister is not going out into society at present, I believe?"

"She expects to be confined in July," said Edward briefly.

"Her third child, I believe? Yes. Has she a son?"

"She has two," said Edward with a smile. "Young rascals they are, too,"

"And strong healthy boys? She is a fortunate woman."

"Oh, yes, Daphne knows she is."

"I hope she wants a daughter this time," I said, anxious to put in a good word for my sex.

"She's convinced of it; she says her hair has never curled better than this summer, and her old nurse tells her that is a sure sign of a girl."

"Oh, I know all the signs," said Madame Titov, with that dry little smile of hers. "Although, alas, I am childless myself. Sometimes the signs work, sometimes they do not. Tell your sister not to rely on her curls." She had a sly sense of humour, after all. "Miss Gowrie, you have a look of your family about you; you all of you have that outward-looking, pleasant manner. When I was a girl your cousins taught me to speak English. They've talked to me about you and your sister and your brother. I think it gives them pleasure to think of you living still in the old family home. They are *kind* old ladies. Good, kind women." She had run herself into silence.

"I think they are, too," I said, to give her time to get her breath back. And great gossips as well, I added to myself. They seemed to have talked about me to all their friends.

"Of course they know everyone, and go everywhere. In their own style, you know. Oh, yes, you would be surprised at the houses where they are informally received. They are so much respected. Loved, even." She turned to Ariadne. "I believe you are going into the country soon?"

"Quite soon," said Ariadne.

"We shall meet then," said Madame Titov decisively. "Because I am going to the country, too." She held out her hand to me. This time I noticed a very faint response to my own pressure. "Good-bye, till we meet again, Miss Rose Gowrie."

I felt as though I had been inspected and had passed the test. The satisfied little breath that Ariadne drew in convinced me that I was right. "She likes you," the girl whispered to me.

As Madame Titov walked away, she passed close to where the tall monk was still standing. He must have been watching us all the time we talked. He took a step towards her, a broad smile beginning on his face; I thought he meant to speak to her. If so, she gave him no chance. Not for a second did her progress falter. Instead, she seemed to walk faster, and as she hurried on, her skirt gave an angry jerk, as if she had pulled it aside.

I thought I was imagining it until I saw the monk's expression change from anticipation to anger, and turning, saw an amused look on Edward Lacey's face. Ariadne said, "Shall we walk home?" in a breathy, hurried voice.

"Who's that?" I said, looking at the monk.

"No one we know," she answered.

"I am sure he wanted to speak to Madame Titov. So he must have thought she knew him."

"A mistake," said Ariadne.

"Certainly a mistake," agreed Edward Lacey, as if they knew a joke I did not know. "A mistake now, if not in the past and not in the future."

"What do you mean?"

"I mean that Madame Titov has had to know the fellow in the past and may have to know him in the future. But she would rather not."

"She dislikes him, then?"

"She hates him."

Ariadne made a demurring noise. "Perhaps not hates. It would not be wise for her to hate."

"He certainly has powerful friends," murmured Edward Lacey.

"So you *do* know him, Ariadne?"

"Not personally. But he is known at Court, and indeed he often turns up in St. Petersburg where you would least expect. But my mother dislikes him. He arouses strong likes and dislikes, you see." Ariadne sounded flustered. I could see she wanted to draw me away from what she seemed to regard as this man of God's dangerous vicinity. But he was already approaching.

"Good afternoon, Father Gregory."

He raised his hand. "Bless you, child." He had a peasant's voice, but it had rich tones. He held out his hand to her, she took it reluctantly, then dropped it almost at once, but never for a moment did Ariadne take her eyes off his face. Then he turned towards me, holding out his hand again, and smiling at me with his pale, bright eyes. He stank. He looks like a fox and he smells like a fox, I thought, but I took his hand.

I found his touch unpleasant, damp with sweat on this hot day, and withdrew my hand, sorry that I had removed my glove.

"Bless you, my child," he said, staring at me. "You have the face of a saint." Bright and compelling, his eyes held my own, and it was with an effort that I withdrew my gaze. To my surprise, something had passed between us; I couldn't put a name to what I had sensed, but a communication of some sort had occurred. Then I knew what it was: I had recognized a quality in him and he had responded. It was like two metals striking against each other and each giving out the same note. But what could we have in common? I didn't have to put it into speech, I knew it wordlessly. What I had, he had; what he could do, I could do.

He knew, too, and his eyes burned fiercely. "May I see your hands?"

Reluctantly, almost against my will, but certainly unable not to do, I held them out, fingers extended. Tenderly, he turned the right one over, putting palm uppermost. "Yes, there, at the base of the thumb, there is the mark."

"I see nothing." I stared at my hand.

"It is enough."

I wanted to turn my hand over, but for the moment I couldn't do it.

"Come along, Miss Gowrie," said Edward Lacey in a friendly but formidable fashion, "Ariadne is anxious to get home. Good-bye, Father."

I wasn't sure if Ariadne did wish to move, she was still standing there, eyes bright, lips slightly parted, her breast rising and falling in short, panting breaths.

"Get her along, Miss Gowrie," said Edward Lacey.

I put my arm round her waist and gave her a little tug. "Come on, Ariadne."

"Pestilential fellow," I thought I heard Edward Lacey say under his breath. He hailed a *likhachy* and had us on our way home very smartly. "Why did you let her talk to him?" he asked me irritably.

"I don't control Ariadne," I said coldly.

"You can see what he is, the sort of priest who makes up to women. They come in every creed."

Why, he's jealous, I thought, absolutely jealous of Ariadne. He must be the sort of man who showed possessiveness towards any woman in whom he took an interest, even me. It was sad, because I had begun to like him.

"The charlatan," he muttered.

Ah, that's another story, I thought. But I had to remember that he could not possibly know what I knew about the man. For that matter, if hard proof had been required of me, I should have found it difficult.

"Not all priests are charlatans," I surprised myself by saying.

"That's dangerous," he snapped.

Ariadne put her hand gently on his arm and smiled up at him: after a pause he smiled back. I saw how instinctively she controlled the man who loved her. How little of that art I had shown with Patrick. Oh, if only I could have another chance, I thought. But there wouldn't be another chance. Patrick was in India, in bad trouble, missing and perhaps even dead. I would never see him again.

Edward Lacey left us at the door of the Denisov house, and we went in alone.

It was a beautiful house, full of elegance and luxury, of which I felt the charm to the full. But it was also a house of secrets. A house in which a woman had died tragically, a house in which unknown voices spoke to you out of a tube from the depths of the basements, and where an old woman waited at the top of a red staircase for the mysterious gift of eternal life.

Russia was more than living up to any expectations I might have formed for it.

All the rest of that day I waited to see if any more mention was made of Mademoiselle Laure's death, but nothing was said. Dolly and Ariadne, and even Peter Alexandrov. who was still there, seemed satisfied that they knew all the answers to Mademoiselle's death, and that, sad as the event was, it was over.

But I couldn't feel the same, and the more I thought about it, the more the same questions posed themselves. The points which puzzled me were the odd position of the knife on the floor beside the bath of water, the unbuttoned shift that Laure had worn and the medicine bottle by her bed.

As I had knelt on the floor looking at Laure, I had seen the knife on the floor as if it had fallen from the dead woman's nerveless hand. I retained a vivid impression of what I had seen, and the knife was on the floor. Somehow I would have expected it to fall from her hand into the bath of water. Indeed, I found it hard to believe that any woman, however determined, could slash both wrists. I could imagine her cutting into the left wrist with the right hand, and perhaps making an attempt to gash the right wrist, but both wrists looked cleanly cut and in an equal way. The whole thing had a contrived, artificial, *planned* look. That was it: planned.

Then there was the shift, unbuttoned in that negligent, casual way. Now Mademoiselle was, I had already concluded, a prudish lady. It was, therefore, entirely in character that she had dressed herself before committing suicide, so that even in death she must be decently covered. Yes, I could accept that idea, but I thought that, if so, she would have buttoned the shift to the neck. As it was, it had been so undone as to leave her breasts exposed. Shy, prim Laure Le Brun would have automatically covered herself.

Both the doubts led me to the incredible suspicion that Laure had been killed rather than had killed herself. It was murder I was thinking of, and not suicide.

In Scotland the thought of anyone I knew being murdered would never have entered my head. (It was true that a young servant-girl on a farm near to Jordansjoy had been killed by her lover, but one did not "know" servants.) Here, in Russia, anything seemed possible.

The medicine bottle on the table by Laure's bed reinforced the picture that was forming in my mind. If Laure had taken some of the laudanum, either of her own free will or because she was persuaded to do so, she would very soon have become so sleepy that to kill her and quietly arrange her death to look like suicide would be simple.

I told myself I was mad to think such thoughts, but I went on thinking them.

The next day definite signs of our departure for the country became apparent. Great leather trunks could be seen carried up the stairs into Madame Denisov's rooms.

In the stables, the motor car, which had pushed the splendid horses into second place, was being overhauled. The butler began to mutter about packing up the silver. Meanwhile, the routine of the house went on as usual.

"I'm so glad you met Madame Titov yesterday," said Dolly, sailing into the room where Ariadne and I were reading Jane Austen aloud, taking page and page about, from *Pride and Prejudice*. "A darling, is she not? Oh, don't let me stop you. Let me listen. I shall enjoy it."

And for a minute or two she did sit there listening, smoking her cigarette in its long holder, and admiring the flash of the diamonds on her hand. Then she started up again:

"How beautifully you read, Miss Gowrie. And Ariadne, too. What life you put into it, dear. You really should be an actress. In fact, you *are* an actress."

Ariadne laughed. "Thank you for the compliment, Mamma. If it *is* a compliment."

"It's a compliment to Miss Gowrie; you always used to read so woodenly with Mademoiselle Laure." Ariadne pulled a face and murmured something critical about French. "How her English has come on, Miss Gowrie. I congratulate you."

"Her English has always been excellent," I said, which was true. I didn't think I had added much to it.

"And your Russian, too," went on Dolly admiringly. "So good."

"Yes, I understand it pretty well now, and I can make myself understood. Most of the time, anyway. Except that yesterday I caught myself asking for only a little 'cat' at lunch when I meant to ask for a little fish."

Dolly laughed. "Soon you will be able to try your hand with our peasants. I came in to tell you that we leave for the country the day after tomorrow."

"How long shall we stay?" asked Ariadne, playing with a pencil.

"We shall be in the country in all the hot weather," said Dolly. "It depends."

I wondered what it depended on. Not Dolly's pleasure, I thought; she was a city-dweller if I ever saw one.

"Of course we shall have lots of visitors. And go visiting ourselves. You need not fear being dull, Miss Gowrie," went on Dolly.

Two hundred miles to the nearest neighbour, and that one Madame Titov, who had not looked, kind soul though she doubtless was, the spirit of gaiety, I thought.

"Do you know where our estate is, Miss Gowrie?"

I shook my head.

"Ariadne must point it out on the map. Far in the deepest country, near the Polish border, with the most lovely forests all around. You will like it." She lit another cigarette. "But you two girls must remember to go shopping for everything you will need. Our nearest town (and we are not so near that, either) is Shereshevo, and that contains nothing but stuff fit for peasants. No, one can't shop there."

"Mamma hates the country really," observed Ariadne maliciously. "She thinks of it as a sort of imprisonment there."

"Well, we have to go, to keep an eye on the peasants and all that. If one didn't check the steward, he would pick us to the bone. As it is, I dare say he gets away with more than we know. They hand the tricks down from father to son. One never gets to the bottom of it. They are too much for *us*."

"All in all, we don't do so badly," observed Ariadne. And, considering the wealth and luxury that lay all around her, I took this to be no more than the truth.

Dolly Denisov stood up. "Now you know our plans. I must be off: so much to do. I shall be exhausted, a wreck. I don't dare to think how I shall look when I crawl into the train. You two won't see much of me between then and now, nothing, I dare say."

Now was the time to speak then, or never.

"Please, madame," I said hurriedly. She was already at the door with one hand elegantly poised. "Yes?"

I could feel my heart bumping, but it had to be said. I stood up, too. Ariadne looked curiously at me. "Madame, it's about Mademoiselle's death. I don't think she killed herself."

She gave me a long, silent stare. Time enough for me to remember that I was a stranger in an alien country. But so had Laure been. I owed it to her. "She was killed. I'm sure she was killed."

"Miss Gowrie! Think what you are saying."

"Yes, I have thought. And I'm troubled." My voice shook. "The appearance of the room, of her body—it seemed so contrived, so unnatural."

Dolly Denisov shook her head. "Violent death *is* unnatural."

"Then the knife, when it fell from her hand, surely it should have fallen into the bath?"

Dolly shrugged her shoulders. "Well," she began sceptically.

I went on: "But if the knife was used by someone kneeling in front of her, facing her, that person would, naturally, have dropped the knife where I found it."

"Oh', Miss Gowrie," protested Dolly, "such a terrible conclusion from such a simple fact. No, I cannot accept it."

"Yes, Miss Rose," said Ariadne, "it truly doesn't seem much."

"Then there is her chemise—it was unbuttoned; if she was modest enough to put it on to kill herself in, then she would have buttoned it."

Dolly sighed. "Well, no, I think not. It means nothing. She was beside herself. We know that."

"Mademoiselle always wore a white shift when she bathed, Miss Rose," said Ariadne. "She was brought up in a convent and the nuns trained her to do it."

"But the buttons?" I said obstinately. "She would have buttoned them."

"Miss Gowrie, this is all most distasteful. And in front of Ariadne, too."

Peter Alexandrov had come into the room, and Dolly threw an appeal to him. "Thank goodness you are here. Miss Gowrie is trying to make us believe that poor Mademoiselle was murdered. Oh, it is too ridiculous and sad—all about a button and where the knife fell. She is making out such a strange picture."

"Let Miss Gowrie tell us herself what she thinks happened," he said gravely.

"I think that Laure Le Brun had taken some of her headache medicine (I saw the bottle by the bed) and that she was thus drugged and weak. It was while she was in this state her

night-clothes were taken off and her chemise put on by
someone who did not button it, and that this person put her
in the bath and then used the knife on her."

Dolly winced.

"And why do you think all this?" he asked.

Again I went through the reasoning that had made me
form this picture in my mind. He listened carefully, but without much expression on his face. At the end he said sadly, "I
see that Russia has worked its transformation on the mind. It
is easier for strangers to be unbalanced by us than anywhere
else in the world. Do not blame yourself for your fantasies,
Miss Gowrie, it is Russia that produces them. God knows we
have them ourselves."

"I am sure I am reason itself," protested Dolly.

"No, you are as mad as the rest of us," said her brother.
"Still, the servants must know something. Have they been
spoken to? About who ordered the bath water, and why they
were so slow in returning for the bath and finding Mademoiselle?"

"Yes," said Dolly sulkily. "I spoke to them. She always lay
so long in the bath that they were used to it, and they just forgot her. It was negligent, of course, but no more."

"Perhaps we should talk to them again and see if we can set
this poor girl's mind at rest," and he touched the bell.

Very soon they came, two red-cheeked, flat-nosed country
girls. The elder appointed herself their spokeswoman. Yes, it
was they who had carried the bath and brought the water to
Mademoiselle, just as they had already told Madame. Dolly
nodded vigorously. They knew exactly what was expected of
them, as they had done it many times before. Mademoiselle
had opened the door to them herself and stood watching as
they arranged things.

"And what made you take such a time in going back to
empty the bath?"

"But Mademoiselle ordered it that way *always*." The
spokeswoman was voluble. "Always. She liked to lie in the

bath for hours upon end. Relieving the pain of her head, she said. She said that her Tsar Napoleon used to sit in a bath to cool his nerves and that she does the same. I thought it was only us in Russia who had a Tsar, but apparently not. And then after the bath she would take some medicine in a glass, liquid laudanum I think it was, and sleep. That was how it went. Then we brought her tea when she woke up. It was always the same, but this last time we were so busy we forgot clean about her. You can't really blame two poor girls for what happened."

"No, no," said Peter. "That's enough, then. You may go."

I waited for them to go. "I see, then, that the laudanum usually came after the bath. But she could have been asleep in the bed, just as I said."

Peter shook his head. "No, no, Miss Gowrie. It won't do. It's all your imagination at work."

I suppose I looked obstinate, because he went on: "There is something you forget." I looked at him quickly. "What possible motive could there be for killing Mademoiselle?"

I was silent, reluctant to say that I thought it might be because of something she was going to tell me, but I had to in the end. "She was going to tell me something," I said at last. "Something relating to why I was here. What I was really needed for."

"Well, but you are here for me," Ariadne said.

"Princess Irene thinks not," I said. "She thinks I have come here to help *her*."

Dolly exploded: "That old witch! I might have known she was at the bottom of it. I don't know how you came to be speaking to her, really I don't. You had no business to, I am quite vexed about it."

"I was exploring the house. Remember you said I might. And I came upon her by accident."

"It's like a fairy-story," observed Peter, not without humour. "But you must have seen our old great-aunt is crazy? It is the madness of old age."

"You can't believe a word she says. Or only every other word at the most. And Mademoiselle seems to have been the same," said Dolly.

"Come now, Dolly," said her brother, "let's calm this poor girl down. Between two poor sick women and the Russian summer heat, she has fallen into a terrible state. But there's no harm done. Mademoiselle was certainly not stabbed by me or my sister to stop her telling you a further secret about Princess Irene, who seems very well equipped to tell her own."

"No, I never for one moment thought that," I said lamely. "I don't know what I did think." I was beginning to feel very stupid.

"If Mademoiselle herself had been frightened, she would have locked her room," Peter pointed out. "And it was not locked. So no more talk of murder, please."

He smiled at me, and I smiled back. Even Dolly managed a weak smile. Only Ariadne looked disappointed at no more fireworks and revelations.

"I expected better of you, Miss Gowrie," Dolly said, more in sorrow than in anger. And I felt I had forfeited her respect, which saddened me, because I was coming to like my warm-tempered, good-natured, frivolous employer.

I felt ashamed, and yet still reluctant to admit that I was altogether wrong. There was something puzzling about Laure Le Brun's death. Why couldn't they see it?

Dolly had one last message before she sped off on the busy day she professed to have before her. (Playing cards with her friends, I guessed.) "Go off to see your wise old cousins, Rose, my dear," she ended. "And get your head screwed on right again."

In due course I took Dolly Denisov's advice and went to see my old kinswomen; I wanted to say good-bye before we left for the country.

The last few days, since my outburst to Dolly, had not

passed unpleasantly. No one mentioned Mademoiselle Laure again, least of all I. Clearly the topic was a forbidden one. Everyone was very nice to me, as if trying to show me that they bore me no ill will for my outburst. Dolly was even sweeter to me than usual, and Peter hung around Ariadne and me, making jokes and offering us treats, like a special visit to the theatre. I could see as plainly as anything that I had been "forgiven," and I didn't like it. It didn't seem the right answer to my worries about Mademoiselle: I felt she deserved more, and I deserved less.

It was a jolly time for Ariadne, riding in the late morning with Edward Lacey on a spirited black horse, with me jogging along behind on a discreet mare, then walking to tea-parties with her young friends in the afternoons, where they giggled over the tea-cups while I acted the dowager on the sofa. I seemed to enjoy myself, indeed I did enjoy it, but underneath, all my questions about Mademoiselle's death still trickled on, like water over stones.

The big, shabby apartment where my old cousins lived was wearing its high summer look, with English chintz on the chairs, pots of flowers everywhere and curtains looped back at open windows.

Even so, it was hot, and Emma Gowrie in her stiff white shirtwaist and tussore skirt looked flushed, but she was welcoming as ever.

"Come in, come in, Rose. A pleasure to see you, a sight for sore eyes." She was alone in their living-room. "My sister's out: gone to give a piano lesson to the daughter of a wealthy merchant. Rich as Croesus, my dear, but she can't play. Tinkles away, tinkles away, hasn't got the art in her, you see."

She settled me in a chair and gave me a cup of tea, and one of those strange little saucers of jam that seemed an inevitable accompaniment in Russia. But I got a Huntley and Palmer biscuit, too, which I nibbled as I drank the tea. "That's right, good girl," said Miss Gowrie approvingly as I ate and drank. "And how are you settling in with the Denisovs? Shaking down well together, eh? Dolly's a good sort."

"Oh, yes, we get on very well, and I like Ariadne. Madame Denisov has been kindness itself."

"So you said before, so you said."

"But I've been in hot water lately."

Her eyebrows shot up. "Eh?"

"It was about Mademoiselle Laure's death. You heard, I suppose?"

Her face softened, and she nodded. "Poor Laure Le Brun. She never had any stuffing."

Hesitantly, I said, "I thought that perhaps she had *not* killed herself. Oh, well, I needn't go into it now. Better not, anyway, but I talked it over with Madame Denisov and her brother and they showed me I was wrong. At least they tried. I'm not sure if they were right." I stopped. "Yes, I suppose they were. The fact is, though I'm not sure they were right, I'm not sure I'm right either. It troubles me."

Miss Gowrie took some knitting, one of the complicated pieces of pattern she often had by her. "It was a shock, Laure Le Brun's death. But I always thought her an unstable creature. I won't say I expected her to kill herself so terribly, but I was not surprised. Perhaps there is some mystery remaining, and you sense it, being a sensitive creature, and it puzzles you. But as you get older you will find plenty of such mysteries in life, and sometimes one never gets to learn the answer. Not all the answers are sinister."

"No, I understand that; I see what you are trying to say. I wonder, though."

She held up her knitting, appraising the violent geometric patterns of red and orange. I could see it was a monstrous work of art, and that I might even grow to like it. "And was that the end of it, then? Between you and Dolly Denisov, I mean?"

"Not quite." Again I hesitated, then I said, "I've had a sort of question in my mind for some time now, about *why* I'm really employed there. I don't think it's just for Ariadne, it *can't* be, and yet they say it is. I asked, tried to have it all out, said I'd been told there *was* some other purpose laid out for me."

"And *had* you been told?"

"Yes, old Princess Irene said I'd come for *her*."

Miss Gowrie laughed. "You need never mind her. She thinks the whole world exists for her. That's what comes of having been a beauty and an heiress."

"And Laure hinted she knew, as well. But I suppose she was unbalanced and may not have meant what she said. Anyway, I told Madame, and she tried to settle my mind, assured me there was nothing in it all."

"Did she? Did she really?" Miss Gowrie seemed uneasy. "Well, perhaps that was not quite honest of her."

She held out her hand. "Now, don't rush me into saying something I don't mean. I can't say for sure, it's just an impression I got. Or perhaps not an impression, perhaps just a thought." She was floundering. She was such an honest old thing, she hated to lie.

"I'm sure you know something, and I think you ought to tell me," I said decidedly.

She shook her head. "There are some things that are not said aloud. Not in Russia. If my guess—" So it was a guess now, I noticed, not an impression or a thought. "But if it's what I think, you won't dislike it." She got up and started to fuss round the room, straightening the cushions and pouring cold tea on the camellias. Anything to avoid talking any further on the subject.

Afterwards, I wondered if she meant Peter, but, no, that way lay madness. Dolly Denisov, that most worldly of ladies, would never match-make for her brother with a penniless girl from Scotland.

And there was another question that I wanted to ask. I looked at my kind old friend, stumping round the room, and called her back. "Come and sit down. I promise not to ask any more questions about that silly girl, Rose Gowrie. But there is something else I want to ask."

"Ask away." She had taken up her knitting again.

"Who is Father Gregory?" I asked.

"Ah, now that *is* a question. Something of a mystery. But

he is often to be seen in St. Petersburg. So you've met him? Well, it was to be expected. And what did you make of him?" She gave me a sharp look.

"That he is a very strange monk."

She laughed. "Less strange in Russia than in Scotland. You must remember that in the Orthodox Church there is room for many types of religious figures. Our Western notion of a monk as a man living under a strict rule and in monastic conditions is not at all theirs. They *have* strict monasteries, but they give equal respect to wandering religious figures. *Starets* is the Russian name for such people. Or, if the man of God is a poor, wandering pilgrim, he is known as a *strannik*. But both are holy men. Father Gregory is a *starets*."

"He smells," I said. "And he's dirty, too."

"Well, cleanliness is not next to godliness in Russia. On the contrary. And in his case his smell seems to promote the idea of his holiness. He has quite a following. I can't stand him myself," she ended in a detached tone.

"Nor I," I said. "I didn't like him at all."

"He may be a great old fraud."

"No, he is not that. I dislike him, but he is no fraud."

Again she gave me a sharp look. "Yes, he has power. I admit that power. But really, Rose, I would rather you did not dislike him too much. Hate opens the mind so. Indifference is safer."

I did not understand her. "He could never have power over me," I said proudly.

"How did you come to meet him?"

"Oh, at the church Ariadne is so fond of, St. Andrew's. We had just been talking to Madame Titov."

"Oh, was she there, too?" And she nodded her head in a satisfied way as if I had fed one more little fact into a machine that made pictures for her. "What did you make of her?"

"Ordinary," I said.

"Yes, ordinary. You are quite right. They are all of them ordinary, that's the tragedy of it. I wonder what you will make of her when you get to know her better."

"But will I get to know her better?" I was surprised.

She checked herself visibly. "No, no, I dare say you never will. No, most probably you will never see her again. She is something of a recluse in the country. Still, it was interesting that Madame Titov was there in church. And so was Father Gregory."

"Do you mean it was managed?" I asked bluntly.

"Oh, no, the most natural thing in the world. She's always there, and so is Ariadne, and he, too, for all I know."

Before I could say any more, her sister came into the room bearing letters. "The post from England has come. And we have several letters from there and from Scotland, sister. Rose dear, greetings, but you must hurry home, for I expect there are letters for you, too."

"Yes, you cut along, dear," said Miss Gowrie at her most masculine. She was glad to see me go. I think she knew that she had been both too indiscreet and too reserved, at one and the same time. It was an inflammable mixture, but a brew entirely characteristic of her.

As of us all; I recognized the family touch. No wonder as a clan we have come to glory rather than riches.


I did not really think there would be any letters for me, as I had heard so recently, but when I arrived back at the Denisov house I found a letter from Grizel waiting. It was a thick letter, thicker than Grizel usually achieved. I was grateful that Ariadne was out with her mother. In the privacy of my room I opened it and read it.

Grizel's letter was wrapped round an enclosure, another envelope, this time one of dirty yellow as if it had travelled a long way, and been cheap paper to start with. My own name, Rose Gowrie, was scratched out, as if by a broken pen.

I read Grizel's letter first. "I expect you'll be surprised to get this, Rose. I know I was when Mrs. Graham came round with it and asked me to send it on to you. In fact, I almost wondered whether I would. The past ought to bury itself, I think. But Tibby says it's none of my business. So here it is. I may say old mother Graham was pretty cross that the letter had come with one to her and not gone to you direct. But I said perhaps Patrick only had one stamp. From what I gathered, there wasn't much information in her letter, which made her cross as well. Of course, she's always been jealous of you."

There was more to her letter, news about that fox again, about her visit to Glamis (I was right: she had managed to get there), and affectionate messages to me, but I did not read it then. Instead I opened the letter from Patrick. It was very short, and written in pale ink on cheap paper, which made me think Grizel's joke about the stamp not so wide of the mark.

"Dearest Rose," Patrick had written, "now that I know myself to be hopelessly lost and cut off from you for ever, I want you to know that I truly loved you. Even when I broke things off between us and went away, I retained the hope that I might come back. Now I know I never shall. Don't think of me any more. Forget me. I have put a padlock and chain round my own neck, and thrown away the key. Good-bye for ever, dearest girl. Good-bye."

My first reaction was anger: anger at the way Patrick indulged his own emotions at the expense of mine. First offering me love, then taking it away, then giving it back to me again, just as it suited him. I was so angry for a moment that I almost tore the letter up.

Then I saw something bigger in the letter. It was a call for remembrance. "Forget me," he wrote, but it was not what he meant. No, he wanted to be remembered.

"When Patrick wrote that," I said aloud, "he thought he was about to die. Or if not die, to enter some region from which he could never return."

It was a fantastic thought, but I was convinced it was true. We had been like lovers in a fairy-story, going innocently along on our happy way, till an evil spell fell upon us and all our lives were changed from henceforth.

\* \* \*

There was hardly any night now in St. Petersburg. In the small hours a silvery, ghost-like light settled over everything, but there was no true darkness. In this grey gloom the whole world seemed unreal and insubstantial. Restless and unable to sleep, my mind full of unresolved problems, I stared out of the window. My bedroom window looked down on the street. Even at this hour a few people were moving about below. The streets of St. Petersburg were never empty. It was very hot and airless; I thought I would, after all, be glad to be in the country.

Preparations for our move were well in hand. Since it was now known that I had met the Princess Irene (my intrusiveness was tacitly forgiven), there was no need to maintain a reserve about her existence, and mention of her even appeared in the conversation.

"It seems impossible either to take her or leave her behind," I heard Dolly grumble, and I knew whom she meant.

"Oh, the journey would be impossible for her," said Peter. "I believe strong sunlight would cause her to crumble away. In any case, she won't come."

"Oh, she stays, of course," said Dolly with irritation.

Although they talked about the old lady and called her mad, I felt that I was the only one who was aware of her true oddity. She was not just mad with old age, but she had created a mad atmosphere, a mad world around her. Other people were in her strange world. This Dolly and Peter seemed not to know, but I was convinced of it. She wasn't alone in the Red Tower. Or not always.

Confirmation of these thoughts came soon to me.

"We are off to our last St. Petersburg gaiety," Dolly announced the evening before we were supposed to leave for the country. "But I expect you will be glad to have a quiet evening to yourself."

From which I gathered that my company was not desired that night. Sometimes I was invited along with Ariadne, sometimes I was not; there seemed no rule about it. St. Petersburg hostesses were all charming, well-dressed worldly women, and I found it difficult to distinguish one from the other. By the end of this first, short season of introduction to them, I had a confused impression of one beautifully be-jewelled lady after another, swimming forward with hand outstretched in friendly greeting. They were friendly and made me feel welcome, but whether they remembered my face once I had turned away, I took leave to doubt.

"Yes, I will be very glad of an evening on my own," I said in reply to Dolly. "I have a lot of last-minute things I want to do."

"And did your new frocks arrive from the dress-maker?" She was straightening her bracelets over her gloves, and a delicious smell of French scent was wafted from her.

"Oh, yes, they came this afternoon. Every one of them is a joy. I don't know how to thank you enough."

"Nonsense, no thanks are necessary. You will need all of them. We *live* in those plain little dresses at Shereshevo, they are quite the thing."

Dolly, after a quick look at my scanty wardrobe, had insist-ed on ordering me some summer dresses from her own dress-maker. She had called them "plain little dresses" and by her standards they were, but to me they were the prettiest dresses I had ever had. I had inspected them carefully, and had already conceived the notion of copying these dresses as a present for Grizel. The short, tight skirts (mine barely came to the ankle) and the masculine tailored tops would set off her delicate looks marvellously.

I thought that Grizel would be needing some new clothes. (Distantly I seemed to hear her amused, mocking voice say-ing: Dearest Rose, you and I are constantly in need of new clothes.) Well, a particular need, I answered this far-away Grizel. Her letter had contained more than a hint that she might be going to be married. "Harry Ettrick brought me back from the Bowes-Lyon dance," she wrote. "He has a new motor car: a Daimler, he said it was, but they all look alike to me. He's really very rich, you know." I did know; we had been neighbours of the Ettricks for generations, they had al-ways been rich and getting richer, it was a way of life with them. "And he likes me, Rose. He thinks I am a 'deucedly pretty little thing,' but it's more than that; I can tell, he watches what I say, and he went quite white when I accidentally let my cheek touch his as we were dancing." Poor Harry Ettrick, I thought, he had delivered himself over, bound and helpless, to my cool-headed sister. "And it's time he was married, for he's thirty if he's a day, and you can see he fancies the idea if he could only pluck up the courage." Oh, poor Harry, I thought again. A gallant soldier, a rich landowner, the heir to a baronetcy, and after one dance at Glamis, my sister had him so twisted round her little finger that she could talk about his needing courage. Grizel had something in common with Ariadne: they both shared an instinctive ability to manage a man that I thought I lacked.

So I was making paper patterns from my new dresses, and if I got time tomorrow before we set out, I would buy some inexpensive cotton in which to copy the dresses. Nor could I let the dresses themselves remain a present to me from Dolly Denisov. "Neither a borrower nor a lender be" was one of Tibby's axioms most firmly dinned into us, and backing it was the almost unspoken assertion that we never accepted presents which we could not hope to return. Pride came into it somehow, I dare say, and I had always abided by the rule, although I noticed it never stopped Grizel accepting anything she really wanted, from a ride on a horse to a spanking pair of new white gloves to wear at a dance at Glamis. ("Miss Blair up at the school-house insisted I should accept a pair of long white chamois gloves she had had by her for years to wear at Glamis. 'It will be an honour for them,' she said. She has such a quaint way of putting things. But I did truly need them, Rose, for my old pair had been cleaned so often I *smell* of benzine. I didn't tell Tibby." So Grizel had written, and I could hear her light, clear, confident tones almost as if she had been in the room talking to me.) But I must find some way of paying back Dolly Denisov. I had an old seed pearl brooch of my grandmother's. I might sell it and buy her a present.

I sat on the floor, surrounded by paper and pins, with my scissors in my hand, happily engaged in my work, when I was interrupted by a soft tap on the door.

Not Ivan, I thought, he doesn't tap, but raps hard.

"Come in," I called, scrambling to my feet.

The door was opened by the Princess Irene's squat old maidservant Anna, who looked no more well disposed to me than she had ever been. "Her Excellency desires your presence," she said.

"Well, I don't know if I can," I began.

"Come!" said the old woman in a peremptory voice. Frail as she was, she looked capable of trying to drag me up the red staircase if I refused to obey. Her gentle little tap on my door had been from want of strength rather than any weakness of purpose. She must be very nearly as old as her mistress, and very nearly as eccentric. Certainly she had it in her to be, but life had not allowed her as much licence as Princess Irene. "The Princess desires and you must come."

"Is she ill?" What a question, I thought. She was dying. "No," she repulsed me with the word. "Not for years has she been so strong."

"Oh, really?" That took some thinking about.

"But you are to come." While Dolly was out, I thought, as the old lady up the red staircase probably knew very well. "Quickly now, don't keep Her Excellency waiting."

"I'm coming." I allowed her to lead me up the stairs, following meekly behind. Every few yards she stopped and looked round suspiciously to see if I was still there. If she was truly the product of the life she had led, then it had been one full of disappointments.

We had reached the heavy door. She opened it. "Here she is, Excellency." She gave a bobbing curtsey. "I have brought her. Your old Anna has brought her to you."

For the first time the Princess Irene was out of bed, and was sitting in an armchair in the corner of the room by the pot-bellied porcelain stove, which seemed to be alight in spite of the summer heat.

"Good." She clapped her hands. "Fetch some tea. See it is very hot, now. She can make tea," she confided in me. "She is a fool about anything else, but she can serve tea. So you are here." She sounded satisfied.

"You are lucky I could come. I might have been out with Madame Denisov and Ariadne."

"Foolish girl. They are at Countess Alice Atabekian's and she did not ask you. She knew better; she is an old friend of mine."

"I wanted to come anyway to say good-bye," I said.

"Good-bye?"

"Yes, I am going to the country, to Shereshevo."

"Oh, that, but that is nothing, you will hardly be gone long."

"The whole summer, so Madame Denisov says."

"Oh, Dolly says! It is what I say that happens."

She pointed to a chair with a gesture fit for an empress, which I believe in her heart she felt herself worthy to be, and as I sat down on it, I noticed that there was something unusual about the room today. Always it was cluttered, but now it was untidy with chairs and table out of position, and dented cushions on the sofa. I had seen our room like that at Jordansjoy after it had emptied of a party of Grizel's and mine. Also I could smell cigarette smoke, and it did not smell like Princess Irene's either. She smoked a rich perfumed tobacco and this one had a rougher, more masculine tang. I was certain that she had had visitors here, and a good many of them.

"You see how well I look?" And it was true, her eyes were bright and her skin clearer, but there was still a paper-thin fragility to her, as if there were nothing left of her now but dry skin, and hair. "It is all due to you."

"No. Perhaps I gave a very little help, but mostly it has come from inside you. I gave you confidence, that is all."

"Confidence is life, then."

"Yes." I paused and thought. "Sometimes it is."

"But you helped my pain. Took it away."

"I may have done. I can never be sure."

Her bright, gay eyes were fixed on me. What a beauty she must have been in her day. I could see what had attracted all her lovers to her, including my great-grandfather. "You drew the pain away as you touched me. It went through your fingers. Did it go into you?" I shook my head. "Or else you transformed it into something else. Pleasure, perhaps. I know I felt pleasure."

"There was relief from pain. Nothing more."

"It felt like life itself to me."

I shook my head. "I hate such talk."

The maid came back into the room, bearing the tea on a great silver tray, which was almost beyond her power to carry. I hurried forward to help. With a grunt she waved me away.

"I'm afraid Anna doesn't like me."

"She's jealous." The Princess sounded well pleased. I supposed that after the sort of life she had led, the whiff of jealousy, even if only from an old servant and former serf, was a positive necessity, like incense to a pagan god.

"Besides, she is frightened. She is an ignorant, superstitious old woman and she thinks you come from the devil. She wants me to have you whipped and sent into a convent."

Downstairs, I thought, they believe that *you* have an alliance with the devil.

"I won't, of course. No, I am well pleased with what you have already done. I am glad I got you here. And it was I that did so; Dolly may say what she chooses."

"She doesn't say anything very much."

"You must learn to read between the lines with my great-niece," said the old lady, a little grimly, I thought. I wondered if she meant it as a warning. "She pulls and I pull and we will see who wins."

Buoyed up by the new life she claimed I had given her, even some of the facial twitches that I had observed on my first visit had ironed themselves out. She looked at once younger and yet more desperately frail. Perhaps it wouldn't be such a bad way to die, I thought, to go believing yourself immortal.

"Of course you will go to Shereshevo, and a dull time you will have of it, too. No neighbourhood to speak of, none that we could visit, a provincial lot, far beneath our notice. Dolly tells me it has changed lately and that they have some manufactories and some rich men have sprouted."

"But I suppose you couldn't know them either?" I was fascinated by this glimpse of provincial life in Russia seen through the eyes of the ruling class.

She shrugged. "I don't know what Dolly does. Certainly I could not have met them. My own good taste would have prevented me if my husband's position (he was a Marshal of the Nobility and we had no social equals in the neighbourhood) had not precluded it."

Marvellous, I thought with amusement, remembering the village at Jordansjoy where the richest man was a jute merchant from Dundee to whose splendid parties we were all glad to go. None of us would have felt our good taste should have kept us away. Champagne and quail in aspic are great levellers. Of course, we had our own snobberies, and perhaps we laughed behind our gloves at the alacrity with which our jute merchant got himself into hunting pink and offered to underwrite the hounds, but we rather liked him for it. As a matter of fact, the jute merchant, who was called John Heggie, was always particularly nice to me because my father had helped Heggie along the road when he was starting out. It must have been the last occasion on which my father had any ready capital to spare. And so the social wheel went round.

"No, there is nothing to do at Shereshevo but let the peasants curtsey and bring flowers, and to sit under the mulberry tree and gossip. Of course we love our peasants and they love us. We are one family, and though they kick against us, they could not live without us. You wouldn't understand that."

"No, perhaps not." It was certainly not like that at Jordansjoy. We were liked, but not loved. People there had their own lives to live and got on with them. "No, it is not like that in Scotland. People are too independent."

"You have a sister? Unmarried, I believe?"

"Yes, so far."

"If she is as pretty as you, it will not be for long. But then you are poor," she observed, "so there will be no dowry."

"I think Grizel will manage without a dowry," I said with a smile.

"Is that her name? It sets one's teeth on edge."

"Short for Griselda," I said.

"Then why not call her that?" She was getting a little sharp, as she tired. Her false youth was melting fast. "And you have a brother? Still at home?"

"Yes, for the moment. But he will be going away to school soon."

"Oh, that barbarous English habit. A tutor at home would be much better. Of course, we have the Emperor's Corps des Pages, but that is quite different."

"We couldn't afford a tutor. Alec will be happy enough at Eton."

"You can afford that?" she said, sharp again.

"His godfather has offered to pay."

"Then I advise you to ask him to pay for a tutor," she said.

I kept quiet. The notion of "advising" Admiral Norris, that peppery fellow, to spend his own money on a tutor, made me dizzy.

"Ariadne went to a school. Against my advice. And look what it did to her." Fatigue was making her talk jerkily; I knew I must leave soon.

"I think she is delightful," I said, "and I must be glad she left her school, otherwise you would not have had me." I stood up. "Now I will say good-bye and go. I can tell you are tired."

"No, wait. I have something for you." She rang a small silver handbell. "Anna, get the box." She turned back to me. "This is why I asked you to come."

Anna had come back into the room carrying a small but beautifully made wooden box. "Take it," Irene commanded.

I held it up in my hands, admiring the delicate carving. "It's beautiful. And from the delicious smell, it must be sandalwood. And then there is another darker wood."

"Yes, yes, it came from Povarov's; the dark is pear-wood. But open it. It is what's inside that counts."

I raised the lid. Inside was a round ball of onyx threaded with a lattice of gold. Inside each golden lozenge a brilliant sparkled. "Goodness!" I exclaimed. "Is this for me? What is it?"

"Press the gold stud on top and look," she ordered.

Solemnly I pressed a little gold button on the ball, and slowly the ball split into two. A photograph set in an oval frame rose up as if on a spring.

I found myself looking at a young woman in the full pride of her beauty. Dark hair lay in a smooth roll round her face, her eyes were large and expressive, a little smile quirked her lips. In her hair, at her ears, and round her throat, jewels glittered.

"It's you," I said at once.

"Yes." Princess Irene nodded with satisfaction. "I am not yet so much changed."

But it wasn't true: she had changed. There was nothing left in her face of that arrogant young beauty seen in the photograph. I had simply made an intelligent guess.

"But why have you given this to me?" I looked down at the box and the onyx ball. "It's so valuable."

"I know I have to give way to Dolly on taking you to the country," she said, her voice suddenly fretful. "So you must take this picture of me with you. Look at me every day as I was, and think of me."

"I should probably do that anyway," I said, which was almost true.

She returned sharply: "I know enough of human nature to know that this bauble will fasten your thoughts more secure-

ly. No, don't flush with anger. What a girl you are. Just like
your grandfather. You know he fought a duel for me?" She
was beginning to ramble a little. "When I am in pain, you will
come to me, will you not?"

"I will try."

"Promise you will come."

"I promise," I said gently; it was all I could say.

She relaxed, satisfied for the moment. "He fought with the
sword, your grandfather, not pistols; he said it was more
Russian. But he would not kill. He could have given the
coup, no one would have held it against him, but he would
not do it."

"I think you should go to bed now. You are tired." I looked
round the room. "You seem to have had people here already."

With dreamy dignity she said, "I have had a party of my
friends here. We talk politics."

"I'm sure it can't be good for you." I stood up, clutching
the onyx ball in its box. "To bed now, because I am going.
Good-bye." I bent forward and kissed her softly on her
cheek.

Her eyes widened and she smiled, but she said nothing.

"Anna," I called, "I am leaving now."

"She knows, she listens all the time, she knows everything,"
whispered the Princess. "She will come when it suits her.
Anna is one of your enemies now, remember that. And there
are others. Remember that, too. Take care."

"What do you mean?"

"I will protect you, of course. But I cannot do everything."
It was a mutter, half to herself, but I caught it.

Again I said, "What do you mean?"

Quite clearly she said, "But why do I talk of protection?
The Queen of Heaven herself will look after you," and her
head fell forward. For an alarming moment I thought she
was dead, but then I saw that she had simply fallen asleep.

I put the box containing the onyx on the table beside her.
It was my intention to leave it behind. But Anna grabbed it

and thrust it at me. "Take it, take it. Her Excellency wishes
you to take it. You must take it. If you do not take it, she will
die."

Whenever one of us had to travel at Jordansjoy, the whole
house rose at dawn to assist in speeding the traveller. The
luggage, assembled in the hall the night before, was checked
and double-checked, then the voyager was given a special
travellers' breakfast of cold ham and boiled eggs. (Unconsciously we thought of travel as a sharp attack of illness for
which one must be strengthened.) And then everyone sat
around, made restless by Tibby's flow of advice and warnings, until the departure, by which time all concerned had
raging headaches and ill suppressed bad tempers.

How different from St. Petersburg, where the day began
like any other with a leisurely breakfast. Gently, one became
aware that all one's possessions had silently melted away
from the house, and that soon one would disappear from it
oneself. It was almost effortless.

However, it left me with a problem. Dolly Denisov was nowhere to be seen: she was breakfasting in bed. (Tibby would
have been amazed. Breakfasting in bed on a travelling day?
How could she do it?)

"Oh, we shan't see Mamma till we arrive," declared
Ariadne blithely, as we stood together in the hall, waiting to
be transported to the railway station. "She keeps to her own
compartment. She says that travelling bores her, so she always takes a sleeping draught and goes to sleep till we arrive.
Only sometimes she meets a friend and then she plays cards
all the time, and gambles, and that is *not* boring."

A world away from Jordansjoy was such a traveller. Tibby
never closed an eyelid when she travelled in case she should
miss her station and travel on to goodness knew where; and
she trained us to sit erect and alert against the same fate. And
as for gambling, Tibby thought cards an invention of old
Nick himself.

"I had something I wanted to give to her."

Too well bred to question, Ariadne said nothing, but she looked her curiosity.

"What is it, Miss Rose?" Her Uncle Peter had entered the room unannounced. "You look worried. Ariadne teasing you again?"

"I *never* do," protested the girl.

"No: it's this which Princess Irene gave me," and I produced the box from the valise at my feet.

"Oh, she's given you the Fabergé ball," he said with interest.

"You know it, then?"

"Of course: we have been shown that ball and taught to admire that photograph for as long as I can remember. The photograph is much older than the ball, you know, taken of my great-aunt as a young married woman. I suppose the ball is a mere decade or two old," and he handed the box back.

"But I can't possibly keep such a valuable object."

"Oh, it's not worth so much," he said easily.

"I'm glad she gave it to you and not to me," said Ariadne. "I should hate to have her eyes looking at me all night. I dreaded visits to her when I was little. Great-aunt used to tell me I walked like a peasant, and then that old Anna would pinch me with her fingers when she thought no one could see. She has a cast in her eye and never looks at me straight." The girl shivered. "Great-aunt never asks to see me now. I'm not an admirer and answer back, so she doesn't care for me."

The house steward stood by the door, ready to open it for us. Outside, the Denisov motor car was waiting to take us to the railway station. Madame Denisov had already left, driving herself in her little coupé. She had recently taken up driving; she was one of the first women in St. Petersburg to drive her own car, she had told me. (Of course she always had a chauffeur sitting beside her, ready to drive if needed, but I suppose he did not count.) "How it emancipates one," she had said. I wondered what Dolly needed emancipation from: she seemed to have her own way pretty well as much as anyone ever could. Perhaps it was from boredom. That she did suffer from.

"You go off, Ariadne, and take all the luggage," said Peter. "And I will drive Miss Gowrie myself in my own car. That is, if she will allow me?"

Ariadne made a face. "I would rather drive with you in your car and let Miss Rose go in the Rolls with the luggage."

"I want *her*," said Peter.

Ariadne departed with a good grace.

"Very well, I shall have my little dog in the car with me. I always wanted him and he is very good company."

Peter took out his watch. "We will give her five minutes and then set off. I have no idea of riding in her dust."

And he really meant it. He studied his watch and measured the minutes. They could be so astonishingly literal these Russians, and just when one least expected it.

Peter Alexandrov's car was a long, low car, painted pale grey outside and upholstered in a deep blue leather. He told me it was a Hispano-Suiza; he had this car and Dolly had a Delage and the Rolls.

I was amused and excited at the thought of driving alone with Peter in his car. It was a dashing thing to do. Back home in Scotland it would not immediately have sunk me in society, but it was a little what we called "risqué." Here in St. Petersburg, where no one knew me, it didn't matter at all.

Peter handed me in and I settled myself beside him in the passenger seat with frank pleasure. He looked down at me with approval as he drew on his driving gloves. "I like to see a girl who enjoys herself."

"I seem to enjoy everything in Russia," I said, once again almost truthfully. I appeared to have developed a dreadful facility for telling only half the truth. Tact, some people call it, I believe. Still, there again, a great deal about Russia was very exhilarating. "In any case I've never ridden in an open motor car like this one. My sister Grizel went for a spin in one once, but I never did."

"You must learn to drive. Would you like to?"

"Oh, yes. Do you think I could?"

"It's not very difficult. When I come down to Shere-shevo—I'm not coming immediately, but I will be joining you there—I'll teach you. You'll soon learn."

"I would like it very much, thank you," I said, completely truthful now. "But I'll have to ask Madame Denisov."

"Oh, Dolly is usually reasonable about things," he said.

Yes, I thought, probably she is to her brother, but perhaps not to those she employs.

"She didn't like what I said about Mademoiselle Laure, nor my meeting your great-aunt."

"But that was understandable," he said, and added quietly, "Nor has it stopped you from seeing more of Tante Irene."

"No." I felt myself flushing. So perhaps I hadn't been taken in the car alone because he liked me, but to be scolded. "She asked to see me and I went. That's how she came to give me the onyx ball. She thinks I help her, you see."

"I know, I understand. I know what my old great-aunt is like. You must not let her worry you."

"She wants to live for ever," I said.

"She has very nearly done that already," he laughed. "Oh, yes, I know all about her and her fantasies. I keep well away from them, and I advise you to do the same. But she is old and lonely now after a brilliant life."

Carefully, because I did not want to fall into the same trouble as I had done over my speculation about Laure's death, I said, "I think that perhaps your aunt is less lonely than you suppose."

"Why do you say that?"

"She has visitors."

"She is not a hermit," he said dryly.

"I mean that she entertains large numbers of people up there in the Red Tower." The name always had capital letters to me now, but, I suppose, to no one else.

His attention was momentarily diverted from the subject, and even, as I saw with some alarm, from his driving. "Oh, you call it that, too? I always did as a child. My family have always owned that house, you know; Dolly married a cousin. 'Up the red staircase to the red tower,' we used to say. It was empty then, except for its ghost. A ghost is *de rigueur* in a Russian home like ours."

"I think the servants still think it haunted. I got the name from them. Isn't it right?"

"It's hardly its official name. I think it is called the Konrad's tower after the architect." With a neat turn of the wheel, he avoided a horse and cart, and at the same moment came to the subject which I had started. "Yes, I know about my great-aunt's 'entertainments.' They are hardly a secret."

We had reached the Nevsky Prospect and were driving down it. Never had St. Petersburg looked more beautiful to me, with the light reflected from the water that was everywhere in the city, and then striking off the buildings of the pale yellow stone so characteristic of the place. Never anywhere else, either, did I see buildings painted a pale blue, but here, whether in the heat of summer or, as I was to see them, in the frozen winter, they looked entirely in place and very beautiful.

In this short drive with Peter Alexandrov, I seemed to have seen the city with new eyes. Perhaps it was because of my happy excitement.

"Oh, yes, Dolly and I know about the meetings in the red tower; impossible for Tante Irene to keep them entirely secret, although she may believe she does. But certainly people slip in and out of her gatherings that we know nothing about."

I looked mystified.

"My great-aunt entertains her friends up there in her tower, and some of them come secretly because their political feelings are not such as are welcomed by the government. Oh, don't mistake me, they are not emancipators and liberators up there in the red tower. On the contrary, they are *plus royaliste que le roi*. In other words, they want the Tsar to make his government more *imperial* and more autocratic, not less. They think he is soft."

"And they meet in Princess Irene's room to talk about this?"

"As long as they do nothing but talk," he said.

"But they could not want to harm the Tsar?"

"Not harm him, but replace him, perhaps."

"And Princess Irene *knows* about this?"

"I'm not sure, she's a secretive old thing, and would probably like nothing better than to go back to the days of Peter the Great. But I think the people about her make use of her, more than she realizes."

"Is it dangerous?" I asked.

"The police, the Third Bureau, have a spy in there, I expect, but I doubt if they will do anything since their sympathies incline that way in any case. They, too, are in favour of reaction."

"I see," I said thoughtfully, aware, though, that a true understanding of Russian political life was as yet beyond me. The city about me looked so beautiful and strong, but Peter's words made me wonder if the buildings were any stronger than cardboard with strangenesses hidden behind their façades.

"No, it's not people like my great-aunt who interest the Third Bureau, but those who want to overthrow the whole established order."

"Like the anarchists who tried to bomb the Imperial Library?" I asked.

"Yes, they, too, have a long history. The Decembrists, the Land and Freedom Movement, the People's Will, names written in blood in our history, Miss Rose. We Russians are a people in love with secret societies. Yes, that is what lies behind all the structures you see, and these are like rats nibbling away at our foundations."

He was driving much faster now, too fast, I thought. "Careful," I said.

He took his eyes off the road for an alarming minute. "You look quite white, Miss Rose. Are you frightened? By Russia? Or by my driving?"

"Not frightened, no. Startled, I think."

"Oh, come now, Miss Rose, you are a well-informed young lady and certainly knew in your quiet Scotland the way things are with us in Russia. And we are like Russia itself in the Denisov home."

"But it all seemed so far away, and unreal. Now I am part of it."

Seen in profile his expression was impossible to read. The car swung round at the railway station and stopped. Peter turned towards me. "Yes, you are in the middle. But you can go away. You can go away, Miss Rose Gowrie, if you want. Do you want?"

I shook my head. "No, I won't leave."

Peter leaned forward and took my hand and kissed it. "Thank you, Rose Gowrie."

Russian men always kissed your hand and it meant nothing, I had to remind myself.

By the train Edward Lacey was saying good-bye to Ariadne and Dolly Denisov. Today he seemed as interested in the mother as the daughter.

We said our good-byes and the train moved slowly out of the station. I stood at the window, looking out. I was leaving St. Petersburg behind me.

# Chapter Four

riadne leaned back in her seat and took off her gloves. "Oh, Edward Lacey has such panache, hasn't he? I shall miss him at Shereshevo. What a pity they couldn't travel with us. We are going to be nothing but a house of women at first."

The estate in the country was called Shereshevo House, after the nearest town. Or perhaps the town had been named after their house.

"Is there no company for you in the country?"

"Not much. We are miles from anywhere. The Hertzovs are our nearest family and they take a day's driving. One of the Hertzov boys is quite fun. Dull at heart, though, I fear, but better than nothing."

I laughed. "And there's Madame Titov. She said she lives near you."

"Oh, yes, so she does. But nowhere is very near. You will understand when you see it. Now I am going to sleep. I always sleep on journeys. Like mother, like daughter, you know." And she closed her eyes.

The journey by train to Spala, the nearest railway station,

was comfortable but slow. From there we were driven many miles along dusty roads to the estate near Shereshevo. One way and another I had plenty of time both for my thoughts and to observe provincial Russia.

So many impressions formed in my mind that it was hard to summarize them. No sooner had the train passed through a village that looked poor and depressed than we had stopped at a small town that was obviously prosperous, and where comfortably dressed businessmen and merchants waited for the train. Russia was a country of contradictions. But on the whole the small villages which I caught fleeting glimpses of as the train rushed past, with their huddle of low houses, shacks one might better call them, following no plan but just squatting next door to each other, looked squalid places without dignity. The peasants, seen standing about, were badly dressed and worse shod. However, their animals looked healthy enough, and the fields of crops were well tended. I took it all in with a country-girl's eyes.

Ariadne, opening her eyes from her slumber, saw what I was doing. "You are studying us," she said. "I can see it in your clever eyes. So this is Russia, you are saying, what a strange world. And we are, too, I dare say."

"Very different from anything I have ever seen before," I admitted, turning back from the window. "The landscape is bigger, the colours are deeper, not exactly richer, but more of the earth." And it was true: if I had been painting the landscape before me, I would have used ochre, sienna and a deep rich brown.

"And the people?" asked Ariadne. "Are we earthy, too?"

"I think the peasants are," I answered thoughtfully.

"Oh, I am earthy, too, underneath. Wait until we get to Shereshevo and then you shall find out what I am," and Ariadne yawned like a little cat and went back to sleep.


It was dark by the time we arrived at Shereshevo, and I could get only an impression of a low, white house of classic proportions before I was hustled off to bed by friendly servants, to fall asleep between cool linen sheets that smelt of lavender. But already I had noticed the dry, sweet quality of the air, and taken in the great silence that lay all around the house.

As I drifted into sleep, I seemed to hear a grumbling old woman's voice saying, "So this is the one, is it? This is the miracle maker? Well, God help us all, that's what I say." Then the voice receded into the distance as if the speaker had gone away, and I was asleep.

When I opened my eyes the room was full of bright sunlight. I closed my eyes again and thought: I remembered being led up a wide staircase by a couple of cheerful servants bearing candles. One of them had helped me to undress, and the other had opened the bed and then tucked me into it, all with easy good humour.

Afterwards I had a confused idea that someone had come into my room and spoken as I fell asleep. But that might be no more than a dream. Still, it had been a cross old voice, and not well disposed towards me.

"Are you awake, then?" said a soft voice.

I opened my eyes and propped myself on one elbow to look. At the door stood a plump, red-cheeked girl in full blue skirt and white apron, with a little pleated handkerchief on her head.

"I'm Nina," she curtsied. "I look after you."

"Oh, thank you." I supposed I had left black Ivan behind in St. Petersburg. "I think you helped me to bed last night."

"Yes, I did." She came closer to the bed to get a better look at me, studying my face with unashamed curiosity. "Goodness, you did look tired. We could hardly keep you awake enough to undress you." Over one arm she had a pile of my underclothes, miraculously all newly laundered and pressed. "You look more yourself this morning." She put my clothes on a chair. "Shall I bring you some chocolate? Or you can have coffee? And a rusk to eat?"

"I don't know," I said doubtfully. "I suppose I ought to get up. Where is Miss Ariadne?"

"Oh, don't you worry about her, or Her Excellency either, for we shan't see either of them for hours yet. I know how it is with them when they arrive. Sleep! Why they can sleep the clock round. And if they did want anyone, why there's old Nanny ready for them."

So I lay back on my pillows and waited for my coffee to appear. It didn't appear quickly; no one hurried at Shereshevo. But I used the time to get my bearings.

Here I was, then, in the country house of Dolly and her brother. I wondered exactly who owned the house and estate. Dolly spoke as if it was her property, but the Princess Irene and Peter seemed inextricably part of her life and perhaps a common ownership was at the root of it.

The room I was in was large and well proportioned, the walls papered in a dark blue and the paintwork gleaming with white enamel. It was sparsely furnished. Within one window stood a table of some well-polished pale wood, maple possibly, and a mirror on it to make it serve as a dressing-table. In the other window stood a writing-table. A chest of drawers was pushed against one wall and on the opposite wall was a bookcase. My bed was large and with white muslin hangings, all as fresh and crisply laundered as the linen sheets. I thought it a comfortable room but not luxurious, for the boards were bare except for a strip of carpet by the bed. An oil-lamp stood on a small table near the bed. But it was a friendly room, full of light and space. From the windows I could see leaves and clouds and sky. I had the feeling of being high up under the roof, riding among the tree-tops.

I was at the window looking down on lawns and a flower garden when Nina returned. She gave a disapproving cry and put the tray down. "Oh, now, miss, you'll catch your death of cold." She draped a wrap round my shoulders. "Back to bed now." She herself was snugly dressed in thick cotton with a little triangular white shawl over her shoulders.

"Oh, it's warm, warm," I cried. "And the air is delicious."

"Cold air on the body is very bad," she said firmly. "And really, miss, you're mother naked under that gown," and she clicked her teeth disapprovingly. It was my first glimpse of a sort of puritanism which ran together with other strands through the Russian character. And the root of it was, I came to believe, that what was permissible for men was forbidden for women. I often and often saw the young men bathing naked in the river, but the girls never went near the water. If I had taken it into account more, I would have had the servants more on my side, whereas it was I ended by shocking and alienating them. And yet I don't know: from the beginning I had an enemy in that house, that so friendly, welcoming house.

It seemed totally friendly to me as I ate my breakfast of coffee and a kind of rusk with raspberry jam of a beautiful flavour but unusually runny.

I needed a thorough wash after my breakfast. I was sticky with jam and still travel-stained. But without a request, Nina and two hefty friends came into my room with a hip-bath and stone jugs of hot water. Efficiently, but not without a giggle or two, they set out my bath. Bathrooms had been put into the St. Petersburg house by Dolly Denisov, but in this house there seemed no running water at all.

Only for me it brought Mademoiselle Laure back into the room as if she had been living and breathing in there with me. She might even have used this room in summers past. In fact, she probably had done.

Still, I took my bath, using a great tablet of what looked like home-milled soap, full of rough bits like oatmeal but smelling of lilac, and I found the water soft as milk. I stopped thinking about Laure Le Brun and enjoyed myself.

Wearing one of my new dresses, I walked down a main staircase covered in a blue carpet. This led to a wide upper hall, also blue-carpeted, and from this floor opened all the main rooms of the house. The servants slept and worked on the ground floor.

Great pots of flowers decorated this upper hall, and the whole impression was of lightness and space. Ahead of me a white lilac bush was growing in a procelain tub. To my eyes, it seemed late in the year for a lilac to be blooming, but I suppose that in this land the seasons moved to a different moon than at home. I bent forward to enjoy the delicious scent which I specially love. I had meant to have some in my wedding bouquet but my wedding had it happened would have been a winter wedding. The tub stood close to the wide-opened doors of a large room. Flowers hid me from the occupants of the room and also masked the entrance to my view. But suddenly I heard Dolly Denisov's voice. She sounded quite close.

"Well, it is *going*. Not perhaps so well as you and I might wish, but it moves."

She sounded serious, as if her plan (if that was what she meant) was something she was in earnest about. She must have got an answer, because I heard her speak again.

"Dangerous? Indeed we know it has its dangers and not least for the chief character concerned. I have always understood them, and so have you, my dear, but it *must* be done."

She must have been moving away from the door because her voice was fainter, although still audible to me. "No, no, we must do it," she said urgently. "To give up is inconceivable. No, no, I will not consider it and neither must you."

I couldn't hear any response, but I heard Dolly say, "Ah, my dear creatures, we owe it to posterity not to be squeamish." And then, with a sharper note in her voice, "No, the death was of no significance, none at all. And will not stop me. I shall manage, there are ways, and really one has got to."

I thought I had heard enough, probably more than I should have done, and I walked quickly into the room. Dolly was at the far end of the room, near the windows. She turned quickly when she heard me. A look of surprise, quickly suppressed, appeared on her face. Then she came to meet me, hand held out. "My dear girl, good morning, and welcome to

Shereshevo." There was no one else in the room. Whoever she had been talking to had gone. "Did you sleep well?"

"Beautifully, thank you." The open windows led to a terrace, a colonnaded open room, with steps which went down to the gardens. Dolly's visitor must have gone this way.

"And what do you think of Shereshevo?"

I looked at the room. "What I have seen is lovely."

Dolly looked pleased. "Like an English country-house or a Scottish castle?"

"No, quite different. More, more"—I studied the room—"more homelike."

Dolly still looked pleased. "It *is* a home. You are quite right. You have caught the true essence of Shereshevo and what it means to us: it is our family home, and belongs as much to Ariadne and Peter as to me, and will belong to their children." Then she said in a practical tone, "Are English houses so different, then?"

I smiled. "I'm not an expert. But I've seen pictures, of course, and I stayed at Warwick Castle once: Lady Warwick was a friend of my father's. It was very grand. English country-houses are. You know how it is—Chippendale and Sheraton furniture, Boulle cabinets. Family portraits by Van Dyck, town scenes by Canaletto or Guardi: the best of what they can afford, really. It's not like that here. I like it better."

"We keep those possessions in our town-houses," observed Dolly. "But in the country we like to be simple. You will see the same everywhere. I am so glad you like it," and she patted my hand in a friendly fashion.

This was the first hint I had of my changed status which became apparent at Shereshevo. Dolly had been constantly kind to me from the beginning (except when I had angered her over Laure's death), but it had been an aloof, impersonal kindness; now suddenly it became warmer. She truly wanted me to like Shereshevo.

"When that little monkey Ariadne appears this morning, she shall take you round outside and show you the farm buildings and stables. And you must see the Swiss Dairy. Our milk is excellent here. You must drink great bowls of it and become strong."

"Oh, I'm very strong already," I laughed, and it was true; we Gowries are a healthy lot. Considering the large families we had bred, and the lack of money that had been constantly with us, we had need to be.

"Good, good." Dolly was dressed in her country garb, which meant a dress of fine pleated linen in a pale buff colour, a hat of matching natural straw and a triple row of fine pearls. "Health is so important and particularly for you."

"Oh?"

"For any young girl, I mean," went on Dolly easily. "The bloom so easily goes." She picked up a box of papers and account-books that lay on a side table and tucked it under one arm. Seen thus, she looked surprisingly alert and business-like. "Now I have to go down to the estate room and see my steward and go through the farm accounts. If I don't keep a sharp eye, goodness knows what would happen. Oh, they are as honest as the day, but slow, you know, and given to some little tricks one must watch. Of course, I have known them all my life. Why, Gregor was steward when I was born, so I understand their ways."

"And they understand yours, too."

Dolly looked surprised at this, as if it was a new idea to her that the process worked both ways, the observer was observed. "I dare say they do."

She strolled towards the windows, giving a pretty fluting whistle through pursed-up lips as she did so. Two large beautiful dogs immediately appeared from the terrace and awaited her command. "My wolf-hounds," she said, looking at them with affection. "How I miss them in St. Petersburg, but they would never be happy in the city. Come along, boys."

"Shall I come with you, Madame Denisov? Can I perhaps help you?"

She paused. "Well, I expect you would be very good at adding up the figures in the accounts, better perhaps than I, but no, I must go alone. Old Gregor would be so jealous, you see, if I appeared to be getting help from you. And after all, he will have his abacus there, and we can both add up on that." I looked in her face to see if she was serious, but apparently she was. "No, you must explore the house."

I looked again to see if this was some oblique reference to my discovery of the Princess Irene in the St. Petersburg house. No, apparently she meant no criticism. "All the rooms on this floor are used by the family. Below, the servants live near the kitchens. You can go down there, too, if you like, they never mind a visitor. I often drink a bowl of sour milk down there myself if I am hungry after a walk." She waved a hand and disappeared through the window, a much younger and more girlish figure than in St. Petersburg.

It all seemed very different from the formal world of the St. Petersburg house, but already I was learning not to draw quick conclusions about anything in this amazing country. Russia defied hasty judgements.

The sound of soft, shuffling feet behind me made me turn round. A stout, comfortable-looking figure stood looking at me. Her round, chubby face, its plumpness accentuated by the dragged-back hair and little bun, had a cheerful look, which the sharpness of her black eyes belied. It was more an accident of her features than a real reflection of her character, I concluded later, that she looked so good-humoured and was called "Dear Old Nanny" by everyone.

She ignored me. "Excellency, Excellency, come back," she called, shuffling towards the window. "Excellency, you have forgotten your overshoes. You can't go trampling in the damp grass without your overshoes, and you with a weak chest."

Dolly reappeared at the window. "Ah, *kormilitsa,* dear," she said, "take those ridiculous things away. Of course I shan't wear them. The grass is as dry as a cinder." The *kormilitsa* was her own old wet nurse and so dear to her.

"It's old Nanny that will have to sit by you all night and lose her sleep, if you have one of your chests," grumbled the woman, and she held out a pair of rubber galoshes.

Dolly shook her head, but she stretched out her hand, took them and put them on in a good-humoured fashion. "What an old tyrant you are, Nanny," she said. "I shall take them off as soon as your back is turned. Rose, this is Sasha, who was my wet-nurse."

But I had recognized her voice. It was she who had come to stare at me in my bed that morning as I fell asleep, and who had muttered strange comments. I had felt dislike in her voice then, and I felt dislike now.

She bobbed at me politely, and smiled, but her little black eyes observed me coldly.

*Kormilitsa*—wet-nurse—Dolly had called her, so she had had a husband and a child once, and perhaps she still had.

"I'm glad to meet you, miss," she said.

"I'm going," said Dolly from the window. "Nanny will look after you, Rose. Ask her for anything," and once again she was gone.

"I thought you had already met me," I said deliberately to Sasha.

"I don't understand you, miss," Sasha's red-cheeked face was puzzled.

"Surely you came and looked at me last night? I was asleep, or almost asleep, but I remembered it in the morning."

"There were several of the girls as well as me in and out of your room, miss, to see that you were comfortable and had everything as it should be. You were tossing and turning in your sleep, miss, having a nightmare, I dare say. You've had bad dreams, that's what it is."

"I heard you talking about me."

"We weren't talking about you, miss. It's those bad dreams I spoke about."

"I don't remember bad dreams," I said sceptically.

"Ah, we don't always remember what we dream. Tossing and turning you were, and muttering. It's a consequence of the travelling, without a doubt."

"Without a doubt," I said coolly, and went out onto the terrace where I nearly tripped over the pair of rubber over-boots which Dolly had deposited there. No doubt Sasha was reluctant to admit that she had stood by my bed, talking about me. I could understand it.

I walked on the terrace for a little while, conscious that I was observed, and keeping up my dignity, and then, because I was young and happy, I gave a little skip.

Quickly I looked round. Yes, she was watching me from the window. Then she turned round, and, soft shoes pattering on the shining parquet floors, slipped away into the recesses of the house.

Well, I'm out of your sight, I thought, and so I was, but very soon her place was taken by another servant, a pretty young girl, who appeared from another window further down the terrace, and who seemed to have no other work to do in the world but stand and observe me. It was true she carried a duster, so some task had been allotted her, but it was I she was watching.

Presently an older woman appeared behind her and evidently said something sharp, for she went back into the room and very soon I saw her shaking her feather-duster out of the window in a vigorous and ostentatious manner.

I grinned to myself: I knew the mark of a lazy worker when I saw one. I strolled along the terrace towards the room where she was working. A sweet-smelling breeze blew along the terrace, which was really like a room open to the air, because it had a lofty roof supported on classic stone pillars. Indeed, at one end I could see comfortable-looking basket-work chairs arranged around a low table, so it was obviously a family meeting place.

I glanced towards the window where the pretty, lazy girl had stood: she was there again, half hiding behind a curtain and peeping at me. No doubt they had few visitors here at Shereshevo, probably there had never been one from Scotland, and so I was an object of interest.

An angry hand pulled the girl back and a voice adjured her to get on with dusting the dining-room. I was close enough to the window to hear what was said.

"Ah, I only wanted to see the little saint," said the girl.

"Silly girl," said the voice; "there are no little saints these days, the times are against them, and if there were, it would not be a woman."

Sensible woman, I thought, and marched on towards the group of chairs and sat down. Still, it was disconcerting to hear oneself dubbed a "little saint," even if the notion was at once rejected. I wondered what had brought the idea on. I was not thought of as a saint at Jordansjoy. Far from it, as Tibby would have been the first to point out. It is true that one day there we had a visit from an old school-friend of Tibby's who said she was a follower of Annie Besant and Madame Blavatsky and her own gift was for seeing auras. I had an aura, she said, of pale blue tending towards violet. Tibby soon put a stop to talk such as that.

Dolly had left some cigarettes on the table and I lit one and began to smoke it as an experiment. Enjoyable, I thought, but hardly worth making a fuss about.

"Oh, you're smoking," called Ariadne, approaching along the terrace. Her hair was loose on her shoulders and she wore a plain white linen dress; for a moment she looked younger than her sixteen years, then she smiled and her face became older and more sophisticated. "Do you like it?"

"Yes, I do, but I think I need more practice."

"Oh, don't try." Ariadne plumped herself down beside me and sat there swinging a foot. "It makes the complexion go yellow, and you have such a pretty one. Now what do you think of Shereshevo?"

"I think it's delightful."

"I'll take you round it soon, if you like."

"Ariadne, what is a little saint?"

She looked surprised at the question. "Oh, the peasants are always inventing 'little saints' or holy people. They love to do it, but it doesn't mean much; half of them are frauds, or they might have some special gift or the other that gets exaggerated. But the peasants enjoy it, you see, it's part of their life, and although one laughs, one must also respect."

"Oh, I do," I said.

"But, of course, sometimes they do use the term for almost anyone who catches their fancy. They *long* to revere and worship, you see, it is a strange thing about them. And 'little' is a term of endearment," she added. They call the Tsar the *Little* Tsar."

"And they love him?"

"Yes, they do. I don't think you would quite understand, being English."

"Scottish," I corrected.

"I suppose your King is respected, loved, too, in a way, but our peasants think of the Tsar as their special protector. 'We're lucky,' I heard one old woman say, 'we have the Tsar to look after us.' So when they get angry with my mother or the steward, they feel they can call on the Tsar for help."

"And do they?"

"They do petition him, sometimes," said Ariadne. "I don't know if he ever sees the petitions."

Thus opening up a gap between hopes and their fulfilment, I thought. "How dangerous," I said.

"Dangerous?" Ariadne opened her eyes wide. "And is it more dangerous than some of your acts of Parliament, which seem to promise more than they perform?"

It was a shrewd remark, and I didn't think it was original. She had heard someone else say it. Little monkey, I thought.

I stood up. "Show me the house," I asked.

Together we went from room to room on this *piano nobile*; each room was wide open to sun and air, sparsely furnished, plainly decorated, but everywhere comfortable and homely. Even the ballroom, where pots and tubs of flowers stood in the windows, was a place for happy country dances and not for grand formations.

Shereshevo was the most friendly and companionable house I had ever been in. One never felt alone there, the rooms seemed to offer their own communication, silently telling one to be peaceful and at ease and to take some enjoyment in life. There always seemed time for everything at

Shereshevo; even the servants had a leisurely life with plenty
of opportunity for drinking tea and gossiping. They still appeared at the raising of a hand, or even sometimes without
one, and of those sinister speaking-tubes that I had found in
the St. Petersburg house there was no need. "Let's go outside
now," said Ariadne, leading the way. "Of course we can't see
everything, it would take too long. But you can see the Swiss
Dairy, you'd like that, I think." She glanced at me. "You'll
need a hat, the sun is very strong."

"I'll get my straw. Oh, Ariadne," I paused.

She looked at me, laughing-faced.

"I met your mother's old nurse, Sasha."

"Ah, yes. Her old wet-nurse. Do you have wet-nurses in
Scotland?"

"Not any longer. I think the mothers do it themselves
now." Vividly I remembered Tibby (who had a touch of
earthy, country humour about her at times) describing her
life with another employer. "Every night I'd carry the bairn
(and him bawling his head off) into her ladyship's bedroom.
She was a sound sleeper, was my lady, and so was his lord-
ship, helped by the port at his dinner and his day out with his
gun, but I'd get her awake in the end and get the bairn fixed
to her breast. Then I'd wait outside, huddling in a shawl, till
she finished. She was a slow feeder, and by that time his lord-
ship would be awake and grumbling. He'd grumble as if he'd
nothing to do with its arrival at all. I'd wait till I reckoned her
ladyship's breasts were empty, then I'd pop back. Ten to one
she'd be asleep. I was glad when bottles and teats came in." I
smiled, wondering what Tibby thought of wet nurses: she
had an opinion, no doubt. "They do it themselves, or they
use bottles," I said.

The Swiss Dairy was a gem of blue and white tiles stamped
with swans and daisies. The tiles covered the ceiling and the
walls and made up the floor. On great wooden benches stood
cream bowls of blue and white porcelain. In another room
was a butter-churn, and in a third, cheese was making. Ev-

erything sparkled and everything was a perfection of porcelain, but why it was called the Swiss Dairy was not in the
least apparent. Ariadne didn't know.

"I think it may have been copied from a dairy that my
mother saw in Switzerland on her honeymoon."

"Do you remember your father, Ariadne?"

"Not at all, he died when I was a few years old." Shyly
Ariadne said, "I was told he died in an accident, but I used to
have dreams that he was not dead."

"That's natural," I said, yet a trifle surprised: Ariadne had
not struck me as an imaginative girl. "You wanted a father."

"Yes, and perhaps didn't want a mother," said Ariadne
meditatively. "It was a shooting accident. Later on I used to
have fantasies that my mother had killed him. Murdered
him."

I stared at her in shocked surprise. It was my first intimation that the relationship between Ariadne and her mother
was not all it seemed. What was it Miss Gowrie had said about
Russian family relationships? "I will leave you to find your
own way about that murky pool."

"I've startled you," said Ariadne with a faint smile. "Never
mind, I don't have such imaginings now. I know better."

"I'm surprised that you could think such a thing of your
mother."

"Oh, I could," said Ariadne in a level voice. "I judge her by
myself, you see, and I know what I could do and assume that
she could do the same."

"Now you're being a silly girl," I said. "You are only sixteen, and can't have much idea of what you are capable of.
You will grow up and find out." Privately I thought that Edward Lacey, with his robust common sense, might be good
for her. No wife would dare murder him!

All the same, it was a rubbishy sort of thing to say, the kind
of comment one makes when the intention is to repress. I
saw this as soon as I spoke, and Ariadne was clever enough to
see it, too. She made no comment, but said, "Come and see

the rest of the farm buildings if you feel strong enough. We can cycle down there. Do you bicycle?"

"Yes, I learnt some time ago."

"Well, you can always borrow one here if you want. We keep two of them so we can get about ourselves. Here," and she opened the door of a small building a few yards away from the Swiss Dairy where two gleaming machines stood waiting for us.

I wobbled for the first few minutes, then steadied and went well; Ariadne was very proficient.

"Follow me," she said, bowling ahead with confidence.

Probably I had thought the stables would be like those I knew at home, the one at Jordansjoy, for instance, which was a solid, serviceable building; but nothing had prepared me for the elegance and fantasy of the stables at Shereshevo. Beautifully suited for their purpose, they were also toys, just like the Swiss Dairy. Impossible not to think of Marie Antoinette, playing at dairymaids in the Petit Trianon. There were two stables at Shereshevo, one red and one blue: the blue stable housed the work horses and the red the carriage horses. In the red stable every piece of equipment, harness, bridle, reins and so on, was decorated in red; in the blue stable everything was in matching shades of blue. Even the horses had little plaits with coloured bows. They were splendid horses, too, some of the finest I had seen, and they had the indulged, placid look of animals that are not overworked. When, later on, I visited the village, I thought some of the peasants might have envied the horses, for they were housed much worse and looked less healthy.

It was hot in Shereshevo, but the air had a wonderful dry, spicy quality that I found exhilarating. Ariadne saw this; perhaps she wanted to please me because she said, "If we cycle through the gardens, we can reach the forest and ride there."

"The forest?" It sounded like a fairy-tale: to ride in a Russian forest.

"Oh, it's only a tame little bit of forest," she laughed. "Not many miles square, but it belongs to us. There is a wood mill and a paper factory on the further side, but on our side we can ride along bridle paths and feel quite lost. I used to try to get lost there when I was little." Again this disconcerting hint of all not being well. Not quite of unhappiness, one could not say that, but of non-happiness, which was odd to associate with bright Ariadne. "But I never succeeded; someone always came and brought me back."

"My sister and I tried to run away once, because our old nurse had been stern with us," I said. "We packed our bags, and stole some food for the journey, and waited for night."

"And what happened?"

"We never went." I stopped. Even now I could hardly bear the thought of that day. "We discovered that the reason old Tibby had been so harsh to us was that she had just heard our parents had died in an epidemic in India, and she was summoning up courage to tell us. Thank goodness we did not go. Poor Tibby."

"I would have run even further," said Ariadne. "Yes, to be orphaned and free. One might run for ever then." She sounded as if she meant it.

"Show me your forest, and we'll try not to get lost there."

"Oh, I don't want to get lost any longer. No, I have other ideas." She mounted her bicycle.

"I hope you won't talk that way to your husband when you have one," I said, getting onto my bicycle and preparing to follow her.

"Oh, perhaps he will run with me."

He'd have to run hard to keep up with you, I thought, as I pedalled after her. We travelled round the rose garden, round a shrubbery, past a formal topiary and then through an avenue of limes which led to a great bronze statue.

"Ah, the monster himself," said Ariadne. She got off her bicycle and stood there, one foot on the pedal, holding the handle-bars, and looked up.

"What do you mean? Who is it?"

"Peter the Great. He gave this estate to one of my ancestors. So my ancestor put up this statue to him. Not very good, is it? I'm afraid he did not spend enough money on it. And then the birds have used it for years to perch on."

I looked up at the bird-stained, greening bronze. "And was he a monster?"

"I think so, don't you? Great and good for Russia, as she was then, but otherwise mad and terrible. Did you have anyone like him in your country?"

"I don't know. In England there was Oliver Cromwell, but he was a monster of sanity not madness." As a remote descendant of Charles Stuart, and a hereditary Jacobite, I was bound to think Oliver Cromwell a monster, but another part of me admired him.

Beyond the statue the forest started, and although Ariadne had called it tiny and not many miles wide, yet it gave an impression of immensity. Great pines stretched in every direction. The ground sloped gently.

"There is a river down there," said Ariadne, "a great, broad, gentle river. Our boundaries end at the river."

There was a narrow path, and leaving our bicycles propped against a tree, we followed this track down to the river. Ariadne was humming softly; she was not a girl with much of an ear for music, but her little song reminded me of a familiar tune, although I couldn't place it, like seeing a face you know in a distorting mirror.

"What's that you're humming?"

"Oh, I don't know," she said idly. "Just something. Look, there's the river."

It ran in a great loop with low banks on both sides. We stood among the pines looking at a flat meadow on the other side where cattle grazed.

"Not our cattle," said Ariadne. "The Brusiloffs own that land. Nice people, but the house is miles away by road because you cannot cross the river."

In the distance I could see the roof of a long, low building. I pointed. "What's that? A school? Or a hospital?"

Ariadne laughed. "No, we don't have either of those institutions. Oh, I think there is a sort of dame school in the village. No, that is our distillery," and, seeing my look of surprise: "Oh, yes, we make our own spirit, using our own grain. We sell it, of course."

"Ah!" At last I knew where some of the Denisov wealth came from.

Ariadne sat down on the soft carpet of pine needles and stared across the river. Her burst of unwonted energy was over and she seemed disinclined for talk. She had warned me that she would be a different girl in the country and it seemed as though she was. I sat beside her quietly, wondering if I, too, was one person in one place and another elsewhere. Certainly I felt that the Rose Gowrie I had been in Jordansjoy was on the move. That earlier Rose Gowrie had been a little, shall I say it, passive. She had accepted too easily. Patrick Graham in part had already felt that the first Rose Gowrie was a silly child who deserved what happened to her. But I had shed her, left her behind like a carapace I had outgrown. The Rose Gowrie I was getting to know now was asking a lot of questions.

Ariadne rose and shook herself like one of the dogs. "Let's go back now."

I stood up, too. "I'd like to see the village." I had the wrong idea about the village then, and thought it might be a place to stroll and shop and gossip, as at home.

"Tomorrow. Tomorrow we will go to the village," said Ariadne dreamily.

Tomorrow. It seemed quite close; I looked forward to it. But I was to discover that "tomorrow" at Shereshevo meant "sometime" or "any time," it was a hope rather than a definite intention to act. Tomorrow could be infinitely far away.

And in fact next morning Dolly decided that what, above all things, she wished to do that day was to sit under the mulberry tree and draw Ariadne and me as we read and worked. We were fairly caught, with no chance of bicycling off on our own.

"It's very boring being drawn, Mamma," said Ariadne after a while. "And there's something tickling my nose. I long to scratch."

"It's a butterfly, dear," said her mother, crayon poised above the drawing-board. "I am putting it in. You look very pretty with a butterfly on your nose. Ah, there, it's flown away."

"I wish *I* could." Ariadne gave her nose a scratch, which made her sneeze.

"What a fidget you are," said her mother absently. "I've got the colour of the butterfly. Such a pretty shadow it cast."

The timeless day wore on with nothing to break the monotony except the movement of the butterflies, as Dolly drew, and erased what she had done, and then started again. We were not allowed to see what she had drawn, I suspected because we would not have liked it, but Ariadne impishly said no, it was because there was nothing there at all and that her mother had rubbed out more than she had drawn.

The next day Dolly said we must help her sort through the library and begin on a catalogue. "We had one once," said Dolly. "It was begun in 1870, but somehow it never got finished." I was not surprised very little got finished at Shereshevo. There was no need to hurry, there would always be time tomorrow.

Ariadne sat and watched me labour among the books; she said such work made her hands dirty.

"They are dusty," I said, banging two books together and watching the dust rise. "No one has read them or even shaken a feather-duster over them for ages."

"They are mostly Grandfather's books. Except for a few Tauchnitz editions we bring down to read in the summer." Ariadne yawned.

"Most of the books are about agriculture and estate management."

"Yes, my grandfather was a great estate improver. He built the distillery, and the mill, and I don't know what else. And of course, it was in his time that the serfs were liberated."

"I suppose that all his enterprises helped the peasants a great deal?" I was interested in the development of the estate.

"I don't know if it helped them so much, but it certainly helped us: we became much richer. Oh, dear, I can't stop yawning."

The days passed quietly. No mention was made of either Peter Alexandrov or Edward Lacey, and there was no sign of their arrival, but I imagined they were expected. One day I saw the maids cleaning out two of the bedrooms and airing the great goose-feather beds, but nothing more happened, and quietness closed down again.

One morning I looked out of my window as I was dressing to go downstairs, when to my surprise I saw a group of peasant women clustered about the steps that led to the upper terrace. They were sitting there patiently with the air of having waited some time already, and of being ready to wait longer if they must.

But when I looked out again, just before going down, I saw they had gone. Only a servant from the house, with a great broom sweeping away at the steps where they had crouched, gave any idea that there had ever been anyone there at all.

Downstairs, I said to Ariadne, "Why were all those people gathered outside in the garden? I saw them from my bedroom."

"Oh, the peasant women? Yes, I heard they had been to look for Mamma." She looked round the room almost as if a group of peasants might swarm in through the door. "They always come to Mamma when they are in trouble."

"What sort of trouble?"

"Oh, debts. They always seem to have debts," said Ariadne vaguely. "And illnesses, they always have those, too."

"What a responsibility for her," I said. "It must weigh on her."

Ariadne shrugged. "If she is tired or doesn't want to bother, then she just sends them away."

"But what do they do then?" I was shocked at Dolly Denisov's heartlessness, but it was in character.

"Oh, I suppose they go to the steward, or manage on their own." Slowly, Ariadne said, "Really, it is better for them to be independent and not to rely on my mother."

"Yes, of course." Once again I was surprised at the flash of acuteness in Ariadne's observation. She was showing herself a cleverer, sharper girl than I had realized. So often she saw the truth. But Dolly—still it was wrong to judge her, and no business of mine. Would I be any better in her position?

Perhaps it was just a coincidence, but this was the day Dolly decided we should visit the village. We rode in a smart little governess-cart, with Dolly driving. Suddenly she stopped. "Would you like to drive, Rose?"

I was Rose these days, it seemed.

I nodded. "Oh, I'd enjoy it."

We changed places and then set off again. A governess-cart, with its sideways seats, so that one has to twist at the waist to drive, is very safe and easy.

"The reins mark my white gloves," said Madame Denisov, and she sat there looking picturesque and elegant with one hand on the little door that closed us in at the back. At her feet were several baskets covered with linen cloths. "And I see you drive well."

"But the mare is so clever." And indeed she was, knowing the road thoroughly and almost anticipating the slight direction I might give her on the reins.

"Yes, Fanny goes beautifully," agreed Dolly, carefully brushing a little dirt from her white chamois leather glove. "You must borrow her whenever you like and take her for a drive. She won't let you get lost: give her her head, and Fanny will always get you home."

We were in the middle of the village before I realized we had arrived. A few houses stood together as if trying to form the nucleus of a village, but the rest were scattered here and there as if they were toy houses that a giant child had thrown from the skies. I thought of a child because it seemed impossible to believe that a fully adult architect of the village could have dropped down such hovels.

As we drew closer, I saw that I had been unfair to the houses. Although it was true they were mere constructions of wattle and mud, with turfs on their roofs, yet almost all of them were cleanly whitewashed with pots of plants at their windows. Moreover, a small patch of garden with vegetables and flowers had been created around most of the houses. I had to drive with care as geese, ducks and children, together with a wild-looking pack of animals rather like goats, but which I think were a sort of sheep, were swarming along the track that was the road. There were only three structures of any size in the village, of which the most prominent was the village church, a low white structure with a stubby tower, from which a bell was now thinly clapping the hour. Opposite the church was the steward's house which, although small, looked comfortable and prosperous, and where a plump woman was sitting on the verandah shelling peas into a bowl in her lap. She looked of a different status from the group of women clustered round the big iron pump which was the other prominent object in the village, and had three steps leading up to the domed hood in which it was protected.

"My grandfather built that for the village," said Ariadne, seeing my eyes rest on it. I wondered why he hadn't given the villagers taps and running water while he was about it, but no doubt that was expecting too much. After all, one or two houses in Jordansjoy still lacked mains water, although I think they mostly had their own pump.

"Well, now," said Dolly, "we are here on business. Stop, please." And she looked around her as if seeking something.

I reined in the horse and we drew to a stop, very near the pump. Dolly looked at the women, but obviously did not see there what she sought, because she said, "Ariadne, you go into the village shop and find out where is the child that was brought up to the house this morning." Ariadne still sat there. Dolly held out her hand to me. "I'll take the reins. You go with Ariadne."

Reluctantly, Ariadne got herself up and out of the governess-cart, and I followed.

"I didn't realize this was a shop," I said to Ariadne, as she led me up to one of the larger of the huts.

She shrugged. "If you can call it a shop."

As we got closer, I could see that the door was festooned on either side with various saleable objects. A tin kettle and a pan hung above a pair of long felt boots while, facing them, was a bunch of enamelled mugs hanging from a bit of rope threaded through their handles and suspended from a hook. A wooden tub filled with what looked a pile of old rags stood underneath these mugs: the rags were, in fact, strips of felt and were used, as I found out later, for repairing the felt boots. By it was another tub, this time of washing soda.

Inside the shop it was very dark, in spite of the bright sunlight outside, dark and stuffy, smelling of old clothes, and strange, dried foodstuffs, but Ariadne led the way confidently forward, and so I followed.

Then I could see that a waist-high wooden counter ran along one wall of the shop, with a door behind it opening into an inner room, and leaning up against the counter as if she had been there all day and might stay there all night was a burly woman. She gave a little bob of a curtsey when she saw Ariadne. I earned nothing except an inquisitive look; it was a comprehensive one, however, and I felt she had taken in all she wanted to for the moment, and had registered it, and would presently think about it.

"Ah, good morning, Excellency," she said to Ariadne, not with any particular politeness. "I guessed we should be seeing you."

I thought that Ariadne seemed the least little bit nervous of the shopkeeper. Nor did I blame her, she was a formidable-looking woman. "My mother directs me to ask where is the sick child, the one who was brought up to the house this morning?"

"The child didn't come, Little Excellency," said the woman. "Only the mother and the grandmother and a few of their friends. The child was too ill; besides, it was screaming dreadfully, and the mother thought that none of them might be admitted to the house at all if the servants heard the noise."

"My mother wasn't awake at the time; consequently they were sent away."

"That poor little wretch would have woken her, bless its unhappy soul. Oh, what a cry it has, strikes you cold. Sharp, you know, like a knife, and yet thin and wailing at the same time, like a lost cat."

"You always exaggerate, Madame Mozorov. Anyway, my mother wants to know whose child it is."

"The son of the daughter of old Katia who used to work at the big house as a laundry-maid and married big Paul, the carpenter. The girl's husband was taken off to serve in the army as one of this village's quota. He didn't want to go, but he had to."

A string of dark sausages hung from one hook in the ceiling, and by it, another hook supporting a skein of dried fish. Neither sausages nor fish looked very appetizing, but, except for a sack of soft, sweet biscuits and some black bread, constituted the shop's entire food stock. I found the atmosphere in the shop oppressive and unpleasant.

But there was something more than a bad smell troubling me, and I stood there for a moment assessing what it was.

"Miss Rose?" said Ariadne quickly. "Is anything wrong? Are you ill?"

"No, no, not ill at all. I'm perfectly well." And it was true, I was quite fit, but I was just experiencing a very strange sensation. For ages now, Patrick Graham had been very far away from me, but now, suddenly in this ugly, stuffy room, he had come back to me. I had the queer feeling that he was very close to me.

It wasn't a fantasy; I did not believe he was there in the room with me, rather it was a terribly strong intimation of his presence. More as if he had just left me, walked out of the room that minute. I corrected myself: no, it felt as if he were just about to walk in.

I turned to look at the door. Of course there was no one there.

"Are you sure you are all right?" asked Ariadne's worried voice.

"Perfectly and absolutely. If you are ready, shall we go?" And with a firm step, I walked to the door.

Behind me I could hear her murmuring still to the shop-woman, and then she joined me.

"You look better now," she said.

"Oh, yes, I am. Really, there was nothing wrong. I am quite myself." And the awareness of Patrick's presence had gone. But nothing could take away the shattering knowledge of how much I still cared for him. The protective skin I had maintained over the wound had been roughly torn off and for the moment I winced with the pain of it.

Dolly came up to us in the governess-cart. "Well?"

"Yes," said Ariadne, "Madame Mozorov knew all about it."

"She always knows everything."

The women who had been talking around the pump had now picked up their buckets and pots of water and were scattering to their homes. Dolly's presence had somehow put paid to their gossiping. And yet Dolly herself sat there looking friendly and gentle and benevolent. I thought that nothing I had so far seen at Shereshevo marked the chasm between the classes more clearly than this silent melting away before Dolly's gaze. Heaven knows, at Jordansjoy people complained enough about the Old Countess, and said what a stiff-necked old snob she was, and how really there was no pleasing her, but all the same, when she came to the village, she was treated as another human being.

Ariadne was telling her mother where to go. "Old Katia's house. You know which that is? Near the distillery. Well, I know if you don't."

We got back into the governess-cart, Dolly flicked the horse with a whip, and we were off. Old Katia's house was on the other side of the village, and was larger and more respectable-looking than some of the others. She had a trim vegetable garden round it, with sunflowers and poppies growing in it. She herself stood at the door, curtseying and welcoming us. Of course we were expected. A message had got to Katia that we were on our way, probably from one of the numerous children one saw scuffling in the dust of the village street. In the winter that dust must turn to liquid mud.

Dolly and Ariadne prepared to go into the house, but I hesitated. "I won't come with you. I will stay and hold the pony's head. After all, we haven't brought a groom."

Dolly didn't allow that. "No, no. The horse can be tied. She is good at standing and will wait for ever. You must come with us. Pick up that basket for me and bring it with you."

"I'd really rather stay outside."

"I wish you to come, my dear," said Dolly smoothly, and, in case there was any further trouble from me, "I insist," she said, laying her hand on my arm with gentle sweetness. It was said with a smile, but I was left with no doubt that she meant it. And, indeed, my reluctance to go in puzzled me a little.

I picked up the basket, which was heavy. Inside I noticed the shape of a wine bottle and a covered pudding basin, from which I could guess that Dolly was doing the Lady Bountiful in the classic style, although I could not see that either wine or pudding would do much good for the sick child. I had put my finger on the root of my reluctance to go in: I did not want to see the child. Something in me held back.

"Am I to come, too?" It was Ariadne.

"Of course. Bring the other basket." Dolly herself carried nothing. "Katia," she called as soon as she was close enough, "I am sorry about your grandson. It was not properly explained to me this morning. But I have come now." Katia gave a little bob, meant to show gratitude. "And where is the child, and what is the trouble? Girls, put those baskets on the table."

Ariadne was looking around her with interest. I realized, with surprise, that this was the first time she had ever been inside a peasant house.

It was a first time for me, too. Inside the cottage it was cosier and more comfortable than I had expected. Certainly it was crowded with furniture, such as a heavy table, a bed and a wall cupboard, all of dark wood and clumsy construction, more or less home-made, I should think, and everywhere smelt of cabbage, but it was a home.

Katia's dignified reception of us made it clear that it was her home, although Dolly's grandfather had owned her own grandfather as a chattel, and I liked her for it. I was the one who smiled at her; Dolly didn't smile, but continued to look preoccupied, while Ariadne stared around her with a strained expression.

Ariadne and I had placed our baskets on the table, but although Katia gave a polite dip as if to say thank you, she didn't hurry to look at them; instead she stayed and watched Dolly Denisov. "The child needs a doctor, Excellency, and as you know there is not one in the village."

"And you want me to send for one? I'll do that, of course." Dolly sounded thoughtful. "Where is the child?"

Katia nodded towards an inner room. "In there with his mother, poor little thing."

"He's not crying," said Ariadne. "Madame Mozorov said he was crying painfully."

Katia smiled. "Oh, you asked her, did you? Well, you should have known what sort of an answer you'd get: that Mozorov woman always likes to tell a tale. So they didn't tell you that it was Katia who had come to the big house? I left a message with the servants, but they're a hopeless lot you've got there now, Excellency, and you ought to know it. Hopeless. Thieves, too, I dare say."

Clearly there was no love lost between the village people and the servants at the big house.

"No, the little man's asleep now," went on Katia. "Do you want to see him?"

"Perhaps we shouldn't disturb him," I began nervously, but Dolly cut across me.

"Let him be brought in." There was no mistaking the command in Dolly's voice, and Katia could not have disregarded it even if she had wanted to. In any case, the child was already at the door in his mother's arms. The girl stood there shyly for a moment and then came forward and stood by her mother. The two were alike in feature and stature, plump, well-built women. The girl was young, younger than I, I thought, although life had been harder on her. Katia was probably no older than Dolly Denisov, I guessed, though from her red-cheeked, weather-beaten complexion you would never know it.

Of the child there was not much to see; in spite of the heat he was so muffled up in wraps and shawls that nothing more than the top of his head was visible.

His grandmother was wrong, though; he was not asleep. I knew it at once; the knowledge flooded in through my own body. He was not unconscious, but he was at a very low ebb indeed. This, too, I knew strongly. I had been reluctant to come here to see the child, but I was here now and could not turn away.

"What is the trouble? What sort of illness is it? How long has he been ill?" This from Dolly.

"For two days now," whispered the girl. "He could not take his food, and then he began to cry. Now he does not cry, but just lies. And that worries me more."

Rightly so, I thought.

"I wonder if it's a fever," said Dolly.

"He was hot. Now he is deathly cold," said Katia.

She knows he is dying, I thought. And not a fever. Some sort of internal obstruction flashed through my mind.

Almost against my will, I went over to the baby and stared at a pale, shrivelled little face; it was certainly plain. The girl hugged the baby to her more tightly as if she didn't want me to see. Above his head her own face was expressionless.

I lifted the shawl back, although I sensed her reluctance. "Let me see," I said gently.

"He has always been a delicate boy." Katia stepped forward defensively.

"Yes." I held the shawl for a moment, and then softly replaced it. I had already observed the tiny, shrunken, twisted left leg. The child was crippled. "So I see." The mother looked at me in a wordless, piteous plea.

What possible future could there be for a crippled child in a poor Russian peasant household? Was not oblivion better? No wonder I had been reluctant to come in.

"At least he won't have to serve in the army like his father," said Katia, as if she'd read my thoughts.

The baby gave a mewing cry.

"Is he in pain?" said Dolly. She looked at me.

"Yes, he's in pain." I avoided meeting his mother's eyes.

Deliberately, I tried to withdraw myself. I made the cold decision not to help. I could feel my heart beating hard in my chest. This gift of mine always brought anxiety and alarm to me, however composed and calm I seemed outwardly. I was frightened of the power I seemed to have, frightened and puzzled, and many times would like to have closed my eyes to it.

Now I said to myself, No, no, no, nothing shall happen. I gritted my teeth, aware that Dolly was watching me with curiosity. I gave her an awkward smile, but she wouldn't leave me alone.

"Do take another look, Rose," she said. "I'm sure you know about babies. Have you ever seen such a case as this before?"

"I know nothing about infants, nothing."

"But you're not looking." She put her arm round me and turned me gently but firmly towards the child. "And he is looking at you."

It was true: the infant had opened his large, dark brown eyes and was gazing at the room, not as if he saw anything, but certainly with some consciousness. I saw him blink.

His grandmother crossed herself and muttered a prayer under her breath. The mother gave a little cry and started to stroke her son's cheek.

"Oh, do look, Rose!" said Dolly. But I was too preoccupied with what was happening to me to answer. It was as if I were being pulled towards the child. Whether I wanted to or not, some energy within me was flowing towards him. The process was beyond my control, it was quite involuntary. I didn't want it to happen, but it was happening and I couldn't prevent it.

Then slowly the feeling ebbed away; I returned to what was happening in the room. To my relief, it seemed as if no one had noticed anything wrong with me.

The mother was still nursing her child, whose gaze remained placidly open, and Katia was helping Ariadne to unpack the baskets while Dolly gave them orders.

"Put the honey there, Ariadne. Honey is always very good for babies, Katia. See if you can get him to take a spoonful. The wine is for the mother, it will improve her milk, I dare say there may be something amiss there, too, she looks very pale, poor thing. . . . Those are infant's clothes there, and do use them. It is old-fashioned to *swaddle* the child so. Exercise of the limbs is the thing, remember, Katia."

Katia muttered something about the rigours of fresh air.

"And I will send to the town for the doctor there. I don't put a lot of faith in him, a mere apothecary, as I recall, but we will try."

For the first time the child's mother spoke; in a soft voice she said, "He is easier."

Again, Katia crossed herself.

"That's good," said Dolly with satisfaction. "See if you can get him to feed." She looked round, gathering Ariadne and me up with her eyes. "We must be off. I shall send for the doctor, as I said, Katia."

There was a small bustle as we left, an old man mysteriously appeared from somewhere and helped us untether the horse and establish ourselves in the governess-cart again. Dolly took the reins, but before we could move away, Katia came hurrying out of the house.

Quietly, and with evident satisfaction, with the air of one delivering an important announcement, she said, "The child has taken some milk."

"Oh, that's splendid, Katia, splendid," said Dolly. "Just what I wanted to hear. But you shall still have the doctor call."

As we moved away, Ariadne let out a long breath, as if she had been holding herself in all this time. "They are really quite comfortable in there," she said. "It's not at all what I imagined, bût quite clean and homelike."

"I always told you so"—Dolly touched the horse with her whip—"but you never believed me."

Ariadne sounded almost disappointed, which was puzzling, but I had no inclination to think about it. I had plenty to think about on my own account.

"You're silent, Rose," said Dolly.

Ariadne answered for me: "She's thinking. Let her be. Rose likes to think."

"Rose has to think," I might have said.

Today, my strange gift, which I so distrusted, had grown in strength. Hitherto, however little I liked to admit it, my gift had been under my control. An element of willing had to come into the process, I had to wish to help. But today I had not wished to help; on the contrary, I had desired to hold back, but my power had taken control and spent itself spontaneously and freely against my will.

I was frightened; it was like harbouring a dangerous spirit which might, in the end, possess one.

"Very well, we will let her think," said Dolly in a good-humoured way. "I understand. I myself am a thoughtful person."

We trotted, the horse going at the speed it chose, all three of us silent now. I suppose we were all thinking in different ways of the scene we had left behind us.

Why had I been so reluctant to enter the house? I could rationalize it by pointing to the child's infirmity which made my conscious mind judge him better dead. But had I then known of it in advance? It seemed I had. So part of me knew, and this part didn't wish to help, but my deeper mind had apparently taken a different and independent decision.

And how did this resistance, followed by the sudden welling out of power towards the child, relate to the strange feeling of Patrick's presence that I had had earlier? Perhaps there was no connection. Nothing seemed clear, or easy to understand.

In St. Petersburg brightly painted wooden dolls were sold. You unscrewed the dolls, and there was another one inside. And inside that doll, yet another one, and then another. I was like that doll.

"I'm so glad the child seemed easier when we left," said Dolly. She looked briefly towards me and I caught her glance, bright with satisfaction. "And he really did, don't you think so?"

Suddenly I understood: there had been a test and I had passed it. Dolly had taken me down to the cottage to see what happened to the sick child when in my presence; she wanted to know what I could do. And apparently I had pleased her greatly: I had given a good performance.

"Now you're frowning," said Ariadne.

"Am I? It's the sun shining in my eyes, and I think my head aches." It was true; suddenly I felt a dull ache behind my eyes.

"It's the place. Shereshevo takes some getting used to," said Ariadne philosophically.

"Oh, what nonsense you talk, Ariadne." Now it was Dolly's turn to frown. "Shereshevo has a particularly healthy climate."

"It's the climate of the mind I'm thinking about."

Dolly was crisp. "I don't understand you, Ariadne. Here you are with every freedom and extravagance a young girl could wish for, and yet you continually complain."

"I've never heard Ariadne complain," I said.

"Well, she does to me," and Dolly whipped up her placid mare, who took no notice but continued at her usual steady trot. Perhaps it was an epitome of the life here.

Ariadne met my eyes and smiled, as if to say, Well, I don't really complain much, but I wondered; I thought I was beginning to know my Ariadne. Now that I could see further into the Denisovs' inner relationships, they were not such a happy family group after all. But perhaps you should never get too close to any family. I began to see that we were lucky not to have a strong family nexus at Jordansjoy. We had no one, you see, except Tibby, to keep us together, and so it did not matter if we flew apart, as we did, at intervals.

Dolly strode ahead of us into the house, a servant appeared to take the horse and governess-cart, and Ariadne and I strolled behind.

"Your headache will be better in the house," she said soothingly.

"She's worn out, poor girl," said her mother, pausing at the foot of the stairs. "And no wonder. Go and rest, my dear."

I stopped abruptly. "No, I'm not tired. And it wasn't really the sun which gave me a headache. I was just angry."

"What, you, too?" said Dolly.

"*I'm* not angry, Mamma," said Ariadne.

"Yes, you are," said her mother, with perfect good humour. "I can feel waves of it passing over me. Goodness knows why." She turned to me. "Miss Gowrie, Rose, my dear girl, *why* are you angry?"

"Madame Denisov, what happened to the child had nothing to do with me. *Nature* cured him, not I. Some constriction inside him eased. Nothing more than that. It was perfectly natural."

"*You* eased him, Rose. I saw it happen. And it was very interesting, too. Spontaneous and happy. Natural. Yes, it was natural. But by what means?"

"No," I said, shaking my head, "don't go on."

"I *will* say it. You were the means."

"I don't admit it," I said.

Dolly smiled. "You must admit it."

"Mamma, what is all this about?" Ariadne came and stood beside me on the stairs. "You are making Rose cry."

"I don't see why she should cry," said Dolly, with a show of irritation. "Most people would rejoice to think they can alleviate human suffering."

Ariadne's eyes went wide and round. "Oh, my goodness. Can you truly do that, Rose?"

"Except that I don't believe I can. I won't believe. It makes a monster of me."

"I believe what I have seen with my own eyes," said Dolly stoutly. "And I am glad to have seen it."

"But what did you see? A sick baby take a sudden turn for the better. It happens all the time, children are volatile, life-seeking little things, they *want* to live and so struggle for it."

"Do they?" said Dolly dryly. "I've seen plenty die. Especially peasant babies. It's more common than not. I tell you that child's life was not worth a penny piece till you took hold of him." Once again that satisfied note of triumph in her voice.

"I never touched him."

"I meant spiritually."

We were at the top of the first flight of stairs by now and had reached the *piano nobile* on which the family rooms were. Dolly led the way into the big living-room, and went straight way to a side-table where a covered jug of lemon and barley water rested on a bed of ice. She poured herself a glass and drank it quickly. Then she pushed the jug towards me.

"Do take some. I'm sure you need it."

This was showing less than her usual easy good manners, and I judged that, between us, Ariadne and I had managed to annoy her.

Ariadne poured two glasses of the drink and handed one to me. "I don't understand what this is all about," she said, "but I am very interested."

"Your mother thinks that I have the power to cure sickness." The words came out bluntly, more bluntly than I intended.

"I had begun to guess that."

"Somehow she has picked up a tale about me," and I gave Dolly a hard look. "From my old cousins, I suppose. And now she thinks she has seen this power in operation."

Dolly sat down on a soft, low chair and swung one foot casually. "It's true I heard about you from Miss Gowrie, who is a great teller of tales as you must very well know. She has many correspondents back in your own country, and she had heard stories about you. She is always picking up little bits of gossip and information about all sorts of people and passing it on—it amuses her and there is no harm done. She is never malicious."

"Before you asked me to come?"

"Oh, long before that," said Dolly absently.

Why did I not see the significance then of that remark? Yet I did not. I was still driving on at what I wanted to say. "I do not accept that I have any special powers; I will not accept it. I have been over-imaginative, perhaps even thought myself to have an influence of some kind, but this is the twentieth century and in the end I believe in reason," I finished defiantly.

"You're frightened," said Dolly. "I saw it in your face and it is very understandable. What happens *is* very strange and wonderful, and to be the instrument of it . . . Yes, I see how you wish to turn away from it, disown it. That is what you are doing, my dear."

I was silent.

"But one must face life," she went on.

"Other people's life," I murmured bitterly. "It's easy to face things for other people." I felt like a butterfly transfixed on the pin of Dolly's determination.

"I believe in the economy of life," said Dolly. "Nothing is wasted. You have this great gift and it will not be wasted." And she smiled, a sweet smile, but not entirely directed at me; she was smiling for herself and to herself.

"That's a frightening thing to say, if you think about it," said Ariadne. "Every little scrap and tittle of our everyday life all fitting in somewhere and being put to some use. No, I don't think I like that notion. I believe I feel happier with some oddments left over. It nourishes the illusion of freedom, at least."

"You pick up a lot of nonsense from your Uncle Peter," said Dolly.

"Yes, I do."

"He teaches you scepticism," said Dolly.

"I go to church more regularly than you do." Ariadne's voice was half amused.

"I sometimes wonder what you think about there."

"And so you should do, Mother, so you should do." She eyed her mother with bright-eyed defiance, enjoying the clash.

A woman-servant hurried into the room and went straight up to Dolly. "A message has just come up from the village." She bobbed a curtsey. "The postman brought it from Katia, the one you visited. She says the child is dead."

"What's that?" said Dolly. "But we've only just left."

"The minute after you departed. The messenger came running. Katia wanted you to be told. She said he died without pain, poor little creature." The woman crossed herself. "He died smiling. It's God's will." Another bobbing curtsey, combined with another cross. "Is that all then, Your Honour?"

"Yes," said Dolly. "You can go. Well," she went on, turning to me, "so the child died." She was thoughtful.

"You see, I didn't cure him. It came as no surprise to me. You cannot cure death." But I was wretched all the same. "Oh, that poor little baby." I covered my eyes with my hands.

Ariadne came up and put her arm round my shoulders. "Don't cry. Truly, he is better dead."

"I know, I know, but that, too, is terrible."

"Yes, it is," observed Ariadne soberly.

"Dead, after all," said Dolly. She lit a cigarette and strolled up and down the room. "It was, probably, inevitable that he should die in the end, and, as Ariadne truly says, for the better really. No, he was too far gone. It was not a fair experiment."

I looked up sharply at that word. *Experiment*, I thought.

"Yes," went on Dolly, not realizing, I think, how much she was revealing herself. "With a stronger child it would have been different. The easing of the pain in itself might have saved life. As it was, the child died smiling. Did you notice that phrase? I did, and it seems to me very significant. He was happy. Wasn't that a good thing you did? Yes, and it is like the boy who was injured on the London docks before you sailed."

"I suppose Edward Lacey told you about that episode?" I felt bitter that he should have talked, but I suppose it was inevitable. Who can keep a story like that quiet?

"No, as it happens, I heard it first from another source," Dolly frowned, as if the source gave her no joy, and I wondered who on earth it could be, "and then I questioned Edward. Not that he said much, he never does. One always has to *dig* with Edward." She flashed a look at me. "You might have told me yourself."

"You must know it is not a story I would want to talk about," I said.

"Yes, Rose, little as you may expect it of me, I do understand, and I respect you for it."

Ariadne said, "I should leave Rose alone, now, Mother. Let her go to her room and rest. She looks worn out."

"Yes, you rest, Rose," said Dolly, as if she'd got what she wanted from me. "A rest is just the thing for you. I shall have one myself. Soon we shall have Peter and Edward Lacey here, and no rest for anyone. And what will you do, Ariadne?"

"Write letters," said Ariadne demurely.

"Good, good. In English, mind, nothing in Russian or French."

Ariadne came with me to the door of my room; outside it she said hesitantly, "I understand how you must feel about your gift, and why you don't wish to talk of it."

"I'm frightened," I almost whispered. "I feel as though whatever it is is growing in strength and will end in taking me over completely. That's why I deny it if I can. I fear the strength I cannot control. I must keep it down, deny it when I can, it *must* be nothing, or it will become everything."

Ariadne squeezed my hand sympathetically and went away. Perhaps she understood, perhaps she did not, but she was a good child.

Once inside my room I did something I had not done before.

I got the Fabergé ball out of the drawer where I had kept it locked away, and opened it to stare at Princess Irene's photograph.

"If there is any good to be got from me, you might as well have your share," I murmured, staring at her picture; the painted face stared back at me, bland and bright.

Then the top of the box snapped down on my hand, badly bruising it and drawing blood.

The next ten days were very quiet. Ariadne and I worked, and walked together, not saying much to each other but companionable. For long stretches I was alone. Ariadne had a trick of absenting herself when she chose. One couldn't blame her for wanting some solitude, she got little enough of it. I, too, was glad to be alone to think my own thoughts, which were perplexing. Dolly Denisov was elusive. She was certainly in the house and I occasionally heard her voice, but she was never seen. Ariadne said she was "rejuvenating herself." What she meant by this I did not quite know, but it seemed to involve her maid in a great deal of work. I saw her coming and going, carrying an odd variety of boxes and bowls, and once she was superintending the transport of what looked like a small bath of hot mud. Ariadne said that it *was* mud, and that it was to be plastered all over her mother who would then be swathed in towels and left to lie while it dried.

"What, even mud on her face?" I exclaimed.

"Oh, yes, right up to the eyes. The face-pack is *very* important," Ariadne assured me.

"And is it then chipped off?"

"Oh, it crumbles away quite easily, and the skin looks very pretty afterwards, all pink and soft."

So then I knew what Dolly was up to: she was restoring her appearance, always one of her chief interests. Not so much difference between her and her old relative, the Princess Irene, after all, I concluded.

"And then she will bathe in milk. We have plenty of that because of the dairy," added Ariadne, practically.

"Sounds very sticky," I said.

"Oh, but afterwards she washes in verbena water. And then there is her hair." Ariadne was silent on the matter of Dolly's hair, but certainly when Dolly reappeared, her hair was more softly and luxuriantly curling than ever, and its pretty colour an even denser black. Indeed, she did look refreshed. Her maid, however, appeared worn out.

"And what have you two dear girls been doing while I have been very busy?" was Dolly's first question when we met. So I was her dear girl now, I thought.

"Doing nothing, Mamma," said Ariadne, "but doing it very well."

"Ah, if only one could be sure that with you nothing really means nothing," said Dolly.

"Ask Rose," returned Ariadne. "We have been together the whole time."

I looked at Ariadne in some surprise. This was not quite the whole truth; we had been apart for considerable periods. The girl had a knack, not of deliberately lying, but of glossing over the truth.

"Then how do you account for the fact that the stables inform me that you constantly bring back my horses hard ridden and exhausted?" asked Dolly, with asperity.

I turned towards Ariadne sharply; she did not meet my eyes.

"Just touring the countryside," she said to her mother. "Just exploring."

"Alone? And the horses? So exhausted? How far had they travelled?"

"Next time I shall take a bicycle," said Ariadne smoothly.

"There will not be a next time," answered Dolly, turning smartly on her heel and leaving the room.

When she had closed the door, I said, "And where were you? Where is it you went?"

"Oh, over towards Vyksa, where there is a copper mine. One of the daughters of the manager is a particular friend of mine. My mother doesn't like me to go there. She thinks the girl is not of what she calls 'the right class' to be my friend."

"And where did you meet her?" I said, puzzled.

"Oh, she was at school with me, at the Smolny Institute. Yes, occasionally girls from less than noble family are admitted to the Smolny if they have the right letters of recommendation, and her father is an important official. We left together. Well, we were expelled, really." She looked at me from under her eye-lashes, aware she was making a confidence. "Sent away, you know."

"Oh." I considered this revelation. So this was what the old Princess Irene had meant by her sharp comment on Ariadne's schooling. "Why were you expelled?"

Ariadne shrugged. "One never gets a straight answer to that sort of thing. They are so arbitrary. I had done nothing wrong. I expect Marisia was too clever."

I looked at her doubtfully. I saw she was going to say nothing more. "I've heard the institute has very clever teachers," I said.

"You should let my Uncle Peter hear that: it would amuse him. He taught there once for a while."

"Did he?" I was genuinely surprised, not having seen Peter Alexandrov in a tutelary light.

"Yes, he taught European history. He was quite a pet of old Princess Elena Lieven, the directress: Nelly, we called her. But it was only for a few months, until they found a permanent teacher. All the girls loved him," and she giggled. "He's very attractive, of course."

"I'd like to see the Smolny Institute," I said.

"Speak to him about it. He still visits Princess Lieven. He'll be here soon," she finished lightly. "Talk to him yourself."

All I said in reply was, "Next time you visit your friend at Vyksa, you'd better take me with you."

Ariadne gave a small shiver. "I don't think you'd like it. In many ways, it is a terrible place."

We were interrupted then by a summons to a meal and I never had a chance to ask why Vyksa was so terrible. But that was my introduction to that name and place which everyone knew of and no one, except some administrators of the Tsar, wished to acknowledge.

Edward Lacey and Peter Alexandrov arrived the next week and the atmosphere of the house changed. Life and sociability poured in. Visitors started to arrive, many of them motoring some distance in order to get to us at Shereshevo. There was talk of picnics, and tennis parties, and even of a dance. It seemed that people would travel a hundred miles to visit each other in the depths of the Russian countryside.

I was in and yet not in it. Ariadne was gay and cheerful and introduced me to everyone, as did Dolly. I was included in every invitation, asked to everything, but never had I felt so separated from them. Because it gradually became apparent that except for a few idle games of tennis, and one afternoon when we all took tea-baskets down to the banks of the river and ate our tea there (which counted as a picnic, I suppose), none of the projected plans came to anything. Nothing was going to happen. People arrived and they sat around and talked. They certainly did talk. Endlessly, imaginatively, wittily and charmingly, but in the end, boringly.

Not that I found Peter Alexandrov boring. On the contrary, he seemed tirelessly interesting, continually revealing fresh aspects of his character. He took pains to care for people. One of his first actions on arrival was to say, "Here, catch this," and he threw a small bundle at me.

He had brought me some letters from home.

"These were delivered at St. Petersburg just before I left, and I thought you might as well have them."

"Oh, thank you." I grasped them eagerly. A letter from Grizel, one from an old friend in the village and another in a writing I did not recognize, which had been delivered by hand.

I opened this letter first, the dark blue seal on the envelope having given me a clue as to the writer.

Princess Irene wrote in an antique wavering script, which was yet perfectly legible. She had only two things to say and both concerned herself.

"You will be glad to know that I continue in undiminished strength. But I have had a good deal of neuralgia in my arm and I should be obliged if you would turn your attention to it. The right arm, I may say."

I stopped in my reading. Her command would have been laughable if the appeal had not been so naked. And the pain was from her heart, I knew that, and not neuralgia of unknown origin.

Princess Irene went on: "Pray remember to keep up your own strength by drinking two glasses of red wine each day. It seems advisable. Oblige me by keeping away from the peasants, they are full of infection."

She meant she didn't wish *me* to sicken and die. But I supposed at her age it was legitimate to be a monster of selfishness. The letter was signed:

*I. Mikhailovna Drutsko,* in letters about half an inch high, a splendid, baroque, sprawling structure of a signature.

I put the letter aside with a mixture of reverence and amusement. Then I opened my sister's letter. Grizel wrote: "This is to tell you that Patrick's mother, Mrs. Graham, took a heart attack last Tuesday and died at once. The girls are packing up and leaving the village to live in Edinburgh. I suppose we shall never see them again, nor hear more of Patrick. Strange and terrible, is it not, how quickly they are all removed from our lives?" She remained my affectionate sister Grizel, and in that capacity (having dropped the role of sober moralist on life) had a postscript of her own to add: "Dearest Sis, I have refused Archie this first time, but mean to accept him next time round."

Archie? I thought. Who is Archie? Nothing had prepared me for Archie, she had never mentioned him before. But poor Mrs. Graham was my last thought as I put the letters safely away in the drawer of my writing desk. Silence was the best answer to them, for the time being.

Yet perhaps my thinking about my letters was more obvious than I conceived, because eventually Peter said, "You're very quiet these days, Miss Rose."

"Am I?" I was surprised. "Perhaps it's because you all talk so much."

"Yes, we do rather," and he said it with amusement. "It's the relief of being out of Piter." In the country even his vocabulary relaxed and became more casual. Piter was St. Petersburg. "It's an oppressive town. The geography of it, I dare say, with the constant juxtaposition of water and great buildings. In the country we relax, and we drink too much, and of course that always makes Russians talk too much as well."

In the country Peter abandoned the stiff town clothes that were prescribed for St. Petersburg, and wore a casual jacket, buttoned to the neck, and a soft, round-necked shirt underneath. The influence of the peasant dress was unmistakable, but it was practical and cool. Edward Lacey, of course, stuck to his good English tweeds, and sweltered.

"Anyway, you will have no longer any cause to reproach me. I am going to do something positive."

"Really?"

"Yes, and don't raise your eyebrows like that, please. It involves you. Aha, now I've surprised you, haven't I?"

"Yes, certainly you have."

"Don't you remember what I promised? In St. Petersburg? Surely you can't have forgotten? I flattered myself it meant something to you."

"Tell me," I said, laughing. He was impossible in this mood.

"I am going to teach you to drive my motor car." He looked at me in triumph.

"Oh, well, as to that, I don't know," I began, thinking I would really have to consult my employer.

"Say you will learn. You must learn to drive. There are immense distances to cover in Russia, and it will be very useful to you."

"While I am here, perhaps," I said sharply. "Which, after all, will only be for a limited time."

"But, supposing you could be persuaded to stay?" And he looked at me again, amused and coaxing.

What could I say? How could I say that Tibby's last words to me had been to warn me against men of the Russian aristocracy whom she castigated as "unreliable." And unreliable in her terminology meant only one thing, that they were sexually unreliable, seducers and not husbands. Was Peter unreliable? I thought it highly probable he was. For surely he could have no serious interest in me? But I was flattered. And, in spite of myself, attracted to him.

After all, why not? He had wealth, intellect and good manners. As Ariadne said: he was attractive. Why not try for a great match? Grizel meant to, and when I had engaged myself to marry for love, I had been jilted. Perhaps Peter had other plans for me, but I thought that when it came down to it, my will and my determination might be as great as his.

Quite calmly I let a little seed of ambition take root inside me. It was a coldly silent decision and I was surprised how easy it was: Russia was changing me.

And yet, was it really so much out of character? Tibby, for all the way she talked, did not expect us to marry the local dominie or even a poor farmer. We were expected to marry within our class, and to do the best we could for ourselves. This was the unspoken assumption behind much of our behaviour. I might remain unmarried, but convention demanded that if I did marry, I had better do it well.

So I laughed at Peter, and agreed I would let him teach me to drive his motor car, and promised to take the first lesson that afternoon after luncheon.

Another thing that we did at Shereshevo was to eat. Meals were prolonged and frequent. We usually lunched at a long table set under a shady tree in the garden. There was nothing of a picnic about the meal, however, which always ran to five courses, beginning with iced soup and ending with a fruit sorbet. In between came fish (the fish at Shereshevo was always delicious, fresh from the river) followed by game and roast meat. We ate much the same sort of meal in the evening, too, and why Dolly and her family and her visitors were not fat I could not imagine, but in fact they were all remarkably slender. Perhaps it was the exercise of their tongues that did it.

After lunch, Peter said, "Go and get a dust-coat and I will take you driving."

I looked questioningly at Dolly Denisov, but she just shrugged and laughed. "You will need goggles as well, my dear, and a chiffon scarf over your hat; our roads are so powdery and dry that you will be covered with a layer of dust before you have driven out of sight of the house. I wouldn't do it for anything."

"I'd like to try," I said. "But what about Ariadne?"

"Ariadne has some music to practise, and I shall hear her." All objections were being smoothed away.

Ariadne looked rather sulky at this. "I can do it perfectly well on my own."

"Yes, but will you? I shall hear a few bars, played badly, and then when you think I am safely out of earshot, you will melt away."

"You'll never make a musician out of Ariadne," observed Peter.

"There's not much music in any of us," returned Dolly, "but a girl must try."

"Ariadne is quite as musical as is necessary," said Edward Lacey firmly. "I have known her to hum and sing quite tunefully when in a good mood."

Ariadne burst out laughing. "Well, your own voice is atrocious, dear Edward. You try, I admit, but I can say no more."

What a courtship, I thought, not a romantic illusion between them.

"I'll get my coat then, I have a tussore one that will do." I stood up. The men stood up politely also. Over Ariadne's head, I saw Dolly Denisov and Edward Lacey exchange looks. To my surprise, in her expression there was something astonishingly like entreaty, and in his, complicity. I felt a sensation like embarrassment, as if I'd discovered something about them. "I'll hurry," I said, and ran into the house.

It took longer than I had expected to array myself in my loose coat and arrange a soft scarf over my hat. I was wearing a natural-coloured straw boater, which I secured to my head with two long hatpins, and when I had tied a pale cream chiffon silk scarf over that and tied it under my chin, I thought it looked rather fetching. So I spent a little time improving the effect by fluffing my hair out round my temples and rubbing some *papier poudré* over my cheeks. I suppose I ought to have felt ashamed of myself, but I didn't. Instead, I felt quite gleeful.

I studied my face in the looking glass; my eyes were bright, my cheeks pink, and there was just a touch too much powder on my nose. I attended to that with a handkerchief. At that moment I was prepared to say good-bye for ever to Patrick Graham.

I ran down the stairs, and when I was half-way down them I heard someone whistling in one of the rooms on the floor below.

As a whistle, it was not very tuneful. It was true, as Peter had implied, no one in this house was musical. But I recognized the tune.

Someone was whistling "My love is like a red, red, rose." I had heard Patrick hum and sing it so often that to me it was irretrievably associated with him. What was so strange and surprising was hearing it whistled here in the heart of Russia.

I ran down the stairs, and paused in the wide upper hall from which all the rooms on that floor opened. The whistling had stopped, and there was no sound now to be heard. All the doors stood open, as almost all doors did at Shereshevo to promote the flow of cool air. No one was in the library, nor in the smaller room which Ariadne and I used as our workroom.

I hurried into the large sitting-room which led to the terrace. Surely the whistler must be in here? I longed to know who it was. But the room was empty, except for Ariadne who was just entering the room from the terrace.

"Who was that whistling? Did you see?" I asked her at once.

She looked surprised. "I don't know. Someone went out of the further window as I came in. At least I think so, but I really was not looking. And I didn't hear whistling. I'm so sorry. Does it matter?"

"No, no, of course not. So silly of me, but it was the tune," I said, not very coherently. "I knew it of old."

"It reminds you of home, I suppose," said Ariadne slowly. I nodded. "I wonder who it was, then?"

"It was badly enough whistled to be any one of you," I said, with a half laugh, which was almost a sob.

The very strength of my reaction to the tune should have alerted me to the state of my feelings still for Patrick.

"If the tune reminded you of your home, then it is most likely to have been Edward," said Ariadne reasonably. "But I have never heard him whistle. Why not ask?"

But I was calmer now. "Oh, that would be making too much of it altogether. Besides, where is he?"

"Gone off somewhere with my mother," admitted Ariadne, and she added sympathetically, "but people never remember what they whistle; sometimes it's as unconscious as breathing." Then she added, as she skipped off on her own business, "And, after all, perhaps you imagined it and there was no one there at all."

I imagined it—never, I thought. But no one there at all? Yes, that was perfectly possible. A strange idea was forming in my mind.

I stood there for a moment, remembering the exquisite pain of the moment when I had heard the whistled tune: "My love is like the melodie, That's sweetly played in tune." Oh, Patrick, Patrick. Then I collected myself and went on down the steps from the terrace to the waiting motor car and to Peter.

The driving lesson consisted for the most part of my sitting beside Peter while he talked. I did take the wheel on a long, straight stretch of the road, where I managed to control the vehicle more or less steadily. Perhaps I did show a strong tendency to veer towards the right, but Peter assured me that ladies always did this and it was very natural.

The dust rose up from the road in clouds, coating hands and face, and entering nostrils, mouth and eyes. I don't know how Peter managed conversation without choking, but I could not.

"You're very quiet," he complained, half-amused, half-serious, I thought. He had wanted me to enjoy this new experience.

"Oh, but it's the dust. I can't make light conversation with my mouth full of what feels like sand."

"You were quiet when we set out. I saw your face before you draped that bit of chiffon over it, and very serious you looked, too."

"Oh, perhaps I was frightened at learning to drive this great car," I said, as lightly as I could.

"Not you. You handled it as if there were not a nerve in your body."

"You win: it wasn't the idea of a drive. No, just before we came out, I heard a tune whistled that reminded me of "—I hesitated—"of so much that had better be forgotten."

"You looked as though you'd seen a ghost."

"Heard, not seen. Yes, I have considered that, too," I said sadly.

"What?"

"Yes, I heard a tune whistled where no one was. Did I really hear anything at all? And if so, what?"

He turned to stare at me. "Yes, you are serious."

"Mind the wheel. Do please watch the road, or I am sure we shall hit something."

"There are no ghosts at Shereshevo," he said, returning his gaze towards the road, on which an old woman and a goat had materialized.

"No, I rather believe I may have brought it with me." I spoke cautiously, waiting for his reaction.

"Yes, that is possible, I suppose. But how sad for you." I ought to have known that no Russian was going to laugh at me for being haunted.

"I'm not sure if the person concerned is dead or not, but it begins to look as if he is."

"One can be haunted by the living, indeed one can," he said thoughtfully.

"I'm getting fanciful," I sighed. "If the incident had happened at home, I'd have thought nothing of it."

Peter drew the car into the side of the road in the shade of a tree, and stopped. "Now, tell me *exactly* what happened that worried you."

Briefly, I said, "I was coming down the stairs from my bedroom to meet you, when I heard someone whistling the music to which a poem of Robert Burns is set: 'My love is like a red, red rose.' But when I went down to look and see who the whistler was, I could see no one. I don't know who it could have been, either. Ariadne thinks she saw someone leaving the room by another door on to the terrace, but she is vague. It wasn't you, I suppose?"

He shook his head. "No."

"I swear I heard someone."

He said: "You're rather given to hearing things, aren't you?"

"What do you mean?" But I thought I knew.

"You heard a voice speaking to you from the disused speaking-tubes in St. Petersburg, didn't you?"

I turned away from him, and found that I was looking at a great field of sunflowers. We don't grow fields of them back home in Scotland, but here they did. I believe they extracted some sort of oil from the seeds. "I hadn't forgotten," I said. "And indeed I saw the connection myself. It's a little madness, I suppose, invented specially for me. The madness of the voices."

"Don't be melodramatic. And silly as well," he said gently.

"You are a very sensitive young woman. It's not remarkable you should occasionally hear things that others do not. Perhaps you hear them with an inner ear we others lack."

I hadn't told him everything, not whose favourite tune it had once been, nor the exact associations it had for me, but I had the impression that he understood perfectly well what it was all about. I was skating on the surface of things, but somehow he saw what was underneath.

"How rational and simple and easy to bear you make it all seem," I said.

"Most situations are when you seize them by the right handle."

"I don't think I invent things," I said thoughtfully. "I am rather a matter-of-fact person. Our old Tibby always says I have no imagination at all."

"From what I have heard, it seems to me as though your old Tibby underrates you. She sounds very overweening."

I opened my eyes wide. We never criticized Tibby, she was our bed-rock on which we rested. "I love her," I said. "And she loves me. She sees me clearly, I dare say."

"Of course you love her. It's the fault of our educational system, Russian as well as English, that we put sensitive, intelligent children into the hands of peasants in their youngest and most formative years."

"You couldn't call Tibby a peasant. Her father was a sea-captain. Only his ship went down with all hands."

"She has allied herself with them, then. Seen through your eyes she seems a conservative, pigheaded old woman."

"And are all peasants like that?" I asked, thinking I heard a sort of anger in his voice.

"Yes, God help them, they are: conservative, archaic in their ways and customs, obstinate and obstructive. How could they be anything else? One never knows whether to flog them or love them."

"I think you know," I said gravely.

He laughed, started the car and began to drive on. "Forget the outburst. The shaming truth is I believe I am jealous of the love in your voice when you speak of that old woman. I never hear it when you speak of anyone else."

He drove very fast then for a mile or two; I saw the speedometer needle tick towards fifty, then sixty miles. I was half-exhilarated, half-frightened, but there was no expression on his profile at all. Certainly not love.

As we came into the outskirts of the village, Peter slowed the car. In sight of the house, he said, "If Dolly suggests any plan to you, I want you to know that it has my blessing. Fall in with it if you can."

"What sort of plan?" I was puzzled. "A plan for me?"

"She has an idea of how you might make use of your gift."

I considered what he had said. Of course I understood what gift he meant, and I did not try to pretend to ignorance. "Tibby did once suggest I might become a nurse," I said hesitantly.

"That is precisely what I mean about Tibby's attitude of mind," he muttered under his breath, and gave the driving-wheel a sharp bang with his hand.

If Dolly had any plans for me she did not mention them within the next few days, although once or twice I thought I caught her eyeing me in an assessing manner, and it was Ariadne who next made an urgent demand on my attention.

"I want you to come with me to Vyksa," she said when we met early one morning, a few days after my first driving lesson.

"Vyksa?" For the moment I was lost. Where and what was Vyksa?

"Where my friend lives. I want you to come with me. Remember you said I was to ask. Well, I'm asking. I daren't take the horses because they tell tales in the stables. And I am frightened to cycle all that way on my own. One feels safe on a horse. So I want you to come."

"You mean we aren't to tell your mother?"

"Of course not." Ariadne sounded surprised at my question. "She would refuse. She detests Marisia. Not without reason perhaps, as Marisia has been very cheeky to her. Dislike is usually mutual, isn't it? A pity love isn't, too, but it isn't, I've noticed."

"And I've noticed that you always talk too much when you are uneasy." Two could play at Ariadne's game of sharp perception. She looked very pretty, though, when she was so eager.

"Well, I do want to go, and I'm afraid you'll say no."

Trying to hide my dismay, I said, "You must see that I couldn't go behind your mother's back and disobey her."

"Nothing *direct* was said," murmured Ariadne sulkily.

"Sophistry," I said, aware that I sounded more or less like Tibby, stern daughter of the voice of God.

Ariadne muttered something in Russian under her breath, no doubt uncomplimentary to me. She followed it up with, "Mademoiselle Laure came with me sometimes."

"How very unlike her," I said. "I would have said such behaviour was not in her character."

"People always act out of character in Shereshevo," came the reply, delivered with calm convictions. "I told you that. Or they behave unusually, if you prefer to put it that way. It's something in the atmosphere of the countryside which loosens their strings."

"Ah, but you aren't telling me all the truth, are you? Unveil it a little. So Mademoiselle went with you to Vyksa? Well, why did she? She must have had her reasons."

Ariadne smiled and gave a minute shake of her head. I believed she thought she had got the better of me. "So she had *then*. The man she hoped to marry was a dancing-master there once. Although heaven knows what they have to dance about in Vyksa."

"I see." Yes, I could see Laure making a sentimental journey of it.

Ariadne reinforced this by saying, "She always wore black when we went there. Nothing ostentatious, she was clever about it, but I knew." She added naughtily: "I do wonder what sort of man he was to want to marry poor Laure. But it may have been losing him that made her what she was. Yes, now, I surprised you by saying that, didn't I? I only did so because I could see the very words trembling on your own lips. You have no idea how clearly your thoughts are mirrored in your face. So I thought I'd get there first," and she went off into peals of laughter. "So what will you do? Shall we go?"

"Yes," I said.

"Oh, good." Undoubtedly I had surprised her now.

"But I will ask your mother first. I'm sure she will give permission if we put it the right way." And when Ariadne looked incredulous, I said, "I'll seek my opportunity."

Dolly frowned when I asked her. "It's not a friendship I care for. Nor one I wish to encourage. It has brought Ariadne nothing but harm."

"And for that reason you should let them meet openly," I said firmly, "and give Ariadne no reason for secrecy."

"I see you know my daughter," said Dolly. "No, I am not going to ask any questions that will strain your loyalty."

We were sitting together after dinner. I had settled on this cool, pleasant evening hour as the best time to talk to Dolly. We were more or less alone in the dusk, as the others were grouped round the piano where Ariadne was picking out a few notes. Edward Lacey, amazing man, had produced a banjo ("All the rage in town, my dear girl") and was plucking it in rag-time.

"If they meet under supervision Ariadne will be safe and satisfied," I said.

"Very well. If you will do it?"

"Oh, yes." How easily and confidently I rushed upon my fate. Looking back, I marvel at myself.

But Vyksa, and all it was to mean, was always lying there in wait for me, and one way and another I would have got there.

I believe that there is a larger I than this present and local one whose penumbra stretches tendrils far out into the future. Even when I had been back home in Scotland, happily affianced to Patrick, a part of me had stretched out and reached Vyksa.

Dolly sighed. "Perhaps you should see Vyksa. For you have seen something of the best of Russia, now you should see what we have to hide."

Before I could ask the question forming on my lips, her old wet-nurse, Sasha, appeared and announced peremptorily that she had the corset covers ready to embroider and she would be glad if Her Excellency would come and inspect the crest and initials traced upon them.

"Oh, Sasha," demurred Dolly softly. But her nurse bustled between us, forcing me to take a step backwards, and putting a hand on Dolly's arm. "Sasha!" said Dolly, more loudly. "You pushed Miss Gowrie. Watch what you are doing."

Sasha mumbled an apology, but I could see she had enjoyed disconcerting me. She didn't like me, but that I already knew. "It doesn't matter," I said hastily.

Sasha was jealous of me, and I could understand her showing her dislike, just as her counterpart, Princess Irene's maid, had done in St. Petersburg. Sasha was an aggressive, silly old woman, anyway. But what was disconcerting was that I had noticed unfriendliness in the other servants, too, lately. I had felt criticism, even hostility. I'd done something, or I *was* something they didn't like. It wasn't imagination, because I could see the reflection of it in Dolly's embarrassment now. There ought to be a book for visitors to Russia, I thought, called *Rules of Conduct in Town and Country.*

To Ariadne, when we met next, I said briefly, "We can go."

"Oh, good. I'm glad. I want to see Marisia again soon. We have so little chance. It is only when we are here at Shereshevo that I can manage anything. She would never dare come here."

"You're very fond of her?"

"Yes, I am," she said defensively. "Is that so wrong? She befriended me at school."

"And yet according to you, *she* was the one whose background did not fit in."

"Ah, but she is so clever. Nothing mattered to her, you see. She could manage any of us. She was too clever for them, that's why they got rid of her."

"Things aren't usually as simple as that, Ariadne."

She gave me a startled glance, and I guessed I had struck home. She licked her lips. "Rose?"

"What is it, Ariadne?" I said.

"Nothing. After all, nothing. But of course you are right: it was not simple, my being expelled, and especially not for Marisia. Being at the school meant so much to her."

"And she threw it away?"

Ariadne didn't answer, and I left it there. One day she would explain, if she wanted to.

"There's something you can tell me, though," I said thoughtfully. "Is Vyksa such a dreadful town?"

"Oh, the town is pleasant enough. A perfectly ordinary provincial town."

"Then why is it considered so terrible?"

"It's the copper mine," said Ariadne, "That's what makes it so terrible."

"But many countries have mines. We have in Scotland."

"Not like this," said Ariadne with a shiver. "You wait till you see it. Or as much as one is allowed to see."

"Allowed?"

"Yes. You see, all the people who work there are prisoners."

I stared at her, perhaps not quite taking in what she said.

"Yes, prisoners," she repeated. "All of them prisoners. Prisoners of the State."

# Chapter Five

Without a word being said between us, Ariadne and I knew that we would set off early on the next morning. The matter was settled by a look between us. She was wonderfully sharp, Ariadne, when there was something she wanted to know.

"You'll order the horses?" I said.

"Of course. There'll be no trouble now we have permission."

"Or we might take the pony and governess-cart we used before. The pony seemed a canny beast."

For a while in the afternoon, however, it looked as if our next day's visit would have to be put off. Dolly interrupted Ariadne and me at work in the garden.

"Madame Titov wants us all to spend the day with her and her father tomorrow."

Ariadne pulled a face.

"I am aware you don't like her," said Dolly, "but she is one of my oldest friends."

"Whom you never see."

"We meet when our respective social duties allow," said

194

Dolly, with dignity. "Naturally that's not often, considering what her life is, and mine."

While I was thinking what a pity we couldn't go to Vyksa the next day after all and get it over, Ariadne said thoughtfully, "How tiresome that old Sasha won't have finished altering my white poplin dress, as it's just the sort of style for Madame Titov. You know how quietly she dresses."

"You have many other dresses," said Dolly.

"Oh, yes, oh, of course. But that one is so exactly right, if you know what I mean." And I thought that I at least did know, whatever Dolly understood by it. "And then what a shame I haven't quite finished that album of the photographs we took of the holy hermit's shrine at Kazan. I meant to give it to Madame Titov. I was telling her about it and she was so interested."

"The visit to Kazan was three years ago," said Dolly suspiciously.

"I have been slow, but it's almost done. Just a few more days. Bother."

"I suppose it wouldn't matter if we went this day week. She does offer us a choice," observed Dolly.

Ariadne smiled brilliantly. "Oh, thank you."

When I saw how easily she manipulated her mother, I began to wonder exactly how far she did the same to me.

The road to Vyksa was hard, with the sun glaring down on the dusty road all the way.

"This is new Vyksa," explained Ariadne as we drove. "The town really grew up around the mines. There is another Vyksa further north, and some times people confuse the two."

"The road is bad," I said, as we jolted down into a large pot-hole and then up the other side.

"You should see it after the winter snows have melted. Mud, pure mud. Nothing and nobody can move. Even the peasants stay where they are."

As we travelled I became aware that bleak and uncouth as I had thought the village at Shereshevo, it was, compared with some of the places we were passing through, a model village. The peasant houses in Shereshevo were neatly kept and had their little bits of garden about them, but now I saw villages where the houses were no more than huts, and dreadfully dilapidated huts at that, with grass growing on the roofs. Usually there was nothing that could be called a main street, and the pony (who seemed to know her path instinctively) had to pick her way through a huddle of houses. This brought us close to the villagers, many of whom were sitting at their doors, or leaning against the house or wall or, in some cases, standing in silent groups watching us, the only incident of interest in their lives, probably, for weeks. I noticed a difference here, too, between these peasants and those at Shereshevo. Here they looked at us with sullen dislike; I could feel the hostility. At Shereshevo there was a relationship between the Denisovs and their peasant-tenants. Perhaps I had thought it too servile and dependent on one hand, and too demanding on the other, but the bond existed and was strong. These people looked as if they cared for nobody and nobody cared for them.

I studied Ariadne's face to see what I could read of her expression, but she was driving the pony, staring straight ahead, and looking neither to right nor left. She knows, I thought, she is as aware of the waves of hostility surrounding us as I am.

Still keeping her gaze on the road (if such it could be called), she said, "I was quite nervous on this stretch when I came alone, so that I wished I had brought one of the grooms. I rode so fast the horse got all lathered, that was what exhausted him so much and caused all the fuss in the stables when I got back." She gave a quick look about her. "Not nice, is it?"

"No," I said with conviction. Out of the corner of my eye I saw a young boy gather up a stone from the road and nurse it in his hand. He looked at the boy next to him and then back at us. "Get a move on, Ariadne," I said sharply.

Surprised, she turned her head to look at me. "What?"

At that moment the stone sailed through the air and hit me sharply on the cheek. I gasped with pain.

Without a word, Ariadne whipped the pony to a gallop.

I put my hand up to my face to feel a trickle of blood. Another stone hit the side of the governess-cart with a heavy thud. I heard a shout from behind.

But Ariadne kept her head and we drove steadily on. "It's all right. We're through the village now. They won't follow us." I thought she sounded more angry than frightened.

When we were well outside the village and alone on a country road with fields on one side and that great river on the other, she reined in the pony and we stopped, "Now you see how stupid they are," she said, "and what impossible people they are to help, so ignorant and conservative that they would sooner throw a stone at a strange face than think a rational thought."

"I think they threw the stone because we are so obviously what we are and they are what they are," I observed.

"Oh, that, too, I know, and no one grudges them their anger, at least I do not, but it is no answer to throw a stone."

"But a great relief."

"And it hit you! That is what I mean: because they are stupid and dogmatic they would as soon throw a stone at a friend as an enemy." She gave the pony an angry flick with the whip, at which its ears went back. "But how is your face?"

"The bleeding has stopped. I suppose I shall have a bruise." I put my hand up to my cheek. No doubt about the soreness. Russia had drawn its first of my blood.

"Yes, I can see the beginning of it already. When we get to Vyksa we must bathe it. Marisia will know what to do, she's so practical."

"How much further is it?" I had found the journey interesting so far, although the countryside, flat with belts of heavy forest alternating with areas of cultivated fields around each village, was full of repetition. But now I was hot, thirsty and uncomfortable.

"About another twenty minutes' driving." Ariadne added:

"I wish we could have the use of the motor car. Then one could be there in no time. Is it hard to learn?"

"There are a good many things to remember all at once. I think I might master it eventually," I said thoughtfully. "Ariadne, why do the servants seem to dislike me now? Is it to do with driving the motor car?"

"Yes, they think it shameless and unwomanly of you to go off with Uncle Peter in his car to learn to drive it. How clever of you to know."

"I sensed it," I said. "It wasn't difficult."

She shrugged. "Well, that's what they are like, you see. But take no notice."

"But your mother drives," I pointed out.

"Ah, but she's married. Or has been, and that frees her. Marriage makes all the difference here."

"Does it indeed?"

"Doesn't it everywhere? Here some girls make a 'white marriage,' just as a formality, not consummated, you know, simply to be free."

"Good heavens," I said.

"Oh, yes, many of the cleverest and more advanced girls do it. Of course, it causes a great upset, their families don't like it. Still, there's nothing they can do. We young people very often have the upper hand."

"But you wouldn't do a thing like that?" I questioned. "I mean, make a 'white marriage.'"

"No, I'm not clever enough," said Ariadne, whatever that might mean. Except that it was true, of course, there was passion in Ariadne, that would always push through, but an intellectual she was not.

I looked at Ariadne with respect. As I had begun to notice, when she made an observation about herself it was perfectly accurate. I felt that if I could only understand Ariadne, I might begin to comprehend Russia, and that if I watched her the layers of mystery about Russia might peel off one by one.

Presently Ariadne pointed with her whip. "Look, there's Vyksa."

A long wooden bridge crossed the river at this point and beyond it I could see the low-roofed buildings of a small town, where only the bell-tower of the church stood out.

"The mine is on the further side. We shall drive through the town. What there is of it."

We rumbled over the wooden bridge and over the cobbled streets. The centre of the town was a small square lined with flat-faced, two-story buildings. Square, bevelled cobblestones (setts, we called them in Scotland) covered the street surface; they were not very well kept up, and bare, dusty patches appeared at intervals. At present they were dry, in winter they would be full of mud. There were no pavements, pedestrians took their chance. A few carts loaded with sacks trundled through the square. A dray carrying casks of what smelt like beer passed us going in the opposite direction. I saw no private vehicle.

In the middle of the square a small market in vegetables and fruit was being conducted. Great sacks of cabbages, purple and green, were heaped together, with marrows and melons. I saw a wooden bin of peppers and strings of onions. The street market seemed to be conducted by men. To my surprise, I saw no women. Perhaps it was not the custom for women to go to market in Vyksa.

Several of the houses had wooden balconies built onto their fronts, and on them plants in pots were growing. But this was the only sign that the owners of the houses cared much for decoration. Everywhere the paintwork seemed in need of renewal and there was a sad and seedy air about the place, as if no one took much pleasure in it. Across the square from the market and facing the church was a hostelry or inn (it couldn't be called a hotel) with a great painted board spread across its front, on which its offer of hospitality and the price for it were written in gold capitals. It was the only hint of gold in the place.

"Dreary place, isn't it?" said Ariadne. "But what can you expect?"

I didn't answer, because I was watching a strange contraption which had come rumbling into the square from the opposite direction. Two horses draped in what looked like crocheted or knitted coats of thick white cotton pulled a towering structure of silver and black, which ran on two slender, high wheels. Above was raised a curving, curling, highly ornamental rococo shrine. An empty shrine at the moment.

Ariadne saw it, too. "Dear me. A hearse. To see one is supposed to be unlucky. I hope you aren't superstitious?"

"Not at all," I said. "Are you?"

She thought for a moment. "I believe I am, but I must try to grow out of it. I might manage to. When I was little, I believed in Baba Yaga, the old witch of the fairy-tales, and I don't believe in *her* any more."

The town dwindled into a few scattered houses, and then we were back on a country road.

"How bleak!" I exclaimed. The fields seemed uncultivated, full of dust and emptiness. But they were fenced in and the gates had been wired up as if they were not meant to be open.

Ariadne pointed with her whip. "The mine lies straight ahead."

A wooden stockade stretched great arms on either side of the road, which disappeared under a high arch. As we got closer, I could see that strong doors were drawn back under the arch. I looked questioningly at Ariadne.

"Oh, yes, those doors are locked at night. And these are only the outskirts; there are other precautions inside. Not that anyone could escape, of course. Where could they go? Everyone would know them."

"What do you mean?"

"You'll see," was all she said.

Beside the gate was a small house from which emerged a man in uniform with a large bunch of keys hanging from his belt. He bowed to Ariadne, whom he obviously knew. "There you are then, miss. You're expected. In fact, they're waiting for you."

"Oh, good."

"No, nothing's good here, and why say it is?" He came forward and took the pony's bridle. "I'll look after the pony. You know I can't let you take it any further?" He made a noise that passed for a laugh. "You might smuggle a prisoner out. It can be brought round for you when you leave. I'll do that myself. There now, out with you."

"The goods waggons go through," grumbled Ariadne. "I hate walking here. One gets so dusty." Still, she was preparing to hand over the reins.

"But you ain't goods." He took the reins as she scrambled out. I got out the other side.

"You search the waggons. You can *see* that I could not smuggle a cat out in the governess-cart."

"Goods waggons may go through, that's business. Private vehicles may not, that's regulations. I should have the Tsar down on me if I let you through."

Clearly they were old enemies.

"I'll just take the pony round the back for you," and he moved off round the side of his hut, giving a shout to an unseen underling within to keep the gate for him and the Tsar. He seemed to have great regard for the Tsar.

We followed him, and watched while he dealt with the pony. I should think he must have been a groom at some stage in his career. At all events he arranged for the pony's comfort skilfully and easily.

There was a series of stables and out-buildings arranged round a narrow yard. At one end a man was standing by a small cart from which the horse had been released, so that the shafts rested on the ground. I wondered why the man was still standing there; it seemed a strange thing to do.

Ariadne and the gate-man were arguing about the pony; I took a few paces nearer the man. I saw that the reason he remained standing where he did was that he was attached to the cart by a chain. A length of chain was also stretched between his ankles, and another around his wrists. The skin of his hands and face shone with a strange metallic stain of bronze lit with green.

I understood why Ariadne said that no prisoner could hope to escape: the stain and the shackles would immediately identify him.

He was keeping up a constant muttering conversation with himself, which he was glad to extend to me when he saw me.

"God bless the Tsar," he called out in a cheerful, manic voice.

On his bare upper arm I saw he had been branded. The burn was new and inflamed, and I thought he looked mad with a fever resulting from the wound. His cheeks were flushed and his eyes were over-bright.

"Now that's enough, you," said the gate-man, coming up behind me. "Hold your tongue before the young lady. She doesn't want to hear from you."

"Oh, but I don't mind," I said quickly; I was wrung with pity for the man.

"Who is he?" asked Ariadne.

"He's nobody. Not even a political prisoner. Killed a man, he did once, and found himself here. He tried to escape, but he was caught."

"That's right," said the prisoner cheerfully. "I ran away, but I didn't get far."

"Hence the brand," I said.

The gate-man had pushed his way in front of me now and stood between me and the prisoner, half-protective and half-hostile. For the life of me I could not be sure which of us was the object of the protection and which the hostility; he seemed to me to be making a pretty fair division of a little of each to both of us. I suppose he had lived so long among the prisoners that he shared in their suffering, as well as imposing it on them. "It's always done in such cases, the branding, I mean. A matter of routine."

The man held out his arm and looked. "Marked for the Tsar," he said happily. "God bless him."

The gate-man shook his head till the keys at his waist jingled. "I would have told you how it would be if you'd asked. I've seen others try. Do you think you were the first? Now look at you. What have you got to say for yourself, and what good did it do you? What's your state? Bad before, and infinitely worse now."

"I'm to have a hundred lashes," announced the prisoner. "One hundred. And at the end I shall call out, 'God bless the Tsar. Long life to the Little Father.'"

The gate-man shook his head, and pointed his finger in the direction we should walk. "Off with you, young ladies, you're waited for, and I don't need your company."

"Come on," said Ariadne, taking my arm. "We'd better go, and there's nothing we can do for the poor fellow."

"Call a blessing on the Tsar after a hundred lashes, will he?" said the gate-man in a low voice. "He'll be dead after six, you'll see."

Ariadne gave me a swift look and put her hand into mine. "Never mind," I said, hardly knowing what I was saying. "Never mind. It's not your fault."

"But it isn't myself I'm thinking of," she said, "but of you. You want to help him. I can see it."

"Yes, I do want to help, to take away his pain. But I can't do anything. Nothing happens." I was rigid with the effort I was making to efface the pain he was suffering now and to forge a channel between us through which I could drain the agony to me. Let him die painlessly if he must die, I was saying to myself, but it was no good. I had no power; it was gone. What had previously flowed spontaneously and freely had dried up; I realized now that unconsciously all this time I had been thinking of it as a spring within me which I could tap. "I can't help him."

It came as a shock. Yes, I had hated sometimes what had happened, and had even been frightened, but I knew now that I had valued it, and wanted to believe that it was mine to use when I chose. Now I saw that, just as the power could sometimes be summoned up when I did not choose (as with the peasant child), so when I wanted to help, help would not come.

"I can't help him," I repeated to Ariadne.

We were interrupted by a cool, light voice. "Oh, there you are, Ariadne. I have been waiting for a long time. Come here." The speaker, a tall, slender girl, managed to get reproof, command and affection all nicely mingled in her voice.

"Marisia!" and Ariadne ran forward to hug the girl. She threw her arms round her enthusiastically, and kissed her cheek. Marisia arched her long neck, turning her cheek away and laughing.

"It's good to see you, dearest girl, but don't break my neck."

So this was the famous Marisia, the heroine of Ariadne's expulsion from the Smolny Institute. She looked a few years older than Ariadne, and had a thin, clever face, from which her dark hair was drawn tightly and smoothly back.

"Now you are here you'd better come along to the house. I suppose you've got to hurry back? Yes, you always have. But I've got a luncheon laid out and we can talk over that." She held out her hand to me as she spoke.

Timidly (for her) Ariadne introduced us.

"But of course I knew who you were," and Marisia gave my hand a brisk shake, almost masculine in style. Turning back to Ariadne, she demanded, "Why were you so long?"

Ariadne hesitated. "Oh, we were slow in making our way here." I thought for a moment that she was going to tell her friend about the stone-throwing episode, but she didn't. Not then. "And then we were delayed by him." Her eyes went to the prisoner by the cart, a silent figure now.

Marisia took pince-nez from the pocket of her dress and fitted them on her nose. I realized she was very short-sighted. "Oh, him. I advise you not to worry yourself about those you cannot help. Concern yourself with those you can." It was calmly and coldly said, with both conviction and astringent good sense. I admitted to myself that I could understand why she might have irritated her preceptors at the Smolny. "And how did you come to injure your face, Miss Gowrie? Did Ariadne drive you into a ditch? She has done that before now to me."

I put my hand up to my cheek. "No, it was another sort of accident."

She studied the wound through her pince-nez. "It looks sore. Come inside and let me bathe it. I believe in homoeopathy, and follow its precepts. Do you, Miss Gowrie?"

"I don't know much about it," I said humbly, as it seemed to be a subject I ought to know about. "Indeed, nothing."

"Like to like, that is the root of its theory. If you are vomiting, then a drug that would cause vomiting in a healthy person will effect a cure. Or one that will give you a headache will relieve a headache. What do you think of that?"

"I think it sounds dangerous," I said, reluctant to submit my own wound to her treatment.

"In minute doses the drugs are safe enough. But in your case I shall only use soap and water. For your injury, I judge, it is enough," and she removed her pince-nez with a snap and replaced them in her pocket. "How did you say you came to do it?"

"A boy in a village threw a stone," said Ariadne.

"Fool," said Marisia. "Fool."

"That's what I said," answered Ariadne at once. "Didn't I, Rose?"

"Well, come along both of you, then," and Marisia offered us an arm each, and in this way, one on either side of her, the trio made our way to her father's house. It was a very strange way of progressing, but I am sure it was typical of her, and that she always did everything in a style of her own. I had not been in the company of Ariadne and Marisia for more than a few minutes, and witnessed the manner of their meeting, before becoming convinced of one thing: Ariadne and her mother had completely different ideas about a scheme for life. What a long way I had come since the days when I had regarded Ariadne as a light-hearted child.

We stopped before a square wooden house where Marisia's father, who was manager of the mine, had both his home and his office. Facing directly opposite was a long, low hut, through the open door of which I could see a clerk in shirt-sleeves sitting at a desk writing. At right angles to both these buildings was a high wooden fence with a great door in it, and I took this to be the entrance to the mine workings themselves. Everything about us seemed to be made of wood, everything was dusty and dark, nothing pleasant to look at anywhere. A group of prisoners passed in the distance, all of them shackled and all stained with that characteristic dusky stain.

At the door Marisia unlinked her arms, producing a large key from her pocket.

"Welcome to the Lazarev home," she said.

Inside, the house was better than I had expected. True, the rooms were box-like in shape, with ugly windows, but bright colours and well-polished furniture, together with a general feeling of order, made it comfortable if not beautiful. The meal that was served to us, although very simple, was tasty and nicely served.

It was a household of women. They were a family of five girls, the mother being dead, and Mr. Lazarev, a small, mild man, being relegated by Marisia (who managed the house) to his study and his office.

The four younger girls sat in a row at luncheon and were fed by Marisia like birds.

"Soup for you, Alicia. Now, here is your soup, Olga. Soup, Katia, a bowl of onion soup for you, Ksenia."

Each little girl, hard to be sure of their ages, as they seemed so alike, put her head down and supped her soup in silence.

An elderly pug dog called Gubish sat on a chair at the end of the table and surveyed the scene. I quite expected him to be given a bowl, too, but it appeared he had eaten previously. No doubt he did not care for fish soup followed by a sort of pancake filled with meat and then fruit.

A tray of food was carried into Mr. Lazarev's office through the opened door of which one caught sight of him bending over a desk with a green eye-shade on his forehead. Bad eyes must run in the family.

"A glass of tea?" asked Marisia, presiding over the bubbling tea-urn.

"Yes, please." I was learning to like the refreshing and ever-present tea.

"Alicia, take a glass in to your father." Marisia turned to me. "My father leaves everything to me. I manage all." She went on: "It is his way of keeping his two worlds separate, here and"—she nodded towards the window—"out there, over the wall. It's not pleasant, over there, although it's not his fault, you must understand, he is responsible for the commercial management of the mine only. But there is a lot he has to see that he would rather not see."

"So I can imagine."

"He wants to keep us quite apart from it, untouched. But it can't be done, of course. We breathe the same air, walk on the same dirt. That's why he keeps separate in his own rooms, so that he shan't have to admit it."

I nodded, partly understanding.

"And then he plays little games."

"Games?"

"Yes, games with us. Games such as sending me to the Smolny Institute as if I were a noblewoman, and getting governesses and tutors for the other girls. Do you know they all talk English? And dance beautifully. Up here! In this place! Think of it, dancing lessons here."

Ariadne said, with a touch of her old archness, "If you had never gone to the Smolny, we might never have met." She said it much as she might have said it to Edward Lacey. Strange girl.

Presently they disappeared, those two, wandering off without explanation, arm in arm, and leaving me to the four other girls. Their ages were said to range from fifteen to ten years, but they were remarkably alike in appearance, paler, less assured versions of Marisia, and silent.

However, they took me into their schoolroom, and over their books and playthings we managed to pass about forty minutes before Ariadne reappeared.

"Time to go, alas."

Marisia appeared at her side. "Your pony and governess-cart are being brought round to the door." To her sisters, she said, "Girls, Mr. Corvus is waiting for you."

And that was it. The visit, apparently so important to Ariadne, was over. Marisia gave her a friendly little pat on the shoulder. "Good-bye, my dear girl."

"Good-bye, Marisia." The two girls exchanged kisses.

What was it all about, after all? I thought. A nasty, hot drive, a pleasant luncheon, a couple of hours' talk with her friend, was this all? For this Ariadne had been prepared to lie to her mother and defy her rules?

I couldn't see any harm in Marisia, although I had been conscious of a good deal of intellectual force, ferment, I might almost say, and she seemed something of a martinet.

The pony had been groomed free of all the dust picked up on the journey out, and stood fresh and ready in the governess-cart. Even this had been wiped down and dusted. Say what you like, there were some things they did well in Russia. In this case, I had little doubt that our tidied-up appearance was due to our friend, the gate-man.

"You'll be home before dusk," said Marisia, putting on her pince-nez.

Ariadne climbed in and picked up the whip. "I'll come back if I can once again this summer, but it might not be easy. But perhaps we shall meet in St. Petersburg."

"If I can get the money together, I want to attend some classes at the university there."

Ariadne sighed. "If only I could help you. I have so much money; if only I could get my hands on it."

"Oh, I'll get there under my own steam, never fear, and be all the gladder for doing it myself. Freedom, one must have freedom," and she gave the pony a smart pat on the rump to urge it on its way. Ariadne picked up the reins and the wheels crunched on the gravelly dirt.

From an open window of the house I heard the tinkling notes of a bad piano well played. I clearly heard the tune.

"Who's that? Who is that playing the piano?"

"Oh, that's our music-master," answered Marisia. "The girls will just be beginning their lesson. You ought to get on, Ariadne."

"But what's his name?" I cried, as the pony moved away.

"Mr. Corvus: he came to us from Hungary."

"We must hurry," said Ariadne, and she touched the pony with the whip so that it began to trot.

We were just out of the dusty yard, through the arch with a wave to our old acquaintance at the gate, and on the road to Vyksa, when a bird flew up from a ditch straight in front of us, with a harsh flutter of its wings. Ariadne said, "They say a bird flies up when a soul leaves the body."

"Oh." I was remembering the branded prisoner. Perhaps it was his death. "Do you think, perhaps . . ." I began.

"How can we know?" said Ariadne, and flicked the whip on the pony's back.

We were almost out of Vyksa before I spoke again: "Did you hear the tune that was being played on the piano?"

"No." Ariadne sounded surprised.

"I wish you had. I would like to have asked you what you thought it was called."

"I hardly ever know the names of tunes," Ariadne reminded me meekly. "What did you think it was?"

"I thought it was a song of Robert Burns," I said. " 'My love is like a red, red rose.' "

There was a long moment of silence, then Ariadne said, "You keep hearing that, don't you?"

"I heard it on the piano just now. Of that I am quite, quite sure. But I wonder what it means?"

"Why, that you heard the tune, I suppose," said Ariadne blankly.

Ariadne drove us through Vyksa, but just outside the town, I said, "Stop, Ariadne, and change places with me. Here, give me the whip. I'll drive. You look tired."

She yawned. "I believe I am."

For a little we drove in silence. Then I said, "I've just remembered that I heard *you* hum that tune once, Ariadne, rather badly so that it was not easy to recognize. But I'm sure of it now. So, therefore, it was also you whistling it in the house." I didn't accuse her of lying or of evasions. Probably she hadn't been.

Falteringly, she said, "If you say so, I suppose it could have been. Yes, it must have been me. Without realizing it, of course. How strange."

I didn't answer at once, but concentrated on my driving. The first time I had heard Ariadne attempt that tune we had only just arrived at Shereshevo. It looked as though Ariadne had made another and earlier visit to Vyksa that no one knew of. She was capable of it.

Ariadne closed her eyes and leaned back in her seat. "Just let the pony have her head," she said sleepily. "She knows the way."

"I'm sure she does," I said ironically.

The heat of the day was cooling as the sun went down.

"Ariadne," I said, although I guessed she was already asleep and I was talking to myself, "I think I know why I could not help that wretched prisoner. He was demented, mad. I could not reach his mind!"

"What's that?" said Ariadne sleepily.

"Nothing." With the baby, in spite of his infancy, there had been a level on which our minds could meet. Only unreason and reason could find no common ground.

"Is it that tune again?" she murmured. "Don't worry. Perhaps you imagined it all."

I didn't answer, but let her relapse into sleep, so much did I want time and silence in which to think about that tune which was Patrick's tune, and my tune, too.


Because it was my song also, it had a significance to me beyond anything I had said to Peter.

From the beginning the song had clearly meant something to Patrick. The tune and then the kiss, more than one kiss. When next time he hummed the tune under his breath, I suppose I was ready. I remember turning to him as if I had been asked a question and was making my answer. As, of course, I was.

We were walking in the grounds of Standings, the great house near Jordansjoy. Unlike my ancestors, the owners of Standings had held on to their money, indeed it had grown with the years, so that from being simple yeoman farmers, they had been ennobled and had seen their estates grow. The fact that coal had been discovered on a tract of their land at the beginning of the last century had certainly helped the process. Now the family was so rich they lived mostly in London, too grand to see much of us. In the grounds of their house, where we had freedom to walk, was the Chinese pagoda. Patrick and I used it as a meeting place. Innocently enough usually, but not always so, nor always what Tibby imagined.

It would be impossible to say that I did not love Patrick and did not know what I was about. I had had the warning of the first kiss. But then, you see, it was what I wanted. Of course I was innocent, all girls like me are. But I was not ignorant. A country girl I was, after all.

And adventurous, like all my family. I suppose we have all been a sensuous, reckless lot, on whom education and good manners have imposed a certain discipline. Of us all, I would say Grizel had the hardest heart and the coolest mind. I somewhat belie my calm exterior.

Patrick knew it, had always known it, probably it was what had drawn us together. I could be seduced. There was no calculation in our minds, I acquit us both, we were free of any fault except that of being young and in love. Certainly, I don't blame Patrick, and I don't even blame myself, which for a girl of my upbringing is even harder.

But no song should be as powerful as that. Where did Patrick learn to make it so powerful? What other lovers he had had I do not know, but they had existed. Some things one's body tells one without instruction: and I soon knew this about Patrick. As he soon knew the opposite about me.

The air inside the Chinese pagoda was scented and warm. I knew all about the pagoda, all the local girls did. There was not one iota of my behaviour that day that I did not have my eyes wide open to.

There was a long low bench in the pagoda, almost like an altar, and on this we sank without a word, arms, legs and bodies entwined.

"What stupid garments you girls wear," said Patrick, his voice muffled. But it was I who ripped it off. I had to put the buttons back on my bodice next day, and all without Tibby knowing. "What a girl you are," he said then. "There's no holding you back."

Well, there wasn't, and I'd better confess it. But I suppose Patrick couldn't have been stopped either, then.

I remember saying (and I giggled) as I wiped the sweat from Patrick's brow with my petticoat, "You know what, we deserve that Farmer Scrimgeour should come in on us—he keeps his cows in the lower meadow. Supposing he found me in your arms?"

So that was the way it was: the music and all that loving and it led all the way to Vyksa.

Corvus, the crow, his other name is grey-bird. Grey-bird—Graham, the thoughts ran through my mind.

Suddenly I pulled on the reins and turned the pony's head round.

"What are you doing?" cried Ariadne, roused from her doze.

"Going back. Back to Vyksa. I must." I lashed the pony mercilessly hard.

"We can't. We shall be back home so late."

"I tell you I must."

We tore through Vyksa, the gateway was still open, and I clattered through, ignoring a shout from the gate-man.

The door to the Lazarev house stood ajar. Throwing the reins to the protesting girl by my side, I ran into the house.

Incredibly, the piano was still being played, this time a halting, limpid melody.

I followed the sound. It led up the stairs and to a room overlooking the yard. The door was open and I saw one of the little Lazarev girls labouring away at her Chopin at the piano. She had her back to me. By her side sat a man.

He stood up when he saw me and bowed, stiffly and rather shyly. I saw a bespectacled middle-aged man. No one I had ever seen before in my life.

"Monsieur Corvus?" I asked. "I'm so sorry I interrupted you like this. My apologies. And to you, Alicia." For the little girl looked frightened.

"He understands no English," said Marisia, coming up behind me. "Not a word."

I stood there, bewildered and discomfited, utterly at a loss. "I thought perhaps he was someone I knew."

The man smiled and bowed again.

"He doesn't know you."

"No. I see that clearly."

Ariadne said crossly, "We must get home. Rose, are you mad?"

"I'll send a servant to drive you back," said Marisia. "For neither of you looks up to it. You can send the man back tomorrow, Ariadne."

Ariadne nodded. I saw she had been badly frightened.

"I'm sorry," I said. "Yes. Let's go back. Ariadne, you won't say anything of this to your mother?"

"Of course not. But she'll never notice anything. You need not worry. She's so interested in her own life, you see," said Ariadne sleepily.

"I thought that nothing happened in the country," I said sceptically. "That it was all peace and quiet."

"Oh, there's always a great deal going on at Shereshevo underneath the surface," said Ariadne, before she dropped off to sleep.


We were met at the stable-yard by Peter Alexandrov, who had obviously been waiting for us.

"Go on up to your rooms and dress for dinner: I will cover up for you. No, I'm not asking what you have been up to or why you are so late."

"We thought Madame Denisov would not notice," I said.

"From your experience of her you might think so. But people always notice what's not wanted."

"You're very kind and protective of me and Ariadne," I said, shepherding my sleepy charge up the garden staircase.

"I am protective of *you*, Rose Gowrie. Now, hurry up, and I will keep Dolly playing chequers and gossiping. I have some very good Piter gossip that will be news to her."

"Clever of you."

"Oh, I keep some on hand for such emergencies," he said lightly.

And aren't above making it up if necessary, I thought.

Peter called after me: "There are some letters for you in your room. I myself told the servant to put them there." He smiled at me. "Letters should be enjoyed in private, should they not?"

Gratefully reaching the peace of my bedroom, I found my little maid standing beside a ewer of hot water with fresh towels over her arms. I dismissed her and picked up my letters.

The first one, as I saw at once, was from my ancient correspondent in Piter. It was brief but rhapsodic, so much so that I wondered in passing if dementia had set in.

"I am so well, so well. Today I went out for the first time in nineteen years. And my luck at cards! *Incroyable.* Will the power to love return also? *Merci, merci.* Continue to think of me."

My second letter was from Tibby and was much welcomed as offering more news of Grizel and Archie. Grizel had met him at the Bowes-Lyons' dance to which Harry Ettrick had taken her. "He is a barrister in Chambers in Gray's Inn, and with parliamentary aspirations, so they will live in London, which will suit Grizel. There is a baronetcy in the family and ten thousand a year, but unluckily there is an elder brother. He is in the Army, but so safe is the modern Army that (barring a general conflagration, which heaven forbid) there is no hope there!" She ended with the comment that "He is not a bit good looking, but is very clever and can manage Grizel if anyone can."

I put the letter away, glad to have it, but feeling remote from Grizel and her love affairs. I think you could say I was winded by the episode at Vyksa and needed time to get my breath back. I did not quite get it.

A little preliminary unveiling of the plans that Peter had told me of came from Dolly the next day.

"On Thursday next we go to visit Madame Titov at her own estate. Such a beautiful place. Very quiet, of course." She means dull, I thought, knowing enough of Dolly by now. "We shall stay overnight, so get the maid to pack what is necessary. A *small* toilette, nothing grand, she rarely entertains, and I suppose we shall be her only guests." I did wonder why the brilliant, worldly Dolly Denisov and her wayward daughter and the daughter's Scottish governess were to be welcomed by this recluse. Then Dolly went on: "And you won't mind if Madame Titov asks you a few questions of a personal nature."

My eyebrows went up. "I won't mind," I said coolly, "but perhaps I may not answer them."

She looked doubtful at this. "Everyone always answers Madame Titov."

"I shall be a surprise to her, then."

Dolly smoked a cigarette and then looked across to her brother. We were in the great bare room they called the "summer" ball-room. There was no evidence that anyone had ever danced in it, but there were many potted plants around, and it was cool and fragrant. It was evening.

"Peter, what shall we do with her?"

"Leave her alone," he said shortly. "If she doesn't want to answer the old girl's questions, why should she?"

"Ah, but consider Madame Titov's position. She *must* ask questions."

"Or at any rate, she always does," observed Peter.

"In the nicest possible kind of way. She feels it her duty." Dolly looked round the airy room lit, at this moment, by just one lamp. "You know we might give a dance here this summer."

"We might. But we never do."

"Next year, perhaps. Yes, next year would be a very good time."

"I should like it this year," observed Ariadne.

"You're so impatient. It's your age."

Ariadne shrugged. "Next year might never come. Who knows what will happen?"

"Oh, next year always comes," said her mother. "When you are my age, you will know all about that."

"You'd like a dance this year, wouldn't you, Edward?" asked Ariadne of her silent suitor, who was sitting smoking a pipe and removing green-fly from the pelargonium by which he sat. "And goodness knows, you're old enough." She burst into laughter.

"Peter, take them both into the garden, Edward with that awful pipe and your niece with that stupid laugh, and bring them back when they are nicer to be with," ordered Dolly crossly.

When we were alone she said, "I think I must explain things a little to you."

I waited.

"You see," she said, almost shyly, "we are going to see the Tsar."

To be in Russia, and to see the Tsar! My eyes flew open wide at that: I felt like the heroine of an opera or a romantic poem. I was going to see the Tsar.

Characteristically of Dolly, she began with a bang and proceeded to a diminuendo. "That is, we shall very likely see the Tsar, and be seen by him. But it is the Tsarina we are to visit.

Not to stay in the house at Spala, of course. But Madame Titov lives in a lodge attached to Spala when *they* are there, and we shall stay with her. While we are there, we shall be in the Tsarina's company."

Just her company, I thought; that does not sound very lively.

"So now you see why Madame Titov might ask you some questions; she really has to vet all the people who, through her, might speak to the Tsarina. Of course, she may never say a word to you, but if she does, you must answer."

"I shan't know what to say."

"So you say now, but if the time comes, I think you will manage. I have noticed that you have quite a cool way with you."

I supposed this visit to the Romanovs, preceded by "some questions" from Madame Titov, must be the plan that Peter had spoken of in connection with Dolly, and with which he wanted me to fall in. Well, it would be interesting to see the Tsarina, and be spoken to by her, and to see the Tsar and be seen by him. "Very well. I'll try to answer any questions Madame Titov may wish to put," I said.

"Bravo," said Dolly. "I knew you would. You are a reasonable little creature."

Oh, no, Dolly, I thought. You don't know what a feast of unreason I am growing inside me.

"Well, you can call them to come in, now that I've said what I want. I was glad of an excuse to say what I wanted. It was better to talk on our own."

Always wheels within wheels in Russia, I thought. An observation I might have done well to have made more of. But obediently I got up and went to summon the others inside.

I found them sitting in the dusk under a tree, not talking to each other, but apparently waiting for me to summon them; they knew as well as Dolly did that they had been banished. But only I knew really why. It was to give Dolly and me a secret, not to keep Ariadne and Peter from knowing about the visit to the Tsar, which I am sure they knew already. Dolly was binding me to her with gossamer strands, like a pleasant little spider. For some reason she wanted me close to her. It was to do with that gift of mine in which she took an increasingly obsessive interest. I knew it must be so, because it was the only thing that marked me out from other girls. "Are you ready to come in?"

"Oh, we're coming," said Ariadne, jumping up. "I'm being bitten by a particularly nasty sort of little fly, I shall be all blotches tomorrow. We know we were only sent out so that you and Mother could talk."

"We didn't say much."

"No, you weren't long. Oh, she loves her little mysteries. She's like Tante Irene. Don't you think she's like Tante Irene?"

"Why are you talking about her?" called Dolly from inside. "I can hear every word you are saying out there." She appeared at the door. "I hear extraordinary things about Aunt Irene. People keep writing to me and say they have seen her about the town. Actually seen her walking and talking. Princess Kudashev says she's even got a lover. Well, it'll kill her, that's all."

We passed up the stairs and went back into the sitting-room.

"I shouldn't believe a word of it," said Peter, sitting down in a chair and picking up a book. "Least of all the Kudashev."

"I believe the stories that she's about the town," said Dolly in a definite manner, "but not those of a lover. But where will it all end?"

"In a bed," said Peter, "like most of her activities."

"Peter!"

"I meant it most respectably," he assured her with a straight face. "I meant she will die in her bed. Come along now, Dolly, don't pull such a long face. Her bed has been her place of residence for a long time past."

Usually, out of politeness to me when I was present, Dolly spoke English, but now she lapsed into Russian, which, however, I understood easily, although I still spoke it clumsily.

"How I wish she would die. Isn't it sinful of me? But I wish she was dead. I feel her influence on me all the time. I'm frightened of her."

"Everyone is."

"Not you, Peter."

He shrugged. "You shouldn't let her worry you so much. Why do you?"

Dolly said, "She brought my mother up, she brought me up and she tried her hand with Ariadne. Three generations of us. How can I not be influenced?"

"Poor Dolly."

"I ought rather to ask how you are free."

"Ah, you have the Corps des Pages to thank for that. Five years in that establishment is enough to free any man from the influence of women."

"Did you hate it so much, Peter?"

"Hated, loathed, despised, resented it," he said. I had never heard him speak in a tone like that before. "Ridiculous discipline, archaic severity, stupidity rampant and raised to the level of a deity. The whole of my life since has been a reaction to it."

"One must have discipline. And service to the Tsar in the Corps is a responsibility of the nobility which one must respect," said Dolly nervously. "Discipline one must have, especially in this country; we are so wild otherwise."

"Wild? Why, we are a population of sheep," said Peter. "Look at the peasants—any other peoples but ours would have risen long ago."

"Gradually things will be bettered," said Dolly. "Patience is needed."

"The *mujiks have* once risen," said Edward Lacey. So he was listening avidly, too. "Then there was the Land and Freedom movement. Remember what Herzen said in *The Bell.*"

"Oh, that name," said Peter. "So powerful and yet so powerless. People like Herzen have ruined us, I think."

As I listened, I remembered the scene in the village on the

way to Vyksa; I put my hand up to feel my cheek. To myself I thought that though there might not be much open anger, there was a deep, smouldering, sullen resentment. But possibly that was what Peter meant by "sheep." Perhaps that was the only way sheep had of showing anger.

I think they'd forgotten I was there. It was time to remind them. "Who was Herzen?" I asked.

They remembered me then, and expressions changed, slightly but unmistakably, veering towards reserve.

"Alexander Herzen," said Peter. "A famous revolutionary. In thought, anyway. As far as I know he never lit a bomb. Long since exiled."

"Oh, where?" I was interested.

Edward Lacey answered: "England. Then France. He's long dead, and largely discredited by now, but I imagine he has left his disciples. He has a daughter, I know."

"Oh, but they lived in such a messy way," said Dolly distastefully, and in English. "Wives and mistresses all muddled up together."

Edward Lacey laughed.

"No, I agree with Dolly," said Peter. "It is more dignified to have them under separate roofs, but one has to think of the expense, you know. Not everyone can afford it."

This time it was Ariadne who laughed. "I thought Tante Irene once had an affair with her husband's aide-de-camp. *That* must have been under one roof."

"Oh, that woman," said Dolly. "Shall I never be free of her!"

"Perhaps she'll come to Shereshevo now she is so much stronger," suggested Ariadne. Out of malice, I thought.

"What? Never. She hasn't been here for twenty years." Dolly looked at me, and it was obvious what she was thinking. "No, she would never come without due warning."

"But there *was* a letter for you from her," said Ariadne, "and you wouldn't bother to read it."

Dolly gave a shriek and ran out of the room. Presently she was back, the letter pressed in her hand. "No, it's all right.

She just talks about how astonishingly well she is. No pains, great feeling of vitality, she goes on a lot about that, calls it a miracle. As indeed it is, a black miracle." And Dolly stared at me with a glare so remarkably like old Princess Irene's that I quailed. Why be surprised that they were both fascinated by my gift of healing, when they were so alike?

"Of course, she might always take it into her head to come here. I put nothing past her, the greedy old thing. But it won't matter, no, it won't matter, for the day after tomorrow we go to Madame Titov's."

On the way up the stairs to bed, Dolly took the opportunity to say to me, "Oh, by the way, I shouldn't do too much driving around with my brother. The servants hate machinery anyway, think it is the invention of the devil, and are beginning to look at you. Of course, I know that in one way one takes no notice of them, but in another way—" And she shrugged. "They know how to be bad enemies."

"I don't want to alienate them, although I think already they don't like me, but how can it matter if they are my enemies?" There spoke the free, self-confident, misguided Rose Gowrie.

"Ah, my dear, how can you possibly know what your destiny is?"

Her face seemed very close, her eyes big and dreamy. I realized she was as short-sighted as her daughter. Probably Princess Irene was, too, three generations of them.


A quiet day or two passed. We always seemed occupied but never really busy. There was no hurry about anything. We walked, talked together or idled round the gardens. The most active pair were Edward and Ariadne. He was coaching her in tennis and promising to teach her golf, if only he had brought his clubs with him. I thought that her small, compact figure made her a natural athlete.

I wanted to talk to him about Ariadne. Their relationship puzzled me. The girl seemed sure he was her suitor and that she had only to say yes and the marriage would take place. But I wondered. Certainly sometimes Edward did behave as if he was courting, but in such a merry, light-hearted way that it did not seem to me serious. I had an idea that he was a man who, if fully in love, would not play at it.

I saw his eyes resting on her, and took my opportunity. No one was near us.

"She's beautiful, isn't she? And she seems to become more adult every day."

"Yes. One can no longer dismiss Ariadne as a charming child. But then I never did."

"No one who really knows her could do that," I said very soberly.

"You don't find her easy to manage, though, I suppose? No. Her mother sometimes spoils her and sometimes bullies her. It's a bad mixture."

"I'm sure you could manage her better. If you are in love with her, that is."

"Well, she knows I will marry her if she wishes. My cards are on the table."

Thoughtfully, I said, "Somehow I don't see Ariadne settling anywhere outside Russia."

"It would be the best thing in the world for her," he said forthrightly.

"I believe her mother thinks so, too." I was fitting little bits and pieces of evidence together. It was a marriage of convenience that was being planned.

"But why?"

"To save her."

I opened my eyes wide. "But from what?"

"From herself. From her friends. She mixes in bad company."

"From people like Marisia, I suppose?" He didn't answer me. "I can't see Ariadne marrying for such a reason." Nor you either, I thought, but I suppose Dolly will make it worth your while. But what fears she must have for her daughter.

"Oh, I wouldn't be marrying her for her money, which in

ten years' time will not exist, in my opinion. It's not a subject
I usually talk of, but I am rich. Rich enough not to need a
wealthy wife. No, my family and Dolly's have been friends
for generations. My grandmother was from St. Petersburg. I
cannot bear to see things go wrong."

"You're being very frank."

"To you, I am," he said simply and sat back watching my
face.

"Why?" I asked, curious.

"Perhaps I want to open your eyes a little, too."

"To what?"

"To Russia."

He leaned back in his chair and watched Ariadne moving
lightly across towards us. I heard him say to himself, not to
me at all: "After all, she need not stay married to me. I do not
think she would. But I might want her to."

He turned to me. "Are you satisfied," he drawled, "with
my answers? It *was* an inquisition, was it not?"

"I think you *are* arrogant. You think you can judge best for
Ariadne. For me, too, for that matter. Disloyal, too. Why
don't you trust her Uncle Peter to look after her?"

"Don't shout." His own voice was kept low.

But Ariadne came hurrying up. "Why, you two are quarrelling."

He got up. "Don't be a silly girl."

"There you go again," I said quickly. "In fact, she's quite
right. We are quarrelling."

"Over me, I suppose," she said, looking from face to face.

I stood up, too. "Yes, and over me, too. And over Russia."

The dogs came running up to us, and one, a pretty little
bitch of mixed breeding, pawed anxiously at Edward. I
thought for a moment he was going to push her angrily
away. Then, very gently, he pushed the animal down and
patted the creature's head. After which, he took Ariadne's
hand and tucked her arm under his. "Come on, let's go into
the house," he said. "I can see your mother watching us."

All in all, it was impossible to stay angry with him.

In all of Shakespeare's tragedies there is a character who survives the debacles of others. He is the small, still centre at the heart of the storm. Such a character now seemed Edward Lacey.

But this scene precipitated a quarrel at Shereshevo: the first I ever saw there. I followed Edward and Ariadne into the house; they went into the music room where presently Edward began to play. He had a light, modern, syncopated touch on the piano.

I sat myself down—drawn to listen and to read a book I had picked up from the table. One of Peter's books, it was full of statistics and tables of population and paragraphs about the ownership of property.

Dolly and Peter were standing in the window.

Peter said, in a cold voice I had not heard before, "Edward Lacey is a nice enough fellow. I like his company, but I wish you would not encourage Ariadne to be with him so much. I'm not saying he is after her money, of course, but . . ."

In an equally cold tone, Dolly said, "She has none unless I choose to give her any, and I shan't choose unless she marries as I wish."

"You couldn't withhold her money from her."

"Certainly I could, and I will do so if I think it in her best interests."

"That would be morally wrong."

"Who is to talk about morals, Peter? Not you to me."

"Keep your voice down, they will hear you." He glanced towards the other end of the room where his niece and Edward Lacey had paused in their music.

But Ariadne had heard, and she left the piano and rushed across the room.

"Mother, you couldn't mean to keep my money from me. I mean to have it. I *must* have it. I have a use for it."

Dolly shrugged. "You know how to choose," she said.

"No, no, Mother, you couldn't. You couldn't hold back my own money from me." The girl almost threw herself at her mother in a fury.

"Your father left it all to me to do with as I chose."

"He was ill, dying," screamed Ariadne. "You poisoned him. His mind if not his body."

"During his terrible but short illness his mind was quite clear," said Dolly coldly. "We've had all this before. Don't work yourself up."

Edward drummed away at the piano as if to hide their voices. I went over to him and pretended to select some music. We exchanged a silent look. "I mean to keep out of this if I can," he said in a low voice. "But I doubt if I'll be able. You, too."

"Me?" I spoke in surprise.

Across the room I heard Peter say, "Isn't it better that Ariadne should waste her money, as you call it, than that it should be spent on jewels and lovers?" I saw Dolly flush and look angry. "Like our old Aunt Irene," Peter finished smoothly.

"If you keep my money you are nothing but a thief, a thief, a thief!" screamed Ariadne.

Before I could get between them, which I meant to do, Dolly had slapped her daughter's face.

"It is you who has lovers," shouted Ariadne, "and not Aunt Irene. And I will name their names. And Edward Lacey, too."

"Now, Ariadne, that is too bad," said Edward. "You know that is quite untrue." He banged down the lid of the piano.

Certainly not true in hard fact, I thought. But the sudden flaring of the pupil in Dolly's eye convinced me that the physical desire had been there, on her part, at least.

"Ariadne, hold your tongue," snapped Peter. But the girl was beside herself.

"As for you, my dear uncle, don't you go round the countryside looking for—" Peter slapped his hand over her mouth and held it there, but not before she managed to get out "And I have seen you eyeing Rose—"

I jumped, and felt my cheeks burn.

Peter dropped his hand as if Ariadne had bitten it. She did not speak.

We all five stood in silence.

Dolly recovered first. "Rose, take Ariadne upstairs. I think she must be sickening for some little illness. She will certainly have a migraine tomorrow."

"I feel sick," said Ariadne suddenly.

Upstairs, I held her head while she vomited profusely. She heaved and moaned as she retched.

Then I helped her get to bed, with very little said on either side, although she clutched my hand and kissed it passionately. "Forgive me, forgive."

I drew the blind down. "Go to sleep now," I said, and left her alone.

On the stairs outside I met Edward, as if he had been waiting.

"Better," I said briefly, in answer to his unspoken question. "Asleep by now, I hope."

"Poor little wretch," he said. "You don't know what she suffers."

"As to what all *that* was about," I began.

"She didn't mean it," he broke in.

"Yes, she did. Every word. But whether it was true or not—" and I paused.

"A sprinkling of truth, blown up by fantasy."

"But all three of them were as bad as each other. Such a quarrel. Why?"

"They were quarrelling because their nerves were raw," said Edward.

"On the surface it was about money and love and jealousy. I see that. The facts of family life. A too close and confined family life. But what was it *really* about?"

"Russia," he said simply. "It was about Russia."

"How can they meet each other again?"

Edward Lacey laughed. "You don't know them as I do. Peace and tranquillity will be restored, and the scene will never be mentioned."

I shook my head.

"Haven't you ever quarrelled with your brothers and sister?"

"Of course, but never so bitterly."

"But then you aren't an emotional Russian. Accept scenes like this, Rose, for they will surely happen again."

"And does it mean nothing?"

He paused. "I wouldn't say so. No, you have misunderstood them if you think that. But they won't speak of it again."

He was quite right. Next day, beyond looking white and tired, Ariadne was as normal.

I did attempt to open things up with her, unwisely perhaps, but she stopped me.

"Don't go on, Rose. I don't want to talk about me. I do the best I can about myself and my situation and must leave it at that."

It was a saddeningly adult comment.

"You mustn't think I don't love my mother," she said, "because I do. But sometimes there is a chasm between us which she will do nothing to bridge."

"And she loves you, too."

"Yes." Then Ariadne said, "I'm sorry if your name got dragged in, Rose. My fault. Sorry again."

"Oh, please—" I protested.

She smiled. "The trouble is, Rose, you're mixed up with us now. For better or worse. That's the way to put it, isn't it?"

"It sounds like a marriage," I said.


The next day we did what Ariadne, who obviously had experienced it, called "The Titov drill." What it amounted to was first a thorough survey of all the clothes, parasols and handbags which might be used on the visit, to see if they met some unimaginable standard of propriety. Clothes were ruthlessly weeded out for any hint of frivolity. Too much lace eliminated Ariadne's petticoat, although she protested it would never be seen, and an embroidered butterfly ruled out my own best frock. Dolly's handbag and vanity-case were emptied of all cigarettes, and her parasol all but fumigated in case it should smell of smoke.

"Madame Titov is totally opposed to smoking," Dolly said.

The next stage was the quick study of various little books and pamphlets of a pious and devotional nature, which, it seemed, Madame Titov was in the habit of sending out to friends and enemies alike, and which, naturally, Dolly had never looked at until now. Then there was a solemn discussion of them, conducted by Dolly and inflicted on Ariadne.

That was about all, and more than enough, to my mind.

In all these preparations Dolly's old wet-nurse, Sasha, played a prominent part, bustling here and there, full of self-importance. She particularly harried my little maid, even boxing her ears when she dropped some linen she was carrying.

"Why do you let her bully you?" I said, trying to soothe the crying girl. "Answer her back."

"Oh, I'd never dare, we're all frightened of her. And so should you be, miss," and she rubbed her ear. "No, there's nothing to be done but put up with her."

"What do you mean? What was that you said about me being frightened of her?" I said sharply. She was silent. "Come, now."

"She talks about you, calls you names, says you're a loose woman, not a true woman, driving motor cars."

So here was the source of the other servants' dislike; this old woman was influencing them. "She's jealous," I said. "Jealous and spiteful."

"Oh, yes, we all know that. She hates the interest the mistress takes in you. But it makes no matter, she has the power of words. You should watch her. But don't let her know I told you, or I shall be in trouble. The mistress listens to her." She rubbed her ear again. "No, thank you, miss. I'll take my medicine and get on with it. That way'll be better for us both."

She was a realist, that girl, and knew her world, as I should have understood. I hated to settle for anything less than the utter defeat of old Sasha; all my instincts were aggressive and urged me to fight it out with her, but I did not do it.

The day and night with Madame Titov passed with boring

smoothness. If Ariadne yawned once, she yawned a dozen times, and even Dolly stifled a small gape behind a white-gloved hand. I didn't yawn because I knew beyond any doubt now that I was the principal object under inspection.

About thirty versts away from Shereshevo, and across the river, the Titov mansion was much grander than the Denisov country-house which, when all was said and done, was nothing but a comfortable family home; whereas the Titov house was graced by a noble, columned portico and flanked by two wings, lower in height than the main house, and faced by a colonnade of marble.

"How beautiful," I said.

"It *is* beautiful." Madame Titov smiled; she had a sweet smile. We were pacing side by side along the gravel path that circled the house. She had asked me to walk with her. In the distance I could see Dolly and Ariadne yawning together under a lime tree. "A pity I am so little here. And then, I have no child to inherit. That is the tragedy of my family, we have produced no heirs. One should pray for children when one marries, Miss Gowrie; I did, but none came."

"So what will happen to this lovely house?"

She shrugged. "Who knows? It will be sold, I suppose, and strangers will live in it. Sometimes, you know, I feel as if I shall survive the house. That I will live on, for years and years, and this house will be an empty shell. I've had that vision more than once. Nonsense, of course. People cannot outlive houses."

"I think they can," I said, remembering the ruined great house of Jordansjoy, by the side of which I had lived all my life. "Or they can in my country."

"But not in Russia, where things go on for ever and ever. No, we don't change much here."

"I had noticed for myself."

"You are a sympathetic and perceptive girl," she said approvingly. "Ah, there is Dolly waving to us. We had better stroll across."

Dolly waved gaily, hopefully.

"You don't wear mauve much, I suppose, my dear? No, I'm sure you don't. White is much more suitable for your age. Avoid mauve."

And that was the extent of our conversation.

"A lovely house and poor food. Eliza Titov has a soul above food," was Dolly's verdict, as we rolled home in the carriage next day.

But she looked, and sounded, satisfied with her visit.

"And what about you, my dear?" She leaned towards me as we jogged along. "Did you enjoy yourself?"

"She told me not to wear mauve," I said.

Dolly did not laugh or make any direct answer to this, as I suppose I had expected she would; instead she looked serious and said, "Mmmm. We must have a little talk. I think the time has come."

I had to wait, however, till we got back to Shereshevo, when she got rid of Ariadne by saying, "Off to rest with you, my dear child, there is nothing so tiring as being bored." Then, with a smile, she led me to her boudoir, that haven of delicious, scented ease, not hitherto seen by me. Here she sat down on a chaise-longue and drew me down beside her with a confidential little pat on the quilted satin.

"That remark about mauve, well, it was an acceptance. Of you and of your part."

I looked at her warily. I suppose I had always known I had a part.

"You wouldn't have seen it as that, of course. But *I* knew."

"Oh, did you?"

"Ah, you mustn't be sharp. Of course, no girl likes to be kept in the dark about anything, I do see that, but it had to be. I didn't have permission, you see, to speak. Now I have. Tacitly."

"Tacitly," I said. "That word does stick in my throat. So many secrets, so much done underhand."

"One learns to be secretive in Russian society."

"But I am the object of the secrecy."

"No, that is rating yourself too high. You were not the object of it, but the Tsarevich. Rose, he is a sick child, perhaps a dying one. People suspect, there is talk, but few know. I do know, because Madame Titov told me. She told me because I told her of you." And Dolly gave me a hard, direct look. "You know what I mean?"

"My gift of healing," I said reluctantly. "You knew through the Misses Gowrie, my cousins."

"Yes, from them, and one other person, but leave that for now."

It couldn't have been Edward Lacey, I thought, because he never saw me till we met on the London docks, and all this had been in the making long months before.

"Rose, you know what I am asking: help the Tsarevich. Cure him. In God's name, I ask you to cure him."

I just stared at her.

Then she smoothed her hair, and leaned back. "There, it's out. I've told you."

I still didn't answer. I couldn't. She was sitting there as if she had solved all her problems. By offering them to me.

"Rose. Say something."

"I can't. Madame Denisov, you must know nothing in the world is as easy as that, least of all such a thing as this."

"But I have seen you work it."

"And seen me fail. The child died."

"The child was too far gone, the case here is quite different."

"I can't save anyone from death," I said sadly. "I don't know that anyone could."

"But you give life, you've given it to that old wretch in the Red Tower, I saw that with the baby. For him there was no more pain." She was speaking eagerly, fervently. To convince me? Or perhaps herself. "Russia needs this child. He's our hope for the future."

I remembered that Ariadne had reported her mother as saying this. I remembered, too, the frail boy in the English book-shop in St. Petersburg.

"I saw him once in a shop in St. Petersburg. He looks a nice lad. Not like anyone's saviour, though."

"But you'll try? Say you will try."

I didn't answer directly. Instead, I said, "So this is the plan to which your brother told me he had given his blessing?"

"Yes." Dolly was eager. "We have discussed it. I believe he thought I was being slow in getting it in hand. But I told him it moved. And we agreed it must be tried."

I nodded; I had recognized the echo of the conversation I had overheard. Now Dolly had rounded it out for me. So on that earlier occasion she had been speaking to her brother. I was glad of that somehow.

But I had not known he was in the house. Nor had it been mentioned later. Indeed, I had got the distinct impression that his arrival with Edward Lacey was his first visit to Shereshevo that summer. Instead, there had been this secret, unannounced visit.

Then I recovered myself. Dolly was his sister, Shereshevo a home to him. Why should he not come and go? And why should Rose Gowrie expect to be told? But for a moment the picture I had formed in my mind of Dolly and Peter and their relationship wavered and broke up like a reflection in water, troubled by a passing breeze.

"And it was he who told me of the episode on the London docks—the boy who died. He had it in a letter from Prince Michael Melikov. You don't mind, surely?"

"No." Dolly, Peter, Prince Michael Melikov, a chain of observers, all with their eyes on me. "But you make me feel like a monster."

"I thought you'd be pleased." I don't think Dolly ever saw anyone's viewpoint but her own. "You should be proud."

"No." I shook my head.

"I shall never understand you English."

"Scots," I said mechanically.

"You have this great gift and you are not proud!"

"I hate it and fear it. When I want to use it, I cannot, and when I wish nothing should happen, then it operates on its own. It's like some terrible growth inside me, another body in my own that I cannot control."

"But you will come to Spala?" she urged me.

"And when am I to go?"

"I will be coming with you," said Dolly. "But we have to wait."

"And what do we wait for?"

Dolly said simply, "For him to be ill enough." Then she looked at me. "From all I hear we won't have to wait long."

Before we parted, she took my hand and said, "You're a good girl, Rose. God bless you."

I didn't see Peter that day.

One of the things I missed at Shereshevo was the company and ministrations of my black Ivan. He had a sense of humour and sharp powers of observation. My present little maid was no company. She liked watching me, breaking off her work to give my underclothes a long, hard stare, as if anything of mine must of necessity be different from anything she had known before. It made her services slow. And, to me, boring. I used to count one, two, three of her heavy breaths before breaking in on her. A test of my patience, she was. I would really have preferred to be independent, as I had been in St. Petersburg, and manage my own dressing, but it seemed impossible to get away from her.

"Did you look after Mademoiselle Laure like this?" I asked. I was sitting up in bed watching the girl tidy the room that night of my conversation with Dolly.

She shrugged. "I did my best. A proper misery, she was."

"She's dead now."

The girl crossed herself. "I know that. We heard. Poor soul."

"Yes, I think so."

"But what a terrible way to go. Still, she wasn't a bad old stick. Not one to cheer you up, but she wasn't much trouble, either. Wouldn't let me do a thing for her."

"And I do?"

"Ah, but I enjoy doing it for you, it's so interesting. Besides, anyone can see you're a lady, in spite of what old Sasha says. And all ladies cause a bit of trouble, it's as natural as breathing to them. It's what they're *for*."

It was a new philosophy to me, but I could see what she meant. From her point of view ladies were nothing but trouble and hard work.

"Last time she was here she left something behind," said the girl.

"Oh? What was it?"

"A book with writing in. I kept it. The cover was so pretty. Would you like it? I'll get it for you."

She was gone so quickly and back so soon that I saw she had had it ready and wanted to give it to me.

When she laid it on the counterpane in front of me, I saw at once it was a diary, nicely bound in morocco leather.

Tentatively, I opened it, aware she was watching me. The first twenty or so pages were filled with closely packed writing; after that it was empty.

"I *can* read, but I couldn't read that."

"It's in French," I said, turning the pages.

"She left it behind last summer."

"Yes, you see the last entry is for early September."

"That's when they went back. She forgot it, I suppose. I found it in a drawer."

I started to give it back to her, but she shook her head and put her hands behind her back. "No, I don't want it. You keep it. Read it."

"Read it? No, I couldn't do that, it's private."

"She's dead, it can't hurt her," pointed out the girl, practically. "Sleep well, miss."

When she'd gone, I sat for a moment, looking at the diary, and then I took it up and began to read.

Laure Le Brun had written every day, sometimes only a little, sometimes at length, giving factual accounts of her quiet life.

She wrote beautifully, in a plain, spare, elegant style. That was my first surprise. The second grew on me slowly as I read; I realized that I was reading the diary of a devout and gentle woman. Laure had been deeply religious, but without emotionalism or excess.

I had misjudged her during the short time I had known her. She wasn't a hysterical woman.

The days she depicted were commonplace in their activities: her reading, walking in the gardens and by the river, her drawing and her little attempts at water-colour painting. "A failure," she recorded prosaically.

Dolly figured in her diary as M.D., Ariadne as A., and Peter as P.A. She didn't mention Princess Irene, which was not surprising, since she was writing about Shereshevo last summer, and last summer Princess Irene had spent in the Red Tower.

Only I had freed her from that place.

I closed the diary and put it away in a drawer before going to sleep.

"She wasn't a hysterical woman," I said sleepily, as I turned on my pillow. "Not at all the sort to kill herself; I wasn't wrong to be surprised, not wrong at all."

We did not have to wait long for the summons to Spala. Madame Titov sent us a message. It came by hand, delivered by a bearded servant in a tall hat, and it was written in her beautiful, clear handwriting on violet coloured writing paper. I didn't read it, but it was handed to Dolly at breakfast one morning when the colours of autumn were beginning to be hinted at, and I saw her face grow white, so I knew what it was.

She looked up and gave me a little nod, as if to say, "It's come." Peter Alexandrov stood up. "At last," he said. "I thought it would never come."

"It seems wrong to have wished for it," said Dolly in a flutter, "when one knows it means pain and suffering, but one can't have an end before one has a start."

"I'll travel with you," said Peter.

"Oh, it's not necessary. Oh, no, I don't think you should do, nothing was said about your coming . . ."

Peter held up a hand. "I'm coming. I shall be very useful to you on the journey. You're a poor traveller, you know, Dolly.

And you'll be glad of my company, won't you, Rose?" His eyes met mine with amusement.

"Yes. But I could look after Madame Denisov, you know. I am a very capable traveller. I got myself from Scotland to Russia on my own," I said.

"Well, I was there," put in Edward Lacey. "Not that I did much, I grant you. I'll come with you and keep you all company if you like."

"No, thank you, Edward," said Dolly with decision.

"Come to think of it, I ought to get back to Piter anyway."

"You mean I am to be left on my own?" put in Ariadne.

"Certainly, do you good, my girl," said Edward. "You can set her some very hard lessons, can't you, Miss Rose? Keep her occupied and all that."

Ariadne drew herself up. " Edward Lacey, I am long past that sort of thing. Lessons, indeed. I don't do lessons."

Edward got up, too, and held out a hand. "Come into the garden with me and I'll give you one. Oh, it's all right, Dolly, only in croquet. She's shocking bad at it."

They went out, hand in hand. I noticed there was no longer much pretence I had been brought here to be with Ariadne. As she said herself, she was "long past that sort of thing." I had been brought here for one reason and one reason only: to be a servant to the Tsar.

The idea gave me a very strange feeling. I felt as if I should stand up and say: "I am a subject of the King of England. *Civis Romanus sum*"; but instead I just sat there feeling like a dumb fool.

"Certainly it is an exhausting journey from here to Spala," said Dolly uncertainly. "I suppose you would be useful on the train."

"I shall drive you there by motor car," anounced Peter. "You'll get there in half the time."

"Yes, so we shall. But the roads . . ."

"All right, at this time of the year. I shall manage the roads. We shall speed along at about fifty versts an hour." Dolly gave a soft moan, and he laughed.

"We shall be there before we are expected," she protested.

"What could be better?"

Dolly laughed. "Only a man could say that. Consider your poor hostess." A calculating look settled on her face for a passing moment. "But, yes, you may be right. Not a bad idea to get there quickly."

"As quickly as possible, I'd say." A look was exchanged between them.

"Yes, where pain is concerned no one must be slow," said Dolly thoughtfully. She rose.

"No one." Peter went to the door and opened it for her. "That's settled, then. I'm driving you. And, Rose—you shall sit beside me and be instructed."

I followed Dolly to the door. I could see in her eyes that she was waiting for me to turn the offer down, thus accepting her advice. But the devil got into me and I said, "Yes, I should enjoy to do so." Then I followed Dolly out and up the staircase.

Peter came up behind. "Yes, I shall take you safely there and then drive away into the night." He had caught up with me and was looking into my face. "Well, it will be night by the time we get there. And Madame Titov won't ask me to stay the night. She doesn't much like me, you know."

I shook my head. "No, I didn't know. I'm not on those terms with Madame Titov. She never mentioned you."

"All the same she dislikes me. I had the misfortune to serve in the Imperial Corps des Pages with a young cousin of hers. Dissipated young devil," and Peter scowled. "He disliked me on sight, it was mutual, I may say, and then handed on his dislike to his relative. She's a sort of sponge, that woman, and soaks up impressions."

"I liked her," I ventured.

"Oh, liked, one may like her, but don't expect any real humanity from her, it has all been sucked out of her by the life she leads. So take note, I am warning you, they will none of them treat you with common humanity. You are there to be of use to them. Everything there is subordinated at the moment to one end."

I looked at him, not really comprehending.

"Oh, well, you will understand," he said with a sigh.

We were off in a surprisingly short time, considering how Dolly usually conducted her departures.

"I was all packed in readiness," she confided. "And I'm not taking my maid. I shall dress myself." She seemed impressed with her own hardihood.

Peter said with amusement: "That will show you how seriously she takes the trip."

"No, I was told to bring no one. Discretion, secrecy, you know, the fewer eyes the better."

Peter gave a little quirk of his eyebrows. "Oh, they think they can keep a veil of secrecy over everything there. Don't they see the dangers of such a way? That people gossip all the more because they aren't told? The stories I have heard going around and known to be untrue, and not really able to nail them as false because of the constant cry of secrecy and discretion—openness and frankness would benefit everyone."

"Ah," said Dolly, stepping into the car, "there I don't agree with you."

"The stories that go around about the monk Gregory . . ."

"Hush," said Dolly.

"I've met him," I said brightly.

There was a dead silence, and they exchanged looks. "Have you, indeed? And where?" asked Dolly.

"At church. With Ariadne," I added hastily. "But it wasn't anything to do with Ariadne. I think he came to see Madame Titov; she was there, too."

"Did he speak to you?" asked Dolly sharply.

"He looked at me."

Peter said, under his breath, "I'm sure he did, the bounder."

"But Madame Titov cut him. Or as good as. I'm sure she didn't want to see him."

"No, she wouldn't want to. She's a sensible creature at

heart, and knows he's dangerous," and she motioned me to step into the car. "Do get in, dear."

"Why is he dangerous?" I asked, as I seated myself.

"Oh—I'll explain later. But that man, he *would* be at the church when you were there with Madame Titov. He seems to be drawn by instinct to a sensitive spot. Do you think he has second sight?" she demanded of her brother. "They say so."

"I think he has good spies," said Peter, getting into the car and settling his favourite fox-terrier into the seat beside him.

"Must you bring that creature?" asked his sister.

"Yes." A short answer but decided.

Dolly was quiet for about thirty seconds, then said, "You're driving too fast."

"Not fast at all, considering the distance we have to travel. Wind yourself into all those wrappers and the scarf you've put on and go to sleep."

"I shall never sleep a wink," grumbled Dolly, but she relapsed into silence, and when I peeped next, her eyes were closed.

"Some people always sleep when they travel," said Peter, "and Dolly is one of them." He smiled at me. "We're as good as alone."

He drove on a little more, then said, "Just as well, as I want to talk to you."

"Oh?"

"Yes, I couldn't let you set off on this trip alone, unguarded except for Dolly, without anyone to help you."

"But will I need help?" I was surprised.

"Yes, you might. Your very existence poses a threat to some people in that inner circle. To begin with, not all of them want the Tsarevich to survive at all. Some would like him out of the way, and one of the Tsar's brothers proclaimed as heir. And then even among those most fervently praying for the boy's health are a group who want Father Gregory to be his saviour. Yes, that's *his* secret, he, too, is a healer. A foul-mouthed braggart but with strange powers."

"I have seen him look at me," I said, "and not liked it."

Peter drove a space without speaking, then he said, "Yes, I dare say he has heard of you, and that's why he came to have a look, but once he'd seen you, he would get other ideas. You understand what I mean? And he is insatiable." Peter's voice shook. "I'm warning you."

"Oh, but surely. . . ." I began.

"No, he has friends. God knows what secrets give him power over them, but he has it. Don't trust him. I don't say he will be at Spala, but if he is, avoid him. I mean what I say."

"I'm not afraid," I said, having been brought up by Tibby not to show fear even if I felt it. "Keeping a stout heart," she called it.

"You should be. Even the young Grand Duchesses have had to be protected from him."

I looked up at him doubtfully, wondering if he could be serious, but apparently he was. Forcibly it was brought home to me that I was moving in a strange world. How little I as yet understood Russia.

"You heard what I said?" Peter asked sharply.

"Yes, I was thinking about it. I will be prudent, I promise."

"Stay close to Madame Titov. She's honest, even if stupid. Although I am coming to think that stupidity is the ultimate vice."

Again I looked at him doubtfully.

"I have a right to be anxious about you. I am taking the right. Dear Rose, you must have noticed how I feel about you."

And he moved his hand from the wheel and took my hand firmly in his own. The dog, which was sitting between us, growled softly.

"She's jealous. Babette is always jealous of those I love. She bit my last—" Here he stopped.

"Your last mistress," I said calmly. "Is that what you were going to say?"

He took his hand from mine, returning it to the wheel, and drove straight ahead in silence for a few minutes; I saw his lips tighten in a thin line.

So I had angered him; I felt a moment of excitement, almost pleasure at what I had done, before doubt crept in. He was smiling.

"I believe you led me into that on purpose," I said.

"I own I did want to see what you said."

"And now you are pleased!"

"If you had kept a polite silence, I should have been disappointed," he admitted.

"I blundered into it," I said.

"No blunder: I wanted you to speak." He reached out his hand questioningly again; I took it in mine. "I couldn't let you go to that place without trying to build a bridge between us. Something you could scramble back on to if you felt unsafe, something that could never break."

He raised my hand to his lips and kissed it gently. The dog leaned her body against me, staring into my eyes and growling softly.

"She likes you," he said.

"I'm not sure," I said breathlessly, half suffocated by the warm fur and my own emotion: Peter was still holding my hand to his lips. Anxiously, I looked over my shoulder towards Dolly.

"It's all right; she won't wake up. She took one of those tablets of hers. She always does when she travels."

True enough; although Dolly stirred and her lips parted, she did not waken.

"Happy dreams," said her brother to her. "Rose, may I dream? No, I won't use that word, I don't want dreams, I want you, Rose, solid, real, provoking as you often are."

"Provoking?" I was surprised.

"You do withdraw, you know, just as you are taking your hand away now. I look round and you are gone. In the spirit, if not the flesh. But sometimes that, too. I want you always, Rose, and in the flesh, yes, certainly in the flesh." I didn't answer. "Rose, you do understand me?"

"I'm not sure if I do."

"I want you to be my wife. Will you marry me, Rose? Marry a mad Russian."

When Patrick had asked me to marry him, he had taken me for a walk in the moonlight and the air had been soft with may-blossom. He had kissed me before he asked me with the sure instinct about my body he always possessed. I had accepted him without delay.

Now I sat dumb. I was being offered position, wealth beyond anything I had dreamed. When I had imagined anything like such an offer, I had made up my mind to accept it. But the truth was, I had not really expected it. I was no Cinderella. Now it had happened, and I was silent.

"It would not be fair," I said slowly. "I don't love you."

"Rose, I know that. I am not an inexperienced boy, who thinks love is a thing of moonbeams and gossamer; I know it's not. I know what it is made of and what will carry us through. In Russia we say marry first and enjoy love afterwards."

"You forget: I was to be married once. I do know what love is. After my own fashion. And I'm not sure if I want to love again. I found it painful."

"Inside marriage, you would be secure. It would happen to you. Naturally. I promise you."

"I haven't forgotten Patrick. I suppose I am still in love with him." Now I'd said it aloud, I knew it was true. "I thought I'd been so hurt that love had turned into hate. Perhaps it has, but hate is too close to love, isn't it?"

"No," he said, decisively. "No. Anyone who says that has never known true hate."

It was my turn to be silent now, and all the time the dog kept up that slow, crooning growl. "I don't understand why you want to marry me," I said wistfully; I suppose I wanted to be assured it was for my matchless beauty and supreme attraction.

I was a little hurt, therefore, when he burst out laughing. "What a girl you a.e, Rose, I adore you. I don't know why. It just happened. Isn't that the best way of all?"

"And what about me? What shall I do?" I said, naively stung by his belief that only his emotions mattered. Men were all alike; Patrick had been the same. He had whirled me along in a delicious dance while it suited him, and then, the moment it did not, he had dropped me, never mind what I felt. "I'm just to come because you call?"

"You do like me, Rose, though. I'm not wrong about that. You haven't tried to hide it."

"No, I haven't," I admitted. "Perhaps I should have. Tibby would say I should show more pride."

"Oh, that old Tibby. She's bad for you, Rose. She *limits* you."

"She's a very sensible woman," I said with conviction.

"It's no, then, is it, Rose? When you speak with the voice of Tibby, I know it must be no." He sounded sad.

"No." I nodded.

"Mind, I don't give up. I'm not like your Scotsman." I thought I caught a note of contempt.

"Ah," and I turned on him fiercely, "don't criticize him: I may do so, you may not."

"I see you do still love him," said Peter. "I was wrong. It's not quite over for you. I've been too quick."

For a while he concentrated on the road ahead, and we were both silent. Then he said, "Forgive me."

"Nothing to forgive. There is something I must say to you: your offer hasn't been such a surprise to me as I let you think. I wondered when you started to teach me to drive. . . . I began to ask myself what I would say if you did propose to me and I meant to take you. For the position, you know, not for love. But when it came to it, I couldn't do it. No, I couldn't."

He was very quiet, his expression unreadable.

"Are you angry?"

"No. No, I was thinking that I admire you, Rose Gowrie. What an honest girl you are." There was a note in his voice I had not heard before. "So you had to say no?"

I nodded.

"I think you are half-way to saying yes, Rose."

"I don't know." I shook my head. "Perhaps I am tied to Patrick for ever, whether I like it or not."

The dog leaned against me, an inscrutable expression in

those shining amber eyes. Behind us, Dolly murmured in her sleep. I looked round and saw that a chiffon scarf had blown across her face, disturbing her. I leaned across and removed it.

"How she can sleep," muttered her brother.

"Do you think she has heard us?"

"No. Or if she has, then only as in a dream. It will *be* a dream."

"I think she knows, anyway," I said.

"About me? Yes, I dare say Dolly has her speculations. She understands me pretty well. Not as thoroughly as she thinks, but well enough. But not you. No one knows you and your feelings, Rose."

"Am I such an enigma?"

"To such as Dolly. She has her emotions on the surface, whereas you hide yours. And you frighten her, of course., Just a little. But it's good for Dolly to be frightened. I wish someone could frighten Ariadne."

I laughed. "You should meet her friend Marisia."

"Ah, yes, Marisia. The clever one," he said thoughtfully. "And she frightens Ariadne, does she?"

"Ariadne respects her," I said. "And I'm not surprised. I was inclined to be frightened of her myself. I should say she rules her family with a rod of iron."

"She does," said Peter absently.

"Oh, you know?" I was surprised.

"Yes." Then he added gently, "I taught for a little at the Smolny."

"So you did. I'd forgotten. Ariadne told me. You were much admired.

He laughed. "More than I deserved. They were so bored, poor things, shut up for years in that fossilized world. Do you know the girls still wear the same costume with the same white fichu and bare bosoms that the Empress Catherine devised for them? Of course, it's charming, they look delightful, but they are all living in the past."

"Was that why Ariadne was asked to leave?"

The road ahead was suddenly full of a flock of geese, being escorted down the road by a barefoot peasant girl. The whole lot of them were covered in a cloud of dust as we sped past.

"She was a difficult pupil," said Peter. "She can be awkward, and then she was a friend of Marisia's."

"Is that all?"

"I suppose Marisia's political beliefs were a little extreme for the Smolny," he said carefully.

"Revolutionary, you mean?" Yes, I could see Marisia advocating revolution.

"Almost anything would seem revolutionary to those ultra-conservatives in the Smolny," he said. "But once it was discovered. . . . " He shrugged. "Out they went. Expelled with ignominy. Dolly was quite frantic. For a little while, anyway. Fortunately, her natural calm soon returned," and he glanced backwards to where his sister lay, the picture of happy ease. "Of course, Dolly thinks Russia should change itself, but she thinks it should do it with the least possible trouble to herself and her property. Occasionally she will stretch out a hand to preserve the status quo. As now. As in sending you off to Spala. You realize your function, don't you, Rose?"

"Oh, yes. Madame Denisov explained: she sees the Tsarevich as the only hope for the future," I said. "I'm to save him, and through him, Russia. It's a formidable task. I told her I don't think I'm up to it."

I seemed to irritate him; he gripped the wheel of the car and drove forward at an increased speed. "Oh, I hate that dry little note in your voice," he burst out with. "One day you will grow out of using it, and grow out of that ferocious honesty of yours, dinned into you by that servant of yours. Oh, yes, I recognize the voice of your old Tibby when it speaks through you. It's the voice of a puritanical old woman. And you are young, Rose, you have passion. One day you will realize that honesty is not enough, nor consistency the only virtue."

I was silenced, and puzzled, too. When you are behaving,

as you think, well, it is very hard to be criticized for it.

Behind us Dolly stirred. "What is that you are saying about virtue?" she asked.

"Only that it's not always what you expect," said Peter.

"Don't I know it," grumbled Dolly, unwinding herself from some of her scarves. "The troubles I fell into as a young girl because I did not realize that what you are taught in the schoolroom does not hold good in adult life. The truth is, it is safer to be wicked in an adult way than good in a childlike way. It invites less trouble, anyway."

"Dolly, I never suspected you of such cynicism," said Peter. "What will Rose think?"

But I thought she was talking for my benefit, and I wondered how long she had lain there listening to our conversation.

We lunched at a small hotel in a country town. To get there involved a diversion from our route, but the needs of our machine had to be considered. It needed feeding just like a horse, and this small town had a supply of the petrol it needed which, it seemed, was not always the case in Russia.

"Journeys in Russia have to be planned between petrol pump and petrol pump," said Peter. "But my tank is large, although the engine is greedy."

"And what would happen if you ran out of petrol?"

"We should stop. Did you think we should blow up?"

"It smells alarmingly of hot metal," I said. "And of petrol fumes."

He gave the gleaming radiator a pat. "Yes, but you can get to like it. To an addict like me, it smells better than a horse."

Around the hotel was a small enclosed patch which they called a garden. Peter and I walked around it, while Dolly restored her appearance to its normal high gloss, after the dusty journey. Presently she would reappear with her lips and cheeks pink and smelling of eau-de-cologne. "I always wash in eau-de-cologne when travelling. One never knows what the local water contains."

The walls of the garden were made of rough hurdles of

wood over which climbing plants, roses, red and white, and
purple convolvulus were trained. There had been a shower
of rain just before lunch and the damp had brought out the
sweet smell of growing things.

"This rain will lay the dust and make the journey more
bearable for Dolly," said Peter. He reached out and took a
rose spray between his fingers, bending and twisting it before
letting it spring back to where it was before. "That's a wild
rose, unscented but strong."

I saw a small bead of blood forming on one finger. He saw
me looking. "Yes, and the thorns are strong, too. Well, that's
the way with wild things. You're not a wild rose, are you?" Silently, I shook my head. "You've been bred to be what you
are. But one day I think you might throw off the influence of
that old woman who has laid her hand on you so strongly
and taught you so much about honesty and common sense."

"Don't laugh at Tibby."

"I wouldn't dare. Nor was I laughing. The thought of her
terrifies me. Sometimes I can hear her speaking through
your voice, and she makes you into an old woman."

"I haven't always done what Tibby would have approved
of," I said thoughtfully, remembering how I had let Patrick
love me.

"No?" He was studying my face closely. "I wonder what
you did that was so wrong." A flush rose in my throat and
travelled up to my cheeks. "Perhaps I can guess," he said
gently. "Because while you only pretend sometimes to be old,
I really am old. Ten years older than you, Rose." He picked a
spray which was thickly budded with tiny white roses. "Here
you are: a present from nature. Give it back to me one day if
you can and I'll accept it gladly." He spoke lightly, but his
eyes were serious. I took the spray and tucked it in my belt;
when we were in the motor car again I put it in my pocket for
safety. He pretended not to see.

It had been morning when we set out, evening when we arrived at Spala. For some time we had been travelling along
quiet roads through thick forest, then suddenly there were

soldiers on guard, obvious policemen, even if in plain clothes. Swiftly we were passed through all the checks, we were expected guests in spite of our early arrival, and were drawing up on the gravelled path before a small, stone-built house.

"Oh, I'm stiff," complained Dolly as she crawled out of the car. "What a wretched-looking house; I hope we shall be comfortable."

I watched as two footmen appeared and removed our luggage from the car.

"Good-bye," said Peter. "I'm off. My love to the Tsar and all that. Oh, just a joke, Dolly, no need to look shocked."

He kissed her hand, then under Dolly's interested gaze, he kissed my cheek and went away.

"So, here we are," said Dolly; she put her hand on my arm. Certainly she seemed more nervous than was her wont. She looked at the open door, the darkness inside lightened by one small lamp. "We might as well go in."

# Chapter Six

Madame Titov came hurrying towards us. "Oh, I am so pleased to see you. How kind of you to make such good time." The smile of welcome faded from her face. "Things are very bad here. You could be too late." She led us into a comfortable sitting-room, where a small fire burned in the hearth. It was cool here in the great forest. "The poor child. If you see how he suffers, and hear his agony, your heart would break. Even I can hardly bear it and I have trained myself to show nothing." In the dim light her face looked white and drawn. "You'd like some supper; I'll order it," and she went to the bell-pull.

"We're travel stained," said Dolly. "I must wash and make myself orderly."

More eau-de-cologne, I thought, but possibly the water in her old friend's house could be trusted.

"Dolly, of course. Stupid of me. I'm so troubled, you see. It drives every other thought straight out of my mind. I'll take you up myself," and she bustled forward. "I've taken a risk in summoning you," she said as we followed. "All off my own bat. Took my own line. I knew I must *act*."

"Do you mean *They* don't know?" asked Dolly.

"They do and they don't. That is, the Tsarina really knows and is willing, she will clutch at anything. The Tsar has been told, let's put it like that, but no details. It's a subject he will *not* think about: he relies entirely on the doctors, only gives way to his wife in this matter."

"And the Heir?"

"The child does not know," said Madame Titov sadly. "One could not torment him with any promise of relief that might fail." She turned and gave me a worried look. I could see that she was assessing what chance I offered of giving relief, and that she was finding it hard to believe I could do anything at all. I wondered myself. Then from studying my face her eyes went back to Dolly's, whose expression was now of her usual insouciance. I guessed from this by-play that she wanted to question Dolly further about me.

She escorted Dolly and me upstairs before returning to her sitting-room, with the polite remark that a meal would be served when we were ready. I was not surprised, when on going down again, I heard her and Dolly talking, and realized that they were talking about me. Dolly was in mid-sentence.

"—an imaginative girl," I heard her say.

A low murmur in response from Madame Titov, and Dolly went on again: "Oh, there was some fantastic story she invented about poor Madamoiselle Laure— Yes, suicide without doubt, but Rose imagined she had been murdered. Imagine: murdered! In my house. As if I wouldn't have known. We soon made her see sense. And then there was some story my brother told me about her hearing voices coming from a speaking-tube. Nonsense, of course, and so I told him."

Oh, traitor, I mentally apostrophized Peter.

"No, there has been nothing since we came to the country," I could hear Dolly saying. "So, it was probably just the initial excitement of arriving in Russia."

You little know, I thought, remembering the episode at Vyksa, when I had dreamt, for one mad moment, that Patrick was playing the piano. Ariadne, then, had remained loyal and not diverted Dolly's ears with the tale. For this, I was grateful. But Dolly was going on:

"And perhaps there will be a closer relationship," I heard her say.

"You mean your brother Peter?" A note of sharp interest in our hostess's voice. "And how will you like that?"

No answer was to be heard from Dolly; I could just imagine her silently shrugging her shoulders.

I found myself wondering how much Dolly had slept in the car, and how much she had overheard. It seemed the right moment for me to enter the room, and I did so.

Both women turned on me bland, unconcerned faces, as if their conversation had not related to me, which goes to show what natural liars really good women can be.

"We shall go over there this evening, after you have dined." explained Madame Titov nervously. "We won't wait. What is it?" she asked, as a manservant came into the room. He whispered in her ear. "Oh, dear." She stood up. "We are summoned now. Dolly, Miss Gowrie, I am sorry to give you no time to rest, but we are called for: I'm sorry you can't stay to eat."

"Oh, food doesn't matter, does it, Rose?" said Dolly hastily.

I shook my head. "Let's go," I said briefly, beginning to walk towards the door. Unconsciously, I was beginning to take charge.

"We walk across," said Madame Titov, almost whispering, she was so nervous. "It's hardly any distance, and it will be more private. Discretion is important."

Our wraps were brought down by a servant and silently draped about us.

"And I'm to come, too?" asked Dolly, her voice low. She seemed almost overcome with nervousness.

I felt calm now and practical, as if nothing could stop me doing what was right.

"You mustn't be nervous, Miss Gowrie," said Madame Titov as we walked, all three abreast, along a broad gravel path through the trees. "Just behave naturally."

"Oh, I will," I answered calmly. "I wouldn't think of doing anything else."

"How ruthless you sound, dear," murmured Dolly. "I have never heard that note in your voice before."

Oh, Dolly, I thought impatiently, this is real, not some game you are playing. Isn't it better I should know what I am doing, and be certain of myself? Not certain of curing pain, you understand, but convinced of the power I had. Surprisingly, doubts had gone, I was sure of myself. "One must be practical," I said. "How many people will be in the room with me?"

"Does it matter?" asked Madame Titov.

"I think so."

"Well, then, very few, I imagine," she said in a flustered kind of way, as if she was not sure of the answer. "Just the boy and his mother. Possibly his nurse. You understand I have never myself been admitted? But I have been in the ante-room and seen and heard much."

"And now?" I questioned. "Will you be there?"

"Oh, not now. Nor you, Dolly. I am sure we will wait outside." She turned to her and Dolly made a murmur of assent.

"Good," I said. "The fewer the better." I strode forward. Inside myself I was thinking that it would probably be better if I could get the mother and the nurse out and have the child to myself. "I wonder if I could get rid of the mother," I said aloud.

Madame Titov gave a shocked cluck. "The Tsarina, you mean? Oh, never. You could never ask her to go."

"I could," I said calmly.

"But will she go?" asked Dolly.

Madame Titov was horrified. "But only his mother keeps him alive," she said.

"I wonder," I said.

Madame Titov moaned. "Oh, I don't think I can let you go on."

"You can't stop me."

"No, I believe I can't now. You are expected. But you must behave reasonably. For God's sake, use discretion."

"I've always understood that the Tsarina responded well to firm handling," said Dolly surprisingly. "And that Father Gregory bullies her."

Madame Titov drew in her breath sharply. "Don't mention him to me, please. And certainly never to *her*."

"Still, it's as well Rose should know," observed Dolly.

"I know all there is to know. More or less. Remember, I've seen him," I said. "I'm not thinking about him now. How long has the illness been going on? It doesn't matter, but I want to know."

"A week, less than a week. As far as I know. I'm not always told everything, but one learns to guess. Oh, I know the signs." And I was sure she did: I could see her keenly observing, so sharply focussed on that close family group that she knew all that could be known without being told. I felt a sudden pity for that family beneath the scrutiny of those birdlike eyes.

"And what is the illness?"

Madame Titov said hastily. "I don't know, it is never disclosed, but there are sometimes great swellings in the body, I believe, and always great pain." She spoke in a low, sibilant voice, as if she wanted only me to hear, but I was to hear with clarity.

We had come out on to a wider area of gravel, and ahead of us, only dimly lighted, sprawled a substantial stone house. A shrubbery grew all round it, and here and there in the gloom it was possible to see the silent, unobtrusive presence of guards. A policeman in plain clothes was tucked away in a sort of wooden niche beside the front door, his hiding place decently obscured with laurels so that one might not have seen him had not the light from the lamp beside the door shone on his spectacles.

No one made a move towards us, so I supposed that we were expected and that everything was known about us.

There were, however, wheels within wheels, as I discovered when Madame Titov whispered, "We will follow the path round to the right; there is a side door open for us there. It will be more private."

Private? Private meant secret, I thought. So our visit was to be kept secret from some. And yet the men outside unmistakably knew who we were and where we must go. They had been informed. So they were in on the secret. But inside the house, close to the heart of it, were those who did not know, who were not meant to know. Perhaps even the Tsar himself did not know. A strange world where a humble policeman might know more of the whole picture than an emperor himself.

Or perhaps it was not the Tsar from whom I was to be hidden, after all; *I* had been told that I might be "seen" by him. A part of the Imperial household, then? So it looked as though he had servants close to him that he kept secrets from which lesser servants might know.

I was thinking all this as I hurried after Madame Titov, but I was not so naïve as to be surprised for long. Courts always have secrets, and back ways in, such as the one we were approaching now.

I suppose we looked like conspirators as we filed through the door. I could hear Dolly breathing behind me in nervous puffs. The door was unlocked and led into a narrow hall where a silent servitor sat on a great leather chair as if waiting for a summons which had not yet come. He neither promoted nor hindered our progress but merely bowed us in.

Madame Titov gave a brisk little nod of her head towards yet another door at the end of the hall. "We go through there."

I halted her with my hand on her arm. "You may wait here."

"What's that?"

"You wait here," I repeated. "I will go alone."

"But I must come with you."

"No. I want to be on my own." And before she could stop

me, I had pushed through the door and let it fall behind me.

I was in a square room, lit by a lamp hanging from the ceiling and furnished with ugly heavy chairs lining three walls. Along the fourth wall was a big writing-desk. A tall girl of about my own age stood by the desk studying a piece of paper. A long white overall covered her from head to foot, buttoned at her throat, and going down to her toes.

She looked up as I came in and gave me an appraising stare. Not a pretty face, I thought, but well modelled and fine skinned. She would be a handsome woman and perhaps a beautiful old lady.

"I've come," I said. She didn't introduce herself, but she was sufficiently like the girl I had seen shopping in the English book-shop in St. Petersburg to let me know she was one of the Grand Duchesses.

"So I see." She looked at me deliberately, taking in my face and clothes with a calm scrutiny. I returned the gaze. "Good," she said, as if I had satisfied her. She spoke English with very little accent. "You are to come with me." Then she said, "Where is Madame Titov?"

"I left her outside," I said firmly.

A faint smile moved her lips, but she said nothing. More human than she looks, I thought. "And she stayed?" she said. It was the only comment she allowed herself.

I smiled back without answering. Without another word, she turned on her heel, motioning me to follow her. We went through a door in one corner of the room. This led us to a staircase.

At the bottom, she stopped. "I should tell you that I do not wish you to be here. I do not approve." Her accent was much clearer now. "It is against God and nature. I think what you do may be a mortal sin."

"Possibly. I do not think so."

She gave me a hostile stare; I suppose Grand Duchesses, even young ones, are not used to being argued with.

"I gave way, consented to join in the charade" (I flushed at that word), "because you are, at least, better than the other one," she said bitterly. "You are not a wicked girl, I can see that in your face, nor mad, nor stupid. Before I saw you, I wondered about all those three things." The colour ebbed away from my face. "Now I see you are honest. I dare say you believe in what you do: I do not."

For a moment, we stared at each other, my eyes held hers, and it was hers that eventually fell. "You have one thing in common with that other one," she murmured, "you know how to use your eyes. Come on. We are late."

She hurried up the staircase, at a trot, so that I almost had to run to keep up with her. We went through a door into an ante-room in which a servant was sitting, who rose and curtseyed as we passed, and then paused momentarily before a double white door. From behind the door came a cry of pain, then silence.

As we went through the door a long, low moan opened up the silence of the darkened room like a wound.

Against one wall was a bed, the curtains of which hung about it half drawn. The bed-clothes were rumpled. A small, dumpy woman sat on a chair by the bed; she wore a voluminous blue and white apron and the head coif of a nurse. Her back was towards me as she leant over her patient, tending him, but I could see her feet, and they were tiny, plump, elderly feet, and her face when she turned to look at me was old and expressionless, but wrinkled, crumpled like a dried-out walnut.

Slowly, deliberately, she turned her back on me. The snub direct, I thought.

I took a tentative step into the room.

Standing at the foot of the bed was another woman, swathed from head to foot in a white overall. She, too, was intent on the boy.

"Who are these?" I asked.

"The nurses."

"Both of them?"

"Both."

I moved forward again.

"Don't speak to them," warned my companion hastily. "Don't speak to either. Deal only with the boy."

I took no notice. "There has to be trust," I said slowly. "Here there is distrust. Make up your mind. Either you will offer me trust or not. If not, I will go."

The boy cried out again.

"Please do your best for the boy," said the girl in a low voice, grudgingly, the words wrung out of her. "I trust you."

"She doesn't." I nodded towards the figure standing, motionless, at the foot of the bed.

"Hush."

I looked again at the woman, who had a pale, worn face; she was pressing her lips together as if she was holding emotions back. She had the closed-in look of someone who had been holding them back for years. One hand gripped and pulled at her white apron, in an unconscious, mechanical gesture. The white material did not quite cover the dress beneath, which was of a pale mauve colour.

I walked up to her, and after a moment's thought made a deliberate curtsey.

For a moment there was silence, then the Tsarina said slowly, "So, like *him*, you know how to tell who I am. It is a mark, I think, of the true power. Perhaps you are genuine, after all."

Dryly, I said, "If that is the test of validity you use, ma'am, I should advise you to be careful what you wear. Do you not think you are always picked out in a crowd by what you wear? Your appearance, is that not known?"

The girl behind me gave a shocked gasp, and pulled at me.

"No, leave her." The Tsarina's mouth curved in what was almost a smile. "She is atrociously blunt. But so is *he*. It is a mark; I almost believe in her."

"Mamma," said a weak little voice from the bed.

At once her attention drained away from me to him. The child was the only person real to her in that room; the rest of us existed only as we served him. At once she was bending over him, answering, "I'm here, lovey: Mother's here."

The nurse wiped the beads of sweat from the child's head.

I looked at the boy for the first time; he moved his head on the pillow so that he could see me.

"Stay still, lovey, so nursey can wipe your head."

"Who is that girl? I want to see," he said. In spite of the weakness, it was a composed and self-possessed voice, making a nonsense of the distracted diminutives used by his mother. I thought I even detected a resentment that his dignity was reduced by her.

"You shall, you shall."

If he'd said he wanted to eat me, I expect she would have said he should do that, too.

Without waiting for another word from her, I went forward and stood by his side. "You're looking at me now," I said. "What do you see?"

"Don't torment the child with questions," said his mother sharply.

But the boy only smiled faintly without answering. Then he said, "I see a nice face. You look jolly."

"I see a nice face, too. And it *could* be a jolly one."

He moved on his pillow, raising himself a bit. "I am when I'm myself. I'm very happy when I'm let be."

I saw then that a small cat was nestling by his side on the bed, and that his hand was resting on her delicate little frame. His fingers rose and fell with her light breathing.

"Who's that?" I asked.

"Her name is Pickles. I have another cat called Samson, but I left him behind in Tsarskoye Selo. He will be there when I get back. Papa says I have too many pets."

"But he doesn't mean it?" I questioned, studying his face. I thought the tense lines of pain on it were already relaxing.

He considered it. "I think *not*," he decided, "because he always gives me more. I have four cats and two dogs."

"Three dogs at least," put in his sister.

"They have puppies, you see," he explained. "And the cats sometimes have kittens. Only not as many as you'd think."

"No?"

"I believe they take away the kittens before I see them, but I can't be quite sure." He stroked the creature by his side. "This is my new, little cat, my new, dear, little cat." On his face was the dogged, patient look I had seen on the face of other children who had had to suffer prolonged pain.

"When I came into the room," I said, "I heard you call out. Do you feel like calling out now?"

"While we've been talking I had forgotten the pain."

There was silence; I could hear his breathing. "Is it not less?"

"But it hasn't gone away," he said quickly.

"Of course not. But you were able, for a while, to forget it. To feel nothing. That was good."

He said carefully, "I'll tell you something: even when it is very bad, there are moments when it seems to go away. Only moments. If they didn't happen, I should scream all the time."

"I don't blame you."

"I'm supposed to be brave, not call out or shout. It's expected of me."

"I think you're being brave now."

"Yes, I am," he said, slightly surprised. "Because the pain is bad, but more bearable, somehow."

"I'm so glad." I was beginning to feel tired. My legs were heavy, the lightness had gone from my body.

"You're not a doctor, are you?"

"No. Couldn't be." I meant only that I was temperamentally unfitted for it, but he took it another way.

"Girls *can* be, I know. One of my sisters would like to be a doctor. But, of course, she won't be allowed. It can't be done." His tone was grave: he took the position of his family seriously. And his own, too, no doubt. "Her rank, you see."

What colour there was in his face had drained away, leaving it an ashen grey. He closed his eyes.

His mother screamed. "He is dying. This is death. You have killed him." She rushed forward hysterically. "Baby, baby—"

I seized her arm and held her strongly. "No. Stop. Leave him."

The girl, after one horrified look, said, "Let my mother go. Nurse, help us."

But the nurse seemed frozen by my boldness in laying hands on the Empress.

"She's simply hysterical," I said coolly to the girl. "Take your mother off my hands and leave me to be with your brother. Take her away altogether, if you can get her to go."

I think my voice steadied the girl. Moreover, she could see her brother was not dead, because his eyes had slowly opened. There was no meaning in them, but he was there.

Between her teeth, as if it was an effort to talk to me and only the extremity of the occasion made her do so, the girl said, "Mamma, come to the corner of the room and sit down."

"That creature, that creature," sobbed the Tsarina. She was weeping uncontrollably.

"Now, Mamma, be calm." Over her mother's shoulder the girl looked at me with hostility. "What have you done?" she said.

"Get Papa, get help," sobbed her mother.

"No, no. Now, stop crying, dearest. See, you're frightening *him.*"

And it was true: comprehension had come back into the boy's eyes. "Why is Mamma crying?" he whispered. "Is she ill?"

With a scream, she wrenched herself away from her daughter and threw herself upon him, literally blanketing him with her body.

"For God's sake take her away," I said. "Get her off."

Between us, the nurse and I lifted the struggling woman and left her to her daughter.

"Your mother's all right," I said to the boy. "She was frightened, that's all. You went very far away just then, and it alarmed her."

"Not really far away," he said. "I was here all the time. I could hear you all."

"Of course you could." I put my hand on his; I had expect-ed it to be cold: to my surprise it felt young and warm. I was pleased.

"What a funny person you are. Your cheeks have gone all pink. Why?"

Idly, lightly, I spoke: "Pleasure, I think."

Between our hands a small warmth was growing. It *did* give me pleasure to help him. What I felt was physical, not of the mind. My body enjoyed itself. This had never happened before. And even now I question if it would have happened if it had not been released by the hysterical attack on me by the mother. But it was a release: a rush of warmth like hot water running all over me. Did he feel it, too? I think he did.

And I knew I had done what I had come to do: stayed for a moment the pain and the dying, postponed the victory of the enemy.

"You'd better go to sleep now," I said, leaning back, flushed.

He closed his eyes obediently. "I believe I could now. I feel so happy."

"I know."

"The happiness has made the pain go away, or begin to go away. But the happiness came first. That's strange, you know. I am not happy because the pain is going, but because I am happy, the pain is less. That's very strange. I wonder why?"

Euphoria, the Greeks called it, I thought, and watched him with compassion; a mere bundle of bones, he was, with one still-swollen limb, the knee, I think, but it was hard to see un-der the bed-clothes.

"Will it always be like that?"

"I can't promise," I said sadly.

He opened his eyes wider at that, and gave me an assessing look. I had his measure then, and knew that he was a life-denier, he wouldn't hang on, in the end he didn't want it enough.

"But I will be better for now?"

Who can really tell, I thought. "I believe so," I said to him.

I had done the job for which I had come, and it was time to go. The boy saw my intention at once: he was as quick as a needle at times. "You're better than the other one," he said. "I don't really like him."

"Who is the 'other one'?"

"Father Gregory," he said.

"I thought so." The Tsarina had jerked her head around at the name; I thought that there was a mixture of anger and real fear in her eyes. This was a name not to be named.

"Mamma likes him."

"I wish you hadn't said that."

I was anxious to go now, but I was far from sure I should be allowed to leave. I was inside the inner circle now, treading on sacred ground, and perhaps I already knew things I should not know.

"Good-bye," I said. "Go to sleep and forget me." I moved towards the door.

The Tsarina dragged herself to her feet; I saw she was trembling. "I should be thankful to you, but it is not easy . . . there is something about you." She put her hand over her eyes. "Never mind. I will teach myself to thank you."

Belatedly, crazily, I remembered the way I should behave. I gave a little bob, and said, "Good-bye, ma'am."

The Tsarina looked at her daughter, who obediently came with me to the door. The girl's face was quite expressionless (which I should have seen as a danger signal) till we got outside the room, when she closed the door deliberately and leaned against it, and began a tirade.

"I want you to know that I hate and despise you. At first I thought you were better, now I see that you are as bad. You are an animal like the other one." She was furiously angry, her face flushed, her lips twisted.

I stared, fascinated. It was difficult to believe this finely bred, reserved girl could so lose control.

"You are an animal like him. And like him, when the excitement is on you, you smell. I noticed it there in the room, the smell."

I swallowed, feeling sick. "I don't—" I began, then stopped. It was true what she said. Now it was said, I had noticed it myself. There was a body smell, not strong, nor unpleasant, but perceptible. I think this was the first moment when I began to realize the essential nature of my power and the source of my energies.

I found my own way out. It wasn't very difficult, really. Down the stairs and through three doors. Once I took a wrong turning, opened the wrong door and found myself in a large room lined with racks of guns with a man in a green baize apron standing at a table polishing the metal of one. After all, it was a hunting-lodge. He looked up when he saw me, but before he could do more than look amazed, I had backed out. Then I found the right door and was back with Dolly and Madame Titov.

At once they rushed at me with eager questions. "How did it go? What happened? Did you succeed?"

Disastrously in one way, I could have answered, and I wondered I was not shot for treason.

"He will recover," I said briefly, which was all I wanted to say.

"I thank God," said Madame Titov.

"You may also thank Rose," said Dolly. I was her property, in a sense, and she wanted some acknowledgement of this fact.

"I *do* thank her," answered Madame Titov, in her gentle, modest manner, "I think she knows that I do."

I felt exhausted now, physically and mentally. I didn't want to talk.

But they prodded me as we walked back, Dolly in particular, and because she knew me so well by now she eventually wrung out of me what I didn't want to say.

"Yes, this time he will recover, but in the end he will die, he's against life; I felt it. He won't be here long—doesn't wish it himself."

"Ridiculous talk," began Dolly, running to keep up with me as I strode ahead.

I rounded on her angrily. "Trust me one way, then trust me another," I said; I was so fierce that she stopped in mid-sentence. In all this strange business, everything was closely bound together: if one thing was ridiculous, all was ridiculous, and this she knew.

I saw Madame Titov give us a puzzled look, as if she did not understand the interchange between us. She was a kind woman, but a stupid one. "One must not look ahead in that way," she said nervously. "What happens is God's will. We move from crisis to crisis, getting over each as we may. That is the best we can do."

I walked on: I wanted to get away from this place.

Next day, at breakfast, just before we set off back to Shereshevo, a small packet was delivered to me. The two older ladies watched me open it. Inside was a small oval photograph, set in a gold frame, of the boy and his mother. It was unsigned, something which Dolly remarked on at once.

"Pity she didn't sign it."

"Even as it is, it is a signal honour," said Madame Titov stoutly.

"Oh, do you think so?" I answered coolly. I was turning the framed photograph over in my hands. I didn't say so, but it *was* signed. An initial *A* had been scratched on the back with a pin. The photograph was from the boy. His mother had sent it, but somehow he had made his mark on it. "I shall keep it, at all events. I have given a good deal. I might as well get something back."

"I hope you will stand by ready to help again, if need be," said Madame Titov.

"I may not be in Russia," I pointed out.

"Oh, you must persuade her to stay." She turned to Dolly who smiled and nodded, but very wisely did not attempt to put what she meant to say, if anything, into speech.

"The Tsarina does not like me, I must warn you," I said bluntly. "She used me this time, because the boy was *in extremis*, but another time she may not." I felt as though I had had enough of the Romanovs and their quirks. I do not say

that the Tsarina did not know of the sending of the photograph, because I believe she knew of every breath the boy
drew, and she had almost certainly authorized the picture's
despatch, but she did not know he had scratched his initial
on it. He had good manners, even if she had not.

"What *is* the matter with the Tsarevich?" asked Dolly, as
soon as we were driving away towards the railway-station.
(No Peter to drive us on this journey.)

"I never discovered. Nothing was said."

"They say it's a disease of the blood," said Dolly in a confidential voice. "Inherited."

"Very likely."

Dolly sighed. "Oh, dear, and such a journey ahead of us
now. And with no company to keep us cheerful."

"And we never saw the Tsar," I said.

"No, but he saw us." Dolly giggled. "As we crept to the
house last night I'm almost sure I saw his face at an upstairs
window watching. And he was there when we left. He waited,
smoking those endless cigarettes of his. He saw us come and
he saw us go."

But when we arrived at the station, there was Peter in his
motor car, waiting for us, ready to drive us home, after all.
He sprang out of the car the minute he saw us.

"How did you get here?" demanded his sister.

"But I've been here all the time waiting for you. I drove
straight here after I left you."

"But how did you know we were coming today? And at this
precise time? How could you find out?"

"There is such a thing as a telegram, even in this benighted
country." He was laughing. "And I have my spies."

"You must have." But she was settling herself in the car
and making herself comfortable; I saw she was pleased.

The journey back to Shereshevo was unmemorable. I sat
beside Peter as on the way out, but this time there was little
chatter. We were both thoughtful.

Ariadne was very welcoming when we returned. "Been very boring without you all. I've actually had to do some of the work you left me to keep me busy," was her summing up.

Two or three days after our return Peter took me aside and said, "I've had a letter from Piter. The *on dit* is that the Heir has been gravely ill in Spala and been cured because of a telegram sent to Father Gregory asking for his intercession."

I laughed; so much for my efforts, then. I could see the irony of it.

I don't know whether Dolly had heard the rumour, but in the next few days she continually pressed me for details of my encounter with Alexis Romanov, as if she wanted me to prove that the cure was mine.

"Was anything said about Father Gregory? Was his name mentioned? Did you learn anything about his footing with the family?" she asked curiously.

"No." Half truth, half lie. But I felt a reluctant loyalty to that drawn and ravaged woman, Alexandra Romanov. I did not know then of the wild rumour that circulated in St. Petersburg society about her relationship with Father Gregory, that he had bedded her and the young Grand Duchesses, and that the whole family was totally in his power because of the sexual sway he held over the Empress.

The dangers to me from Father Gregory which Peter had warned me of had not materialized at Spala. No physical threat had faced me. Instead the attack had been more subtle and intangible.

The young Grand Duchess had hysterically yelled at me that I was as bad as he was, that we were of the same flesh, that we were both animals.

Now, instead of thinking of my gift of healing as God-given, I saw it as essentially dirty and grovelling, its source was the desire to couple. One part of me resisted this idea, but another part accepted it.

I found it made me shy with Peter. He noticed it himself.

"You've changed since you went to Spala. A visit to Court has made you proud," he said gravely.

I tried to smile at the joke. "No, I'm not proud. To tell you the truth, I like myself rather less since I went there."

He nodded. "It's a strange household. Hard to get into, but difficult to get out of."

I shook my head. "I wasn't liked. The Tsarina will be quite glad to attribute any cure to the other one."

"That woman." He turned away from me moodily. We were alone on the terrace overlooking the garden. "A destroyer if I ever saw one." He turned round again. "I think she knows in her heart what you did, but as always with her, is hysterically unable to accept the truth. She will summon you again. Madame Titov thinks so. She wrote to Dolly."

"Did she? I didn't know. I am glad to have helped the child. But it is something I would rather not have to do again. I don't like what it makes me."

"You never have."

"No, but while it was a private business, my own secret, more or less, as I thought, I could manage—bear it, I mean. But now it is getting beyond my control. So better to put myself where I can withstand it." I thought of Tabitha Mackenzie, my dearest Tibby with her robust common sense as my salvation. "I shall go home."

"No!" The cry of anguish startled me. "No. Stay. Stay with me."

"Peter, I can't."

"Marry me, I mean."

I shook my head. "I'm no wife for you. Perhaps not for any man. No, I shan't marry. The only man I could have married is gone." Patrick, I thought, we were well matched.

"You silly girl." He sounded amused and indulgent, even. "I won't believe a word of it."

"I'm not as innocent as you think."

Peter gave an amused chuckle. "Whatever you may mean by that, dearest Rose, must remain your own secret. I'm glad you *have* a secret. I have plenty myself." He wagged his finger at me, half-amused, half-admonishing. "You're such an imaginative creature."

"Am I?" That word again. "You mean the voices in St. Petersburg and Mademoiselle Laure?"

He shook his finger sternly. "I forbid you to mention that poor woman's name again. She had death written all over her the moment she stepped into this house."

"Now that is a flight of the imagination. She was a *good* woman. Practical and down to earth."

"And how can you know that?" He was amazed.

"Oh, but I—" I stopped short, not wanting to reveal the diary nor that I had read it. I shrugged. "Just thoughts. My impressions of her."

"You are a little puritan, you know."

I thought for a moment. "Yes, I believe I am."

"You think that what is pleasing and happy is bad, and what is stiff and unyielding and difficult is good."

"And that was Mademoiselle Laure?"

"Well, yes, since you force me to say it. To me, she was unpleasant. Now, that's enough about her. But you and I, Rose—"

"Oh, I can't marry in Russia," I cried.

"I think I could make you do a lot of things you don't believe possible at the moment."

I couldn't tell if he was angry or laughing. Suddenly, just for a second, he reminded me of Patrick.

It was a bad moment to remember Patrick, but I don't think Peter noticed. He went on: "But for the moment I shall content myself with teaching you to drive. You are making progress."

Yes, I made progress. It was a beautiful motor car, and really a lovely object in which to make progress.


The hot days wore on.

"It's getting cooler in the evenings, have you noticed? Autumn is coming," said Dolly. "I think we shall have an early winter."

The party was already breaking up. All the young people who had clustered around Ariadne, at picnics and tea-parties, were packing their bags for Moscow or St. Petersburg. Edward and Peter came and went.

I had come to love rustic Russia with its forests and lakes and long, straight, dusty roads. But it frightened me. It was a haunted landscape.

Even Shereshevo, so warm and homely, was threatened by the countryside which hung around its neck like a halter. In the end the countryside would swallow up Shereshevo. I think Dolly sensed this, and it accounted for the sparseness of the furnishings. She kept no treasures at Shereshevo.

Laure Le Brun was one of the ghosts at Shereshevo. The existence of her diary in my possession guaranteed her presence. I read it again.

Once again I laid it down with the conviction that I could not believe the writer of this sober journal had killed herself in the macabre way I knew she had died.

But if she had not killed herself, then she had been murdered. Murdered in the rich, sheltered Denisov house.

I sat thinking about this, convinced it was true. There was a follow-up to this, because if I had not been "imaginative" about Laure's death, then probably I had not been "imaginative" about other things, like the voice in the speaking-tube.

Tibby had a precept: Test what you can, act when you can.

Very well, I thought. I would act. It would have to be next day, but I would do it.


The mechanics who looked after Peter's car were so used to seeing me drive away in it that they let me take it this time on my own without surprise.

Behind I left a carefully prepared scene. I had left a note for Ariadne declaring a headache, and I had bribed my little maid to keep my bedroom darkened and the door locked.

To all enquiries she was to say that I was "resting." The day before I had taken the precaution of assigning Ariadne several paragraphs of Turgenev's *First Love* to translate into English, and I knew she would gladly leave me undisturbed in case I asked to see her prose, which I knew she had little intention of doing. I should get a few sentences out of her, no more. Ariadne was no worker, and not even the influence of her dear friend Marisia at Vyksa had made an intellectual of her.

Vyksa: I felt a shiver down my spine as I turned the car towards that town. I was surprised how quickly the distance between me and Vyksa was eaten by the rush of the motor car. The village where the boys had thrown a stone at me was behind me before I could count ten. Perhaps I went through it faster than I should have done, because the dust of that village seemed to rise up in a cloud and hang over me until almost the outskirts of Vyksa. I was coughing and rubbing my eyes: I remember wondering what infections that dust carried. I knew from Dolly Denisov that typhoid fever and diphtheria and smallpox appeared intermittently in the towns and villages.

I own I was apprehensive of my ability to steer the big vehicle through the narrow streets of Vyksa and I did, indeed, stop once nervously as a hay-wagon drew out before me from the front of a livery stable near the hotel. Then I was able to drive on, glad that today the great hearse, met with last time, was not parading in the streets. The vegetable and fruit market was there as before. Today's main crop for sale seemed to be big purple cabbages. One of the stall-keepers picked a cabbage from his stall and rolled it towards my wheels with a shout. I swerved to avoid it and pressed on.

My heart was beating fast by the time I got to the gate of the copper-mine. My old friend the gate-keeper was on duty; he looked surprised when he saw me.

"So you're in the motor car this time?"

"Yes." I stopped and put on the brake. "No horse for you to look after today."

"Couldn't look after that object if I tried." He patted the gleaming metal flank as if it were a horse. "So ladies drive motor cars now, do they?"

"Well, I do." I got out. "Is the eldest Miss Lazarev at home?"

"All of them are, as far as I know. Where else should they be?"

"May I go through to see her?"

He scratched his head. "You went before, so I suppose you can this time. But I've had no instructions. I like to have my instructions."

"Surely they have unexpected visitors sometimes?"

"No, never. Why should they? Who comes here? Only those that can't help themselves."

"I've come."

"Then you can't help yourself, I say. Go on, in with you, then. She's there. I heard her shouting at her father this morning. Yes, and he was shouting back as well. You'd never think it when he goes past, all stiff in his uniform, that he could shout, but he can. Well, if it wasn't him, I don't know who it was," and he gave an asthmatic, wheezing laugh. "I don't know who else she'd shout at."

I walked forward towards the Lazarev house. The door stood open, but there was no sound of shouting, not even a voice. I stood on the threshold and listened.

I didn't really want to see Marisia, or her father, but I wanted to see the younger girls and ask them about their music-master.

The house seemed deserted. I could see through an open door into the dining-room where we had all lunched that day, but it was empty, with the big wooden table, made of some pale yellow wood, shining and bare.

But distantly I could hear the sound of a flute and a piano. The noise seemed to be coming from outside the house. I turned round.

Behind were the huts remembered from my other visit, one of which seemed to be a clerk's office, but it was from the open door of the other one that the sound of music and, as I walked closer, the sound of dancing feet also were coming.

My own feet dragged; now I was so close I didn't want to look. I had been quite mad to come.

The Lazarev girls, with the exception of Marisia who was not present, were solemnly going through the steps of a rustic waltz. The main burden of the tune was being carried by the piano, but a second part was being picked out by the flute whose gay notes cheered up the whole scene. Piano player and flautist were near the door. Both men had their backs to me.

The little girls were moving with leaden feet, nothing would make dancers of them, and the flute player seemed to be urging them to lightness with one uplifted hand.

He half turned as I came to the door, and I saw his face. I drew in a sharp breath. He saw me at that moment, and our eyes met.

"Patrick!" I said.

# Chapter Seven

He was dressed in dark blue stuff trousers such as a peasant might wear, together with a soft white shirt open at the neck. He was bronzed and thinner than before, his expression tauter somehow. Nothing could have looked less like the neat Army officer I had known. But he had not lost the deep attraction he had for me; rather it seemed sharper now. I caught my breath.

"Patrick Graham, by all that's holy. Or unholy."

"You might well say that," he said soberly. He motioned to me to come outside, and we stood in that dusty courtyard, leaving the little girls to dance inside.

"What are you doing here?"

"I'm the dancing-master," he answered, not without a glint of self-mockery in his eyes. "And I assure you, I earn my keep; the Misses Lazarev are hard taskmasters."

"But that's not answering my question."

"I've just taught them how to waltz. I was going to move on to the cake-walk next. We must bring them up to date a bit, they are miles behind the times here."

"You taught me the cake-walk once," I said, not without bitterness.

"And you were a good pupil."

"In more ways than one," I snapped. And then I was ashamed, for after all, I had been as much a leader as led.

"Oh, Rose, Rose." It was almost a groan.

"I knew you were here. I knew when I heard the tune of the Burns song. You taught it to them?" He nodded. "I came back on that occasion, convinced I should find you here, but it was another man playing the paino."

"The music-master, a poor little chap, taken in by Miss Lazarev as an act of charity. Of course, she gets the work out of him. He's always hoping to earn his fare back to Hungary, but I doubt he will. He drinks, you see, and in all his years in this country has never learnt Russian."

I had to touch Patrick and I took his hand. "And it really is you and I am not imagining it? I can hardly believe it all, even now I see you. It's so incredible we should meet here."

His hand gripped mine back. "I knew you were here," he came out with. "I was even close to seeing you."

"What? Here? In Vyksa?"

"No, not Vyksa. I'll tell you sometime." He stopped, drawing closer to me.

"You knew I was here? And yet you never tried to see me?" I turned on him.

"Yes, it needs some explaining," he said slowly. I tried to drag my hand away, but he held on to it.

"I heard that you had been in trouble in India and had fled."

He hesitated. "That story isn't quite true. Not altogether."

"I thought it didn't sound exactly like you. But then perhaps I don't really know you. You have turned out to be different from what I might have expected, Patrick."

"Our engagement was at an end, Rose," he reminded me. (As if I needed it; broken by him.) "No tie bound us together."

"Didn't it?" I said fiercely.

Patrick looked at me gravely: he had always had beautiful eyes, and they looked brighter and clearer than ever against his tanned skin.

"Come with me," he said, and drew me by the wrist round the corner of the building. Here we were protected on three sides by walls and could not be seen.

"Let go of my hand," I said in a whisper.

"Don't pull away, Rose, please don't. You aren't really angry anyway. I am so glad to see you, Rose. You don't know."

"I shall, if you explain," I said as clearly as I could. Not so very clearly because suddenly we were kissing each other. I felt his lips pressed hard against mine, and my own responding. Eventually I pulled myself away.

"Patrick, this isn't what I want."

"Isn't it? Why did you come looking for me, then?"

"I wanted to find out, to know . . . I was puzzled. Curious. I still am. Much as I love you, Patrick, and I think I still do, I want to *know*."

"I'm not your property, Rose."

"No, indeed."

"Temper, Rose. You've always had a temper. But I *will* tell you."

We were interrupted by the sound of laughter and of running feet. The Lazarev girls had danced out of their hut, hand in hand, and were skipping around in the dusty courtyard.

"I don't want them to see me," I said hastily. "Especially now, like this." I knew I looked untidy, with my cheeks flushed, my lips bruised and my hair pulled about my face.

"No." He stepped in front of me, hiding me. The young girls danced off to the other side of the yard. "No, it's better if they don't see you. They've gone off now, and I'll follow and get them into the house. Can you come back tomorrow?"

"Well, I don't know." I hesitated; it would mean getting the motor car again. "Yes, I suppose I could."

"They'll be off tomorrow to Vyksa. Out all day. The eldest sister is taking them. Will you come?"

"Yes," I said, "I'll come."

He bent and kissed me again, quickly and gently. "Disappear when I've gone. Good-bye Rose."

"Patrick—"

"What is it, Rose?" He turned back.

"Patrick, I *hate* mysteries. Russia seems all mystery."

"Only till tomorrow, Rose," and then he was gone towards the house in the wake of the giggling girls.

The music-master came to the door of the hut and stared out with a puzzled frown. Certainly he saw me, but as he spoke no word of English or Russian, I suppose it did not matter.

I couldn't get back to Vyksa the next day. When I arrived at Shereshevo after an uneventful drive home, I slipped up to my room. Very soon I was joined by Ariadne.

"I thought your headache was so bad you couldn't be disturbed," she said with reproach. "And now I find you've been out for a drive in Peter's motor car."

"When I began to recover I thought the fresh air and movement would help me," I lied.

"It must have been a nice long drive," observed Ariadne, but she didn't ask any questions and I wondered where she thought I'd been. Never to Vyksa, I supposed. She went on: "I wish I could drive Peter's car. I think I'll ask him to teach me."

"Yes, do." I was sure Dolly would never allow it. There was a sort of natural rivalry between Dolly and her daughter, which increased daily with Ariadne's ever growing maturity. Dolly would never willingly give up even that little part of her pre-eminence that her driving and Ariadne's not driving gave her, when every day Ariadne encroached on her.

"Tomorrow we are all going for a last picnic by the river with the young Carlows. They are staying with their cousins. The Olsul'evs, rather far away from here; you haven't met them, have you?" I shook my head. "They will have to stay the night, I expect, as it's such a long way to come. We shall all be exhausted, my mother says, as the Carlows are so energetic, laughing and joking all the time. But I expect you'll like them."

"Oh, I will." I could see I would never get away.

"It doesn't matter, anyway. The Carlows are only a smoke-screen." Ariadne smiled faintly.

"What do you mean?"

"My mother is bored with the country. Surely you've noticed? Now you've done that little trip of yours to Spala, she hankers after St. Petersburg. She will find the Carlows very exhausting. You and I will be left to amuse them all, they'll do something disastrous, I expect, they usually do, like falling in the river or setting fire to a peasant's hay, and there will be a quarrel. Then the next day she will announce that we must return to St. Petersburg."

So I knew that if I wanted to get back to Vyksa I wouldn't have much time. Why didn't I ask permission openly and just go? I don't know. It was my secret.

We all had our secret worlds at Shereshevo; I realize it now.

The next day turned out more or less as Ariadne had predicted. The young Carlows, three massive brothers, were charming, but as destructive in their exuberance as she had guessed. This time they broke a good deal of china in horse-play, and sank the boat in which we were drifting on the river. The water was very shallow here, so we were in no danger, but we all got very wet as we struggled through the reeds and rushes to the river's edge. Thus Dolly had a good excuse to retire to bed and be seen no more.

"Louts," she said, as she trudged up the stairs with water dripping from her pleated silk skirt. "Barbarians."

Next day I had to wait for the Carlows to depart before finding my own opportunity. This came when Ariadne started to sneeze.

"Bed for you, young lady," I advised. "Like your mother, you are worn out after yesterday, and in addition you've probably got a cold."

"I do feel cold," she admitted. "Hot and cold, all at once."

"Go to bed," I said. "Sleep and I'll come and see you later."

She was sufficiently heavy-eyed and headachey not to argue, but took herself off, still sneezing.

This time it proved less easy to get Peter's motor car. Not

that the servants in charge refused me; Russian servants did not behave in that way. But instead they produced a string of excuses, offering a series of reasons why it would be inadvisable for the motor car to be used. It looked like rain, they said, it was unwise to motor in the rain, everyone knew that, the wheels of the motor car would be stuck in the mud. When I rejected the idea of rain from the deep blue sky, I was told the petrol tank needed replenishing. But I knew that Madame Denisov kept a reservoir of the stuff, and a pump, for her own use. So then there was some nonsense about the tyres.

From all of which I deduced that they had known all along I had no real permission to drive around in that valuable and extravagant bit of mechanism. But I was determined, and desperate by now.

The road to Vyksa behaved in an extraordinary way. Parts of it, the first few versts, seemed to shoot by, and then as I approached the town, the road seemed to lengthen ominously, and then on the other side, as I passed along the desolate stretch of road that led to the mine and prison, the distance shortened again and I was rushing precipitously onwards. I have noticed this before about time: it has no consistency.

Then I was at the gatehouse, and my old friend was looking at me with raised eyebrows. "What, you again?"

"I wonder how sailors manage about time," I said. "Because at sea that's really all you have."

"Miss, you're talking nonsense. There's no sea within a thousand versts of Vyksa."

Not quite true, for the Baltic was nearer. I jumped out of the car. "I've come to visit the Lazarevs. Stand by my car to see me off," and I began to walk, almost run, towards the house.

"If you think I'm going to break my arm winding that thing," he called. In order to start the motor you had to wind up a great handle, "cranking" it was called, and last time he had been very good about it. "They're going away," he bellowed after me.

So the Lazarev family group was about to break up? Perhaps Marisia had achieved her ambition of attending the university.

I had hoped to be able to avoid Marisia this time, as I had done before. Fond hope, for there she was, standing in the hall of the Lazarev house, with her arms full of books as if she was about to pack them.

"Miss Gowrie, you here?" she said with surprise. "How did you come? Is Ariadne with you?"

"No, I came on my own," I said, not answering how I came. "I want to see your dancing-master. I was here the other day and discovered he is an old friend." It sounded lame enough, and yet it was true.

"Yes, my sisters told me they caught a glimpse of you, but I could hardly believe them."

"I was here," I admitted. "I came to see him, and now I would like to see him again. Where is he?"

Marisia put her books down on a table. "But he's gone. Left. He has left us."

A tight, sick feeling gripped the pit of my stomach. I knew then how much I had depended on seeing Patrick. "I should have come yesterday," I cried.

Marisia stared at me through her intimidating spectacles. "Even if you had come yesterday you would hardly have seen him, I am afraid. He left on the midnight train of the evening before."

It took a little while for the meaning to sink in, but I did comprehend then that Patrick had never intended to meet me again. Even if the visit of the Carlow boys had not intervened, I would never have seen Patrick. He had packed and departed the very day of my visit. He had intended never to see me again.

"He went in a great hurry," she added. "I have no address."

"Where does the midnight train go to?" I asked, despairing.

Marisia threw out her hands. "Everywhere and nowhere. Eventually to St. Petersburg, but it stops everywhere first."

I was filled with a bitter hurt. For the second time Patrick had contrived to humiliate and pain me. I hated him at that moment.

Marisia took pity on me. "We are just about to lunch, won't you join us? Just a picnic: we ourselves leave tomorrow."

"Yes, I heard you were going."

"The gate-man, I suppose?" I nodded dumbly. Patrick was gone again. What else mattered? "Yes, my father has given me permission to study at the university at St. Petersburg," she said with satisfaction. "That is, the money for me to do so has been found. So the young ones are going to live with our aunt, and I am off."

I clutched at an idea. "And I suppose that is why your dancing-master decided to leave?"

She squashed that with a swift, "Oh, no, when he left he had no idea; I only knew myself yesterday. No, it was entirely on his own account."

I had not thought that any more bitterness, any more pain, could spring from my relationship with Patrick Graham. I found now that it could. I did not dislike Marisia Lazarev, but there was something wounding in her calm self-certainty as she pressed down into me the hard fact that I had been as thoroughly let down by Patrick the second time as the first. He was calculating and selfish and hard. I hated him.

I retained enough self-control to refuse with politeness Marisia's pressing invitation to lunch, but I remember little of my drive back to Shereshevo. I do recall, however, the look of relief on the part of the servants when I handed back to them their precious charge. Unscratched, too, so I suppose I had driven well.

"Rose, Rose, there you are," screeched Dolly at me, as I walked into the house. "Where have you been? But never mind now."

I had come back into the middle of a crisis. Ariadne was ill. Her temperature had risen very high and she was complaining of a sore throat. When the doctor came, he diagnosed her illness as scarlatina. She was never very ill, never in any sort of danger, but she was uncomfortable and she made all those around her thoroughly uncomfortable, too.

For days we were all incarcerated in Shereshevo. No one came near us for fear of getting the infection. One would have thought it was the plague instead of a relatively mild disease of childhood. Of course, these are always worse when contracted in adolescence, and I suppose Ariadne suffered; she was certainly cross enough.

"I got it from the dust that day we went to Vyksa," she complained to me.

"I expect you did."

"So I've been punished. I wonder you didn't get it, too!"

"Somehow I am protected," I said, thinking to myself that if you are miserable enough, even the germs will find you of no interest.

"And you haven't managed to ease any ache or pain of mine," went on Ariadne, still full of her own woes.

"But I haven't really tried," I said truthfully. "And nor have you really wished it."

"No, true. Clever of you to know. I'm superstitious about things like that. I feel as though I should suffer all the more some time, if I got off anything now." Ariadne, like most of the Russians I had met, had a sense that she must suffer. "Still, we've had a nice, quiet time of it. I've got very fond of you, Rose."

"Thank you."

"Almost as fond as I am of Marisia." I saw she was serious, and in the mood for confidences. "I _do_ love her. More than my mother approves of."

"And what do you want me to answer to that?"

"Ah, never mind." She was turning away again. I had disappointed her. "Of course, you'd have to take Mother's side."

"And what about Edward Lacey?"

"Oh, that's different. Mind you, I like him."

"You flirt with him shockingly."

"Do I?" She smiled. "Do I really? Well, I mean to. And much good may it do him. But you needn't worry about Edward Lacey." She looked at me with sympathy. "You're awfully miserable, aren't you?"

"Yes," I said, gritting my teeth.

"I'm often miserable myself, so I could tell. You didn't guess that, did you?" Silently I shook my head. "One day I'll tell you all about how to be lightly, gaily miserable. You're just grimly miserable, and that won't do at all." There was a touch of seriousness, even hardness in the young voice that kept me silent.

And yet never in the world had I known a more spoilt and cherished young beauty than Ariadne Denisov.

When Ariadne was better, everything was packed up and we travelled back to St. Petersburg. The interlude at Shereshevo was over. We had seen nothing of Peter Alexandrov or Edward Lacey during Ariadne's illness. Messages, of course, but no personal appearances. The cowards, I thought. During all this time, no one mentioned my disappearance on the day of Ariadne's falling sick, so I never had to confess where I had been.

I was going back to St. Petersburg where Laure Le Brun had died, and if I had not been imaginative about sensing the presence of Patrick, then quite possibly I had not been imaginative about Laure's death. She had not killed herself; she had been killed.

Dolly kept awake on the journey to St. Petersburg, more or less. Eventually she explained her insomnia. She waited till Ariadne, still convalescent, was dozing, before she said quietly, "I am really quite worried."

I looked up in enquiry.

"I heard yesterday that Peter had been detained by the Third Bureau and then questioned."

"Arrested, you mean?" I said with horror.

"No, as I say: detained and questioned. They had to let him go, of course. It's all nonsense, but Aunt Irene's friends are so extremely conservative and reactionary (I can say as much to you) and they hold meetings in her room. She thinks we don't know, but naturally we do. And it's one of these 'visitors'" (she almost snapped the word out in her anger), "who has become suspicious of Peter." She sighed. "He's always been suspected of having 'unsuitable' friends."

"I'm glad they let him go."

"Yes." Dolly took up a fold of her skirt and pleated it between her fingers. She seemed reluctant to meet my eyes. "I think it only fair to say it may really have been directed at you."

"What? What can you mean?"

"They have underhand, dirty ways of applying pressure, and for what you have done for the Heir, you may have earned enemies."

"Father Gregory, you mean? Peter warned me against him. But surely the Third Bureau hate him also?"

Warningly, she said, "Rose, in this terrible world no one can be sure who is honest and who has a double face. Yes, many hate Father Gregory, but some of those who hate him may have transferred some of that hate to *you*. Not all of those who wish the Heir to go on living wish him to do so because of help from a girl like you. Your influence could be construed as a threat. And even in the Court itself the boy has enemies who would rather see him dead."

"I am horrified. It sounds so terrible."

The train rumbled on for a few minutes; the carriage was hot and airless, full of stale luxury. Then Dolly said, half to me, but also to herself, "But then Russia is a terrible country. And the revolution, if it ever comes, will be a terrible revolution."

It was a memorable comment to come from the lips of that spoiled, idle and luxurious woman.

# Chapter Eight

Events sometimes creep, sometimes stumble and sometimes march boldly forward. For me, from now on, they galloped.

Dolly was a shrewd observer of the political scene, and she was quite right to greet the news of the detention of her brother with alarm (for, after all, *anything* could happen in Russia) and at the same time, with cool scepticism (for he *was* an aristocrat with good connections at Court). Peter himself was frankly disdainful.

"Oh, yes, they came and requested me politely to go with them. I almost refused, but thought better of it. In the end they were obliged to apologize and let me go. Such rubbish."

"I blame Aunt Irene," said his sister vindictively.

"Yes, it was one of her friends, no doubt, who took exception to me. Probably I didn't bow to him as humbly as he expected of me when we last met. They're a thin-skinned lot."

"I shall speak to her."

"No, don't. Leave the old lady in peace."

"Peace! Have you seen her since her revival?"

"Yes, I saw her flashing past me in her carriage, accompanied by a horseman," said Peter dryly. "And very antique and 1850ish it looked, which I suppose was her heyday."

"Her mind is in the present strongly enough, as I can affirm." Dolly clapped her hands together to emphasize her point. "The minute I stepped into the house I was summoned to her presence and put through my paces about Shereshevo, and what went on there and what we did. I believe I managed to keep *some* things to myself," and her glance at me told me what she meant. My activities at Spala were to be kept quiet. "Of course, she *knows,* she has her spies, but I mean to hold my tongue."

We were sitting at a late breakfast the day after our return to the house, which looked onto Moyka Street. Everyone was there, Ariadne, Peter and Edward Lacey, with Dolly sitting by the bubbling tea-urn and with me managing the coffee-pot. The curiously cozy, intimate atmosphere which seemed to spring up so easily in Russia had made us all linger around the table long after we had finished eating and drinking.

"There is certainly gossip in St. Petersburg about Spala," admitted Peter. "But it remains a bit vague and general; the common herd know nothing specific."

"I expect the tales are the wilder because of it," said Dolly.

Peter nodded. "They are. But within a small, tight circle the truth is known. Or what passes for the truth," he added. "The Tsarina clings to the belief that the real cure was from Father Gregory. Do you mind, Rose?" He turned to me suddenly.

"It may be true. I claim nothing." I moved uneasily. "Madame Denisov thinks that it is really because of me that you were questioned." It seemed better to bring it out and ask him directly. "Do you believe that?"

"No, no, I don't." He gave a startled look at Dolly, who was cross that I had spoken and began to mutter something about having "suggested it in confidence." "No, it was I who was being attacked, no doubt about it. If there was going to be pressure on you, it would come directly, I'm sure. And you will have enemies at the centre of power. But friends, too," and he gave me a sweet smile.

"I'm glad you think it was nothing to do with me. Because if it had been, I would have gone home at once," I said.

"No," said Peter quickly. "Never. We wouldn't have let you go."

"You can't go yet, Rose," said Ariadne more reasonably. "The ice will be closing in soon and no ships can get through then."

"There is the railway," I pointed out.

"But you aren't going, my dear girl," said Madame Denisov. "We want you here, and we hope you want us. I am sorry I alarmed you by what I said. It is sometimes hard to know when to speak and when not. I thought that I *must* warn you a little."

"This is no time to instruct a visitor in the intricacies of Russian politics," said Peter. Hard to tell if he was more amused than cross with his sister, I thought. She looked flustered.

"Well, an unwary step, you know," she began.

"Oh, we all of us make unwary steps," interrupted Peter.

"A British passport is a great protection," put in Edward Lacey.

"In general," said Dolly temperately.

"Yes, there speaks the innocent Englishman," said Peter with a laugh.

"What do you mean by that?"

"If Rose here was to disappear, or if you were, do you suppose a British passport would be any protection then? Or that the British Ambassador could do anything?"

"I think I must go home at once," I said in considerable alarm.

"I am staying for the winter festivities," said Edward, with calm, "and I advise you to do the same."

"The winter festivities?"

"He means the New Year Ball and the Tercentenary celebrations of the Romanovs that are to follow." This came from Dolly.

"And I think I see what you are getting at, Peter Alexandrov," said Edward to Peter as if Dolly had not spoken. "Powerful friends are more effective than police forces."

"In all countries, but in Russia more than most. Russia is a secret country." Peter nodded.

"But exactly what did they suspect you of when they questioned you?" I asked.

"Oh, somewhere, somehow I have brushed against a man, or a woman, who is active in revolutionary politics, and that would be enough. Perhaps I even dined with such a one, or lent him a book or walked in the park with him. A little would be enough. Anyway, my name got onto a list in the Third Bureau's offices. It will stay there now." He sounded quite cheerful. "I dare say it is on more than one list and has been for a long time. But they are a slow-moving, unmethodical lot."

I found his thoroughly Russian way of laughing at what he took seriously both irritating and frightening.

When the party broke up, with Edward and Ariadne planning to go riding together, Edward took the opportunity of all the bustle about us to say quietly:

"If you truly want to go home, I can arrange it for you. My sister's English nanny is returning; you two could travel together."

"No, I mean to stay." My eyes wandered towards where Peter and Dolly stood talking in the window embrasure. I was beginning to realize what Peter stood for now in my life: gentleness, reason, affection, in contrast with the turmoil induced by Patrick. "I think I have a job still to do in Russia."

"Ah." Edward gave me a keen look. "Not Ariadne." It wasn't a question, but still I answered it.

"Ariadne still, but not only Ariadne. I am beginning to see that there is something for me to do in this family."

"You mean Peter? Yes, I've seen how he looks at you."

"Is it wrong?" I said defiantly.

"He's very rich."

"It's not ambition," I said.

"No, of course not, it's very natural. Between you two, I mean. Why shouldn't you love a man like Peter Alexandrov? You do, don't you?"

I hesitated. "I don't quite know. Yet."

"Marriage will settle it," he said bluntly.

"Marriage?"

"Oh, yes, he means marriage. He's asked you already, hasn't he?"

"Yes," I admitted.

"He sounded me out first. Nicely, of course. I suppose he thought I might know more of your mind than he did. I don't, however."

"But perhaps I might bring trouble to him." Still I hesitated. "I think I am trouble."

"Because of the Spala caper, and what lies behind it?" I looked up in surprise and he nodded. "Yes, I know all the background. Plenty of people do. You want to watch your step there."

"I know," I said humbly. "That's what I meant by trouble."

Abruptly he said, "You shall go home if you want."

It would be nice to see Grizel married, I thought briefly, but I said, "No, I shall stay. I feel as though I have to."

"*Have* to?" he repeated.

But at this moment Ariadne rushed into the room, wearing her riding habit and calling on us both to hurry up. "Because you must come, too, Rose."

I looked towards Dolly Denisov with enquiry; she gave a tiny shake of refusal. I was not to go. The two of them were to be left alone. Perhaps the courtship was not going as fast as she hoped. Indeed, I had noticed myself that although Ariadne frisked around and Edward was playful back, they never got any further.

"Princess Irene wants to see you," announced Dolly abruptly when they had ridden off. "I'd rather she didn't, but there it is, she's asked and she'd better have her way."

"I wonder what she wants?"

"I think she wants to say thank you." Dolly gave a little sceptical shake of her head in disapproval of her antique relative.

"I'll go and find out." And I went to my room to collect the jewelled Fabergé ball containing the portrait. In the drawer it rested on Laure Le Brun's diary which I had brought with me from Shereshevo. All the drawers and cupboards of that house had possessed a spicy, scented smell all their own, and I realized now that that smell had come back with the book and the ball. I had brought a little of Shereshevo to St. Petersburg.

And with the smell I realized that Shereshevo was a happy, normal house and this mansion in St. Petersburg was not. It frightened me, and now I was invited to go up the red staircase again. In my mind I made it a proper name and gave it capital letters: The Red Staircase.

I didn't want to go up The Red Staircase, and so I dallied until my black Ivan tapped on the door to remind me.

Almost without words, and certainly without effort, he managed to let me know that it had been a long, dull summer, without incident, except for those connected with The Red Staircase, which had managed to exercise its usual baleful influence. He crossed himself and shook his head before he led me to the bottom of the stairs, making it clear that he was not coming up them and that I could ascend alone. "*Now* she walks about," he said, providing himself with the precaution of an extra crossing of the breast.

But the Princess was sitting down when I went into her bedroom. A pretty little sofa had been drawn up to face the window and she was sitting there in the sunshine with the diamonds at her throat and ears glittering. I thought that she wore her jewellery with more conviction than any woman I had ever seen. She had always worn rings and bracelets in profusion, but they had been antique of setting and in need of cleaning. Now diamonds glittered freshly and rubies and emeralds glowed.

"You've had your jewellery reset," I said spontaneously.

She stood up and held out both hands, for my admiration, not for me to hold. "A mark of my new life, is it not?" She seated herself again and patted the cushion beside her for me to join her. "And I owe it to you. A miracle, nothing less."

"I don't know if I did anything. It's hard to tell. Anyway, I don't want to claim the credit. Let it be your own miracle." I produced the box containing the Fabergé ball. "Here is your portrait back. I shan't need it now."

"But you used it?" she asked eagerly.

"I looked at it occasionally."

"Ah." She leaned back and drew in a satisfied breath. "I knew it. That has always been a happy, lucky portrait." She opened the box and drew out the ball and touched the spring. Then with a blissful expression, she gazed on her youthful face. "I will tell you a secret: for years I have not been able to look at this picture with satisfaction. The pain of seeing what I had been and knowing what I had become was too great. Such comparisons are truly odious. But *now*," and she raised bright eyes to me, "now I can study it with pleasure again. My looks are coming back. Soon I shall look like that again. Don't you see it coming on? It's happening already. Can't you see it?"

What could I say? How could I tell the harsh truth to that eager, aged face? "You *do* look much better. But nothing returns quite the same, does it?" I urged gently.

"Naturally, I don't believe I shall go back to what I was as a girl, or a young married woman. I'm not a fool. But I believe I shall recover the looks I had when I was in my prime," she said complacently. "They depended on my bones, I had beautiful bones, it was always said. Nothing can touch beauty from the bone, you know. Indeed, it was always there, and now that my health and spirits have come back, my looks have come back, too."

"All right," I agreed, laughing. Impossible not to respond to this dogged optimist.

"And no pain," she continued. "No more pain. For that I

thank you, my dear." And now she did take hold of my hands, gripping them tightly so that I could feel her thin old ones, like bits of wood. "I'm grateful."

Gently I disengaged myself. I hoped the remission from pain lasted, but at her age it seemed unlikely, and I knew well enough that there could be no permanent cure. It was not in my power, or perhaps anyone's to offer her that, but possibly I had eased her pain. Pain, I could, it seemed, remove. Sometimes I wondered what I did with it, whether I took it into myself and turned it into a part of me, or whether I burned it up. "I'm glad," I said to her. "I'm glad you have relief." It could hardly be more than temporary. Perhaps she was enjoying one last burst of radiant life before dying. Perhaps this was what I achieved for those I helped?

As if she read my thoughts she said, "But I shall live for ever."

"You know that's not possible."

"For a very long while yet, then." And she emphasized her words with a decided little clap of her hands. She looked at me mischievously, no mean feat in itself at her age, but she achieved it. "And after all, if a long while is long enough, it counts as for ever."

"What would you call a long while?" I asked.

"Ten years," she said in a practical fashion. "Ten years will do me."

Ten years, ten months, ten weeks, I thought.

"Oh, at your age ten years is nothing, of course, but to me at mine it is everything," she said.

"Ten years is a long time, but I can see beyond it," I admitted.

"And I cannot. That is the difference between us. There is my for ever."

In spite of everything, I had come to like her. At times she seemed half crazy, and it was then she believed she could live for ever, really for ever. This was one of her saner passages.

"And what about you?" she demanded. "While I have been flourishing, you have been declining. When I first saw you, I thought: there is a girl who will marry well. Now . . . I am not so sure."

"You should not have been sure then," I said bitterly.

"You mean your first little misadventure? Oh, but such things mean nothing. With the best will in the world such things go off sometimes. Especially where there is no great fortune involved." She was a worldly old thing, but wrong, mine had been no light mishap easily got over.

"I think it marked me for life." I said. "But not him."

"Ah, then you have seen him again?" She focussed on me with passionate interest.

I was startled into an admission. "How do you know?"

"There are some things one woman can recognize in another. You are right, you are marked, and I see the signs that mark you." Her eyes studied me keenly. Matters of love were her absorbing interest. "So, you've met your lover? And in Russia, too. And provincial Russia at that." She was amused. "What a place to meet. Has he followed you, then?"

I shook my head. "No, certainly not. He didn't want to see me. And when I forced a meeting he ran away."

"So it was a lucky chance?" Her tone was thoughtful.

"Chance," I said, "even if not lucky."

"How unlikely that seems when you think of it," she said. "Are lovers' meetings ever by chance? I think not. Where did you meet?"

"In a town called Vyksa."

"That charnel house?" Her eyebrows shot upwards. "Now certainly I do not believe in chance. What were you doing there and what was he doing there?"

"I was visiting, visiting the Lazarev family," I said, considering that she probably knew all about Marisia. She nodded, confirming this·thought. "And he was working there as a dancing-master."

"An improbable occupation."

"Oh, he does dance well. And I suppose he must earn money to live."

"But why live in Vyksa? Very few do," and she gave a dry little chuckle. "Or not for long. More die there, than live."

I was silent.

"Vyksa, Vyksa," she mused. "Why Vyksa?"

"It's a mystery, then," I said with some tartness.

"Marisia must be the clue. She is a strange girl. Not unattractive, though, if you like that type."

"You have seen her, then?"

"I took the trouble to visit Ariadne at the Smolny. She was there, close to Ariadne." She shook her head. "Too close, in my opinion. Yes, you must question Marisia."

"I don't think I'd dare," I said with truth. "Anyway, I don't know where to find her—she, too, has left Vyksa."

Princess Irene raised her eyebrows. "Another exodus!"

"No, no, not with *her*. They didn't go together." I understood quite well what she meant. "And he is not in love with her. There is nothing like that between them, at all."

I started to tell her why Patrick was not, could not be, in love with Marisia. Once started, I found myself telling her everything from the beginning of our love-story in Scotland and the breaking of our engagement to my sensing of the presence of Patrick and my increasing conviction that he was near, culminating in our meeting at Vyksa. I was in tears as I finished.

"It was the song, the setting of Burns's poem, that did it," I said to her. "It meant Patrick's presence. I knew it. And he was there. I was right. Every sense I had told me, and it was true."

I was kneeling by her side, pouring out my story.

"We, too, had our piece of music, my special lover and I," said the old lady, stroking my hair gently. "So long ago, so long ago. And so you sensed his presence? How right. It was the same with me. I could always tell if *he* was near."

"Yes, I sensed it strongly in the days before we met. Even in a place where he could never have been." I was thinking of the village shop at Shereshevo where I had suddenly thought of Patrick.

"Oh, I dare say he had been there," said Princess Irene dreamily. "I remember once thinking of my Alexei at a railway station—and he *had* been there, but hours before. He said afterwards that it was nothing but the smell of his cigar smoke hanging in the air, but I know better. Love has its own sensibilities." For a moment she was lost in a happy dream of her own past, then she recalled my position. "Poor child, poor child, I pity you from the bottom of my heart."

She stroked my head with her tiny, clawlike hand. "Poor child, poor child, how sad it is to be scorned."

"I can't believe it ever happened to you," I said, remembering the arrogant self-assurance of the young beauty in the portrait.

"Oh, yes, it did—once. I fell in love with a poet, and I wrote him a letter. Ah, such a letter, I sat up all night composing it. I offered him myself. Everything for him. Anything. I was just sixteen. He wrote back refusing, saying he had one love, an actress in Moscow, and did not wish for any other. He thanked me, I remember."

"I'm sure he was a bad poet."

"He was, rather. He died shortly afterwards."

Abruptly, I said, "Did you know that your nephew Peter had been questioned by the police?"

"My great-nephew," she corrected. "He is no poet. Yes, I knew of the questioning. It is entirely his own fault. He is very clever, but not wise."

Worldly wisdom, she meant, but was that enough? Did not Peter have something better? "Very often he says things which illuminate a scene," I ventured. "He makes me understand."

"Dangerous. An illusion," she said roundly. "Don't trust him when he seems most lucid. *I* don't. But harm him, no. He has nothing to fear from me or my friends. It is true that we meet here, a group of us, united by our love of Russia. We look back to the *old* Russia, before these weak-kneed, liberal times came upon us, with this pusilanimous government. A strong Tsar is needed, such as Peter the Great, even. *That* is what Russia needs, strength from the top, not petticoat government such as we see now."

"I see." And I felt that there was truth in what she said. Of course I knew that by "petticoat government" she was getting in a dig at the influence of the Tsarina.

"So a group of like-minded spirits have joined together to talk things over, and see how we can provide schemes that might help our country. Our enemies say that we do little but talk, and that we are so old-fashioned we have never looked further than Tsar Peter. They call us the Peter Ring. And it's not kindly meant."

"I have heard the name," I admitted.

"Yes, we have that nickname," she agreed, a little sulky that I had heard it. "But it is not in use among ourselves, I can tell you; we are simply patriots. But I can assure you that no harm could come to my great-nephew unless he means harm to Russia."

A fairly chilling reassurance, I thought.

"Don't make a hero of my great-nephew Peter," she said sharply. "There are no heroes in our family, none. We do not breed them. The men in particular are monuments of selfishness."

"I don't believe it of Peter." I was stung into his defence, remembering his gentle thoughtfulness. "He has asked me to be his wife."

"Yes, I know." And, seeing my look of surprise, "I told you I have my spies." Her voice was amused.

"I can hardly expect you to approve."

She shrugged. "I have no hopes for him at all." The cold dismissiveness was wounding. "Socially, he is hopeless. I regard him as dangerous."

"Nevertheless, I suppose you want someone better as his wife than a poor girl with an awkward gift."

"So you mean to have him?" Her voice was gentle. "My dear girl, take him if you want. And come to me for help, if you want it. You think I would be angry? Not at all. It would tie you and your gift of healing more closely to me." Gently she added, "But your gift is one that may not prosper in the marriage-bed. Remember I say that."

"I hate my gift. I'm sure you know I hate it, you are much

too clever not to guess how it frightens me. I feel ashamed. Aren't you woman enough to understand how I feel?" I shouted. "If marriage will kill it, let me be married, then."

She stared. "Hoity-toity, loud-mouthed miss." There was a pink circle of colour on her cheek. Probably no one had shouted at her for years. She thought about it for a while, then said, "Yes, I do understand, although I think you are a silly, emotional girl. So take my great-nephew and much good may it do you."

We were both hurt, both angry.

When I saw this, I was ashamed of my outburst. Humbly I said, "I will always help you when I can."

She didn't answer but stared back coldly. Presently, she picked up a little silver handbell and rang it. Her old maid appeared, baleful as ever. "I'm fatigued. Show Miss Gowrie to the door."

"Strong, strong, she is strong," I heard her whisper to herself as I went towards the door. "She is stronger than I thought." Then she raised her voice. "Wait. Listen to me."

I turned to hear.

"Your dancing-master lover and the little Lazarev, think about them."

"What do you mean?"

"Listen to what I say. Think about them." Suddenly all her spurious youth had fled and she had aged three decades in a flash. "Think."

That was all; I was left to make what I could of the oracle she had offered me. And I did think as I went down The Red Staircase, and what I thought was that I had been in Russia long enough to know that the term "little" had nothing to do with size and denoted some form of intimacy. Not perhaps friendship or even liking, but knowledge. The Princess Irene might only have met Marisia at the Smolny, but surprisingly enough considering the circle in which she moved, she had heard her talked about.

Yes, that was something to ponder.

* * *

What more was there to think about concerning the relationship between Marisia Lazarev and Patrick Graham? I considered it as I walked slowly down the staircase, claustrophobic as ever (the whole house was becoming ever more oppressive as it closed itself up for the coming winter), and through the hall and up the further stairs to my own room. There was no love affair between Marisia and Patrick, something stern and ruthless about Marisia's profile precluded that, even if I had not known it from Patrick. If he loved anyone still, he loved me. But, of course, he loved no one. No one at all.

Presently old Ivan tapped on my door and offered me some letters on a silver salver. I examined them quickly. A letter from Grizel, one from Tibby, and an invitation to a "musical at home" from the Misses Gowrie. A little note in the elder Miss Gowrie's hand was scribbled at the bottom of their invitation: "Do come and see us. We hear great things about you and your doings, and long to hear it from you in person."

Great things? I wondered what tale they had heard and whether they referred to my visit to Spala or, horrid thought, had they heard some gossip about me and Peter? They sounded happy, though, proud even, and not as if they were cross with me.

By contrast, I had noticed that black Ivan seemed less at ease with me than before I had gone to Shereshevo. He was just as courteous, more so possibly, but the babble of gossip and comment had dried up. Ivan was as reserved and formal in his behaviour to me as it was possible in his nature to be. This time he handed me the letters, bowed to me and departed. At one time he would have spoken about the letters, revealing clearly that he had examined them carefully, knew as much as possible about them without actually reading them, and wanted me to enjoy them.

Grizel was happy; I could tell as much from her letter. She rattled on enthusiastically about her betrothed, his career and future prospects ("he'll be Lord Chancellor, I know he will"), the trousseau she was assembling and the house in London that was being decorated to her taste by her Archie. "How lovely it would be if you could see me married, dearest Rose, but I know it cannot be. But you will think of me on 'the day,' won't you? Three weeks from now, Rose."

I looked at the calendar: her letter had taken a week to reach me, so Grizel's wedding day was now two weeks away. Dear Grizel. Goodness knew what her trouseau would be like without me to hold her in check. All lace handkerchiefs and frilly wrappers and pretty hats without anything solid and warm to underpin it. I dared not think what her attitude had been to woollen stockings and winter chemises, but cavalier was probably an understatement. Well, the London rain and fogs would find it out, and chilblains be the result.

"Oh, I am so looking forward to London and my life there," wrote Grizel. "Just think of the Season, Rose, and how we used to long to be part of it! We shall be 'in' Society, or just on the fringe, anyway, and I mean to take full advantage of it, I can tell you, Rose, money permitting. I hope we don't set up a nursery *too* soon, I mean not to if I can help it and so I have told Archie, but if we *do*, I shall just have to make the best of it."

There was a ruthless practicality about Grizel that convinced me she would deal with a problem as suited her best. Her wildnesses were entirely about costume, and in any other sphere she knew well how to tread.

Tibby's letter, read next, was on much the same lines, full of the wedding plans, but giving a more moderate, less enthusiastic account, and confirming my own thoughts about Grizel's shopping. "Her godmother, old Lady Fourmiles, sent her fifty pounds towards her trousseau. . . . All spent, on ninon and chiffon; and not a bit of warm flannel among the lot. She chose all on a hot day, of course, never thinking about the colds of winter. Well, time will show."

I could almost see Tibby's grim smile as she penned these words. Then she wrote on, with a change of tone: "Rose, my girl, if you want to come home for your sister's wedding, then come. I know we said a year and Madame Denisov would pay your fare, but I have a nest-egg to set against the expense. There is something in your letters lately that has made me uneasy. . . ."

Uneasy? I read her letter to the end, but a little shiver ran through me. Uneasy? Was I uneasy? I rose to walk to the pretty little piece of furniture where I kept my home letters, together with Laure's diary.

A tap on the door, recognizably his own, announced Ivan again.

"Come in." I was still standing by the open drawer.

He came in, followed by one of the maids, who carried a pile of my personal linen which had been newly laundered. She bobbed a curtsey and stood waiting for directions.

"Put my clothes here," and I motioned to the set of drawers by which I stood. She came over and deposited the clothes by the open drawer; I saw her look in, and it was a stare so hungrily searching and eager that I hurriedly closed the drawer. She was *avid* for details about me. Nor was it ordinary, girlish curiosity; I saw from the way that Ivan moved up and touched her arm.

She scurried out of the room like a little animal, but not without a quick look behind her at me.

Ivan had not left with her, but remained, still standing at the open door.

I couldn't stop myself. "That girl would eat me up if she could."

Ivan's black features usually had a plump impassivity, but now an expression akin to sympathy appeared before he resumed his customary blankness. He did not speak.

"Why should she look at me like that?" My hands were trembling. "What reason is there? Are all servants in St. Petersburg so rapacious? Does she hate me personally? Or all women? Or all rich women?"

"Questions, questions," muttered Ivan.

"I think you know."

"Her father was whipped once, that is true, a hundred lashes at the local barracks for breaking a china pot in this house. That was the old master's orders."

"And she still remembers?"

"Ah, she never knew, it didn't happen in her time. She was not born. Still, one never forgets. But that's not the reason. She's half crazy, as all that family are."

"I don't believe you," I said. "She doesn't look it. Besides, I've seen her about the house working. She works well."

He stared at me. "We are all half crazy at times, my lady, our own sort understands it. Let the mistress tell you. Oftentimes I've heard her say: 'The servants are all mad, the peasants are crazy.' It's part of our condition."

"Well all right," I said irritably. "So, you are all mad, by which I take you really to mean you are often resentful, angry and bitter." His eyes blinked, showing me I had interpreted him accurately. "Very well, I understand it. But *that* was not in her look. I saw something different. She was looking at me as one woman should not look at another."

"Ah, but she thinks you are not a woman," he rumbled. Ivan always had a deep voice; now it came as from the depths of his neat velvet house-shoes.

"And who says not?" I asked sharply, knowing at once that servants' gossip had filtered back from Shereshevo. On what side of my life had they concentrated spite? The side represented by the dying baby in the peasant's cottage or the side which had impelled me to learn to drive a motor car?

Ivan shrugged. "They say," he started, then stopped.

"They say? Come on, they say what?"

It came with a rush: "They say you are no true woman. That you can do strange things—lay hands on a baby so that it dies with a smile, but dies. They say you can draw a man's spirit out through his nostrils and make it your own."

"Stop, stop," I said, trying to cover my ears, as the malice spilled out.

"That Peter Alexandrov is your slave, that you drive a motor car like a man. You disappear and drive away no one knows where. Witches dance in the forest near Shereshevo. They think you are therefore a witch."

"Oh, Ivan, Ivan, how can you say all this?"

"It is not I who say it, my lady. I only repeat what they say." He had tears in his eyes.

"They, they, they, this mysterious they," and I stamped with my foot. "They are all liars."

"All? It is all untrue?" He looked troubled: I couldn't answer, and he shook his head. "All *not* untrue."

My anger drained away. How hard it was to make truth and falsehood stick together in the right amalgam. Gimcrack always seemed to result, the base metal drove out the good. "Go away, Ivan. We will talk about it again."

"But, mistress."

"Not now. Later." I sat in a chair, leaned back and closed my eyes. Presently I heard the door close. Ivan had departed. The sourness stayed in my mouth and would not go away.

And after all, was it not true? What was I but a witch?


The bad mood hung on all the rest of the day, even during my walk with Ariadne. We had more or less taken up our old St. Petersburg ways with walks, afternoon concerts, and *demoiselle* luncheons, but nothing was quite the same after Shereshevo. That place and Vyksa had altered me and hence how I saw Ariadne. Either Ariadne really had matured in these last months (and why not? She was of the age for developing) or else she had always been less the insouciant girl than I thought, because I sometimes saw now, at the back of her eyes, the look of a wizened old lady. Not exactly like her aged relative, Princess Irene, who would never be wizened, but approaching it, only colder and even older.

That's Marisia's influence, I thought, and began to consider that the sooner she married Edward Lacey the better.

"You are out of sorts," said Ariadne, striding beside me with her usual physical bounce.

"Yes."

"Grumpy."

"Yes."

We were going to an exhibition of modern French painting which I was really looking forward to seeing, but I could not shake off my depression. A black cloud seemed to hover just over my head and shade the world.

"I know what," said Ariadne, "you are homesick. You are missing your sister and thinking of her wedding going on without you."

"Perhaps it's that."

The sky was overcast, a pearly grey, and the wind was cold, all in tune with my mood, in which the first intoxication with St. Petersburg was over, and it now seemed an alien world. I was a stranger here.

"Is she pretty?"

"Grizel? Remarkably so. Oh, yes, she's the pretty one."

"Then she must be very pretty indeed," said Ariadne, thoughtfully. "But I consider *you* a beauty."

St. Petersburg was a dusty city. A fine dry dust was carried by the almost constant wind that blew as if the marshes and swamps on which the city had been built were drying out and distributing themselves over the buildings. I put my head down against the wind and plodded on for a few minutes. Ariadne obediently did the same.

But not for long. "Rose, let's skip the exhibition and go to tea at Berrin's tea-shop instead."

"We ought to go and have a look at one or two pictures," I said absently. "And we are so close."

In fact, we were at the door of the gallery where an elegant and prosperous audience was gathering; it was a well-dressed occasion. Art was fashionable in St. Petersburg.

"Ten minutes only?" asked Ariadne.

"A little longer, I think." I was examining the catalogue.

"We have to talk about it afterwards, remember, and show

some knowledge of what we have seen. Your mother will expect it."

"What are we to see?"

I read out: "Works by Degas, Renoir, Cézanne and Matisse. Also Seurat and Manet."

The names were fairly new to me, not so to Ariadne, who was in this respect (and possibly others, too, I began to think) the more sophisticated. "And Monet as well, I suspect," she said in a knowledgeable way. "Always Monet."

Slowly we went round the room, looking at the pictures as closely as we could, considering the crowds that were clustering around some of them.

I found the paintings difficult, but Ariadne seemed to know how to look at them. "It's best to stand further back and not put your face as close as you are doing," she pointed out. "Come back, now look. Do you see? Monet meant to give you an impression of the water of the pool as it was at that moment in summer with water-lilies opening."

"It's full of colour and movement."

"Renoir and Degas are really easier to look at, and Manet best of all," she said.

"I find them more difficult to understand, though," I said, as we moved on, thinking of the pictures I had seen in the great houses at home, which were all of people doing something, like a sailor looking out to sea, or countryfolk going to market.

"Ah, you aren't meant to understand, just to feel them," answered Ariadne. "Can't you do that? It's not so hard."

"Who taught you to look at these pictures rightly?" I asked, as Ariadne explained to me what Seurat was doing with his points of colour.

"Oh, I did it myself," she said lightly. "No, that's not quite true, I must be honest. Mademoiselle Laure instructed me, although I was an apt pupil. They are mostly French painters, you see, so she felt it her duty to get to comprehend them, although between you and me, I don't think the liking was natural. What she really liked were very careful, intellectual paintings where every detail means something, like Poussin."

Everything I heard about Laure Le Brun now seemed to confirm her value. "What an interesting and good woman she must have been."

Ariadne did not answer. "Oh, look," she said, "there's old General Rahl over there, and he has seen us. Let's escape through this side door." She had me by the arm and was pulling me. "You've seen enough? Yes, now you must come away to digest it."

But over tea and delicious almond tarts at Berrin's, I said, "You never talk about Mademoiselle Laure. Whenever the subject comes up, you sheer off. I wonder why."

Ariadne drank her tea and ate another cake. "Why, because I feel guilty, I suppose," she said in the end.

"But why are you guilty?"

"Ah, yes, why do I feel guilty? Because wasn't she paid to feel guilty about *me*?"

"That's heartless, Ariadne. The woman's dead."

"Oh, but I am heartless," Ariadne said lightly. "But I can feel guilt, none the less. She died in our house, so I feel guilty. I should think you could understand that."

What a puzzling girl Ariadne was. Sometimes so sensitive, sometimes selfish and heedless. I felt I only skated on the surface of her personality.

"Your mother doesn't feel guilty." I was thinking things out.

"Well, I think she does: she doesn't want to, but she does."

It was a fair summing-up of Dolly Denisov's light-weight but essentially kind character: always more caring than she wished to be.

Our table was in the window so that we could look out from our comfortable nest to the street already becoming dusty. A street-cleaner was working his way along the gut-

ters. I had noticed that he kept his face turned towards the
tea shop as he worked, as if even to look at the delicacies on
display was a pleasure. One hardly ever saw beggars on the
streets of St. Petersburg, at least in the fashionable districts. I
suppose the police chased them away, but one often saw
hawkers of brooms and dusters, sellers of fowl and game,
even a sturdy milkmaid or two, and many street musicians,
and many of these looked desperately poor. I saw the street-
cleaner lick his lips thirstily.

The sight made me say, "I'd like to give that man one of
these almond cakes."

Ariadne looked out of the window. "What good would that
do him?"

"Why, he'd enjoy it."

"If you could teach him to think logically and be a rational
human being, instead of a bag of superstitions and bigotry,
then you might help him. Otherwise leave him alone." She
pushed away a half-eaten pastry. "I've had enough. Let's go
home." She tired easily now, a reminder of her illness. I followed her, silenced by her abrupt words.

We went out into the street and I looked around for a likhachy to take us home.

There was more of a crowd about than I had expected,
and I noticed a large number of policemen stationed at intervals along the broad street. Then I heard the sound of
horses' hoofs and a troop of soldiers began to come towards
us, moving at a smart trot. As the group got closer I could see
that two motor cars were moving within the net of men and
horses. A little muted cheer arose from the crowd.

"It must be one of the Imperial family," said Ariadne. She
sounded excited. "I mean Them, Themselves, the Tsar and
Tsarina, not one of the Grand Dukes, and *They* are not often
seen on the streets of St. Petersburg."

"Oh, why not?" I was aware of the increasing interest and
tension of the crowd.

"Bombs," said Ariadne succinctly. "Or so they say. But I

think it's really *Her*." *Her* was always the Tsarina, in Russia.
"She hates us, you know," and, as I looked at her doubtfully,
"Oh, yes. It's true enough. She's so German."

Russia, that year, before the Tercentenary of the founding
of the Romanov dynasty, was in a fervour of Pan-Slavism,
and I suppose Ariadne had been infected by it. Thus everything Slav was admired and the Teutonic influence resented.
There were a lot of Tartars in evidence in the streets of St.
Petersburg, although usually in the humblest of positions,
the street-cleaner was such a one, but I noticed nothing
much was ever said about their claims to being quintessen-
tially Russian. It did not do to remind Russia that she was
also an Eastern country.

The second of the two motor cars was level with us now,
and I saw a short man sitting in the back. He had greying fair
hair, pale blue eyes and a short beard. From his resemblance
to our own King, I recognized the Tsar Nicholas. He made
some slight recognition of the crowd, inclining his head
slightly, but unsmilingly.

The Tartar road-sweeper took off his hat and waved it. As
if this were, in some strange way, a threatening gesture, two
of the policemen moved closer to him.

"There goes the Tsar, God bless him," said the old man admiringly. "He is a Father, though he takes the shirt off your
back."

I slipped a coin into his hand: the policemen moved away,
then a *likhachy* appeared, its way having been blocked by the
Imperial procession, and we went home.

"I would like to see Grizel married," I said in the cab to
Ariadne.

"Ah, I can't allow that," Ariadne answered. "For you
would never come back."


The lamps were lit in my own room when I went into it on
our return, the curtains were drawn, and it looked warm and
pretty. I was glad to find it empty and myself alone.

I sat down and tried to write my letters home to Grizel and Tibby. It was easy enough to reply to Grizel, who was wound up in her own happiness like a skein of silk and not mightily observant, either. But Tibby was another matter. Should I tell her about seeing Patrick Graham again? Should I hint to her of the proposal from Peter Alexandrov?

But it was hard to write to her. There was one thing I knew: if I went home I had let Patrick Graham wreck me. To outsiders, it might look no more than a little boating accident, but to me the wreck would be total.

My reading lamp made a comfortable pool of light on my desk, the porcelain stove sang in a corner of the room, but it was all false comfort. Inside I was ill at ease.

Outside the room I heard the soft, slippered feet of a servant pass, then from below caught a snatch of music from a gramophone, probably Edward and Ariadne dancing to it: they went round and round the room endlessly absorbed in practising their steps: it was their latest craze.

I had begun the hard letter to Tibby when I heard a rustle. I raised my head and listened, but there was silence.

Yet when I had written a few more words, again I heard a rustle. I looked up quickly and was sure that I had felt movement behind me. I stood up and spun round.

The curtains were moving slightly.

It would have been very easy either to have called for Ivan or to have run from the room. I don't know why I didn't do either of these two things, but instead I stepped forward to the curtains.

My hand was actually on one curtain, ready to pull it aside, when I looked down.

A small animal's foot, a paw, was just to be seen protruding from under the fringe.

Then I did scream, a good healthy, strong scream.

Ivan appeared at once at the door; he must have been immediately outside. "You called out, *baryshna?*"

Without answering him, I pulled the curtain away: a small animal crouched there, one with long ears and bright eyes.

Ivan came into the room and stood beside me. "The *baryshna* thought it was a rat or a mouse?" he queried, a little maliciously.

"I know what it is: a baby hare, a leveret. A white leveret. What's it doing in my room?"

Ivan did not answer; he stood there and looked from me to the leveret, letting his hands hang by his side and giving no answer.

"Ivan! I asked a question."

"I could give you an answer," he said.

"Come on: what is it, then? How does this animal come to be in my room?"

"Ah—how? I thought you asked why?" And he relapsed into silence.

"Why, then, Ivan? Why?"

"White hares are the mark of a witch," he said slowly. "So I have heard."

"Thank you for telling me. Now I know why the creature is in my room, and I dare say you know who left it here, too. Oh, don't worry: I won't ask. Because you wouldn't tell me." I walked round to take a closer look at the little creature crouching there. I could see by its stillness how frightened it was. Suddenly I was angry: not for myself, but for the animal. "How did they find a baby hare in St. Petersburg?"

Ivan shrugged. "The country's not so far away, all the maids here are country-girls, perhaps one of them brought the creature in from her home. And then, there is the market on Vassily Island; there they sell everything alive on four legs or two that you can eat or pluck."

I was a country-girl, too, and, the first surprise over, was not frightened of the leveret; I picked it up, stroking the soft, warm fur.

"And what will happen to the animal when you take it away?"

Ivan looked doubtful for a moment, and then made a twisting movement with his two hands.

I felt sick. "Go away. Leave the animal with me." He started to depart from the room, glad enough, I thought, to get away. "No, I've got a better idea. Go and get some straw and two boxes; the leveret can stay up here."

"Oh, but, *baryshna*," he started to protest, but I brushed him aside.

"Get what I ask."

I stood holding the baby hare till he returned, bearing two wooden boxes and a great armful of straw, together with hay, and with his grumbling help we created a pen for the hare where it was soon peacefully installed, apparently quite happy.

"Now, go back downstairs, and tell them what a witch I am," I said to Ivan. "And what this witch can do." He departed, grumbling.

I felt better because I had met hostility head on and outfaced it. But the episode sickened me with Russia. Holy Russia, I thought. Unholy Russia.

"You are writing a letter," said Ariadne, coming into my room at that moment. "I'm sorry to interrupt, but I had something to ask."

"Just a letter to my old nurse, Tibby," I said, without telling her that it was to say I was coming home in time for Grizel's wedding, if I could. I knew I must tell her mother, and speak to my old cousins, the Misses Gowrie, before I said anything to Ariadne.

But she had been diverted. "Good heavens, Rose, are you keeping a farm in your room?"

"It was a sort of present. It won't be here long. I shall find another home for it. What is it you wanted?"

"I should think it would smell." She dragged her gaze away from the hare. "It's my Uncle Peter and Edward Lacey. They want you to come down. We are going to have some music and to dance."

"I thought you were doing that already. I heard music."

"Uncle Peter can't dance alone," said Ariadne plaintively.

"But I can't do that new dance you and Edward do."

"The tango. You can learn. We'll teach you. Come on. The music's delicious."

She held out her hand, and I let her lead me down. But before I went, I took my letter to Tibby and handed it to Ivan, who was, as usual, lurking outside, and ordered him to see it was posted. I felt safer now that it was off.

Peter met us at the door to the big drawing-room, where they had the carpet rolled back and the boards shining and bare. He had a gramophone record in one hand. He looked flushed and happy, younger than I had ever seen him look. He was ten years my senior and six years younger than his sister Dolly.

"Ah, good," he said, when he saw me. "She's got you. Come along now. Lesson number one." He put the record on the gramophone and put his arm round me.

"But I didn't come to Russia to learn the tango," I protested, as I let him lead me into the dance.

"Not the tango," he corrected. "We've done that. This is the maxixe. Just as new and a shade more vulgar."

"Vulgarity is in the eye of the beholder, my boy," said Edward, dancing past with Ariadne.

"I have a question to put to you," said Peter as we twirled. I shook my head. "And again."

"No."

"And again," he said gently.

"It's no good; I'm going home."

"No." He stopped dancing. "Now it's my turn to say no. And I say it with great fierceness: no, no, no."

"Let's go on dancing. The others are looking."

"Listening, too, I expect, and I don't mind." He looked determined and angry. "Edward and Ariadne know all I want to say to you. Or they can guess."

"But I might mind," I said, exasperated.

He dropped his arm from my waist and gave me a hard look: too, too perceptive, as always. "There is the conservatory next door. We could always step in there if you prefer," he said politely.

"Thank you, no, I didn't mean that." I was struggling to get back the position of advantage I had lost. "Shall we go on dancing? And not talk."

"I don't promise not to talk." He had never sounded happier, nor been a more entertaining companion. He was rich, very nice to look at and in love with me. And, after all, Patrick had betrayed me twice. "You're a very apt pupil, Miss Gowrie. Don't we dance well together?"

"You don't expect an answer to that," I said breathlessly, as we sailed around the floor.

"Don't I, though? Don't you think I've earned one?"

It was true, and it brought me up short. There must be an end to my procrastination.

"I'm going home to see my sister married," I said, standing still. "I've had enough dancing. I'll go to my room. I have some more letters to write."

"That's an excuse."

"Yes, of course it is," and I hurried out of the room, closely followed by Peter, who stopped me at the foot of the stairs.

"Rose, don't run away." He stopped, put his hand to his head and said, "My God, there's water dripping on me."

We both looked up the stairs and there was Ivan, on the curve of the stairs directly above us, carrying a shallow bowl from which water slopped.

Some fell on me at that moment.

"Now, you've been christened. . . . Ivan, what are you up to?"

"Carrying water to the animal, Excellency," called Ivan. "Animals must have water."

"Water, animal?" Peter was hurrying up the stairs, with me after him, and Ivan plodding doggedly on, and with every step the water in the bowl swung to and fro more dangerously. "Put the bowl down, man, and explain yourself."

"I'll tell you," I said hastily, and in as few words as possible, but without mentioning witches, I told him about the hare.

He burst out laughing. "My dear girl, do you mean to say that you are planning to share your room with a hare?"

"I wanted to make sure it was safe."

"The creature can live in the kitchens of this house. I promise you it will be safe. I give you my word."

"I am afraid it will be lonely."

"Then it shall have a companion: we will get it a mate."

I was laughing myself now. "Oh, Peter, the kitchens will be full of leverets, the whole place will be overrun."

"The kitchens of this house are big enough to contain a few hares if that is what will make you happy. This house is like Russia: there is room for everything in it."

I thought it was true: the old Princess in her tower, Dolly and Peter on their levels, the servants in the basement, all shades of opinions were represented in this house and could live together.

I felt happier than I had been for days. "Oh, thank you truly," I said to Peter. "You are kind."

Before Ivan's interested gaze, Peter took my hand in his. "Do I have an answer?"

"Yes. The answer is yes."

Peter gave me a long, sweet look, then, without taking his eyes from my face, he said, "Ivan, you can continue up to Miss Gowrie's room with your load."

Then as Ivan reluctantly took himself off, Peter kissed me.

It was not a passionate kiss. It was gentle and affectionate. Exploratory, I thought. I raised my head like a child for another one.

I heard Peter say something in Russian under his breath. Then I remembered something.

"Oh, Peter, I've sent off a letter saying I am coming home."

"Very well, then we will send another saying that you are not."

"Yes."

"And, Rose, since you cannot go to see your sister married, for I can't spare you and won't let you go away for a moment, then we must get her and her husband to come to your wedding here."

"Grizel and Archie? Oh, Peter, do you think we could?"

"Nothing is easier."

And when he said it like that, it seemed so. Tentatively, but with pleasure, I began to appreciate the power and pleasure of my new position.

"Oh, thank you, Peter," I said.

Although Peter was enthusiastic about welcoming Grizel and Archie, he was adamant about not including Tibby in the invitation, and nothing I could do would make him change.

"No. I am not allowing that old woman near you until my position with you is firmly established," he said. "She has a bad influence on you. If she comes out now, you might never marry me."

"Oh, Peter, no. You misjudge Tibby."

"Let her wait. When you and I have been married for a good time, she can come on a visit. But I want to be sure of myself first." He smiled at me. "I want you all to myself."

So, when my letters home went off, they included an invitation to Grizel and her Archie, but there was no offer extended to Tibby.

The pain she would feel (but never admit to) was a blot on my happiness.

There was one other thing I had to stomach, and I surprised myself by my reaction to it. I had always thought of myself as a sceptic, not declared agnostic, for Tibby would never have countenanced it, but not quite a believer, yet when I was required to join the Russian Orthodox Church I found out I was, at heart, a member of the Church of Scotland.

The two were not incompatible, however, Dolly said, and one faith need not drive out the other. It was she who made my duty clear to me and organized my reception into the Russian Church. Peter said very little; I don't think he cared, but he didn't say no, either.

# Chapter Nine

Soon, with all necessary speed (which was not, after all, so very fast, this being Russia), the formalities connected with a wedding between a British subject and a Russian were set in train. The British Embassy had to be told. I went there myself. Fortunately, I knew Muriel Buchanan, the Ambassador's pretty, talkative daughter, and she eased my path, looking at me with frank interest as she did. "I keep a diary, you know," she said, "and you and your wedding will certainly be in it." I was surprised how much I had to do, and how many documents I had to produce, even my birth certificate (to prove myself born, I suppose), which naturally I did not have with me. The Misses Gowrie were a great help here, as it appeared that one of them had been present at my birth, or more or less, and so was able to prove I existed. I had expected them to show more excitement than they did. They were certainly pleased for me, and said so, but their pleasure was moderate. I explained it to myself by saying that closely as they identified themselves with their adopted country, they were yet passionately proud of being British.

In fact, I fancied the elder, Emma Gowrie, looked at me with a certain pity, although she said nothing. "But think of the position, sister, and the jewels," sighed Alice Gowrie in answer to what had not been expressed.

My reception into the Church and my clothes seemed to be the chief things on Dolly's mind. All she let show, anyway.

Our announcement seemed to have caused her no surprise. "I'm so pleased, my dear," she said. "Marry soon. I should. No sense in hanging about."

"Oh, we're going to," said Peter. "Almost at once, don't you think, Rose?"

"Just time for Rose to be received into the Church (they can do you quite quickly) and arrange your clothes."

I realized at this moment what a staunch countrywoman of John Knox I was. "Is that necessary? The Church, I mean? Peter, is it?"

He shrugged. "I would do what you think best."

I had yet to discover his gentle capacity for disappearing on points where he did not want to make a stand.

Dolly appealed to him. "Peter, it will make all the difference at Court. As you well know."

"Well, you must have lovely clothes, anyway," said Peter to me.

"And they shall be my gift," said Dolly in triumph, having, as she knew, got her way. "A present from me."

"No, I can manage that for myself, thank you." I still had a tiny reserve of money left and it would have to do. I could just see Tibby's face if I let Dolly pay for my wedding dress. Sadly, I remembered that she would not be here to find out. However, the Misses Gowrie would be and would be certain to let her know.

Dolly was graceful. "It's true that there won't be time for anything elaborate. Not that simplicity is cheap. But just a few things now, then afterwards . . ." She looked at me appraisingly. "I have always wanted to see you in one of Poiret's Oriental ensembles, they would suit your style. You have the necessary panache to wear them, and the height," and here she sighed, for she herself was small and inclined to plumpness.

We were to have a whole floor of the Denisov house made over to us to live in, this being the custom. Our living there was quite taken for granted, and never discussed at all. In fact, I saw now that Peter's living *en garçon* in his own flat had been unusual in his class. As our rooms were already fully furnished I had no duties of the sort Grizel and Archie had in getting their home together.

"A pity, really," I said to Peter, as we strolled round the set of rooms, viewing what would be our home. "I should have enjoyed it."

"Later, later." He gave me an affectionate smile. "You shall have carte blanche." He waved a hand. "Throw this lot out."

"They are valuable antiques."

"Perhaps we won't actually throw them onto the streets." He traced an idle finger across the dust on top of a piece of onyx. "We might keep them better dusted. Really, Dolly's servants are an idle lot."

"They seem to work hard enough."

"Oh, seem. But you have to keep after them. Don't want to bother. Inertia is their chosen vice." He drew me down beside him on a damask-covered couch. "Forget them now." He covered my face with soft kisses.

A little of the remaining reserve I still felt towards him melted then.

"You're sometimes quite nervous, aren't you?"

"Yes."

"Of me?"

"A little." He was pressing for an answer I didn't want to give. I had not been nervous with Patrick. Too bold, too free, perhaps.

"You mustn't be."

"I can't help it: sometimes it springs up of itself."

"I can never resist you when you look like that, so surprised and shy." He got up and pulled me to my feet with him. "Come on, let's continue looking around these rooms. You will have your maid with you, of course. This will be her room."

He showed me a square box of a room with no window. "It's not very big," I said doubtfully. "Anyway, I have no maid yet."

"Well, you must choose one. Dolly will help."

"And what about Ivan? Shall I still have his services?"

Absently he said, "I may send Ivan back to Shereshevo. He has served his purpose here." He was studying the room thoughtfully.

I was surprised. "What purpose was that?"

He brought his attention back to me. "Why to look after you, of course. We had to provide someone for you who could speak some English."

"How carefully I was prepared for," I exclaimed.

He took my hand in his. "Yes, you were, my love, indeed you were." He tucked my arm under his and together we strolled round the half-dozen rooms that made up our apartment.

"I suppose I shall get used to being surrounded by Louis Quinze furniture and sleeping on a bed that was built for Marie Antoinette," I said finally.

"Only built for her: she never paid for it," said Peter. "I'm not sure if my ancestor did either, to be quite truthful. I rather think that it was one of the spoils he brought back from France after Napoleon had been defeated. Still, it is a bed of state, and we shall take our state in it. Now I've made you blush."

"Not at all. I never blush. This is the twentieth century." I sneezed twice and then again. "That's the dust. I hope they'll clean the bed-hangings."

By the bed was a large porcelain figure of a little black boy wearing a turban and carrying a flambeau. Behind him was a round gilt mirror in which Peter and I were reflected. Between the mirror and the bed the gold enamelled mouth-piece of one of the speaking-tubes protruded.

"Only the speaking-tube is free of dust," I said.

"I suppose it's the newest thing in the room," pointed out Peter.

"Does it still work? It might be useful." I went over, re-moved the cap and spoke down the tube. No word was re-turned to me, just silence.

"I told you they are never used," said Peter, watching me; he sounded uneasy.

"Oh, don't worry," I said, putting the plug back in the tube. "I won't start that again." But I thought to myself some voices never stop calling, and I still remembered the voice I had heard. "All the same I don't like these tubes."

"Then they shall be ripped out."

"No, leave them. I can see they are beautifully done, and who knows, they may be useful in the end."

Peter was delighted. "Spoken like a true Russian. That's the spirit that has preserved them all these years."

"Just as well, really," I observed. "Father Theo at St. An-drew's Cathedral says I am a bad pupil. Not that I would call the Russian Church a proselytizing church exactly."

Peter laughed. "There speaks the Scotswoman again."

My reception into the Orthodox Church proceeded in a leisurely, calm fashion. In fact, I got quite fond of my young instructor, Father Theophilus. He was plump and idle, but genuinely devout. Also sensible. "Faith must come with liv-ing," he said. "I can only explain, the rest must be for you." He was lazy, and I used to fancy that he drank a little, and he certainly over-ate, but who would not in the increasing cold of the Russian winter? If that is, he had few other pleasures of the senses, which I took to be the case with Father Theo-philus, although I wasn't quite sure about his celibacy. He had a wife, I think, for there was a chubby little edition of himself that used to toddle after him occasionally when we met in a room at the back of St. Andrew's Cathedral.

"You'd better go to St. Andrew's Cathedral," Dolly had advised. "They're so nice over there. Sympathetic, you know." She added: "Of course, the neighbourhood is not quite what one could wish . . ."

When I had got there I was surprised Dolly had ever visited the cathedral, for Vassily Island was frankly slummy. Moreover, close to it was that perpetual institution, St. Andrew's Market. Sometimes after a talk with Father Theophilus I would stroll through the crowded lanes between the rows of stalls, which were always crowded with shoppers. I felt as though I were rubbing shoulders with Russia itself. Pedlars, stall-holders, beggars and shoppers, I absorbed their manners and faces with fascinated interest: I wanted to know them all. I loved to hear the snatches of conversation.

"Buy this lovely little leg of lamb: take it home with you now and give your family a better meal than the Tsar gets."

"I'll wring the hen's neck while you watch. Now, what could be fresher than that?"

Perhaps my baby hare, now flourishing comfortably in the capacious kitchens of the Denisov house, its neck unwrung, had come from here. Ivan had thought so, and looking at St. Andrew's Market now, I thought so, too. In fact, I had a look round to see if I could buy him a companion, but hares, or anyway white ones, seemed hard to find. Perhaps mine had been specially bleached.

Walking through this market I had a startling encounter. It was a dusky afternoon with the dim tapers already lighting up on the stalls and the braziers burning. Autumn it would have been still in Scotland, but it was winter here and chill with it. Frozen water was already winking its way down the Neva, soon the river would be solid enough to walk upon, and then paths would be laid out on it for people to cross. But the market was lively this evening with hawkers shouting their wares and the stall-owners leaning out and beckoning and trying to make a sale with me.

"Come on, buy this beautiful shawl, lady. It will make even

your beautiful face more beautiful. Oh, what eyes you have, bluer than sky in summer, this blue will suit you. Come on, now, buy."

I never answered, because to answer was half-way to buying—but I could never resist smiling, which, of course, encouraged them almost as much, so that my progress was always marked by wheedling calls and shouts.

There were cooked-meat stalls and bakers selling trays of hot buns and other stalls, much patronized by the men, selling drinks. The drinks were hot and produced red noses and cheeks in their drinkers. I never felt any temptation to linger by these stalls.

Forming a separate group, in an enclave all their own, were the stalls where live animals were sold. Trays of tiny kittens, hutches of dozing puppies, boxes of fluttering birds. There was a ready sale for all of these. The poorer inhabitants of St. Petersburg seemed to love their domestic pets. Here I sometimes lingered, in amusement, to watch the byplay: the little girl trying to persuade her mother to buy a kitten; the two young brothers triumphantly bearing away a puppy covered with ginger fur and with huge paws, which gave promise of great size to come, while being assured by the stall-owner that the animal was guaranteed to live in a small flat "like a lamb."

Except for trying to sell me their wares, no one spoke to me or took any special notice of me. I was just a face in a crowd, and that was what I enjoyed. I was learning about Russia.

And I was anonymous. Or so I thought until that day which seemed darker than usual with a thin white mist drifting in from the river. The crowds round the booths selling drinks seemed thicker than usual and the customers drunker. I could hardly blame them on such a raw day. A group came away from a stall as I passed. I hurried on.

Then from behind me I heard a laugh. A deep, rich laugh, rippling from the chest: I turned round to look, half knowing whom I would see.

A step behind me stood a tall, burly man. He was wearing a rich silk shirt open to the waist, with a fur-lined robe thrown over all. Soft leather boots reached to his thighs. Every garment was of the finest quality but stained and soiled. His hair was uncombed and his beard matted.

"You have come too far away from your own country, *baryshna,* you should go home." He was rocking on his heels, still laughing deeply.

"Father Gregory."

"You should go home," he said again. "To your own country."

It was a mistake to have spoken to him, silence would have been wiser as I knew too late.

"You should go home, little lady. You are not safe here. And I am not safe while you are here."

He was speaking in Russian, but with a thick accent, previously unknown to me. This fact, together with nervousness, meant that I followed what he was saying much less easily than usual.

"I know my enemies," he rumbled on. "That is one faculty the good God gave me; I can tell them even when they sneak up behind."

"I'm not your enemy," I said stoutly.

He laughed. "Little lady, you do not even know your own enemies, let alone mine."

His drinking companions, two men, were with him, one on either side. Guards? Protectors? Or friends? One looked like a young peasant, the other a lad of education, but they were both equally drunk.

I began to move away, but Father Gregory growled something to the others and I felt my skirt held. I tried to pull it away, but it was held tight by the peasant, on whose face was not a flicker of expression, and who was not even looking at me.

"I want to talk to you," said Father Gregory, "but not here. Inside." And he nodded his head towards the row of houses that bordered the market. "I have a room in one of those houses there. One of my rooms. I have little nests all over the town like the old rat I am," and his eyes glittered at me.

"No!" I was frantic. "I won't come."

Jovially he said, "Give her a pull, lads."

The peasant still hung to my skirt, drawing it towards him so that we were close together. The other man put his arm round my waist so tightly that the constriction made it difficult for me to breathe. I managed to gasp out, "Help! Help!" No one took any notice. They didn't understand. I was calling out in English.

But I don't think they would have helped me if they had understood my pleas. Father Gregory was known here, and I was not. In this world he was not a person to be interfered with by anyone.

The men half pushed, half dragged me into the darkness behind the market stalls. Father Gregory followed behind. "I don't wish you any harm, my little bird, so don't flutter," he whispered in my ear.

In a louder voice I heard him say, "Better blind the little bird so it can't see," and a silk handkerchief, smelling strongly of musk and tobacco, descended on my head, covering my eyes and nose, and robbing me of what little breath I had left.

When it was whisked from my head I was in a narrow, high-ceilinged room, which was crowded with old-fashioned furniture, including a great bed. Every surface was covered with small objects: photographs, china pots, wooden boxes and packets of cigarettes. Over all was dust, and every piece of over-decorated furniture looked battered and kicked to pieces. I was pushed up against one table which was itself pushed against the wall. My host pulled a low chair forward and straddled it as if he were riding a horse, leaning his chin on the top and staring at me. His eyes were bright and compelling: I wanted to look away and found I could not.

I imagined myself describing the scene to Peter afterwards. I could almost hear him saying, "You should have driven to St. Andrew's or else taken Ivan with you; you should never have been walking alone in the market on Vassily Island."

A small but heavy-looking metal and wooden box was within reach of my right hand; I considered picking it up, hurling it at the monk and running for the door. True, there still remained the two younger men, but of those one had lain down on the bed and the other was standing by the porcelain stove warming his hands.

"Don't try and fly away yet," said Father Gregory, "for I won't let you," and he slapped his side and gave a loud laugh. "Let's all have a drink. Boris, get off your backside and give us a vodka all round."

Boris rolled off the bed, found the bottle of vodka, which was under the bed, and poured out the spirit. There was only one glass, which had to go round all four of us. They watched carefully while I drank mine. I could feel the strength of the spirit as it went down my throat, but the impact was no worse than whisky, and we used to be given that by Tibby sometimes in the winter as a precaution against taking cold.

"For your looks, you have a strong head," said Father Gregory admiringly.

I kept silent. I saw that although his companions were drunk, the monk was sober, for the vodka (and certainly he had had a good deal of it before he came across me) had had no effect on him. His was the strong head.

"I was waiting for you. You've been coming this way regularly, haven't you? I know all about that."

I was still silent.

"Your friends are not my friends," he said suddenly. "Slit my throat for me if they could. *If* they could. Yours, too, if it suited them. Remember I said that. But I have eyes in the back of my head; I know my enemies. Remember that, too. Get me in the end, no doubt. But not yet. Of that I have certain knowledge." He tapped his forehead. "The information comes in here. I need no one to tell me. You also know things of your own knowledge?"

I shook my head. "No."

"But you have the power. You could know, if you wished."

I thought of Tibby then: to her it would have seemed like necromancy and dealing with the devil. As it was, I suspected she dwelt with shame on my power of healing.

"Something holds you back always," he said, shrewd bright eyes roving over my face: he was free with his looks, no one had ever looked at me quite like that before, with almost open lust. And yet there was humour in his look, and humanity. He was terrible, but likeable, too. "Well, no doubt it doesn't matter with you. I dare say as a woman you have other methods to protect yourself. As for me, I need every trick I can lay hands on, whether it comes from the devil or not."

I gave him a startled look: it was as if he had read my mind.

"And as to that, who can know?" he went on. "But I do know that you are one like me. One of us can always smell out another. Agreed?" I nodded. "But where this power of ours comes from, whether from heaven or the other place, I don't know, and nor do you. I always say that it comes with prayer. The truth is, it comes like the wind. Divine wind, eh?" And he gave a wink and a belch simultaneously. "Oh, I'm a wicked sinner, I am."

He had ridden the chair towards me like a wooden horse, and now he abandoned it and stood in front of me.

"Yes, I'm a wretched sinner: I repent regularly of my excesses. But the trouble with me is I *must* have what I want. And I want you."

I took a step backwards, but like a good general was careful only to retreat where the way was open. I now had my back to the bed but I could see the door.

He put a hand on my breast.

"Don't," I said.

For answer he started to fondle me; so close he was now that I could smell the spirit on his breath and his own peculiar, rank, animal smell. I could see my own image reflected in the gleaming protuberant iris of his eyes.

Out of the corner of my eye I could see that the other two, having stayed faithful to the vodka bottle, were now comatose.

"Come to bed," he said. He gave me a little backwards push.

I was half incredulous of the position I found myself in, and in this was my salvation. Because I did not quite believe in my danger, my mind was not frozen by fear, and I was able to act.

He had thrown me off my balance. To steady myself I grabbed at the bed-post. A part of the ancient, neglected decoration on the post came away in my hand. I had a curving piece of wood in my clutch, and I could feel a nail at the end.

I gripped it firmly and stabbed it sharply in one of his ears, rolling sideways as I did so.

He gave a howl of pain and clapped his hand to his ear, trying to make a grab at me with his other hand. He had an enormous hand and it spread over my thigh, gripping a fold of my skirt. But I happened to be wearing a skirt I had sewn myself, and as Tibby had often pointed out, my sewing was careless. "You're a *flabby* sewer, my dear," was how she put it, "and your clothes'll fall off you one day, mark my words." I was glad of it now as a whole pleat ripped away.

I had a moment of freedom and in it I leapt, literally jumping for the door. Thank God it was unlocked and I rushed through. Behind me I heard an angry roar, followed immediately by a deep, deep laugh and a shout, reaching out to me: "Remember, I am your friend, not your enemy."

The market outside was wrapped in fog which was growing thicker with every minute, but I was lucky and on the edge of it, near the quay looking towards the Admiralty Building, I managed to get a *droshky* and had myself driven home.

Home. I was already beginning to call it home.

When I got inside I examined my state: I was untidy and my clothes were torn. I had been frightened and shocked, but I had come through unhurt except for a bruise on my hip and another on my left breast. Nothing had really happened, I was unhurt, but inside me a little flame of alarm had been set alight. This was the true damage. "Remember, I am your friend, not your enemy," he had called. What was I to make of that?

At first I thought to rush and tell Dolly Denisov, but as I tidied myself and waited for the flush on my cheeks to subside, I thought that the proper person to tell was Peter. But the minutes ticked by as I sat in my room, letting my pulse quieten, and I knew I was not going to speak.

I wasn't going to say anything about it to anyone. I would not complain about the attack on me. I think women often suppress episodes of this sort.

"You look tired tonight, my dear girl," said Dolly when I met her later that evening. "It was ridiculous of you to walk to St. Andrew's Cathedral. You should have driven."

"I did drive back," I said.

The winter routine in the Denisov household was taking its shape. Dolly was hardly ever at home in the evening. Sometimes she dined with us, but very often she was out. Peter usually joined us for dinner, even if he was absent all day. Then, occasionally, all four of us went out to a reception or a small party: there was nothing large in the way of entertaining at the moment. St. Petersburg, although insatiably gay, was holding its energies in reserve for the short but brilliant winter season which centred on the New Year festivities.

But Dolly went out alone to the houses of her smart friends, to play cards and gamble. I was just beginning to realize how much she gambled.

"An inherited folly, I'm afraid," Peter had told me. "My father carried it to an obsession. He would disappear into his club for days." It was a folly he was not immune to himself: I had seen his eyes glitter as he took his place at the card-table with Dolly.

Tonight, however, the thick and increasing fog was keeping Dolly at home, thus depriving her of her favourite occupation. But she had had the card-table set out and was shuffling the cards hopefully. "Perhaps someone will call and I will get a game." She knew better than to ask Ariadne and me to take a hand. Edward Lacey could play as keen a game as any Russian, but he was on duty at his sister's tonight.

"I've heard from your sister, a delightful letter, what a charming girl she must be. Looks forward to coming here for your wedding, excited at the prospect. The letter was written on her honeymoon." Dolly's tone expressed wonder at this, and it was a remarkable phenomenon, coming from my sister. Archie must be exercising an improving influence.

"I know. I have had a letter also." To me, Grizel had expressed her pleasure and excitement at coming to St. Petersburg. "Fancy you, married, and in such a remarkable way. Oh, we shall certainly come. Archie says he wouldn't deprive me of the pleasure of seeing you for all the world, and that for his part it will be well worth his knowing Russia as he means to specialize in foreign affairs when he gets into the House. Of course, we pay our own expenses and don't accept your Peter's kind offer and all that. Archie says we can easily stand it." Which I did not believe, but I had never expected other from her Archie.

Grizel had seemed happy and pleased with her lot, although venturing a comment that honeymoons were "mixed blisses." At the end of her letter she had scrawled, "What about Tib and your wedding, Rose? She's very cut up."

Peter Alexandrov had ordered me a motor car from France (coach work to be made in London) and an opal parure was being reset for me at Fabergé's (only I have never liked opals, thinking them unlucky), so in every material way I was a lucky girl, but about Tibby he remained adamant. "Not until I have been married to you for a very long time: I am frightened of her power over you."

I had already learned that he was a man hard to influence; he had a way of disappearing into his own thoughts that baffled me. He was away a good deal lately, "attending to affairs," as he put it himself. I was alone more than I had expected to be.

So it seemed to me, to paraphrase Grizel, that engagements also were times of mixed blisses. On every side people were congratulating me on my good fortune and letting me know, more or less directly according to their good manners or bad, what a lucky girl I was. Every time Peter came to the Denisov house, he brought me a little present; even the old lady in the Red Tower had relented in her anger towards me and announced that she would be giving me a tiara of rose diamonds in the "antique Russian style," as she put it; I was loved, cherished and spoilt. But inside I was uncertain of myself, more than a little frightened and *cold*, as if the winter cold of Russia were seeping into me. I was always cold. The house was hot, the porcelain stoves burnt day and night. When I went out in Peter's company I was wrapped in furs. Dolly's furs, they were, but my own were ordered and in preparation, made of the darkest, finest sable, fringed with black fox. But inside my furs I was always cold.

Oddly, I began to feel lonely.

One day, walking into my room, I found a strange servant waiting there for his orders.

"Who are you?"

"I am Augustus, madam, your new servant," and he bowed. He was a small, thin-featured man, of German birth, as I later learned.

"And where is Ivan?" I demanded.

He bowed without answering, letting me know politely that it was not a question to which he had the answer.

I never saw Ivan after that; I was sure he was still in the house, because I fancied I heard his voice from afar, but we never met. Anyway, Peter had not yet sent him back to the country.

Dolly, when I asked her, only replied vaguely that "he had returned to other duties."

"And who is this Augustus?"

"Oh, Peter chose him specially for you. He is a splendid servant."

"I preferred my old Ivan. He was lazy, and he drank, and he was superstitious"—here Dolly looked at me sharply—"but he had some warmth."

"My dear, I don't know what you are fretting about," said Dolly. "You have nothing to do now but enjoy yourself." She added happily, "Soon we shall have to be getting our ballroom opened. We shall give two balls, I think. One for you and Peter, after your wedding, and perhaps while your sister is still here."

"Thank you," I murmured. I was standing in the hall, dressed, ready to go out. Ariadne and I were going shopping.

"And one for Ariadne: a *bal blanc*."

Ariadne groaned. "Oh, I envy you: you will have a *bal rose* (named for you, even) and nothing but a dreary old *bal blanc* for me. Oh, how I dread it: all the old chaperones sitting around the room yawning, and not even a proper orchestra, but that old *tapeur*, whom we have all known all our lives, banging away at the piano. And nothing to dance but a quadrille. 'Advance. Retreat. Join hands. Form a circle. *Chasse.'* Oh, it's not a ball, it's a military display."

"Poor Ariadne. And you know all the latest steps, too," I said.

"Oh, don't imagine even you will get anything more exciting than a waltz or two. The two-step is vulgar, they say, and the Tsar has forbidden the tango and the one-step. But never mind, when you are married you will be able to give the most delicious little private dances where anything can happen. Oh, how I long to be emancipated."

Dolly gave an angry little click of her teeth, and took another of her incessant yellow cigarettes. "You only talk that way to annoy me."

"Not at all," said Ariadne. She looked at me. "Marisia is in St. Petersburg."

"I knew it," said Dolly, throwing down her cigarette. "I detect her influence on you."

"She's studying at the university; she's going to be a doctor. I think I'll go and join her."

"Never," said Dolly. "Not with my permission."

"Then without it. I'll contract a 'white' marriage and be free. It'll save me from the white ball, anyway."

"Rose," Dolly looked at me imploringly, "help me."

"Why don't you let her go?" I put on my gloves and adjusted the buttons. "She'll soon be back."

"Rose, you beast!" A reproachful cry from Ariadne.

"You know you are not in the least equipped to be a student. I have never seen you study anything."

"Just for that I shall insist on going to the English bookshop and ordering some very dull books to read. Macaulay, I think, and Gibbon, and I shall make you read them with me."

Dolly said, "I am driving out myself. The motor car can take us all. You may leave me first at my dress-maker and come back for me."

I was seated next to Dolly in the motor car, wearing my *shuba*, and Ariadne was in the little seat facing us.

"Must you disfigure yourself with that garment?" she asked disapprovingly. It certainly was an ugly old garment but I had paid for it with my own money.

"It's Rose's gesture of independence," said Ariadne. "I think I shall get one myself."

Dolly ignored her; in a low voice she said, "Rose, I think you may get a call to the palace at Tsarskoye Selo any day now."

"The boy is ill again?" I said quickly.

"No, not ill. Trouble of some sort, though. I am not quite clear. But they may want you."

So I was not to be let off that particular hook.

We put Dolly down at her dress-maker, or one of them; she kept about three, as far as I could see, all hard at work for her.

"Why are you puckering your face up like that?" asked Ariadne as we drove away.

"Am I?"

"Yes. I call it your 'Rose about to do battle' look."

"I was wondering if I am really suited to Russian life: I mean, where the Tsar tells you what you may or may not dance." I shook my head.

"You could rebel," said Ariadne shyly. "Would you do that? You could make a practical gesture."

I looked at her doubtfully. "How?"

"By dancing the tango: revolutions have to start somewhere."

"Well, that would be better than throwing a bomb," I said. "I don't think I'm the sort of person who could do that."

"I suppose we none of us knows what we could do, or might be obliged to do." Her voice was thoughtful.

The English book-shop was crowded, but Ariadne was quick with her shopping (no books by Macaulay or Gibbon, I noticed, but some French fashion magazines), and I collected the invitations to my wedding, which had been engraved and reproduced in their workshop. We were soon ready to leave.

As we drove away, and the car was moving slowly away through the crowded street, I caught sight of a young man just walking away from the shop with a newspaper under his arm.

I leaned forward and rapped on the window so that the chauffeur turned round in surprise. "Stop the car; I want to get out."

"What is it? What are you doing?" said Ariadne in surprise and alarm. "Rose, come back! Where are you going?"

I was running through the street, weaving my way through the crowds, trying to catch the man I had seen walking briskly away from the English book-shop.

But he was gone. For a moment he had been there, almost within my grasp, Patrick Graham, but I had lost him again.

# Chapter Ten

Ariadne and I drove home in silence. I had little I wanted to offer her by way of explanation for my behaviour. "I thought I saw someone I know," I said lamely.

"Seeing things again? Oh, Rose." But beyond this mild reproach she said nothing.

"Leave me be, Ariadne." My heart was banging. How could I marry Peter Alexandrov when I was willing to run through the streets after Patrick?

I could think about nothing else. Dolly, Peter and I had a round of engagements that evening and on the next day, but I could tell by the puzzled look I occasionally caught on Peter's face that my abstraction was apparent to him.

I was wondering how I could get in touch with Patrick again. Suddenly I knew: The newspaper. He was carrying a newspaper. He will go back for another newspaper.

I knew that the English newspapers (over two days old) appeared in the book-shop early in the afternoon. If I hung about the book-shop at this time, sooner or later I should see Patrick again. Every day, on some pretext or the other (excuses increasingly lame, I fear), I made my way down there. But I never saw Patrick. Perhaps I never would. Or perhaps I came at the wrong time in spite of all my planning.

"We should be growing closer together," said Peter sadly, "but I see we are not. We are not making progress."

"We are progressing negatively," I said.

"You have coined a phrase: you mean we are going backwards."

"No: we are delineating the outlines of each other's worlds."

"And is that a good thing to do? Are we like animals then, walking round and round each other?"

There was no answer to that, nor did I attempt one.

That same day, when I arrived at the English book-shop, I saw Patrick, his newspaper tucked under his arm, standing about twenty yards away. He was with Edward Lacey.

I watched: they talked for a few minutes, then I saw them shake hands and part, walking off in opposite directions. Surprise and shock kept me still, till by the time I moved towards them, they had gone beyond catching up.

I made up my mind to take the first opportunity of speaking to Edward Lacey. My chance came that evening at a small private concert held in one of the grand ducal palaces. (The Grand Duchess Vladimir I think it was who was our hostess; she ruled St. Petersburg society in the absence of serious competition from the Summer Palace.) Ariadne was seated next to Edward, and I had Peter on my right hand. But in the interval when the singer was resting her voice before embarking on a fresh flight of trills from Donizetti, Ariadne walked off to talk to some young friends, and our hostess bore down upon Peter and Dolly.

Ariadne's seat was empty and I moved into it on the pretext of asking Edward to translate some piece of Italian in the programme, which he obligingly did.

"My Italian is rusty, but that's it, I think, more or less."

"Oh, thank you: beautifully clear. I believe I saw you talking to a friend outside the English book-shop today."

He must have felt surprise at my question but was too well-mannered to show it. "Yes, I believe I did stop for a few words."

"I thought I knew the person you were talking to, but I couldn't be sure," I said, confused and embarrassed but determined to press on. "Who was it?"

"A young Englishman I have come across in St. Petersburg," he said, with a shade of awkwardness.

"I thought it was someone I knew and that he is not an Englishman but Scottish," I blurted out.

He was silent for a moment. "Yes, he is," he said in a quiet voice.

"And he is called Patrick Graham?"

"I call him Graham," said Edward briefly.

"Do you know him well?"

"No," he said, even more briefly.

"But I do; I think I know him very well indeed, but I was surprised to see him in St. Petersburg."

"He's a young man who has, I think, been very badly treated," said Edward Lacey.

"Did he tell you that?" I demanded.

"Yes."

"But is he telling the truth?"

"I don't think he's a liar."

"I wonder what story he has spun you," I exclaimed.

Edward looked startled, as well he might at the ferocity of my reaction.

"He told me the story of a young soldier who fell into debt in London and made doubtful friends. Unwise friends, I think, and certainly unusual friends for a young man in his position. In consequence of which he felt obliged to break his engagement to marry."

"So you know about that?"

Cautiously he said, "I know you were the girl."

We stared at each other; I wondered exactly what Patrick had said.

"I don't want you to think Patrick has talked about you."

"We were going to be married, but suddenly he jilted me and went off to India with his regiment. Then I heard he was in trouble and had disappeared, perhaps was even dead. Now I find him in Russia, and you say he has been badly treated. Not by me."

"It's all part of a continuing story," said Edward seriously.

"Did you know Patrick in London?" I asked.

Edward chose his words. "I knew of him. Enough to know who he is. And was."

"And did you meet by chance in St. Petersburg?"

"Not entirely by chance, no."

"That's strange," I said tartly, "that you two should meet by some sort of plan in a foreign capital." I looked at him, waiting for a response, and got nothing. I was up against a wall of masculine silence, which angered me into saying, "Did he tell you of his job as a dancing-master in Vyksa, and how I met him there and how he ran away from me?"

"I believe he was frightened."

"Now you have silenced me: I have never thought of Patrick as a coward."

Very seriously and quietly Edward said, "The others are coming back, so listen to me: there are circumstances in which it is very wise to be a coward, not only on one's own account. A fear for others can make most men cowards."

I leaned back in my chair while this sank in.

Edward went on: "I think he should explain what he can to you himself. If I can arrange a meeting, will you consent?"

"There is nothing I should like more," I said.

"Very well, then. Now lean back in your seat and let me translate a little more Italian to you."

Two days later I had a note from Edward Lacey, discreetly handed to me by his manservant, advising me that if I went riding with Ariadne on the afternoon of the day after I received the note I would have my chance to see Patrick.

I had my own reasons for keeping it all from Peter, and Dolly and my pupil; I did not ask myself what were Edward Lacey's motives for secrecy, but I thought he was one of those Englishmen to whom discrètion and silence are a game always to be played. "Never let your right hand know what your left hand doeth." Now I came to think of it, he had that kind of face.

So I agreed readily to Ariadne's idea that we should ride together. When Edward Lacey, as I expected, joined us, I watched warily for my cue. Presently he said, "Let's gallop, Ariadne."

"Oh, but Rose hates to gallop," protested Ariadne.

"We'll come back. We'll have our ride and then ride back. Rose will hardly be alone at all, I promise you." There was not a flicker of any expression in his face except hope for a thundering good ride.

But I was not deceived. I let my nag amble placidly along the track, which was fringed with trees and shrubs. There were few other riders that dull afternoon. A scatter of snow-flakes was already beginning to drift down. I scanned the trees, searching for a sight of Patrick.

The cold was starting to reach through my cloak. Edward and Ariadne would be returning. Patrick *must* be here.

From behind a voice said softly, "Rose, I am here."

I turned my head to see a figure standing among the shrubberies. Slowly I moved my horse on through the trees to his side. A delicate curtain of snowflakes was hanging between us, as cold as my heart.

As cold as his, too, I thought, as I saw the look on his face: blank, dispirited and tired.

"You look cold," I said spontaneously.

"I'm frozen. I've been waiting for ages. You're late." I thought it was like Patrick to go on to the attack, rather than be defensive. "Get off your horse."

"I can talk perfectly well from up here," I said, looking down on him.

"But I can't." He took the bridle and stood there commandingly. "Come on, now: down." He held out an arm.

"But I can't get back on the animal without a mounting-block." I was riding side-saddle, as ladies always did in Russia.

"I'll help you back. Be glad to." And suddenly he grinned at me.

I slid down in his arms, and for a moment we stood together in silence, close. Then the grin faded, and for the first time, anxiety appeared. "Oh, Rose."

I drew away. "You left me. Twice. Once in Scotland and once in Russia. That's enough, I think."

"I don't excuse myself." He kept his voice quiet.

"I should think not, indeed."

"But I could." A flash of anger here.

I could show anger, too. "Edward Lacey thought we should meet and talk. I wanted to and so, I suppose, did you, since you are here. But it is you who must do the talking; I have nothing to say."

"Edward Lacey is a good friend to me, to us both."

"It was a surprise to me that you knew each other."

"I don't really; I knew his name and he knew mine, you know how it is."

Yes, I knew how it was, or could imagine. Both men moving within the small confines of London Society. Just passing each other in the same clubs, without both being members. Entertained by the same hostesses, but not on the same night. Never meeting, but hearing of each other.

Patrick began to speak quickly, pouring out what he had to say in a rush, as if he was anxious to get it over. "In London, just before we were to be married, I got in with a gambling set, a strange, polyglot set they were, Russians and Poles among them. Not the sort I usually mixed with at all, and yet I liked them. They were free and liberal in their ideas, not believing in a lot of the old shibboleths that you and I were brought up with. They have to go, Rose."

"Well, some of them, perhaps," I conceded.

"As well as talking politics, we played high. I lost. I was lent the money to pay my debts by one of the fellows, a Russian called Vladimir Ozerov. I thought he was my friend." Patrick paused. "I must be honest: I still think of him as my friend, he had something about him that I loved. Only I pray God we never meet again, for I should probably feel obliged to kill him. Or he me."

He paused for a moment, then went on: "It was after my debts were paid that Ozerov told me the money came from the secret funds of a society formed to promote red revolution and that I was now an equal brother in it. That was my situation in the week before we were supposed to marry."

"You could have told your colonel. He would have been bound to help you."

"What, tell Colonel Maddox?" He laughed. "You don't know him. Oh, he would have got me out of one sort of trouble, and then put me straight away into another. I'd have been out of the regiment."

"Or you could have told *me*," I said.

The snow was falling fast now; I brushed the flakes from my cheek.

"That was the worst of all. How could I marry you? Or tell you? Or ask you to wait for me? No, it was best to break it off. Besides, Ozerov had let me see plainly enough that you could be in danger. He advised me to break with you." Patrick added in a low voice: "I was very close to you in that village shop; I was carrying a message from Marisia Lazarev to the big house. She had her own ways of communicating with that house. I *longed* to speak, Rose, and I dared not. The old woman in that shop would have told."

"I *knew* you were there in Shereshevo," I said slowly. "I wish you had spoken then. . . . How much money did Ozerov lend you?"

"Three thousand pounds."

"So I was paid for," I said bitterly. "There was some truth in the story, after all." He stared at me, puzzled. "Didn't you know your sister Jeannie was telling such a tale? That you had been paid to throw me over?"

"The little beast," said Patrick. "She must have read a letter.

to me from Ozerov and put her own interpretation on it. But it wasn't true. You didn't believe it?"

"Yes. What do you expect? Oh, yes, I believed it. I came to Russia believing it. And it turns out to be true."

"I went out to India half crazy, Rose. And if you are half crazy when you go to that country, Rose, then you are mad when you leave it. My regiment was what is known as a strict, good, clean regiment, one where the discipline was tight. I found the atmosphere terrible. I didn't like India, Rose. It got on my nerves. I never thought I had much imagination until I went to India, and then I found I had. More than enough. Not that I blame India for what happened. I struck a man in the regiment, Rose, a common soldier. That's a serious offence."

"I know," I said.

"Bad trouble. It was an accident, really. Or so I thought." He paused. "Ozerov had already been in touch with me. He advised me to get out altogether, leave India and the Army. Back to London, if I liked, where they would hide me. Or Russia. I chose Russia. He told me where to go and where I should find friends." Thoughtfully, he said, "It was made pretty clear to me that I had no real alternative. I sensed the menace, without understanding it. I still thought of them as friends, for whose ideas I had much respect."

"So I discovered at Vyksa," I said sardonically.

"Yes, Vyksa." He frowned. "There's a lot to explain about Vyksa. Rose, it was in Vyksa I first knew, to the full, how dangerous my friends are. Murder is nothing to them, and then friends are the first to go. I think now that the episode in India, as with the business in London, was a put-up affair, to get a hold on me. For my own sake? I doubt it now. I think it was because of you. And now I fear them. They have no faithfulness and no loyalties except to revolution. I was afraid for you, Rose."

"So you say. But how much can I believe you."

"Rose—" He tried to reach out and touch me. "You don't know, you don't understand—"

All the hot emotion that could so suddenly break through my calm now showed itself, but it was anger, not love, that I felt.

"Leave me alone. I am going back to my friends."

I met Edward and Ariadne riding back towards me: she was laughing at the snow accumulating on his moustaches and calling him a "snowman." I joined them without a word. When he had an opportunity, Edward said, "How did you get on?"

"We quarrelled," I said briefly. "What else did you expect?" I added: "He told me to talk to you."

Edward said, "It is very hard to talk with you. But I think I should try." His face was troubled, even though he was watching a laughing Ariadne superintending the handing over of the horses to a waiting groom.

"If you are going to tell me that both Dolly and her brother are deep in political plotting, then I know."

"*What* do you know?" he asked.

"Well, they're liberals, both of them, aren't they? Of course that brings them into trouble with the authorities, we both know that, and without doubt they both have enemies, especially Peter. I expect Marisia Lazarev is one of them. She is hostile to everyone, that girl, I felt it in her. I don't trust her, or like her. Neither does Madame Denisov."

"Yes, Dolly has some sense," he said, still gravely. "I'm sorry you didn't make it up with young Graham. I hoped you would. And that might have taken you away from Russia." He paused, as if to let the words sink in, and I listened incredulously, wondering if I had really heard what I thought I heard: "Go back to Patrick," was that what he was saying? But did I want Patrick or did he want me? Then Edward went on: "But if you are determined to stay in Russia and make your home here, then you ought to learn more about it and trust to appearances less."

"What an alarming thing to say," I said, trying to keep my voice light.

"In the situation in which you may find yourself I do not

know who you can trust. You will have to find out for yourself, if you can."

"I shall do that," I said, and I know my voice shook. "I will
trust those I love."

Then he said something terrible: "Remember that Russia
as a society is closed, full of secret lies and secret betrayals.
The revolution, when it comes, will be full of secrets and lies,
and so the society it creates will be the same. That is the
world you may have to live in."

"Dolly said something like that once," I said, remembering.

"I told you she had sense."

For a moment he had dented my confidence, and I seemed
to move in a hideous, haggard world of shadows, then
Ariadne came running over, making a teasing joke to Edward, and brought me back to a normal, happy world in
which girls laughed and flirted with their lovers.

"But I'm going to be married," I said.

I suppose I said it wonderingly, innocently, as a young girl
would, as if marriage were the end of a chapter.

Anyway, he laughed, a dry, resonant laugh. It was a thoroughly sceptical, masculine sound, such as might have echoed round the club-rooms of St. James's, and it silenced me.
Never had I felt the gap between our sexes more strongly,
because it was full of sympathy, too. Women do not laugh in
that way.

Amidst a confusion of cardboard boxes and crisp folds of
tissue paper, my trousseau was arriving. Every article, from
tailored suits to tea-gowns, was inspected and appraised by
Dolly and greeted with rapture by Ariadne. By Dolly's standards it was a meagre wardrobe, but to me it represented the
last of my small capital.

"You have such style, Rose," declared Ariadne enthusiastically. "It's having such lovely long bones that does it."

"You make me sound like a giraffe."

"No, more like a race-horse. Now, I'm such a squat little thing," and she looked down at her young, rounded figure with disgust. "I shall be *fat* when I am middle-aged. However, I don't propose to live that long."

"Oh, Ariadne," and I laughed, "I never knew anyone who liked life as you do. You'll hang on." I was going to question her then about Marisia Lazarev, but Dolly interrupted us. "I am glad that silk and alpaca walking-dress has arrived." (It was a pretty confection of anthracite-grey, tailored coat and skirt with a frilly lace jabot; I had chosen it with pleasure.) "It will be just the thing to wear to Tsarskoye Selo."

So the summons to the Summer Palace had come. But in my mind this thought was obscured by another. "It is part of my trousseau," I said. "I can't wear it yet."

As if the question was beyond dispute, Dolly said, "You have nothing else to wear more suitable."

"Some of my old clothes—I wore nothing very grand to Spala."

This was dismissed. "Spala is the provinces. Here in St. Petersburg you must be properly dressed to go to Court."

"Even sneaking in through the back door?" I said.

"We are honoured guests," said Dolly reprovingly.

"And Father Gregory, is he an honoured guest, too? Will he be there?"

Dolly looked flustered. "You should never mention his name. Not above a whisper. He is banned from St. Petersburg, must not come within miles of the capital. Thank God," she added.

You don't know, I thought. If he ever left the city, he has come back.

"So when do we go to the Summer Palace?" I asked.

"Now, at once. We are to go with all speed. There is a motor car sent." For the first time, she hesitated. "That is, when I say 'we,' it's not the case: you are to go alone." She seemed nervous. "You don't mind, Rose?"

"Not in the least. I'm sure it's best."

"As you say. Still, I don't know, it makes me uneasy for you."

Ariadne was radiant. "Such promotion for you, Rose. You must be sure always to go alone in future."

"If there is ever another visit."

"Oh, there will be, I'm sure of it." She sounded excited. I suppose it was exciting, my contact with the Tsarevich, in this Imperial city. Even for irreverent Ariadne a little glitter remained. "But it means you won't be able to come to the luncheon party that Cousin Louisette is giving for Peter and you."

"I shall explain that," said Dolly. "A diplomatic illness for you, I'm afraid, Rose."

"Cousin Louisette already thinks anyone under fifty is likely to die of galloping consumption, since we don't wear flannel undervests as she does," said Ariadne.

"Can you be ready in fifteen minutes, Rose?" Dolly looked at the little jewelled watch on her fob.

"Someone will have to explain to Peter," I said, going towards the door.

"Then explain to him in person," said his voice, and there he was on the threshold. "Or rather, don't bother, save all excuses and explanations for Cousin Louisette, for I am coming with you." To Dolly's protesting voice he said, "Yes, yes, I know all about it, or guessed, because I saw the Imperial car parked at the back of the Moyka Prospect. Such secrecy was an indication in itself." He was in rattling spirits.

"Oh, you lovers," said Dolly. "Well, I suppose you can go with her in the car, but you won't be allowed in. On her own, that's the fiat."

"I shall always go in the future, shan't I, Rose?"

"If you say so."

"Spoken like a good little wife."

"I don't know why you're so happy at the prospect of a cold drive and a boring wait," I said.

"Because of you, Rose, because of you."

As I ran up the stairs to change, I thought: they are all of them happy, because of me, and only I am not happy.

The great house oppressed me. I could not imagine a happy family life being lived in it. I supposed there would be a family for me. I pushed the thought away from me as bringing with it all sorts of associations I did not wish to dwell upon.

Peter held my hand in his all through the drive out of the city to the royal village of Tsarskoye Selo where palace after palace lay scattered in opulent park-land behind tall railings along whose boundaries mounted guards rode in continual alert.

"What a cold little hand," he said, smiling. "I hope it means a warm heart?"

I don't know why he was so pleased with me, as I didn't think I had been behaving very well.

We drove through the great gates which were permanently open, rusted so, I expect, like the huge gates of Versailles which thus failed to keep out the revolutionary mob when required. Snow lay everywhere, mantling turf, trees and buildings, so that the bright uniforms of the soldiers stood out against the grey and white landscape.

The officer on duty seemed to know Peter and nodded to him as we passed.

"Which regiment is that?" I asked.

"The Preobrazhensky Guard," he said absently. "The loyallest of the loyal. Never mutinied, you know, not like some of the others."

"And he knew you?"

"We were in the Imperial Corps des Pages together, only he went on to make service to the Tsar a career, and I did not. He thinks me an idle, lazy man, no doubt."

"And what do you think of him?"

"I never think about him at all," said Peter, showing, just for a moment, a touch of ruthlessness that lay beneath his gentle manner. "All the same," he said, as he scrambled out of the motor car after me, "I shall go and talk to him while you are on your errand of mercy. There, will that convince you that I am not such a bad fellow after all?"

As I walked away, led by a servant who had been awaiting me, I thought what a lot Peter saw, and how little he ever let one guess it.

I was shown into a pleasant-looking room, furnished with English chintzes and pale furniture. In appearance it was somewhere between a schoolroom and a nursery. The Tsarevich was sitting at a table occupied with a jig-saw puzzle; with him were Madame Titov, who rose as soon as she saw me, and the boy's English tutor, who gave me a pleasant smile. A table near the window was set out with the tea-things. It was clearly to be a social occasion. The boy looked up when he saw me and smiled radiantly.

"So you're here, you've come. *I* asked for you to come, and for once I was allowed to have my own way. I'm not often allowed." He left his puzzle and came over to me and gave my hand a hearty shake.

"I don't believe that," I said, looking around the cozy room where two cats and a dog slept happily on a furry rug by the porcelain stove. "I think you have lots of cossetting, and are spoiled in all sorts of ways."

"So many things I may not do, though," he said with a little sigh. "Not run too fast, not jump, I may not ride on my own, and *never* above a trot." He sat down on a stool near the cats and put out a hand to stroke one. "I'm glad you've come. I'm pretty well, as you see."

"Good," I said.

He put his head on one side. "But there's the little matter of my leg, don't you see, my dear? One leg is shorter than the other."

Madame Titov made a demurring noise. "There is nothing wrong with your leg, Your Imperial Highness, nothing."

He gave her a sidelong look. "No, very well. I am not allowed to say so, neither is anyone else. Nevertheless, my bad leg is crooked and shorter than the other, and that is that."

He stretched out both legs and looked at them, inviting me to do the same. I could see that the muscles of one leg were drawn and twisted so that he could not flex it properly. The distortion was a mute testimony to the terrible suffering he had endured.

"Yes, I see what you mean," I said.

"There is nothing nature will not cure," said Madame Titov.

Behind the boy was a door leading to an inner room and that door was a crack ajar. I could just see the edge of a pale violet skirt protruding. So the Tsarina was there watching me. I thought there was a whole world portrayed in that silent, secret watch.

"I should think exercise would help," I said. "Walking and swimming."

"Ah, but I can't walk very well. I hobble. And that makes them ashamed of me. I mustn't be seen to hobble. *They* think I don't know, but I know all about it." He gave me a hard look. "They think I'll die of this illness I have. They don't say so, but they think it. I won't, though. I don't know how I know it, but I do know it. So I suppose I'll live to be an old man. I might even become as big and strong as my grandfather."

"Of course you will, sir," said Madame Titov, at once both hearty and unconvincing; I could see how she must depress the boy.

"Can you help me?" he said directly to me. "To walk better, I mean. I'll manage the living."

I bent down and looked at his leg. Then I peeled back the thick, knee-length woollen sock he wore, and put my hand on the muscle. At first I felt nothing. Then heat seemed to gather beneath my fingers. It felt like a slightly vibrating ball of warmth whose outlines were almost palpable. My hand became numb. I felt dizzy, and angular bands of light jerked in front of my eyes. Then my vision cleared; a pulse began to bang in my temples. Deeper within me something seemed to open and forces flooded away, leaving me empty. The heat went from my hand. That's the end, I thought. I shall never do this again. It's over. I looked at the boy. He smiled at me. I said, my voice unsteady, "Do you know, I believe Madame Titov is correct; now nature will do the job. As you grow, I believe the leg will right itself. You may always limp a little, but you won't hobble."

"Oh, I'm so glad. It's undignified to hobble. Besides, *they* mind."

From behind the door I saw the flicker of mauve move away; the Empress (and surely she was the chief of *them*) had withdrawn.

A rattle of silver against china announced the arrival of tea, supported into the room by two tall footmen.

"Ah, tea," said the boy. "You'll take some with me?"

"I should be glad to. I missed luncheon."

At once he was apologetic. "Because of coming to me? I'm so sorry."

I drew near the tea-table, which Madame Titov was superintending. A plate of plain bread and butter and some soft-looking biscuits made up the eatable part. I was surprised at the dullness of the food. He saw my look.

"No one cares about food here. I saw what delicious food you *can* have when I had tea on my English cousin's yacht. Scones, short-bread, Dundee cake." He made a tasty catalogue of it, just like any ordinary, hungry little boy. "But no matter how much I ask, I never get anything different from this. I suppose I'll be able to do something about it one day," he said, without much hope.

"Are you always on your own?"

"Well, except for Mr. Gibbs." He gave his tutor a smile; relations between them were good.

"Except for Wednesdays," the tutor reminded him gently.

"Oh, yes. Every Wednesday at five o'clock Mamma and Papa take tea with me. If their engagements permit," he added carefully.

Shortly afterwards a nod from Madame Titov gave me the hint to leave. I looked at the boy, his eyelids were heavy. He was tired and so was I.

Because I was tired I did not talk over-much on the drive back to St. Petersburg. Peter was curious and I answered his questions.

"So he takes tea in state once a week with his parents?" he said with amusement. "I had heard the story. And so it's true?"

"Every Wednesday, at five," I nodded. "Poor little soul. What a life."

Peter did not answer, but he took my hand in his and held it tightly. "Still cold," he said. "If anything, colder than before."

"Doesn't matter. I don't mind."

"How independent you are, Rose," he sighed.

"It's the way I was brought up," I began. "Tibby says . . ." then stopped; a small frown puckered his face and he dropped my hand. I was learning not to use that name.

I was cold all that night in my scented and over-heated bedroom, cold in spite of the heat, and I slept badly. When I did sleep it seemed as though a high wind were whistling in my ears. Then the wind seemed to change into a whispering voice. "Rose," it called, "Rose, Rose."

I woke up once and listened, and it felt as though a sibilant whisper were just completing its sound in the empty room.

# Chapter Eleven

Edward Lacey had a quarrel with Dolly Denisov the next day. I heard them at it from behind closed doors. It was impossible to make out much, but Edward's voice was easily identifiable and so was Dolly's. Then the door opened smartly and Edward himself appeared. He saw me standing at the foot of the stairs; I didn't try to pretend I hadn't heard.

"Oh, it's you," he said.

"You've been quarrelling."

"I've been shouting at Dolly in English and she's been fishwifing me back in Russian," he said. "That tells you we meant it."

"But what was it about?"

"Why don't you ask her yourself? I'm off," and he swung towards the door.

When I went into the room I was at once sorry for Dolly: she looked quite haggard, with little patches of red standing out on her cheeks.

"Oh, what is it? You look almost ill. I heard the noise."

"He has been saying such things, such things," and her

hands trembled as she straightened her hair. "I can't tell you."

"About me?"

"No, of course not about you."

"I thought I heard my name."

Dolly got a grip on herself. "You did." She swallowed once or twice as if some words were hard to say. "He thinks that your marriage with my brother is not a wise act."

"What's it to do with him?" I cried indignantly. "And why doesn't he say so to me himself, instead of to you?"

"Now, how could he? Be reasonable, Rose. A young unmarried man who is no relation. No, of course he was right to speak to me: I am your natural guardian in Russia." Then she said, with an obvious effort, "He thinks you are in love with someone else."

"No, I'm not, I'm not," I said passionately. Clearly Edward had not told Dolly of Patrick's appearance in Russia. He must have wanted to, though.

"He thinks you are marrying for the wrong reasons. Are you, Rose?"

"Not for position, or wealth, or anything like that," I said. "Indeed, I am not."

With considerable dignity, Dolly said, "I believe you, Rose. If you want to get out of this marriage, then, at whatever cost to myself, I will help you."

I stared. "What *has* he been saying to you?"

"Never mind that. Do you want to break your engagement? Just answer me, and I will manage it for you."

"Of course not. Never. I mean to marry Peter. And if I did want to be off with it, then I'd do the telling myself. I know what it means to be jilted. Why should I hide behind you? This is all rubbish, Dolly."

"So be it, then. Speaking for myself, I am delighted you are to be my brother's wife. You can bring him nothing but good. And if you can stand up to him, so much the better. I find it difficult sometimes to talk to him; I know he always does what he wants." Amazingly, there were tears in her eyes.

"He's not a bit like that," I said, thinking he was far more reasonable than his sister.

"I'm glad to hear you say it: he must truly love you. And you him. I should never have doubted it." She patted her tears dry, kissed my cheeks and got herself out of the room. At the door, she said:

"You won't repeat anything of this to Peter?"

Doubtfully, I said, "Well, I don't know."

"It would really be much better not."

"All right then." I supposed Dolly meant well, with her Russian love of scenes and emotion, but I felt played out by it all, and tired, not radiantly happy like a bride at all.

Lest you should think that I was a poor girl, alone in a strange land and bereft of family, let me tell you that a spate of letters and telegrams had been flying between London and St. Petersburg, from Grizel and her husband, and the more august of my relations, who were not coming to my wedding but wanted me to know of their approval and happiness, showing some relief in getting me off their hands. But they sent handsome presents and the British Ambassador himself was coming to my wedding, and had already sent us, as his gift, a beautifully carved wooden box from Povarov's.

I ought to have been floating in a bubble of happiness, but I was not. The physical and mental unease continued, my sleep seemed full of voices. I was keeping so many things from Peter: my meeting with Patrick Graham, the encounter with Father Gregory and now this conversation with Dolly. I told myself this was the reason for my unease. Secrets are like the pea under the Princess's mattresses in the fairy-story. At first they can be ignored, but gradually they came to be un-endurable.

Twenty years after, my son said that the way I dwelt on

restlessness and beds and sleep in describing all this was quite "Freudian." This was the first time I had heard the term.

But "imagination" and "nerves" were the phrases in current use then and they had been hurled at me. "Rose imagines things," Dolly had said about Laure's death and the voice which spoke from the tube.

Did I imagine things? Were some of the manifestations that alarmed me my own fault? Perhaps the wretchedness was self-imposed, I accept that idea, but not the happenings.

To add to my anxieties in these weeks before the wedding was the notion I had that Ariadne was meeting Marisia. I was sure of it; I could detect the other girl's influence in every excited and wild tone in Ariadne's voice. In a short while she would cease to be my responsibility, but while she was, I felt I must keep an eye on her. I fancied they met in the English book-shop, so whenever Ariadne went there (which was almost daily) I went, too.

In the shop I would stroll around reading the books and studying the other shoppers; I never once caught Ariadne with Marisia. Perhaps they didn't meet there after all.

"It's nice to come to the English book-shop so often," said Ariadne one afternoon, just one week before my wedding. She spoke innocently enough, but I thought I saw laughter at the back of her eyes. Did she know exactly what I was up to?

I made a non-committal noise.

"I am just going over there to choose a novel for Mamma."

"And I am going to study all the latest fashion magazines from Paris. Princess Irene wants me to bring back a verdict on the 'new' look."

"Yes, very flat-chested, isn't it? Won't do for me. Nor her, either, I should think. She *does* use you for her errands, doesn't she?" No mistaking the amusement in Ariadne's voice now. And it was true that the relationship between her elderly relative and me flourished. I believed I loved the old creature, strange as it may seem. I thought her false Indian summer was ending, though. "Well, I shall be over there with my nose in the novels, Rose, so look for me there." Yes, Ariadne was laughing at me.

Patiently I studied the drawings of what the smart modistes of Paris were creating. Very bright and gay and funny they looked. I knew I could wear them, tall, angular creature that I was, but for my aged friend they would be disaster in petticoats.

"I'll take this magazine," and I handed my choice to the assistant. He bowed, tied it up and handed it over. Then quickly and silently he slid a letter on top of it, bowed again and disappeared.

The letter was addressed to me in Patrick's hand. I put it in my purse; I was glad Ariadne wasn't watching.

In my room I opened the letter and read:

My dearest Rose,

This may well be the last letter I shall ever write to you. For I shall certainly never write to you when you are the wife of Peter Alexandrov. Did you ever guess, Rose, how I treasured your letters in the past? Those short, inarticulate, shy letters. You never wore your heart on your sleeve, did you, Rose? You would have put more into words, my dearest girl, if you had known how I studied each word for its meaning. But we have both misunderstood each other and I was the most stupid of men. I see my way out of my troubles now. Only trust to me, Rose. Please, please, my dearest love, break off your engagement. Your marriage to Peter Alexandrov cannot be what the Rose Gowrie I knew would wish for. Trust me and accept me again with a love more thoroughly your own than if there had never been a break.

Just send me word and I will come and get you.

Patrick.

The devil, I thought, how well he knows how to pull at the sinews of my heart. And I *did* respond, I *was* moved, I wanted to accept. Against right, against good feeling, against loyalty to Peter Alexandrov, I wanted to say, Yes, Patrick Graham.

People who don't cry much often turn out to have a great flood of tears inside them waiting to be shed. Out flowed mine now.


After this, time, which had been galloping, took off on wings. Seven days to my wedding, six days, then five, then four, then three, and my trunks were already neatly packed and ready, waiting for the final touches, the second day and my wedding dress was delivered, and within the hour Grizel and her Archie had come.

I went to meet them at their hotel. They were staying at the Hotel Geneva, a modest establishment run by a Swiss, which Archie had selected for himself rather than one of the grander hotels where he would have been Peter's guest.

"Rose?" Grizel came speeding down the staircase, arms held out to me; we gave each other one swift glance before hugging each other, midway between laughter and tears.

"Ah, you look bonny," I said spontaneously to Grizel. Her hair was fashionably curled, her skirt stopped just above the ankle, her cheeks were pink and her eyes bright. She looked prosperous and happy.

"And you look thin," was the response.

"Ah, well," I said, wondering what to say.

"It suits you, though." She stepped back and gave me an appraising stare. "Yes, Rose, you have become what my horrid mother-in-law calls a 'thoroughly elegant woman.'"

"Is she horrid?" I asked, amused.

"Yes," said Grizel briefly. "But I am more than a match for her, and mean to go on being so. A thoroughgoing old snob, she is, and don't we have the Maid of Scotland in our family tree? I don't let her forget the blood royal, I can tell you."

And then I was being greeted by her sandy-haired Archie and being given a brotherly kiss.

The rest of the day was pleasant: Dolly was always a delightful hostess and Peter was a courteous and attentive host, and I, for my part, was happy to have my sister and her husband with me. Ariadne roamed around the outskirts of our group, making little conversational forays into it, but not really joining us, so that I thought to myself, with surprise: that girl's not happy.

When I was helping Grizel into her cloak, she said, "And what do you think of Archie?"

"He looks very clever."

"Oh, he is, but so am I clever. We shall do. He's very much in love with me. I love him, of course, but he loves me more. That way I have him nicely in thrall." She sounded pleased with herself. "I hope you don't love your Peter *too* much," she asked anxiously. "Better not, you know. I expect you got over all that with Patrick."

I did not answer, but helped fasten her cloak; she did not press.

But as she went off with her husband, and I saw Archie's confidence with her and Grizel's joyful acceptance of it, I thought that she did love, quite as much as she should.

All the same I was thoughtful as I brushed my hair that night. I knew my Grizel, and there had been a sort of self-consciousness about her. Either she had a secret, or she was plotting something.


I found out the next day. It was something I might have expected, knowing all the characters concerned.

I went round to the Hotel Geneva because I had promised to take Grizel shopping; I was given the use of Dolly's car and chauffeur. Dolly knew now that I could drive, but she said she wasn't going to let me drive her car round St. Petersburg where everyone knew her; I could wait until I was married, after which I could do anything.

I was early by a few minutes, and I was ushered into their

room before Grizel expected me. Archie greeted me, and
Grizel called to me from the inner room that she was almost
ready, "just putting my hat on," following it up with the comment that "Archie will amuse you."

Archie, who had been holding a newspaper, from which
my arrival had torn his attention, politely put it down and
prepared to do his bride's behest.

The more I saw of my brother-in-law the more I liked him.
Not only did he look clever, but there was distinction of mien
and manner. He had, or at least it was in the making, that
subdued, grand seigneur air which one hardly ever sees now
but which I remembered from one of my grandfathers.

"Rose, I want you to see something." And there was Grizel,
her face half exultant, half frightened.

Behind her was a sturdy, beloved figure: Tibby.

"Oh, my darling girl." And in a moment I was in her arms
being thoroughly hugged.

"Tibby, Tibby, how I have longed to see you."

"What, let my girl marry without me seeing her wed! No, I
had my little nest-egg and I've come under my own steam."

There were tears of happiness between us, with hugs and
kisses from an unexpectedly demonstrative Tibby, she who
hardly ever showed emotion. Grizel, of course, was always
overflowing with tears and laughter. Archie looked on in a
friendly fashion.

"He's got three sisters," whispered Grizel. "Nothing puts
him out."

But I knew I had to tell Peter about Tibby, and I did wonder how he would act.

I took Tibby and Grizel on a sight-seeing tour of the city,
ending up with a visit to Fabergé's where were being prepared the little golden crowns for my wedding (brides have a
sort of crown held over their heads in the ceremony in
Russia), which made them gasp, although Grizel assured me
afterwards that her own mother-in-law's diamonds were better than any she saw there. Archie had disappeared on his
own into a men's world to which, as I later discovered, he al-

ways found access in whichever city in the world you set him down.

I watched the meeting between Tibby and Peter, and on her face I saw caution, and behind his formal politeness, anger.

"Why did you let that old woman come?" he asked furiously when we were alone for a minute. "Why did you not order her to stay away?"

"No one *orders* Tibby to do anything."

"She's your servant."

"But so much more than a servant," I said, wondering how I would ever bridge the gap between Scotland and Russia. "I couldn't stop her coming. I didn't even know."

"I don't believe you."

Anger put an edge on my tongue. "I think, at heart, you still believe in serfs and slavery. Or you could find a use for its rules. Tibby is no serf."

He gripped my wrist so hard that it hurt. "That's unkind and untrue."

"A lot of the attitudes remain; I've noticed it." I dragged my hand free.

We stared at each other with open rage; it was our first quarrel.

"I knew if that old woman came here she would bring nothing but trouble. She influences you too much. Look at you now, changing before my eyes."

"Then I'd better go back to Scotland with her," I said.

"Oh, yes, so you admit it. If it comes to a choice between her and me, then you choose her." He was beside himself with fury, and, as I thought, jealousy.

"Perhaps I really ought to go," I said thoughtfully. "I'm not jealous enough, and that must mean something. If you had a mistress in Moscow, I don't believe I should mind, and that can't be right."

"Oh, you are a ridiculous creature," he said, laughing, his bad mood breaking. "And you would mind. Women always do."

We made it up then, in itself an enjoyable process, and nothing more was said about Tibby. Tibby, for her part, said nothing at all about Peter.

I took her to see Princess Irene, to whom, these days, I paid frequent friendly visits.

To my surprise, as we went up the red-carpeted staircase, which I had once so disliked and now took for granted, Tibby said that it was "a fusty enough place," and that she didn't think she'd care to go up it too often. And she gave a genuine shiver.

With Princess Irene herself she was silent, not saying one single word. But none was demanded of her. The Princess contented herself with doing what she always did on my visits now. She held my hand, as if a new infusion of vigour came that way, and talked to me about her lover.

"Ah, but he's so beautiful. A soldier, of course. My first lover was a soldier. No technique, but they have such vigour."

Whether he existed or whether he was part of a fantasy world in which she seemed now to be living, I was not sure. Perhaps it was old General Rahl, although his vigour looked doubtful. But I knew he visited her, coming up the other staircase straight from the Moyka Quay. I saw his back once, shuffling away as I came into her room, no mistaking him, I had seen him at many St. Petersburg gatherings now. People talked about him, and avoided him because of his association with the Third Bureau.

"What did you think of her?" I asked Tibby as we went down the staircase.

After a pause, she said, "She's near death, I think."

"She thinks that she's going to live for ever. Certainly she has had an extraordinary revival of life lately."

"The last flicker of the flame before it dies."

"I think so, too." Then I added, hesitantly, "She believes it is due to me. That I have done it for her."

"And have you?"

"Just the idea of me has helped, perhaps. I don't think it's been any more."

We walked down the stairs and then stopped at the bottom

in that lower hall where I had paused so curiously the first time.

Tibby said, "You know I should never ask you to help me in that way, don't you, Rose?"

"I believe I do."

"I'll go when the Good Lord wants me. And in the way he wants."

"Everyone does in the end," I said. "Do you think what I do so very wicked then, Tibby? Somtimes I have thought that to you it seemed"—I hesitated—"unclean."

"No, no, Rose, no. There's more things in this world than Tabitha Mackenzie comprehends. Aye, others wiser nor me, too. And because I don't understand, it doesn't mean I condemn. It came from God, your gift, you did not seek it out, nor take profit from it, and you are right to use it. But if I seem to fear it at all, it is only because of what it does to *you.*"

"Yes. Sometimes I think it has ruined my life."

"That's a strange thing for a girl about to be married to say."

"Yes, isn't it? But you forget: I have been about to be married before."

I took Tibby to my room; it was filled still with boxes which had contained clothes, and evidence of packing. "Look, there is my wedding-dress."

It was hanging up, white and sumptuous, heavy satin, Dolly's taste.

"It doesn't suit me at all. I look a frump in it. But you'll help dress me in it?" She nodded.

Then I told her all I knew about Patrick, the whole story, including about Vyksa and our other meeting in St. Petersburg. I ended by showing her his letter, which she read soberly and then returned to me.

"Of course, I have sent no answer," I said.

She looked sad. "I've known Patrick Graham all his life. He always was a merry, reckless little boy, I mind some of the wild things he did, but there was aye a tenderness in him. I always thought he was the best one to deal with you when that intense mood takes on you."

"Am I intense?"

"You wouldn't be aware, but a strange look comes over you at times, as if you were taking all pain into yourself and enduring it."

"Two wild, giddy things together?" I said with a sob.

"Yes. It often works best that way," said Tibby soberly. "Ah, my poor lass—don't greet so."

I suppose I'd got all my tears out of my system, because on my wedding-day I did not cry, but allowed myself to be dressed by Grizel and Dolly's maid in good spirits. But I fancy there was a good deal of repressed ill humour battling away inside, because I was quite sharp with Grizel when she tried to embark on reminiscences of her own wedding.

She was hurt. "I thought you'd like to hear. After all . . ."

"You married for love. My case is quite different."

Grizel blushed, her trick when startled or embarrassed. "What are you marrying for, then?"

"I don't know; I wish I did."

"Oh, fiddle," said Grizel. "Nerves, just nerves."

"Where's Tibby?" I demanded. "Why isn't she with you?"

Grizel didn't answer, then she said, "I had to leave her with Archie. He needed someone to dress *him.*" Meeting my eye, she said smoothly, "Well, full morning dress, darling; he's doing you proud. He could never manage on his own."

The wedding was in the private chapel of the Dournkovs' palace. I had been taken there previously to view it; the palace seemed to have a great number of empty rooms.

Now I was taken there again, led through suites of shuttered rooms and corridors to the chapel. It was bright with candles, and the priests and the chanters were already there. By the altar two young men in pages' uniforms, *garçons de noces,* as they were called, bore golden images, one for me and one for Peter Alexandrov.

In all Russian weddings the bride and bridegroom have what is known as *un père assis* and *une mère assise,* who are proxy parents and stand as witnesses to an event which the real parents are presumed to be too emotionally overcome by to testify to. I could see Grizel and Archie and Tabitha lined up beside them, with, to my surprise, Edward Lacey.

The singing started, a candle was placed in my hand, and one in Peter's. At this point he looked at me and smiled. Then we moved into the centre of the chapel and the service began.

I remember so little of it, and yet at the time it seemed endless. There were three magnificently dressed priests, and three times we exchanged vows. Our hands were joined and rings passed between us. Then two jewelled crowns were brought in from the sanctuary and shown to us. Following Peter's example, I kissed my crown, after which they were held over our heads by the bridegroom's men. Then, our hands linked together by a silver band from the priest's robe, we were led three times round the reading-desk, carefully followed by the *garçons de noces* holding our crowns.

Then there was the sermon, the hymns, the prayers, on and on it went.

At last Peter was holding my hand and triumphantly leading me out.

At the reception afterwards, I whispered to Tibby, "Why did you not come to me before to help me dress?"

"I tried, my dear, but they would not let me in at the door." Her face was pale, but without expression.

Peter Alexandrov was standing only a few feet from me and heard it all. I looked up and saw the anger at the back of his eyes; I know there was surprise and resentment in mine.

So our marriage got off to a bad start, and the difficult business of the honeymoon was made even more difficult.

Our wedding trip took us to the protected and sheltered Crimean coastline. I had wished to go to Moscow, but Peter said it was a full-time occupation just keeping the snow from the streets at this time of the year, and he wanted to go somewhere warmer, and he thought I would, too. It was as if my whole being were still penetrated by the extreme winter cold of Russia. So we went to the Vorontsov-Dashkov palace at Alupka. They were Dolly's friends and she had arranged it all. "It's so beautiful there, so romantic, ideal for a wedding trip, you will be so happy," and she looked at me as if urging me, above all, to be happy.

It was dark when we got to Alupka after our long journey, but the air smelt spicy and warm, different from any other smell of land I had ever known. As if I were in Asia, I thought, as, indeed, I almost was. When I first saw the house, early the next day, the walls seemed to reflect the pale blues and greens and beiges of the landscape like an opal.

We were alone there together, except for the customary army of servants, none of whom were ours; we had brought none with us.

The journey was a torment, with both of us shut up in our overheated compartment, locked in our anger. A good quarrel would have cleared the air, but that, alas, was impossible, so after a while we lapsed into silence.

I stood at the tall window of my bedroom, looking out at the building with its turrets and cupolas and curving arches.

"Fantastic structure, is it not?" said Peter's voice from behind me. "Part-Gothic part-Moorish."

"Yes, like a palace in a fairy-tale."

"I'm glad you said fairy-tale and not nightmare," he said soberly.

I kept my eyes on the view from my window. "It's very beautiful."

"Or a fairy-tale in which I am the monster," he went on, putting his arms round me. He turned me round to face him. "Come on now, Rose. You are angry, and when you are angry, you become very cold and far away. I think I'd prefer a hot temper."

"You have to accept me as I am."

"As you do with me? I see exactly the implications that you mean."

"I didn't like you stopping Tibby coming to me to help me dress."

"And I was angry that she should come between you and me, and that you should allow it."

I was silent.

"Yes, I'm jealous, Rose."

"That's a wicked fault," I said slowly.

"But a very human one." He tightened his grip on my arms. "Come now, Rose, admit it: aren't all lovers jealous? I am your lover. Or I will be, if you will allow anything like free, active love to happen between us."

"I'm not jealous," I said.

"I shall make that happen. You do not know what you are."

"I am not entirely to be manipulated," I said.

"No, but it's natural, Rose. You are changing, I am changing, we shall both change."

He drew me towards him, holding me against his chest, so that I could hear the hard little thuds of his heart. Or was it my own heart?

Gently he kissed me. "And undo that ridiculous garment buttoned to the neck that makes you look like a little nun. Whose taste was that, the spirit of that old woman's, I suppose?" Tentatively, he undid one button and stood waiting.

"Your fingers are cold," I said, but did not stop him unbuttoning the others.

"What pretty little breasts. Come away from the window, Rose."

In the great warm bed, the hardness inside me melted and was replaced by softness, and my anger and Peter's anger transformed itself naturally into passionate love, and spent itself.

When I next looked out at the Vorontsov-Dashkov palace the sun was bright and the sky a clear blue.

Inside myself I was slowly accepting the idea that I might, after all, be a happy woman.

We stayed in the Crimea for one week.

"How lovely it would be to stay longer," I said the night before our return to St. Petersburg. "Must we go back?"

"I think so. The Christmas and New Year celebrations at the Winter Palace will be coming on and we ought to be there."

"I have never thought of you as bothering about Court functions," I said.

"Ah, but I want to show off my wife. And then after the New Year Ball, which will be magnificent, I promise you, and you will enjoy it, comes the Tercentenary of the Romanov dynasty, and no loyal Russian can fail to celebrate *that*." I looked at him suspiciously, but there was no trace of irony on his face. "I believe it's what has been keeping Tante Irene alive."

"She thinks it's *me*," I observed. "I think she won't live very long."

"I shouldn't preserve her life for one moment," he observed ruthlessly. "Not at the expense of any energies of yours."

"Won't you miss her?"

"Not for a minute. Such women deserve no remembering. She's had her good fun in life, now let her go. She should have gone long ago."

I was silenced. It was true, but part of my life had gone into her whether I liked it or not, and her death would diminish me by that much.

All the festivities in St. Petersburg were as was usual dominated by the Grand Duchess Vladimir, widow of the Tsar's uncle. Throughout that late autumn and Christmas season a brilliant series of balls and receptions took place, but at none of them was the figure of the Tsarina seen.

"I've heard she's not even going to give a ball in the Winter Palace for the Tercentenary," said Dolly, sounding worried. "The Tsar is to give two, but she won't attend, so they say. Won't or can't. Perhaps she's mad."

We were seated around the luncheon table, just a family group, Ariadne, Dolly, Peter and I. Last night we had been at a costume ball at the palace of Madame Brianchaninov; she had been born Princess Gorchakov and was immensely rich. We had all worn eighteenth-century costume.

"No, she's not mad," I said.

"Have you ever *seen* her?" asked Dolly

"Yes," I said briefly, "once, and another time I think I saw her feet."

Peter gave a short laugh.

"But she isn't mad. Dreadfully emotional and even hysterical, but not mad. She loves the boy and he loves her."

"What *is* the matter with him?" asked Dolly.

I shrugged. "I don't know. Some bone trouble, I guess. It's strange no announcement is ever made."

"Not so very strange," said Peter. "Since there would probably be a revolution at once, big or little, according to the state of the country."

"What's a little revolution?"

"A failed one," he said. "We have had several. But it is not an experience to be repeated too often."

"No, there would not be an announcement," said Dolly, "although not necessarily for the reasons my brother gives— you shouldn't joke about such things, Peter. No, that lot always keep things close to themselves. It seems to be their nature; a mistake, I think."

"It's such a formal, unnatural life. You know, the boy told me that once every week on a Wednesday his parents take tea with him 'in the English style,' as he put it, but only if 'their engagements permit.' He said that, too."

"I didn't think she ever had any engagements," said Dolly.

"I wonder if the whole family attend, girls and all," said Ariadne to Peter. "What a jolly family party." She yawned. "Oh, dear, I'm tired."

"I don't know why," Dolly said sharply, "for you didn't dance once with your partner, you left him to me. I didn't see you dancing at all."

"I think Edward really prefers you, Mamma. He's got so dull lately since he came back from that stay with his sister, and he used to be so amusing."

"It's you who is dull, miss," said Dolly, even sharper than before. I thought that her match-making for her daughter was not going well. "Edward Lacey is quite unchanged."

"No, he never does change," said her irrepressible daughter. "That's his trouble."

"Of course, if Great Aunt dies, we shall be in black," said Dolly, apparently apropos of nothing at all. "And the pain has come back."

She looked at me and I shook my head.

Dolly sighed. "Fading away, that's what they say, isn't it? And with her, it's true: every day more evanescent. Do you ever see her now, Rose?"

"No, she never asks for me now, not since my marriage." I'm of no use, I thought, and she knows it.

"Rose will fade away herself," said Ariadne. "She seems so tired."

"It's all this gaiety," I said. "Night after night. It's exhausting if you aren't brought up to it."

"Yes, you look a little ghost today," said Peter affectionately. "Go and rest now. I won't disturb you. And you have to look your best tonight."

Lying on my bed, eyes closed, but not asleep, I thought I had not been telling the whole truth. First, about Princess Irene: true, she had not sent for me, but I had felt silent signals, tugs at my mind, for the last week. One day I had crept up the Red Staircase to stare in at her from the door of her room, only to have her glare ferociously back, dismissing her whom only she had summoned. Then there was my fatigue, which was not entirely due to the vigour of the St. Petersburg season.

In our splendid set of rooms, I was not at peace. Peter was often away, and alone in my great bedroom in that gilded bed, I slept badly. A voice seemed to call to me.

Sometimes it was just a soft wailing, sometimes I thought I

heard my name: I thought it was real, but it was so soft and elusive I could never be sure.

I lay there, and with eyes wide now, stared at the elaborate mouldings on the ceiling. On the surface, I was a self-possessed young woman who had made a good marriage, and enjoyed the luxuries of her life, but underneath was a girl whose memories contained secrets and whose hopes were ambiguous. I was two people, one was cheerful and matter-of-fact, the other girl heard voices whispering in the night. Since my marriage I felt as though I had split into two halves, which did not match.

There were never any voices in the daylight, though, and if there ever should be, then it would be a hard case: I should know then that either I was mad or I was being tormented. I suppose everyone has his or her tormentors, the Furies, as the Greeks called them, and you are lucky if they come from the outside. I know what I feared most, and that was that they were in my own head.

Peter came to me as I was finishing dressing for our evening's entertainment. I was very nearly finished and was fastening my necklace when I saw his face reflected in the mirror. His expression was such that I turned round, startled.

"Why are you looking at me like that?"

"What is that dress you are wearing?"

I looked down at myself. "My dress for the ball? What's wrong with it?" I was wearing a green and white silk dress with a low-cut white fichu and a white flounced overskirt.

I stood up and turned to face him. "It's a little old-fashioned, perhaps, but pretty, I think. Ariadne persuaded me to order it."

He gave a furious exclamation: "She has dressed you up in a parody of the uniform of the Smolny Institute. How could you let her do it?"

"But I didn't know, I never saw what the girls wear," I faltered. "I suppose it was a joke."

"Joke!" he exploded. Then he controlled himself. "Get it off."

Bewildered, I said, "But I have nothing else to wear that's new. Dolly says it's not done to repeat . . ."

"Take it off," and he turned his back on me.

"No. It's a silly joke, but after all, it's a pretty dress and no one but you may draw a comparison."

"It doesn't matter whether they do or not. Ariadne knows—" Again he controlled his rising anger, and stopped.

Slowly I said, "I don't understand why you are so angry. What is there about the Smolny?"

"It doesn't matter." He was breathing quickly. "Take it off."

Fumbling with the buttons, I undid the bodice and slid it from my shoulders; I undid the waist-band of the skirt and stepped out of it.

Peter grabbed my arm and drew me sharply towards him. "No, Peter," I said before my voice was muffled against him.

He pushed me on to the bed and pressed himself against me.

"Peter, you're hurting." My voice died away. I felt as if he hated me. I couldn't respond, my other self was in control and I was willing to hate back. With angry bursts of energy we consummated that hatred.

"Peter, do you love or hate me?" I said at the end.

"Rose!"

"Perhaps it's Ariadne you hate." I knew I had punctured my way to some truth there, because he drew away for a moment. But then he lowered his head and kissed my lips. "Rose, you are essential to me. Through you and by you everything that matters most to me will come true."

I consented to be bewildered: it was too much for a young girl to understand.

In this state of love and perplexity I went out to the ball, at the Pozharskys', if I remember correctly, leaving the ravaged green and white gown on the floor.

Because of what had followed, I was shy of raising the matter of the dress with Ariadne. But at supper, at the ball, I tackled her. "Ariadne, the green and white dress you persuaded me to buy was a mistake."

"I thought it must be, as you didn't wear it." She sounded innocent enough, too innocent, I thought, and I gave her a sharp look.

"Peter said it reminded him of what the pupils of the Smolny wear. Did you do that on purpose?"

"No, Rose," and she laughed.

"Why should he care? Why should he hate me to wear something that reminded him of the Smolny Institute?"

"He remembers I had an unhappy time there, I suppose," she said calmly. "But it's over now."

The next day I was confined to bed. The cold had been increasing with each day that passed and now was nearly thirty degrees below zero. Within, the house was warm, overheated almost, but outside, thick furs felt like light cotton. The eyelashes became rigid, the breath froze, even to draw a breath was painful. How the horses and the coachmen and the poor of the city stood the great cold I could not conceive. Or the sick or the old.

To myself I thought that when the cold reached its greatest intensity, which they said was after Christmas (Old Style), then the Princess Irene would die. I even thought I might die myself, so great was the tension within me.

I was propped up against my pillows when a note was handed to me from Madame Titov. After the rather elaborate formalities which prefaced her letter and which she never omitted, she went on: "You are invited to call, on any day you choose, on the boy. You know to whom I refer? Discretion is best. Simply announce yourself, the way is prepared. But go soon."

"Physician, heal thyself," I groaned, dragging myself upright.

But I felt better when I was on my feet, and wrapping myself in my thick fur, I decided to drive myself that afternoon.

I drove on the snowy roads to Tsarskoye Selo, had my car escorted by a mounted soldier to a side door and was quietly admitted.

I didn't expect to enjoy myself, but found myself taking part in a happy nursery tea.

"Huntley and Palmer biscuits, you see?" my young host pointed out proudly. "I ordered them specially for you."

"Delicious," I said. "May I have another one?"

"Oh, please." And he took one himself and then one for his little fox-terrier. "It was as you said: my leg isn't exactly better, but it's a good deal more use to me than it was. That's why I asked for you to come. I wanted to show you."

"Oh, good." A trio of little cats were wreathed round his feet. "Do I recognize that kitten? Is it the one I saw at Spala?" He nodded. "How it's grown."

"She had fleas," he said prosaically. "I caught them, too. Did you."

"No." I shook my head. "Never an itch."

He laughed merrily and held out his hand. "You will come again, won't you? It has been such fun."

After that, in the weeks leading up to Christmas and the New Year, I did several times go to take nursery tea.

On one occasion Peter drove me out to Tsarskoye Selo, saying that I looked too tired, which was true. I had had noisy dreams the night before, with my name whistling through my sleep: *Rose, Rose.*

"Do you ever fancy our bedroom is noisy?" I asked him as I drove. He had been away visiting his estates in eastern Russia and had only just returned.

"No." He sounded surprised, and it was true the voice never seemed to be audible when he was there. "We could move, if you wish, but I should not like to trouble Dolly."

"I think I should prefer a house of my own," I said decisively.

"In the New Year." He nodded. "When the spring comes."

We were passed through the great gates, as usual, by the sentry, silent and expressionless. Or was it just one of those mask-like Russian peasant faces that I couldn't read?

"Would he shoot us, do you think," I asked, "if we didn't have a *laissez-passer*?"

"I've never heard that it happened," said Peter. "But then no one comes here without invitation. This is the most un-visited palace in Europe."

"I'm privileged," I said. "I don't know how I'd like the rest of them: not much, I suspect, but I've got to like the boy."

As usual my young host received me gravely, then let his face break up into a broad smile. I didn't stay long on this occasion, mindful of Peter outside.

"You'll have some tea, though?" came the usual question, and he watched my face as I took a biscuit.

"Short-bread," I said. "How delicious."

"Scotch short-bread," he said triumphantly. "I had it ordered specially for you. Is it good?" He was nursing a tiny black kitten. "Do you like it?"

"It's the best I've had since I left home." It was a trifle soft, but otherwise authentic. "You ought to tell them to keep it in a tin, though."

"Oh, I will." He stroked the cat's head. "Do you like my newest little cat?"

I stroked its head. "How many does that make?"

He frowned. "Six, I think, but they come and go. This little creature has no bed yet, so I keep it in my pocket. See?"

He had a large, square pocket on his loose jacket and he popped the kitten in so only its head could be seen. Both of them looked at me with big, confident eyes. "Its name is Katinka."

"And what else is that I see in your other pocket?" I said in surprise. "It looks like a cigarette case. Smoking, are you now?"

"*No.*" He doubled up in mirth at my suggestion, delighted I should make it. "I took it off Papa for smoking all the time at tea. I am to keep it three days as his punishment. Not that he'll stop, of course, but when he's at it one can smell nothing but those horrid gaspers of his. Can't you smell it now?"

"A little," I admitted. It was quite strong, as a matter of fact.

I told Peter on the way home. He liked to hear details of life inside the palace; I was surprised but amused at his passion for detail.

"And still tea and biscuits at the five-o'clock with his parents? How English."

"I think it's rather nice. And anyway, by all accounts, the Tsar smokes more cigarettes than he drinks tea."

"Oh, everyone knows about those cigarettes. I've smelt them. Like burning rope."

"You're a gossip at heart, I believe, Peter."

"All Russians are." He drove on carefully. "The kitten obviously needs a bed. Why don't you get one made at Knopf's and give it to him as a present?"

"Oh, Peter, what a nice idea. Yes, I'll go there tomorrow and choose. I can buy some Christmas presents there as well."

Peter came with me to the shop. To my surprise, Knopf's had a number of beds for pet cats for me to choose from. Some were simple and rustic (but craftsman-made), while others were luxurious and ornate. I swithered between a comfortable little bed covered in quilted silk and a solid wooden four-poster, complete with hangings embroidered with mouse faces. But then Peter drew my attention to an even more fascinating structure made like a Chinese pagoda. Made of wood and metal, it was gleaming with red and gold and decorated with tiny bells.

"How pretty," I said. "Certainly it is fit for an Imperial cat. But it's very large."

"He has six cats," pointed out Peter.

"Perhaps it is the best one to choose. I do like it, I must say. Yes, I'll have it."

"And we will have a big *K* for Katinka Kat painted on the side of the pagoda," suggested Peter.

"Oh, can we?"

"Certainly, madame." And the salesman nodded and bowed. "You must allow us a little time, however." He consulted his books. "I don't think we can have it ready for Christmas or the New Year," he said apologetically. "So many orders. We are rushed off our feet."

"After the festivities will do very well," said Peter.

As we left the shop together he said, "You mustn't let anyone guess for whom you have designed the present. It is entirely your own secret. Don't even tell Dolly."

I shook my head. "No, I won't. Not that your sister will ask. She likes to find things out and not be told them. Haven't you noticed? However, at the moment Ariadne preoccupies her. That girl's not happy, Peter. Dolly knows it and so do I."

"Oh, all young girls are unhappy. Especially Russian girls. It's the green sickness."

"If ever a girl was made for happiness, it was Ariadne," I said, but I had grasped that there were shadows over the Russian character that I did not fully comprehend.

That same night there was a great reception by Countess Betsy Shufalov in her palace on the Fontanka. As Dolly said, "everyone" was there, adding that "she gives the best parties in St. Petersburg, the liveliest and the most fun." I must confess that I did not find it much fun. It was so crowded that we were pressed against each other and could hardly move, but everywhere was the flash of fine jewellery and the splashes of colour of the men's uniforms.

Edward Lacey was there with his sister, a beautiful blonde woman who towered over her short, dark Russian husband. But I'm bound to say that they looked very happy together.

Dolly whispered in my ear: "She has inherited an estate in Ireland and is going to make her husband remove to there: she thinks it's a better place for the children to grow up. That purpose has been part of the reason for Edward's long stay here. To take them from Russia."

"And do you approve?"

"Oh, yes." Dolly sighed. "I should be happy for it for Ariadne."

"Is that why you encouraged"—I hesitated to say it, but after all Dolly was now my sister-in-law—"a marriage between them?" I knew what Edward had told me on this matter. Now I wanted it in her own words.

"Yes, part of the reason. I'd like to think of Ariadne settled." Dolly seemed vaguely troubled.

"But she's such a happy girl." And yet— "Dolly, what did happen at the Smolny Institute? What happened that still distresses Peter?"

Dolly gave me a look of alarmed comprehension. "I hoped it was long ago done with. If you have heard of it, then it is not. Why, she fell in love, that's the long and short of it."

We were interrupted by Edward Lacey's coming over with his sister and introducing us. "I have wanted to meet you so much," she said brightly. "I was sorry I could not be at your wedding." Her eyes were studying me carefully. "And even now I am afraid I am on the point of leaving. I love Betsy's parties, but they are an exhaustion!"

"Yes, we are going, too. I can see my husband appearing with my cloak."

Together we all strolled towards the entrance. Peter was sent away to direct the servants to get his sister's furs and Edward went with him on the same service.

Dolly and Ada Fedotov stood talking idly. "Yes, next year Betsy is planning a black and white ball, just black and white, no other colour permitted," I heard Dolly say.

I wandered forward to look at the long line of carriages and motor cars drawing into the *porte-cochère* to see if I could recognize the Denisov car.

I heard the Shufalov manservant calling: "Madame Fedotov's motor car awaits her." I looked, to see that the chauffeur standing by the door of the car was Patrick. He saw me, too.

"Why are you masquerading like this?" I said. No one was near us.

"It's no masquerade," he said coolly. "I needed a job and Edward Lacey has gotten me one. When I go back to England I think I'll set up a garage. It's a coming trade and I'll need something. This job with Madame Shufalov is only while her chauffeur is sick. I also drive for Edward."

"Are you going back? Dare you?"

"I must go. Edward Lacey has friends in the right places. I shall go through the mill, I expect, but they won't shoot me."

"Patrick," I began.

"I sent you a letter and there was no answer. That's it, Rose." He touched his cap, the complete chauffeur. "Now, I see my employer coming."

I had no Christmas letter from my family in Scotland and I felt strange marking Christmas on January 7. This apart, on Christmas Eve I had a shower of valuable presents from Peter, Dolly and Ariadne, and if jewellery, blonde tortoise-shell and sables could have made me happy, then happy I should have been. The girl on the surface was happy, and drank champagne and was merry, but the one underneath remained ill at ease.

At last the long-looked-for ball at the Winter Palace took place. The cold was more intense than ever, and we hurried into Dolly's motor car, which was drawn up outside the house, and were wrapped about in rugs. Even so, my eyelashes felt stiff and heavy as if they were frozen. Dolly was wearing a diamond band in her curls and the diamonds glittered quietly in her dark hair. She had lent me emeralds. So far, I had no really valuable jewels of my own. Those I had received as wedding gifts were more pretty than valuable, such as my opals.

We drove to the door and staircase of the Empress Mother and from there were admitted to the Salle Blanche, which seemed already crowded with people and blazing with a thousand lights.

I took a deep breath. At least it was warm, and I looked about, trying to take it all in.

The Salle Blanche is one hundred and thirty-three feet long with columns supporting a gallery on which crowded more spectators. The room was decorated in pure white and alabaster, heated by four huge stoves.

"It gets stifling," whispered Dolly in my ear. "They really ought to modernize the heating and the lighting, but the nineteenth century is sacrosanct here."

"They're still living in it," said Peter. He was wearing uniform himself. Having been in the Emperor's Corps des Pages, he was obliged by strict etiquette to do this when appearing at Court.

"The uniforms make everything very colourful," I said. "Who are the ladies in green and gold with little red and gold trains? It must be rather uncomfortable wearing such heavy-looking dresses."

Dolly took a look. "Oh, those are the Maids of Honour of the Empress. The Dowager in this case, as the Empress herself isn't present. The Maids of Honour of the Grand Duchesses wear pale blue. All right if they are young girls, which some of them are *not*."

When the whole company was assembled, the doors opened and the Imperial family walked in. The Dowager Empress wore white satin decorated with diamonds, with which she glittered from head to foot, literally, for even the toes of her shoes had a brilliant or two studding them. She had an antique-looking crown on the back of her head in the Russian style and a small crescent of jewels on her forehead. The Emperor held her hand and led her in, and behind her trooped the rest of what Queen Victoria called "the royal mob." On the whole a tall and good-looking lot, I thought.

"One bomb would give Russia a new government," I murmured absently.

Both Peter and Dolly gave me a horrified look. "We do not say those things *aloud*," said Dolly.

But where had my remark come from? I didn't know myself.

The dancing began with polonaises performed by members of the Court; the rest of us watched. After the polonaise came another set of complicated dances.

The ball had begun at ten. At midnight we went through another long salon and an even longer gallery, filled with pictures, to the supper room.

This room, which was very large with scagliola columns and blue glass lustres on the walls, was got up as an orangery. The scent and the sight of the flowers were delicious.

After the supper, dances more modern than the polonaise and the quadrille were allowed, and I danced with Peter.

"I feel like Cinderella," I said dreamily. "And at twelve o'clock all of this will disappear, and I shall be left alone."

Peter tightened his grip on me and whirled round in the dance. "I promise you *not*," he said. "Dear Rose."

"Only dear?" I said.

"Dearer, dearest Rose." His voice was very low.

"A progression of love?"

"That is how it has been," he said. "For me, at least."

We finished the dance in silence.

The coachmen, chauffeurs and footmen of all the guests were stationed up the great staircase as we left. With us wrapped in strange furs, booted and hatted, they stared in our faces as we passed, trying to recognize their own families and crying out happily and eagerly when they did. It gave a strange insight into the relationship between master and servant. Nothing was simple or clear-cut here.

I began to study the servants' faces, searching, before I stopped myself, for Patrick's face. But of course he was not there. Edward Lacey had not been invited to the Winter Palace.

# Chapter Twelve

In the days that followed there was muttering in St. Petersburg society, which set so much store on such rituals, about the absence of the Tsarina from the New Year Ball at the Winter Palace. Rumours abounded of a more or less scandalous nature. *She* was not going to appear at the Tercentenary celebrations in March, *She* was ill, mentally or physically or both, *She* was in thrall to the monk, Father Gregory. The one hard fact seemed to be that the latter was exiled from St. Petersburg, although the general consensus seemed to be that he wouldn't go, or, if he did, would come back.

The temperature dropped below even what was considered the usual winter cold in St. Petersburg. A heavy, pallid sky hung low over the city. Inside the house it was warm enough, but the cold seemed to arise like a barrier through which one must push.

I had not altogether broken off my old relationship with Ariadne, although naturally I saw less of her. We read together on convenient mornings. We had left behind the quiet world of Jane Austen and embarked on Charlotte

Brontë, which was more to Ariadne's taste. She performed all the tasks I set her with a detached good humour, as if nothing was worth arguing about.

In addition, she went docilely about every social duty her mother demanded of her. From luncheon parties to musical evenings to grand receptions, she followed where Dolly led.

But Dolly was no better pleased with her than I was. "She has closed her mind," said Dolly. "I can bang on the door, but it is not opened. Nor do I really know what goes on inside."

"I think it's often like that with young girls of her age," I said. "I've noticed it before."

"Yes, I know what girls are like. But they change, fall in love, they marry. I thought it would be like that with Ariadne. But I don't think so now. She always had this notion that she would be a completely free and emancipated woman. She had it long before you came. But I thought Edward would change her mind for her. I don't think so now." She shook her head. "And yet there is a happy, pleasure-loving side to Ariadne, which should have worked in my favour."

"Yes, I know. I see it in her even now."

"But there is something stronger operating on her."

With sympathy, I said, "You know, I should leave her alone. Let her be as free as she wishes. It's probably the best way to control her."

"It's not as simple as that. You don't understand. You still don't understand the terrible trouble Ariadne could so easily fall into."

"But I think I do, Dolly. You mean that she and Marisia might become politically active. But only in the most harmless way, surely, Dolly? They are only girls."

"Do you think Marisia so harmless, then?"

For a moment, I thought about it. "She isn't the sort of girl I readily like. There is something hard and alien in her. Although she seemed eager to like me." Dolly gave a short laugh. "But in spite of all that, I think she is *good*, Dolly."

"Sometimes I think terrible things, Rose. Worse than you can guess."

"What about, Dolly?"

"About my own family, that's what. Never mind, you would only think me mad. 'Mad, bad and dangerous to know,' that's what they said of Lord Byron, was it not? He must have had Russian blood in him."

"No, Scottish," I said dryly. "Now, Dolly!"

"Well, as it happens, I have already taken your advice and let Ariadne have some freedom, and do you know what has happened? I have barely seen her for two days."

But that morning, I saw Ariadne in the hall, just as I was going out. I was coming down the staircase, drawing on my gloves, when I saw her talking to Peter. She was in a dark cloth coat and skirt with a heavy cloak and looked as near to shabby as any Denisov ever could.

I saw her shake her head at Peter. What he said in reply I couldn't hear but from his serious expression I imagined it to be a reproof of some sort.

"Where have you been?" I demanded as soon as we were face to face. The girl looked tired.

"Oh, I've been helping Marisia with some poor people on Vassily Island."

I knew that it was only a half truth she was telling me, and that probably she was already involved in the type of political life that Dolly feared. But it was hard for me, reared in a democracy and believing in liberation, to condemn her.

I went out with Peter; we were choosing some china for our use when we had a home. It was to be a present from Dolly, and I thought Peter was reluctant to accept such a handsome gift. Or perhaps the thought just bored him. At any rate, he seemed to pay scant attention as I debated this colour porcelain or that one, finally deciding on plain white, rimmed in gold, with our initials and crest, also in gold.

That evening, when we were alone, he said, "Would you do something for me? Perform an errand?"

"Of course." I was eager. "Just ask me."

"It may be something you will not enjoy to do. Going among people of the sort you have not met before."

"Like Ariadne on Vassily Island?"

He hesitated. "Something like that."

"Then you need not worry. I haven't led such a sheltered life as you seem to think."

"It will involve a journey. Oh, not a long one. To Moscow."

"But that's exciting. I shall look forward to it. Shall I drive? How many servants shall I take?" Already I was Russian enough to expect to take servants with me.

Again he hesitated. "I believe you will be best on your own. It's not quite that sort of journey."

"On my own." I was surprised, but calm. "Very well. If you say so. Just tell me what you want me to do. I'm ready for anything." I believed I was, too.

He kissed my cheek. "Go to bed now. I'll join you later. I have work to do now. We will talk it all over tomorrow."

I waited, trying to keep myself awake. But I was asleep when Peter came to bed.

In the morning he was up before me, and I found him studying my wardrobe.

"What are you looking at? My clothes, Peter? All my old ones, too. The nicer ones are over there, my dear."

He turned round to me. "I was looking to see what you could wear today."

"Oh, don't you worry," I yawned, "I will decide."

"I've chosen already." He put his arm round me and drew me away from the closet. "Go and drink some coffee. You're only half awake. Have your breakfast, and I will join you."

When he appeared, he had a pile of clothes over his arm which he laid out on a chair before me. I saw a thick tweed skirt, a tailored jacket of grey wool that I had brought from home and a shapeless garment which I recognized at once.

"My old *shuba*!" I exclaimed. "I kept it out of sentiment. But why on earth am I to wear all those things?"

"Drink your coffee and I'll tell you."

I poured another cup for Peter and sipped my own. My

breakfast tray was on a round table in the window. We usually breakfasted alone now. It was the household concession to our married state.

"I want you to take a message to Moscow. I will give you the address and also draw you a map. There will be no difficulty about finding the way."

"And how am I to get to Moscow?" I said, staring at him.

"By the railway. You will go to the central station in St. Petersburg and get your ticket. It won't be a comfortable journey, I'm afraid, nor short. You must travel overnight."

"How long does the journey take?" I stood up, trying to think myself into the position of someone about to undertake a long journey.

"Long enough," he said absently, as if his thoughts were elsewhere. "About the clothes, Rose."

"No need." I was studying them. "I've worked it out for myself. I am not to look like your wife. Nor anyone of importance. I am to look like a poor, negligible woman. A kind of disguise, in short. You don't want me recognized, either when I go or when I come back."

"If you can manage it."

"Oh, I'll manage it." I picked up the *shuba*. "I don't believe this was new when I bought it. I believe I can still see the shape of the first owner embedded in it."

"It's no joking matter, Rose."

"I'm not joking." But I was excited. "Is it such a very dangerous and secret errand?"

He was silent. "Not dangerous, Rose, or I would not let you go. But secret it must be."

"Even from me?"

Peter took my hand and held it tight. "For the moment, Rose. In the end, I expect you will know all. Yes, I'm sure of it. You must."

"I hate not knowing what I'm doing. But if you say I will know in the end, then I'll put up with it." An idea had come to me. "Tell me, was it in connection with this errand of yours that Ariadne went to Vassily Island? Was that what she was really doing?" He was silent. "There was something in the way you two were talking when I saw you in the hall that made me wonder."

"She brought me some information in connection with what takes you to Moscow," he said reluctantly. "I tell you the truth as much as I can," he said, with evident pain.

We stood looking at each other in silence. I could hear a pulse banging in my ears. I never doubted for a moment that if I went on this journey I should be taking part in a secret plot. So Peter was actively engaged in working against the government? I suppose I had always known, or guessed, something of the sort.

"I know that the government of Russia must be liberalized," I said. "Must it be done this way?"

"You know it must. You can't compare Russia with what you know of your own country. We must do things in a secret, quiet way."

Suddenly I had a memory of that day soon after I had arrived in Russia when there had been a bomb in the Imperial Library. I remembered the police and the students they had arrested. One of them had been a young girl.

"I couldn't be part of anything violent," I said.

"No, my love, no, Rose. Nothing like that, I swear. Don't you trust me?"

I took a deep breath. "Yes, I do trust you."

"You need not go if you don't want to. I'll put no pressure on you, Rose. Say no. Just say no, and there shall be no more mention of it."

"Oh, I'll go."

"Very well, then, here is what you are to do. You are to go to Moscow to an address I will give you. You are expected. A man will be waiting for you there. You must give him the letter I shall give you." Peter hesitated. "The man may not be there when you arrive. He may come later. It's possible you may have to spend one night at the house. Or even two. Prepare yourself for it."

"Write it all down, address, names, everything, while I pack a bag," I said briskly. "What will you tell Dolly?"

"Nothing," he said, "for Dolly will not ask."

I stared in disbelief.

"I shall lie if I have to," he said in a hard voice. "And so must you. But silence is best."

It was my first lesson in conspiracy.

When I set off a few hours later, I had a carefully written and detailed list of instructions tucked into an inner pocket.

"Destroy it as soon as you can," said Peter.

This was my second lesson in conspiracy.

In the small travelling bag at my feet was secreted the letter containing the message I was to deliver.

No one had seen me leave the Denisov house. I had slipped out, carrying my own bag, and taken a public tram to the railway station.

I attracted no special notice in the tram, or later, when I bought my ticket for Moscow. I was just a shabbily dressed young woman, travelling on her own. A third lesson for a conspirator, I thought: look like everyone else.

My first moment of fear came as I was sitting in the compartment waiting for the train to draw out of the station, and two policemen came down the platform, looking into every carriage.

I shrank back into my corner-seat and tried to occupy myself with a newspaper. But they only put their heads round the door and withdrew, barely looking at me.

I drew a sigh of relief.

"Searching for an escaped prisoner, so I heard," said a fat woman sitting in another corner. "That's the tale. Don't know if it's true. You can't believe everything you hear."

"May be nothing at all. Sometimes they're just finding work for themselves, looking important," grumbled an old man, sitting opposite.

"Something, nothing," nodded the fat woman. "We shall never know. Swine, I call them."

"Now, now," said the old man. "I suppose we'd be angry if they let us get blown up, or if they let criminals rob us or murder us without them doing anything about it. Not that I like them, mind. Any little experience I have had of them has not made me think them charming fellows."

"My brother's a policeman," said a woman opposite, who was nursing her baby. "He's not a bad fellow. A man must live."

There was a murmur of assent, a man must indeed live, and we all settled back in our seats as the train started.

For the journey was uneventful, if exhausting. My fellow-passengers took a mild interest in me, but were easily satisfied to be told I was changing position from being a governess in one household in St. Petersburg to another in Moscow. The baby, a girl, was restless and took up most of her mother's attention. We all of us slept as much as we could.

Every so often we were offered glasses of hot tea from the little old lady who had a great samovar at the end of our carriage. There is a little old lady like this on all Russian trains, but this was my first meeting with one. I knew so little of public transport in Russia that I had to be on the alert not to show my ignorance. The hot tea was welcome. I had no food with me, but the fat lady in the corner had plenty, and she gave me a roll with meat in it.

"It's the best quality beef, my dear, you may be sure of it, for my husband's a butcher."

Inside the train it was very hot, but I was conscious all the time that we were trundling across the snowbound countryside of Russia. I had never felt so lonely and alien as I felt then. What was I doing, travelling through the night, with my message? I wanted to be at home, even back in Scotland, with familiar things around me again. I was lost, a stranger here in Russia.

A hot glass of tea at this, my low point, was a welcome restorer.

"Ah, you look better now," said the butcher's wife. "Poorly, you looked. I dare say we all do. No, for these journeys, I always say I start on them a young woman and end an old woman. Well, it's not so far now, and you'll need all your wits about you in Moscow. Those Muscovites!" and she shrugged. "Rob you as soon as look at you. You be careful, my dear."

* * *

There was winter daylight of a sort when eventually I arrived at Moscow, pushing my way through the crowds that filled the railway station. Nervously, I saw that there were a number of policemen on duty at the station. A pair stood talking by the big arch of the exit, scanning the crowd with bored, cynical eyes. But they took no notice of me as, feeling self-conscious, I pushed past.

As luck would have it, I dropped Peter's list of my instructions almost at the feet of one policeman, but he did no more than pick it up and hand it over politely with scarcely a look. I felt better after that, and breathed more freely.

"You can make your way on foot to the address I've given you," Peter had said, as he had drawn me a map.

Dry, hard snow was falling as I made my way out into the square. I knew I must turn to my right and then look for the street. I hadn't walked more than a few yards before I could tell that Moscow was a very different city from St. Petersburg.

The very air smelt different: drier, colder, full of spice and wood-smoke. The street I was walking in was narrow and twisting compared with the broad, straight roads of St. Petersburg. On either side the buildings were low, dark-stoned and irregular in shape. The sky-line was not a bit like that of St. Petersburg. I had the sense of being in an ancient city whose life seemed closer to the Middle Ages than to the twentieth century. This was the Russia of the Boyars and the Old Believers, the supporters of the archaic Russia and the unreformed church that Peter the Great had tried to sweep away, but which remained there, for ever, underneath.

I was getting weary. As I trudged through the streets, deeply rutted with dirty snow, I put my bag down at intervals to rest.

I felt afraid as I turned the corner into a narrow street and looked up at the house which was my destination.

"It lies between a tailor's shop and a baker's," Peter had said. "So you will know it."

There it was, number thirty-one, Little Arbat Street. A dim light shone behind the fanlight of the front door. I could see a bell-pull. I tugged at it.

Distantly, far away in the house, I heard the bell sound.
Then there was silence for a long time, while I waited.

I rang again. The bell spoke again.

Then I heard the sound of soft, slow footsteps behind the door.

Slowly it opened. "I was coming," said a quiet, complaining voice. "No need to keep ringing."

I was looking at a very small man; he was not a dwarf, just tiny. His head, however, was disproportionately large, like a child's really, which in many ways, except for the sharpness of his eyes, he resembled.

"I was told to call here," I said nervously.

"Come in, come in. I've been expecting you."

He was carrying a lamp and he walked before me, showing me the way along a dark, narrow corridor and up a staircase covered in slippery linoleum. The house smelt damp and stale.

"You were expecting me?" I asked. I suppose I was surprised not to be questioned and checked up on.

"I was expecting *someone*," said the little man. "I knew it would be a young woman. It usually is."

"Oh." Somehow this was a dispiriting thing to hear as I trudged up the stairs. But it was stupid to think I was unique: I could not be.

"I am . . ." I began.

"Don't tell me. Do not give me your name. I do not wish to know it. Nor will I give you mine."

"But I was told it," I said hesitantly. "It was written down for me." I looked at Peter's instructions.

"No matter. It's not what I'm called. You need not use it. Call me Doctor."

"Are you a doctor?"

"No."

He had led me to a small room, where he placed the lamp on the table.

"Well, give me what you've brought."

I put my bag on the table, opened it and began to fumble round for the envelope Peter had given me. Soon I should have achieved my mission and could leave. I wouldn't stay a minute in this depressing house. "You will be taken care of," Peter had said. But I didn't want to be taken care of here.

"Hurry up. You know you have to get on. This is not the end of your journey."

I had the letter in my hand, but I just stood there staring at him. "No, I didn't know. I can't go on. I don't know where to go."

"I'll tell you, of course. When I've had a look at what you bring me." He took the letter from my limp grasp. "Here, sit down." He pushed a chair towards me.

Silently, I sat down, my legs trembling. As he tore open the letter in the light of the lamp, I saw a sheaf of bank-notes. So I had brought money as well as a message. What was the important information I had carried? I studied his face as he read. The large features were expressionless.

"Good," he said as he finished reading, "now I know what this is all about. That is, I know as much as is good for me, which is not much. I will tell you where to go next. That is really what is demanded of you. I'll write down the address. You can take a tram. Ask for Mr. Jakob when you get there."

"No. It's no good. I can't go." I felt sick. "I don't know how I should manage."

He looked at me for a moment, then put on a pair of large, round spectacles and looked at me again. "Were you followed here? Did anyone see you come?"

"No one as far as I know."

"I believe you. Who would notice *you?*"

"No one," I repeated, wretchedly.

"A foreigner, too. German?"

"No." I left it there; the less said about me the better.

"Just your accent, you know. No offence meant." He was fussing round the room. "Very well, I will come with you and show you the way. You look harmless enough."

"Oh, thank you." I stood up, strength returning to me, and a new confidence that I would fulfil my mission.

"Come on, then." He turned out the lamp, and taking my hand, led me downstairs in the gloom.

At the front door he turned as he opened it and looked into my face, illuminated by a gas jet from a street-lamp.

"You will know me again," he said.

"Yes." I drew back a little. Close to, his face was pock-marked and yellow. His breath smelt.

"Forget me. That's my advice. And a warning, too."

"You needn't tell me."

He shook his head as he motioned me to go through the door and closed it behind us.

"So young," he said. "So young. A mere girl. And already you are a conspirator."

We emerged from Little Arbat Street and walked back to where the trams stopped in the main street. Each one as it clanged past seemed crowded.

"Don't sit with me," he said. "Better safe than sorry. Just watch me. When I take my handkerchief out, prepare to get out. Here, take this." He gave me a couple of coins. "This is your fare. Then you need not speak."

We stood there waiting in the cold. He let several trams go past before he deemed one safe. They were all as crowded as each other, and when we got on there was no question of sitting down, and I wondered he had bothered to mention it as likely. We were squeezed up against each other, but I kept my eyes on his handkerchief.

When he signalled, I followed him off the tram and down the street, walking a pace or two behind. I towered above him; the effect must have been ludicrous. The idea grew on me, swelling irrepressibly inside me, so that I had to bite back my giggles. I began to stagger with the effort.

"What's the matter with you?" he said, swinging round.

"Nothing." Exhaustion and a sense of being totally torn from my own life had brought me to the edge of hysteria.

"Good. For we have arrived." He nodded towards a small house, next door to a greengrocer's shop. To my great relief, I saw that the house appeared clean and respectable. A woman's face peeped at us from behind a curtain.

He rapped on the door. It was opened almost at once by the woman. She was grey-haired and plump, with a starched white apron crackling over a dark woollen dress. Little fat folds of flesh almost masked her eyes so that their expression was hard to read. But she admitted us silently, with a nod.

Inside the house the Doctor handed over the envelope I had brought with me from St. Petersburg; I could see the money was still there. He muttered a few sentences which I could not hear, except I made out one word, "Jakob," said more than once. She shrugged and protested. But his only answer was to make his way to the front door, open it and disappear.

The woman and I looked at each other. "So you want to see Mr. Jakob?" she asked.

"I have been told so," I said carefully. "All I *know* is that I was told to go to the house in Little Arbat Street. The rest has followed from that."

"Well, he isn't here. You'll have to stay the night." She put her hand on my arm with a tight grip.

"But I've delivered my message," I said, trying to draw away. "I can go now."

"It is not what you have delivered, but what you must take with you that matters," she said. "Follow me and I will show you your room. Are you hungry? Would you like to eat?"

"No," I said. "All I want is to do what I was asked to do and leave."

"Tomorrow," she said stolidly. "Here," she opened a door, "in here you may sleep."

She lit a lamp on a table by the bed, drew the curtains and left me.

I was alone in a low-ceilinged room in which, except for the table with the lamp, was nothing but a bed and a washstand.

I took off my outer clothes, washed my hands and face and lay down on the bed.

Within minutes I was asleep.

I was awakened by the sound of a voice from below. I could hear a man talking. I lay there listening to the low, bass sound of his voice. At intervals there would be silence while, presumably, another quieter voice spoke. Then he started speaking again. The conversation went on for some time.

I had the sensation of having slept for hours. I had no way of telling the time, for when I consulted my watch it had stopped.

Then I heard footsteps on the stairs. In a hurry I got off the bed and went to the door. But the feet passed me by and went on and up.

I felt the lock, but there was no key. With profound unease I went back to bed and lay down again. I could have dragged the wash-stand across the door, but the idea struck me as ludicrous. After all, I was a conspirator myself. Why should these people here harm *me?* I was one of them now.

As I lay there, I had for one brief moment a flash of something like recoil from Peter for having introduced me into this world. And yet I had gone willingly, even eagerly, on this errand. How perverse my own nature must be that in performing it I should feel betrayed and dirtied.

In the morning, I was roused by the woman (I never learnt her name) bringing me a tray of breakfast. The meal was beautifully laid out on a crisp white cloth, with coffee, eggs and fruit. The way she served it confirmed the thought I had already had that she had once been in good service. So if the man last night was "the Doctor," I would call her "the Servant."

"Eat your breakfast," she ordered, "then I will bring you a jug of hot water so you can wash before your journey."

"Oh, I can go then?" I said with relief.

"Yes. Mr. Jakob is ready for you."

Ready for me, I thought as I ate quickly, why ready?

I soon saw when I got downstairs. A pallid-faced man of about thirty was standing there, looking at his watch. He was wearing a shabby overcoat and cloth cap. At his feet was a small case.

"Good morning," he said politely, "my name is Jakob. So you're ready. We can set off."

"Are you coming with me?" I said, with some surprise.

"Oh, yes. We travel together. Everything is arranged according to instructions."

The woman came bustling into the room with a long woollen muffler in her hands. "Now wear this, my dear young man. You must look after yourself. Too much is asked of you. Remember how close you came to dying."

He ignored her, not even touching the scarf. "We must make a start," he said to me.

Bluntly, I said, "Did I bring instructions or did I bring payment?"

He gave a shrug and a cool smile. "What do you know?"

"Hardly anything," I answered. "I am only guessing that I brought a message asking for you and for you to do something. But it seems logical." I saw by the look of anger on his face that my guess had struck home. "And the money was to pay you."

"I am never paid," he said at once.

"Then you are bringing something that cost money." And I looked at his case. He made no move towards it; a lesser man might have done, I suppose, but I saw his muscles tense.

"You should know better than to talk like that," he said coldly. "We can go together as far as the railway station. After that we had better separate."

From then on there was silence between us until we were approaching the forecourt of the railway station.

"From the way you speak you are English by birth?" he said.

"Scottish," I answered.

At once his face lit up. "Ah, a countrywoman of Robert Burns. *Now* I understand why you are one of us. You know what it is to be oppressed."

"I don't think so," I said. The idea was new to me.

"Of course, it is so," he said with force. "But you are wise to be discreet. No doubt your government has agents here, all governments do." He took my hand and gave it a vigorous shake. "I am only sorry now that we cannot travel together."

\* \* \*

The journey back from Moscow was tedious and long. I had plenty of time to think.

As the wheels of the train rattled interminably beneath me, making a monotonous song, thoughts drifted in and out of my mind.

To begin with, I thought I saw the position of Edward Lacey more clearly now. I was convinced that he was one of those men that the British government used to report on the state of Russia. He had more or less said so himself, when he told me of his contacts at the British Embassy. Perhaps he had been warning me, and I had been too stupid to see the significance of what he had said. But whether he had meant me to understand or not, I thought I saw now what he was.

I suppose Peter guesses, too, I thought. And this explains the coldness I have often felt in his attitude to Edward Lacey. I suppose Dolly knows as well.

To call Edward an "agent" and to think of his activities as "spying" was probably to distort his function. I was sure that Edward saw himself as performing a natural service to his country: watching out from whence danger might come. Indeed, once I thought coldly and rationally about the nature of government, I saw that there must always have been the need for such informants. Hadn't Christopher Marlowe been such a man?

And probably the best governments are also the best informed, I thought.

So I felt I had an insight into Edward Lacey now, and one which explained his interest in and help to Patrick.

Nothing about him is false, I said to myself, listening to the dreary roll and rattle of the carriage. His relationship with the Denisovs is as it seems, but there is this extra layer.

I closed my eyes and tried to rest. I had done what Peter had asked of me. And I hadn't enjoyed it.

With a terrible clarity I knew that to be a conspirator, to act secretly and deviously, twisted my true nature. I couldn't do it, and Peter would have to be told.

Without pleasure I contemplated the rift this must create between us.

At last I slept and awoke only as we arrived at St. Petersburg.

To my surprise, Peter met me at the station. He was pacing up and down the platform, and he had pulled me into his arms before I had quite grasped that he was there at all.

"How did you know I would come on this train?"

"I have met every possible train from Moscow since you left." He kissed me on the lips. "How are you?"

"Weary, but I did what you wanted."

Even in the excitement of our meeting I noticed that he had drawn me into an alcove where we could not be seen.

"But is this meeting safe?" I asked. "Isn't it all supposed to be secret?"

"I have been very careful," he said, "and I have my car tucked away in a most discreet spot. Presently, we can walk there, and I'll drive you home."

When we were in the car and had drawn well away from the station, he said, "Now take off that terrible old garment and make yourself my Rose again."

"What about Dolly?" I said, as I divested myself and tried to settle my hair. "Any questions?"

"Luckily Ariadne has kept her so on the go she hasn't had time for any," he said coolly.

The servants must know I've been away, though, I thought, especially that German manservant of mine. But I did not say so aloud.

It wasn't until we were alone and in our own suite of rooms and I had changed all my clothes that I began to feel myself again.

Peter sat reading and waiting for me to be ready.

"Are you hungry? Do you want to eat?"

"I feel as if I could live on air," I said, stretching my arms out wide.

"You're excited. I'm glad."

"Yes. I'm back again and I did what you wanted." I was ready to dwell on that side of it: the rest I had hated.

"Dear Rose, my own Rose, back again." I stood up straight and proud, while he put his arms round me. "You know, I think you grew a little taller while you were away. You are so young, Rose, that you can still grow." It was a lover talking.

"I've thought myself tall," I said. "I certainly didn't grow."

"You know what I should like to do?" said Peter. "I should like to draw the curtains and close myself up in here with you for twenty-four hours."

"I'm timeless," I said. "I have no idea whether it is morning or afternoon."

"You are out of this world. I can see it in your eyes. You look wild and free."

"It's fatigue, I think," I said, pushing my hair away from my temples. My hair suddenly felt hot and heavy. "I think I shall have it all cut off. Dolly says it's going to be wildly smart to have short hair. Then we shall all look like boys."

"Love, not fatigue," said Peter, holding me very close. "What a beautiful boy you would look. But I adore your hair," and he pulled out the comb and pins which held it. "Hair should be seen against bare skin, not this silly silk of your blouse, wild and free to match your eyes."

It was a strange, violent love-making we inflicted on each other. But even while I allowed myself to be dragged along, perhaps even taking my turn at provocation, I knew that what I was really doing was postponing the moment when I must talk to Peter and tell him that never again could I be a conspirator.

When I spoke, I was surprised to hear how nervous my voice sounded. "Peter?"

"Yes?" His thoughts had been far away from me; I could tell it by the sound of his voice.

"There is something I must say."

"That sounds ominous. Is there anything left for my Rose to say? Or do?" He was half laughing.

"Don't joke. There must be none of the wrong sort of jokes between you and me. No secrets, either."

"Go on." But he was frowning now. "What secrets have you got?"

"None, of course." Not true; I had Patrick, too deep a secret even to mention.

"Now you are being less than honest, Rose," and his tone was severe. "Everyone has some secrets." Was he hinting about Patrick? Did he know? "Even if it is only what you have paid for a hat."

"I want you to give up your work with people like this man Jakob whom I went to meet," I said bluntly and suddenly. "It's a terrible world they live in. I hate and fear it. I felt the blackness and coldness and wickedness so strongly I could not breathe in that house where I stayed. It was a revelation to me."

"Blackness, coldness, wickedness. What a catalogue," said Peter, his tone icy. "You don't know what you are talking about."

"But I do. I was there and sensed it. If we don't stop we shall be as bad."

"You are talking of something you know nothing about," said Peter slowly. "First impressions count for nothing."

"I think they count for everything. Please, Peter, please. Get out of all this, leave it all alone. Try some other way."

"Or?" he enquired.

"I never said that."

"But it was implied. What will you do if I say no? Go away and leave me?"

"Of course not," I said wretchedly.

"Do you think you could do that? Answer, I have a right to ask." His tone was savage.

"I have said no."

"And meant yes. Oh, Rose, Rose."

There was a long silence, during which I had nothing to say that would not make matters worse. It was very hot in our rooms with the shutters drawn. Outside, a wind was whining as it laid the snow.

"I wish I hadn't spoken," I muttered eventually.

"No. I'm glad you did." He took my hand and caressed it. "I'm sorry it was necessary to send you on that trip. But it looked best that you should go." I stared at him, puzzled to know what he meant. "I know now that I could not easily lose you, Rose. Bear with all this just a little longer. Oh, such a little longer, and then we might both be free."

"You mean you will put all this planning and conspiring behind you?"

"Yes." He let go of my hand. "Rose, I promise."

I took a deep breath. "Thank goodness. I won't say another word. You don't know how happy I feel."

We sat again for a while in silence, but this time the moment was peaceful. Then Peter stirred, as if changing the subject.

"Your present for the young man has come."

"The Chinese pagoda for the Tsarevich's cat?"

"Exactly, and very handsome it is."

"Oh, I'm so glad. I'll take it to him tomorrow." I yawned. I was very tired.

"Unfortunately the pagoda was a little broken in the arrival here. Luckily it can be set to rights here in the house. But I'm afraid you can't take it tomorrow. Why don't you go out on your own to see the boy and prepare the way for it. A big object like that going into his room—won't there be questions asked?"

"Yes, that's true," I said, as I thought about it. "The guards do check anything that arouses their interest. They are dreadfully curious. I wouldn't like it damaged again. He can give orders that it's to be allowed straight through."

"And then you can take it out and give it to him. You will need help in any case. A couple of men to carry it. It's very heavy. So you will have to get permission for them, too."

"Oh, yes, I will. That's a good idea. Although the guards

know me by now. They are such simple country boys, you have no idea."

I followed Peter out of the room and down the stairs.

"Well, they are my countrymen and I think I know them. Ignorant and unreliable, poor things. Better to have full authority for you all to pass through. Well, here we are."

Downstairs was a strange world to me and I looked around curiously. Then Peter opened a door in the short passage that led to the vast cave of the kitchens, and I saw my Chinese pagoda gleaming in the gas-light, all red and gold.

Working on it was my German manservan., silen.. as always. He gave a bow when he saw us, and stepped back so that I could look, but was otherwise taciturn. He did not improve on acquaintance. With my trip to Moscow behind me, I was in an edgy mood, not willing to accept this man and his ways any longer.

On the floor were the wrappings which had enclosed the pagoda. I thought I could tell from the broken seal that he had disturbed the wrappings put on by the shop, Knopf's. Out of curiosity, no doubt, in which case it was he who had damaged my present.

I complained to Peter, who shrugged. "It is his job to check the packages."

"But I don't like him and would rather he did not serve me. Dismiss him for me, will you?" I kept my voice low but the servant heard. I did not care.

"Well—" Peter hesitated. "That's hard, I think."

"Then send him to work elsewhere. But not with me. I mean it."

Peter gave in gracefully. "Of course. I'll do what you say. I'll tell him myself. But it wasn't he who damaged your present, you know."

"Nosey old thing. I'm sure it was his fault somehow. I'd rather he left it alone. I suppose he must finish the repairs on it, and then he can go away."

"If you say so."

"I do."

We stayed a few minutes longer while I examined the piece of furniture, which it really was, much more than a toy or bed for an animal. Knopf's had made it beautifully, every detail delicately carved and painted. Inside, the sleeping quarters were padded in dark red, quilted silk. I only wondered if any animal would dare to sleep in it.

As we left the room I could see on one hand the lights of the kitchens and on the other the dark stairwell. Low pillars supported the ceiling, making many dark shadows.

As we walked towards the stairs I glanced back. I saw a figure move out of the shadows and slip into the room we had left.

"Who's that?" I turned back. Peter caught me.

"Now, Rose."

"No. I want to see."

I marched back and threw open the door. I found myself looking into the sallow face of Mr. Jakob.

Peter took the door from me and firmly closed it.

"Why is Mr. Jakob here?" I said. "Why didn't I know?"

"Where else should he be?" said Peter quietly. "Where else can it be safe? It is only for a little while."

"You've made me feel a fool. You could have told me."

"The fewer people who know the better. To the servants he is the German's brother. Soon he'll be gone."

"They both will," I said fiercely.

"Yes. I promise. I have promised."

I thought I had heard a note in his voice that aroused a question in my mind.

I looked in his face, scrutinizing him hard. He must have seen doubt there, because he took my hand and held it firmly in his own.

"Rose, I cannot live with a wife who doubts me. I must have all your trust. All your life too, perhaps."

But this did not accord well with my Scottish independence. "That I cannot do," I said. "I can never give my life. Not as you mean it. I must keep some freedom of judgement."

"Then judge wisely of me, Rose. And trust. Do you trust?" He made it a direct question, and as he offered it, he had a sad, serious look which I had never seen before. That look pierced my heart.

"Yes, I do," I said. "And you are quite right. Between you and me, there must be trust. Come on," I went on gaily. "Let's go and surprise Dolly."

The next day, feeling thoroughly recovered, I went off on my mission with a pleasant thrill of expectancy; it is enjoyable to give presents and this present, I knew, was going to be welcomed.

One of the pleasant winter ways of travelling was by horse-drawn sleigh. Dolly Denisov, of course, had such an equipage, and for a moment I thought how delightful it would be to sweep out to Tsarskoye Selo in such a style, like St. Nicholas himself. One made good speed on the frozen snow by sleigh, but the distance really was too far: it was better to go by train or motor car.

A cold, chill mist hung over the city as I set out, reminding me that Peter the Great had built his city on the marshes. I was glad to drive fast, glad that Peter had given me, as if by foresight, a closed motor car.

I got the usual salute from the soldiers at the gate, and was waved on. I didn't know the sentry's face, but he knew me, and recognized me as a permitted visitor.

I found the boy with one of his tutors, a man I didn't know, with grey hair and a fat face. Both of them looked up, surprised.

"I've come to tell you that I am going to bring you a present: a bed for your little cat," I explained. "I needn't ask if he's still here, because I can see him sprawling across your work." I smiled at the tutor. "I suppose I shouldn't be here."

"This is my German tutor," said the boy. "We only talk German together. He is not permitted to speak Russian or English to me. Perhaps he cannot talk English," he added with a wicked look.

Or not willingly, I thought, seeing the man's sour look.

There was said to be a lot of German influence at the Court, a source of much criticism. The Tsarina usually got the credit for it. But this man was some evidence of it.

"I can't bring it today, but I've come to get permission to bring it to you tomorrow, together with my servants who must carry it."

"Oh, *you* don't need permission. You are always welcome."

"The extra people with me, you know, seemed to make this trip necessary," I reminded him. "The guards could make difficulties."

He thought for a moment. "They can be stupid. Unluckily no one takes any notice of me. Still, he can tell them," and he nodded towards his tutor. "They take notice of him. Monstrously unfair, isn't it? Because *I* am the Heir." Then he chuckled. "Still, he more or less does what I tell him. Don't let's bother with him now. I'll do it later. He's *so* cross at the moment. I'm idle, you see, and that annoys him." Again he gave a chuckle. "I don't like German. No true Russian does, I tell him that."

"No wonder he's annoyed."

"Ah, well, I make it up in other ways, because I don't dislike him when he's not cross. For instance, I always let him smoke his pipe when he wants and considering the smell, I call that very good of me. When he and Papa are both at it, my goodness," and he wrinkled up his elegant little nose. "Whereas you always smell delicious, and I am sure you never smoke."

"That's true. Still, you never know."

I was amused and touched at his show of affection. "Goodbye. I must go now." I bowed to his tutor, who made a sort of grunting noise.

Alexis walked to the door with me. "My leg's not so bad," he said. "I don't walk too badly, do I?"

"Very well," I said, and meant it.

"But I don't know if I shall be allowed to go to all the celebrations in March, because Mother is ill. *I'd* like to go, but she can't bear the idea of it all," and he sighed, a strangely adult noise. "Think of it, three hundred years. I'm not much like Peter the Great, am I? He liked cats, too, though, did you know that? Napoleon hated them, but Peter the Great liked them. Well, so I've heard anyway."

There was a growl from the table, and in English, too: "Sir, you are talking too much."

"When my parents come to tea tomorrow, as they will, I'll ask Papa to give me a bed for each of my cats," he called, as he limped back to the table. "And he'll say, What, six beds! But he'll let me have them."


Dolly was waiting for me when I got back, appearing from her sitting-room with an anxious look. "Where have you been? Driving around at this hour?"

Briefly I told her.

"I think you'll never understand the ways of Russia," she said. "You never seem to know what is done and what is not. The servants don't like it, to begin with."

"Does it matter about them?"

"It does and it doesn't. Oh, you'll never understand us." She was almost wringing her hands. I had the feeling that, although she was expressing worry about me, the source of it was really something else.

"Oh, Dolly."

"Yes, you can look amused. But here you are off from home on your own, Ariadne away with that detestable Lazarev girl," she almost spat these words out, "and Peter saying that he is going to carry you off to Paris with him."

"Did he say that?" I was surprised. "He never told me." But then I thought: he promised he would give up conspiracy. This was his way of doing it.

"I think the world's gone mad," said Dolly, at her most Russian.

"Oh, Dolly," I said again.

"No, you listen to me. Things do break up, crack into little pieces and float away from each other, friends from each other, from their family, from their country. And when they do, it is never a good sign."

When I got to my own room the first person I saw was my German manservant, standing among my possessions.

"What are you doing here?" I said sharply. "You are dismissed. I do not want you."

He smiled and bowed, and very slightly shook his head.

Incredulously, I thought, he's not going to go; he's just not going.

"Leave my room at once," I ordered.

Still smiling, still managing to convey that he was not leaving my service, he edged himself out of the room, to me, now, a sinister and alarming figure.

I walked over to where he had been standing by the bed, but nothing seemed touched, nothing disarranged.

Then I saw that in fact he had been nearest to the mouth of the speaking-tube which protruded from a recess near the head of the bed. The plug-on cap, which usually hung on a cord beside it, had been inserted in the tube, so wedged in that it was now impossible to move it.

I noticed all this without understanding why he had been tampering with it. I had once heard a voice answer me from such a tube in another room, or I had thought so. Perhaps the noises that had disturbed my sleep had come from this tube by my bed. Echoes of the servants' voices, it could be.

If so, it had been a kind gesture on the part of Peter to get this tube sealed up. I touched the mouth of it, the plug of which now seemed cemented in. No more voices would be heard through this instrument.

A sort of sullen heaviness descended on the household that night. Dolly and I dined alone with the silent company of Ariadne.

Peter did not appear and I was too proud to ask Dolly if she knew where he was. Just before we had finished eating, a note from him was handed to me.

Dolly looked at me, waiting.

"Just a note from the English Club to say I shall see him later," I said.

Dolly's lips tightened. "Gambling. It is one of the curses of our family. My father would stay at the table for days on end. Alas, I play myself, but I mean to play no more."

I stayed awake all night, waiting for Peter, hoping he would come, but he did not. Of course there were no voices.

The house was very quiet, except for the soft rustle of ash in the porcelain stove. No noise came in from the great city outside. The triple depth of the winter windows with their double glass and wooden shutters kept out the noise as well as the cold. But I never was able to forget the ice and snow that covered this grey city. However hard I tried to shake off the notion, the cold seemed to be entering into me, changing me into someone I hardly knew who must face, with her perplexing husband, a strange new world.

# Chapter Thirteen

It was still dark when I woke. In my dreams I had been back at Jordansjoy, and for a moment I lay there confused. Then I remembered what was ahead of me on that day: another visit to the Summer Palace and this time bearing my gift.

I got up and dressed myself. And if we *were* to go to Paris, I might as well start to sort out my possessions.

After I had gone through my own property, selecting what I should need for Paris and what could be left behind, I went into Peter's dressing-room to do something of the same for him. I had been married long enough to know what were the small possessions he liked to carry about with him: his ivory-backed hairbrushes, a small chess set carved in jade, a leather-bound note-book (a diary, I thought) and a little leather bag with his watch and a few gold coins in it.

But as I went in I was surprised to see him lying on his bed, fully dressed but asleep. He stirred and woke as I stood there.

"So you are here. I didn't know."

He swung himself up, trying to shake off sleep. "I was very late; I didn't want to disturb you."

I came up close. "You weren't gambling at the English Club? Dolly said you were."

He laughed. "No, not gambling. Not with money, anyway."

"What do you mean?"

"Nothing." He stood, looking tired and shaky. "Rose, do you think you could make me some coffee? There is a little apparatus for doing so over there on the table in the window. I use it when I get up early."

"Yes, of course I will," I went over to the table, and lit the little spirit lamp, and poured coffee into the top of the copper pot; the bottom half already contained water. "What a secret life you lead, Peter, with your early rising and coffee making." I was half laughing, I was so relieved to see him.

"You're dressed yourself."

"Yes." I remembered why I was dressed. "Are we going to Paris, Peter? Dolly said so."

"Dolly again! But would you like to?" He was taking off his soiled and crumpled shirt and putting on a fresh one. "Can you hear the church bells?"

I listened. "Yes, I can hear something."

"It's morning." He took the coffee I handed him, and drank it. "Not light yet, though."

In midwinter it was sometimes almost noon before a grey light broke through the darkness of St. Petersburg.

"I have to go out again, Rose. You'll wait for me here?"

"Of course." I was puzzled and frightened. "But I have to deliver my present to the boy. The pagoda for the cat. I promised."

He smiled at me. "Drink some coffee and don't look so scared." He was putting on a fur-lined cloak and drawing on gloves. "We can see about your present to the Tsarevich. Don't worry. I have the arrangements in hand."

"Are we running away, Peter?"

"We are running to Paris. Would not all true Russians do

that if they could? And then we will have a stay in London. Good-bye. I'll be back soon."

"What shall I tell Dolly?" I said, as he went to the door.

"Nothing. Leave Dolly be."

When he'd gone, I stood in my own room with all the signs of packing about it, and wondered what to do with myself. I felt puzzled and lost, the two people who had warred inside me merging into one unhappy girl.

If I was going to leave St. Petersburg I knew I must say good-bye to Princess Irene. I was drinking some coffee when I heard a timid little tap at the door.

"Come in," I called.

The door opened a crack, and through the crack peered the sour face of the old Princess's woman-servant. "My Excellency wants you: you are to come."

I hesitated.

"I am to bring you with me. Come," and she turned away, confident I would follow.

Up The Red Staircase we went, she leading, bobbing along with her awkward walk. She was slightly lame on one side, from some rheumatic infection, I suspected, which must be painful.

The old Princess was in her bed, propped up on pillows, wrapped in a fur-lined cape, a pack of cards near one hand and a glass of dark brandy near the other. She had been smoking the little black cigarettes to which she was addicted. There was one now, burning itself out between her fingers.

"You'll kill yourself," I said gently, looking reprovingly from drink to cigarette.

She gave a dry, ironic laugh. "But I am dead already." I was silent. "Yes. It is all gone, that lovely, false, last life you gave me."

"I gave you nothing."

"Don't worry. I shan't ask for any more help."

Sadly I said, "I have none to give. I am empty."

"I know it: I told you how it would be with marriage. All gone. So now you are like everyone else."

She couldn't help that flash of malice.

"But I really prefer it," I said.

"Ah, you think so now, when you do not know what you have lost."

The room was stiflingly hot, with lights burning, shutters all drawn and a fire burning in an open hearth, as well as the more usual stove.

"But what I have gained is a husband," I reminded her.

She opened her eyes as wide as she could to give me a meaning look; I could see the tiny red veins threaded across the eyeballs and smell the brandy on her breath. "Then if you wish to keep him, you should look after him." She gave a groan.

I put my hand quickly on hers. "Is it the pain again?"

"No, I have no pain, that, at least, you did for me. No, no pain in the body, only in the mind."

"What do you mean?"

"You know I have my informants? I have many old friends and we meet here, a little circle of those who loved the old Russia. We have friends in the Third Bureau." I nodded. "And the bureau has a friend among us. Oh, yes, we all have our spies." She managed a grim smile. "And spies have spies upon their backs. Like lice, you know. Lady Londonderry said we all had lice."

"Yes, yes, I know, but what is it you are trying to tell me?"

"But I have told you," she said irritably. "Look after your husband. In his circle also, the bureau has a spy."

"His circle?" I said stupidly.

"Yes, madness, madness." She was rambling a little. "Can Russia do without a revolution? Yes, it must, it must. Tell your husband, tell Peter."

From behind me I heard movement. I turned round to see a tall old man pushing open the door that led, eventually, to the back staircase on to the Moyka Quay. I knew him.

"General Rahl," I said.

He ignored me and made his way over to the bed. "Irene. My old friend, my dear old friend." He looked as frail as, if not frailer than the Princess herself. I thought I saw in them and their relationship the nucleus of "the Peter Ring" which had met up here.

"Ah, my lover, my last lover and my best," came from the old lady's lips.

Perhaps he looked surprised, perhaps he did not. "She doesn't know what she's saying," I murmured.

"Irene," he said tenderly, "always your own."

By now I was alarmed by the old lady's appearance; the rouge stood out on her cheeks in streaks, beneath it she was grey.

"Love and treachery," she said clearly. "Remember, Rose, love betrays."

Her head fell back on the pillow.

Ignoring General Rahl's protests, I took her wrist. I could feel no pulse. I stood there for a second, holding her hand. The old soldier, tears now beginning to run down his face and into his beard, the servant wailing on her knees, a cigarette still burning on the counterpane, formed a macabre picture.

"I'll tell Madame Denisov," I said abruptly. "She must call a doctor."

I ran down The Red Staircase, through the upper halls and down the main staircase to Dolly's room. She had just finished dressing, and when I flung the news at her, she gave a little scream.

"How did it happen? How did you come to be there?"

"She sent for me. We did talk for a little, then she just collapsed, Dolly."

"Oh, but I should have been there." Tears were already rolling down her cheeks. In spite of all she had said in the past, I knew it was genuine grief.

"It was very quick, or I would have sent for you," I said apologetically. "As it is, I have come at once."

"I must go to her. She must not be left alone, not in death."

"General Rahl is there. Can I help?"

"No, no." Her hands were trembling. "I will give all the

necessary orders. But you could tell Ariadne for me." And she hurried away.


I went then to tell Ariadne. How can we now go to Paris? I thought.

As Dolly hurried up the great staircase, Ariadne appeared at her own door to ask what the noise was all about. "Is it Aunt Irene?" she asked. I nodded to her without speaking. It was obvious that some quarrel had taken place between Dolly and Ariadne, because through Dolly's upward rush I heard her call:

"Now, we shall have an end to your foolishness, miss. *Now,* I shall get you out of Russia."

As I came up to Ariadne, I said, "What did your mother mean?"

Sullenly Ariadne said, "I suppose that we couldn't leave Russia while my great-aunt remained alive."

"Certainly *we* seem to be leaving," I said. "Peter is taking me to Paris."

"What? I don't believe it. Never. He'd never leave Russia. He couldn't do it. Doesn't he remember what happened to Herzen and to Bakunin? Out of Russia he would have no more credit."

"I don't know exactly what it is you are saying, Ariadne," I said coldly, "but whatever it is, you have said far too much." I pushed her into her room, closed the door and stood with my back against it. "Now, explain yourself."

Ariadne was quite silent.

"Tell me why you left the Smolny Institute. Tell me really why. Was it because you and Marisia Lazarev had friends who were more than liberal in feeling, who were revolutionaries?"

"That was partly it." She shrugged. "But perhaps they *suspected* more than they could prove. Of that side of things they really knew very little. Marisia is so clever."

I pressed her. "Then what? What else was there? Your mother says you fell in love. With one of the tutors there?"

"No, with Marisia, of course. Who else?"

I stared at her.

"We were all in love with her, but I was the one she chose."

"Do you mean what you say?"

"Yes. She calls me her little wife."

"She's a monster," I said.

"Oh, don't be silly, Rose. Do you suppose she is the first I loved? What do you think we thought about at the Smolny, shut up there for ever as we were? Not lessons, I assure you."

"I see," I said slowly.

"I don't suppose you do. I could have loved you, too, Rose." She gave me a sideways glance. "And someone, you see, had to make sure of you once we had got you here."

I couldn't say anything to her.

"I do truly like you, Rose. I've never pretended. But we had to be *sure* of you, don't you see?"

"What do you mean, sure of me? You were sure of me: I was doing what your mother brought me here to do—she pretended it was only to help with you, but I soon learned it was really to use what powers I had to help the Tsarevich."

"You really still think that? You think Peter Alexandrov wants that? Why he knew of you from Prince Michael Melikov in London and got Dolly to invite you here? But not to save anyone."

"Don't accuse Peter of anything to me," I said loudly. "He is my husband."

"He is one of us."

"He is a good, kind, gentle man. He let me keep my hare. Don't you remember the white hare?"

"Your hare," said Ariadne contemptuously. "Have you ever been to see that hare? Did you ever go and look for it again? I expect its neck was broken within a minute of its being taken downstairs."

"I don't believe you." I was almost shouting.

"Go and look then." She gave me a push towards the door; she was as angry with me as I was with her.

I had been but once before, and that recently with Peter, in the deepest regions of the Denisov house, when I suppose I expected it to be like the kitchen regions of any English or Scottish town house: it was not. Instead of the labyrinth of narrow passage-ways and pantries and kitchens and servants' halls with which I was familiar, I saw a stranger scene. The room which was everything—kitchen, wine-cellar, buttery and servants' dormitory (for I saw several slumbering figures)—was dimly lighted and over-hot. I was noticed, I suppose, as I stood there, but no one spoke to me.

I knew at that moment that my little white hare was not here. How stupid I had been to believe in that fantasy for one moment.

I stood there with the nasty taste of deception in my mouth. Automatically, and without taking conscious thought, I went down the short passage to the stairwell and went into the room Peter and I had visited before.

It was empty of people. The Chinese pagoda was gone. So was my German servant, and so was Mr. Jakob. In what passed for daylight in these subterranean regions I saw a small room with a large, plain wooden table surrounded by upright chairs.

Against one wall was one of those large, hooded leather chairs in which the door-man used to sit in great houses. On the wall above was an array of the mouth-pieces of those allegedly disused speaking-tubes, set in rows of four, one above the other, with the names of the rooms to which they led written by them. It was quite true that most of these speaking-tubes looked as if the dust of decades were lodged in them, but one or two were bright, as if handled recently. Above one such I read, in ancient Russian script, The French Room.

Surely my bedroom was the French Room?

I think I knew then that some of the whispers and sibilant calls of my name had come through this tube. The voice had been real, not just imagination. And if this were so, then that first voice I had heard had been real also, and not imagination.

There was something about this room which stank of quiet talk, of company.

Truly this house *was* like Russia itself, with extreme conservatism in the attics and anarchy in the basement.

I turned and went back upstairs. I was sorting out the facts of betrayal in my mind. I went straight to my own room, the so-called French Room, walked through it and into my husband's dressing-room.

On his table was the leather-bound book I had called his diary. It was locked, but without hesitation I picked up a paper-knife from among the litter and ripped it open.

It was not a diary, but what you might call an *aide-mémoire:* a list of names (members of his group, I supposed), a list of place names, which I took to be of safe meeting-places, and then a series of cryptic notes, probably of meetings or plans for the future. These I could not make much of. But I studied the list of names, beside which the occupations were listed. Doctors, lawyers, writers, soldiers and gentlemen of leisure, this was the list. One or two men were called artisans or shopkeepers. There was a sprinkling of students. A few were women. I saw Marisia's name among them, but not Ariadne's. She had been one of those women "used," I thought, but not fully trusted. Of this motley group of anarchists, Peter had hoped to make a revolution. I could imagine the excited, feverish plans these people had made. At once intelligent and dedicated, yet also unrealistic, they were desperate and dangerous.

At the end of this book of Peter's were many closely written pages. They were headed: "Catechism of a Revolutionist."

I took the book to our room, sat down and read it through. There was much to read, for the catechism was split into sections and then subdivided again. Whether it was Peter's own composition or not, I did not know, but the writing was his, and it was on the principles I read here he had organized his life.

> The mechanism of the organization is concealed from idle eyes, and therefore the whole range of contacts and all the activities of the cell are kept secret from everybody.
> Members undertake specialized duties in accordance with their social class.
> The left hand shall never know what the right hand does: this is a general principle.

With appalled eyes I read:

> Conditions necessary for a cell to commence activities:
> The infiltration of clever men into affairs.
> A knowledge of the town gossips, clubs, etc.
> Influence of high-ranking persons through their womenfolk.

This last sentence, about women, had been underlined. I couldn't stop reading, although every word was an act of destruction to me and of me.

"The revolutionary is a dedicated man," Peter had written, as if chiding himself. "He has no interests of his own, no feelings, no attachments, no belongings. He is not a revolutionary if he feels pity for anything in this world . . . all the worse for him if he loves."

Does he love? I asked myself. Can Peter love?

The last section I read was, for me, the most painful of all. This section was headed "Those We Must Manipulate."

The sixth category was that of women. "We must use these as instruments, play on their weaknesses, use their affections, for thus we may enter circles otherwise closed to us, even into that innermost circle of all, i.e., the Imperial family."

I read those last words again. I suppose I shall never forget them. I knew well what it meant to me: I was a woman who had been "used," my affections had been manipulated, and I had, indeed, entered "that innermost circle of all."

I raised my head from the page and tried to see the whole picture. I had been brought to Russia by Peter's will; he had heard of my gift from the Misses Gowrie. In this arrangement, Prince Michael Melikov had been his London agent. I suspected that it was he who had deliberately embroiled Patrick and contrived the breaking-off of our engagement, thus freeing me for Russia. I no longer believed that anything had happened to me by chance. All of it had been contrived. Even, and most of all, my marriage, by which I was chained to the revolution. But for my marriage, I might have gone off again with Patrick.

Another and even more terrible thought was shaping itself at the back of my mind when I heard a timid knock at the door.

Ariadne came in.

"Oh, Rose, I'm so sorry for all those things that I said. I lost my temper."

"I know you did."

"You'll forgive . . ." Then her gaze fell on what I was reading. "Oh, Rose, what have you done?" She sounded frightened.

"You see for yourself." I threw the book away from me and stood up. "Poor girl, I am sorry for you. You have been as thoroughly manipulated as I have been myself. Tell me what you think of your Uncle Peter?"

Her face came to life. "He is my star."

"A dark star. Oh, Ariadne, tell me about Laure Le Brun. There is something to tell, isn't there? I didn't *imagine* that she was murdered in this house. It was only too true."

"One must not mind violence if it serves the revolution," faltered Ariadne.

"She discovered something that was dangerous, didn't she? And it was you who killed her? She trusted you. *You*, Ariadne, she would let you into her room when she felt ill. I believe she loved you, poor Laure."

Ariadne was shaking, and she began to cry, but I felt no pity. "But I've been used, too, Ariadne, so I can't waste emotion on you. I must think of what *I* have done. What present is it that I have got ready for Tsarskoye Selo?"

Ariadne stopped crying and stared at me. "What do you mean, Rose?"

"What is its real purpose, this present? What does it contain? And how deeply have I been involved? I ordered it, apparently of my own free will. I went to Moscow to bring back Mr. Jakob. Did he bring explosives with him? Was that his real purpose in coming?"

"I don't know," she whispered.

Nor did I, but I was making a terrible guess. A bomb, one planned to explode when the mother, father and child were all taking tea together. That was what I had fetched Mr. Jakob from Moscow for. It was I who had gone to fetch him and I who had given him the money. I had thought of myself as bringing life to that child, but really it had, all along, been planned that I should be the bringer of death.

I had made my decision. "I shall have to stop that plan. The Chinese pagoda shall never be delivered."

Then I saw Ariadne's face. "What is it you know, Ariadne?"

She didn't answer; I took her by the shoulders and shook her. "Tell me, I order you."

"Can't you guess?"

I thought of that empty room below, with only the smell of paint remaining to hint of the pagoda.

She saw I understood. "Yes," she whispered, half in triumph, half in terrible fear, "you are too late. Your present is already on the way."

I almost threw her from me.

"Where are you going, Rose?"

I didn't answer, but hurried to the door, and started to run down the stairs.

"Rose, I shall tell Peter," called Ariadne after me.

In the coach-house which gave on to Moyka Street I found my car. My husband's car was still there, but Dolly's was out. I got into my own car, and ignoring the anxious pleas of the mechanics who were cleaning it, I released the brake and drove away.

It was daylight now, and I could hear a clock striking the hour: midday. I had five hours.

At the corner, when I was slowing down to thread my car

into the stream of carts and carriages making their way out of the city, I saw Edward Lacey.

He saw me, and waved to me to stop.

"I've just heard the news about the old lady, and I'm calling on Dolly to see what I can do to help. Where are you off to?"

"I'm going out to Tsarskoye Selo," I said deliberately. "Something terrible will happen there if I don't get there in time to stop it."

His features seemed to sharpen. "Why, Rose . . ."

I interrupted him. "I know now what a good friend you have been to me and Patrick. If you see Patrick, tell him that I got it all wrong. Just say that."

And before he could stop me, I drove away.

A sky the colour of pewter, grey roads, with fresh fallen snow on the roofs, were what I remember of the drive. Every so often I passed a peasant cart, jogging back home from market. There were very few cars or carriages on the road, and those there were I easily overtook.

I thanked whatever gods had given me the chance to learn to drive. (It was Peter, Peter, who encouraged you, a hard little voice said inside me. He was both for me, and against me.)

Very soon I saw the roofs of the palaces of Tsarskoye Selo appearing through the trees. To my relief all appeared peaceful and quiet. I must be in time.

The soldiers let me through with cheerful smiles. They knew my face. But I had to put a question to them, and while I was wondering how to phrase my query so that I did not alarm them, one of the men poked his head into my car and with a broad, peasant's grin said:

"Your servants have gone inside, Excellency. I saw them myself, and gave them a wave."

"How long ago?" I said. So my question was answered. Jakob and the German had arrived.

He looked vague. Time as such meant little to him. "One hour, or half that, perhaps. Long enough for me who had just come on duty to get cold feet."

418    *Gwendoline Butler*

Not so very long, then, I thought, because in this climate the body temperature dropped rapidly.

"Where did they go?"

The young soldier looked surprised, and then pointed. "Why, to where the Tsarevich is. They were taking him your present as we were instructed to expect. Fair bent their backs, it did, too," and he laughed.

"Can I leave my car here?" I asked. "Just inside the gate?" I could see Dolly's car there already, so I knew how Jakob and his companion had travelled.

"Yes, I'll watch it," he said with childlike pleasure. "How beautifully it shines. So does the other one. I can see my face in both. What it is to be rich."

I walked away, trying to move with unconcern. Everything must look normal, and no one must be put on the alert by my behaviour.

If I could remove any explosive device concealed in the pagoda without anyone seeing me, I might still save Peter and, incidentally, myself. Because who would believe me innocent after my trip to Moscow?

As I walked towards my usual entrance I could see bleakly the alternatives that confronted me. The explosion might take place at any minute, before I could stop it. That was the first and most likely happening. My ears were strained for the noise even as I walked.

Secondly, the whole device might blow up in my hands the minute I touched it, taking me with it. This also seemed appallingly likely.

The best I could hope for was to get away with the explosive and throw it away somewhere in the snow-covered countryside.

It was no use planning: I had come to that decision as I drove out. I had to meet the situation as it unfolded before me and deal with it as best I could.

For a moment I considered going back to the gate and telling the sentries. But I knew what would happen: they would question me slowly, send for someone in higher authority to question me again, and by that time anything could happen.

All my senses seemed sharpened. Behind me I could hear the ring of the sentry's boots on the iron-clad earth; I could smell the smoke from the chimneys of the palaces that lay scattered across the park; I could even smell something that seemed to emanate from my own body, and it smelt like fear.

There was a shout from behind me and I swung round to see one of the young soldiers lumbering towards me, a gun in his hands.

"Stop, or I fire!"

I stood absolutely still, terrified. I didn't know what the soldier had discovered, or what this command meant.

He was laughing as he ran. I thought how terrible to be my friend one minute, as I passed his sentry post, and then to rush at me ready to shoot, all grins. It seemed to me absolutely in line with what I had seen of the Russian character that it should be so.

"What is it?" I managed to say in a cool voice.

He waved the gun. "The young Heir's toy. He was playing soldiers with us, and he left it behind. Will you give it to him?" I suppose he saw my pallor then. "I hope I didn't frighten you, Excellency. Just a joke, you know."

I accepted the toy. "Of course," I said. "Only a joke. I knew that." But I also knew that if I had run or screamed, he might very well have shot me in earnest. Things were balanced very finely in Russia, on a knife edge. By now I could have been dead. One incautious movement to cause him alarm and a shot would have rung out.

With an appearance of calm, I walked on, but I was badly shaken.

When I got inside the palace there was no one about. I was standing in a small lower hall from which a flight of stairs led to the boy's room. It was a side entrance with which I was thoroughly familiar and it was often deserted in this way.

Now I looked at the gun; it was manifestly a toy, a good

quality one, of German make probably, but still clearly a little carved rifle made of wood. But the bayonet at the end was of sharp metal.

I went quietly up the staircase. It led to an upper hall lined with tall cabinets filled with Chinese porcelain. I was young and ignorant then and thought the china, the figures and bowls and vases, ugly. But I had no doubt they were priceless.

I was walking quietly, but very fast, when I saw a man standing in the recess between two great cabinets. I knew him at once for my German servant.

He was standing, quite composed, as if he had every right to be there. So unobtrusive and natural was his appearance that if I hadn't been expecting him I might have ignored him.

He blocked my way. I knew I had to get past.

As yet he had not seen me. He was strong and determined. I had one advantage: he had not seen me, nor did he expect to see me. But I had expected him.

I took one soft pace forward. He had muscle, but inside me was a consuming anger.

Quiet as I was, all the same some noise must have alerted him, because he came out of his hiding-place and saw me.

He looked surprised, and I, because I was very, very angry, smiled at him.

He understood my smile, because his movement towards me was unmistakably one of menace. He knew why I had arrived.

"Touch me and I'll scream," I said. I drew the gun in an automatic gesture of protection.

Just for a moment it halted him, but he soon saw it was no more than a toy. I had underestimated him. One hand was clapped across my mouth and the other got a stranglehold on my throat and started to squeeze. He pressed his body hard against mine, thick sinewy limbs engaging mine, and the smell of old, tired sweat and tobacco. His weight pushed me backwards. I think he was prepared to kill me.

The world about me was going black, and I was gasping, choking, drowning. It was in a desperate attempt to get free that I brought the toy rifle up and plunged the point of the bayonet into his side. I felt it go in.

His eyes opened wide, he looked surprised, then the pressure eased on my throat, his hands dropped away and he fell to the ground.

I thought he might even be dead. Perhaps I had killed him.

But I didn't stay to check, because in terms of what I was doing this was only an interim engagement.

At the end of the corridor were the boy's apartments. There was no sailor on duty outside. He was probably out walking with his young master and the tutor.

I guessed what Mr. Jakob and the German servant had planned. Probably from other sources than I they knew the ways of the palace, but from me, and transmitted through Peter, they knew of the afternoon tea-parties when the parents visited their precious son. The present I had planned so innocently for the boy, the little Chinese pagoda, was to contain an explosive to be ignited by a length of fuse, so that Jakob and the German could be gone before it went off. What with the tutor's pipe and the Tsar's cigarette, the smell of the smouldering fuse would be masked.

I opened the door. Inside, the room was empty of boy, tutor and animals. But my present, the Chinese pagoda, a gleaming gold and red, stood in a window enclosure.

Kneeling before it was the man Jakob. He was in the act of replacing a wooden panel in the base of the cat-bed. Above was the quilted cushion, and rising above that, the pretty structure of curving roofs and bells.

I think I hated him as much as anything for turning such an enchanting object into one of horror.

He looked up and saw me, and rose slowly to his feet, dusting down his hands. His face seemed more sallow and pinched than ever.

"Putting the finishing touches?" I said. "I suppose it wasn't safe to do that as you travelled. You used my sister-in-law's car, I presume?"

I suppose it was stupid to show my hatred so clearly, but I couldn't stop myself. Besides, there was a streak of blood on my skirt.

"I didn't know who you were before," he said. "I know now." His eyes took in the blood-stain.

"Yes. In his own way and in his own good time, my husband lied to us both."

"No lies," he said proudly. "Not to me. I do not expect the truth. Only to be given a task." And he couldn't stop himself looking at the cat-bed. "So you have turned traitor?"

I didn't answer, my whole mind focussed on what to do next. But to whom was I a traitor? Myself? My husband? Or to the cause of anarchy to which Peter belonged? Jakob would kill me if he had to. I could see it in his face.

"You can't kill me and leave my body here," I said. "There is already a dead man outside. The place would at once be searched, and the bomb found, even if you got clean away. Your whole plan is already wrecked."

"In an hour the boy and his tutor will be back from their walk," he said in his prim little voice. "In another hour after that his parents will arrive, and then my bomb will go off. The fuse is already lit. A clumsy device, but quite effective. I shall be out of here, and so will you." From his pocket he drew a revolver and pointed it at me. "You do not think I would come into this rat's nest without some protection."

"You can't shoot me, you can't afford to. I've told you that. The noise, a scream from me—and someone will come running. I'm surprised we've been alone so long."

"Even in this place people can be bribed. Or perhaps I should say in this place above all."

I thought he would shoot me, he was ruthless enough. I was frightened; I didn't want to die. But you can always pretend.

He walked straight to me and poked the gun in my chest. In an instinctive and spontaneous movement, I brought my arms up and put them round him so that we seemed to embrace.

It was probably the only gesture I could have made that could surprise him. I think he was not used to being close to women. I felt it in the instinctive stiffening of his body.

Then I saw his eyes widen and lose focus, his mouth drew itself into a grimace, and his breathing altered. I could see his yellow, crooked teeth: sure token of a sick childhood. No wonder his skin was so sallow.

The hand holding the gun went limp. Moving my arms down, I took both his hands in mine. They were deadly cold.

"Let the gun fall," I said. I think he had no choice but to obey. "There is pain like cramp around your heart, isn't there? Don't answer. I know. I feel it in my own hands." He stared at me balefully, speechless. "I feel as though I am giving you warmth now. Take it from me. The pain is passing now. No, don't try to speak."

He was almost leaning against me. I was surprised how light and frail he felt.

"You've had that pain in the past and know all about it. Now it's gone, but it will come again. And again."

In slow, slurred words, he said, "I don't fear to die."

"You don't fear death, but the dying you do fear. Of course you do. I eased the pain now. That can happen sometimes. I can do nothing about the death, but the dying I can help. I promise I'll make a bargain with you: remove your explosive, and I will help you die."

He looked at me like an animal that has been badly whipped and now sees a show of love being offered: he could hardly believe it.

Moved by compassion, I wiped the sweat from his forehead and mouth with my handkerchief. How could I judge from what a pain of neglected, wretched growing-up, from what depths of misery and poverty, both his sickness and politics had come?

"I'll help you," I repeated. Not without urgency, and with one eye on the pagoda.

The room was very quiet, for the double windows and the heavy silk curtains prevented any noise from outside getting in.

"So there is a God, after all," I heard him say. "We are not left alone in the universe, to make our own way. Help can come."

"Then you will remove the explosive," I said. "If you feel like that, then you *must*. Now. Quickly. And we will leave." I stood back from him and bent down to pick up the gun, but I didn't threaten him with it. Threats were now of no consequence. "Come, Jakob," I urged.

For answer, he held out his hands: they trembled without stopping.

"Too dangerous?" I said. "You mean you couldn't do it? Physically, you can't touch the thing? I'll do it then. Show me what to do."

I went over to the Chinese pagoda. At the base a panel of wood slid out. Once it had been screwed into position, but these screws had been removed so that the piece of wood moved at a touch. The job had been neatly done.

I pulled the panel out. Then I looked back at Jakob. "Please help me," I said.

"I no longer know how to act," he muttered. "You have destroyed my faith. You have taken away what I did have, but what have you left me in its place?"

In front of me, I could see a small, dark metal box resting on the floor of the toy pagoda. It was taped into position and from it led a long snake of what looked like narrow cord dipped in wax. One end of this was already alight and smouldering. I think I knew as I looked at it, though it had been carefully and neatly done, that it was the work of someone who had learnt about explosives from books and not from practical experience.

It made it all the more dangerous.

From the edge of the box a pale grey sort of paste seemed to be oozing. It had an unhealthy sheen on it.

Gritting my teeth, I put my hand on the burning cord and

pressed it down. But it smouldered on grimly. Whatever oil
or wax it had been treated with, it was efficient. I stood up
and looked round for a knife or a pair of scissors. In my field
of vision there was the boy's work table and the tutor's desk.

Jakob moved awkwardly over to the table, picked a penknife off the blotter and came over to where I stood. He
pushed me aside, cut the cord, wrenched the box from its position, and held the explosive to his breast. I wondered which
would explode first, his labouring, wounded heart, or the
bomb.

Before we left, I bent down and slid the painted panel into
its place. Perhaps, after all, the boy could enjoy his toy.

If my body had followed its instincts, I would have rushed
screaming from Jakob and his burden. As it was, we walked
sedately and side by side all the way I had come. I was even
able to notice that the German had gone.

"Thank God, I didn't kill him after all," I breathed. But he
represented another danger. Perhaps he was waiting for me
somewhere.

"No," said Jakob with contempt. "He will save himself. If
he can walk, he will survive."

No love lost there, I thought, and was glad, because if I
didn't know quite what I felt about Jakob, I was quite certain
that I hated the German.

To my amazement, the guards saw us through politely,
even assisting me into my car, although what with the blood
on my skirt and the look of death on Jakob's face, we must
have looked a strange couple.

So no one stopped us leaving, or even seemed much interested. I drove slowly for a few hundred yards, and then
stopped the car in the protection of a belt of trees.

"Your husband, does he . . .?" began Jakob.

"No, I didn't tell him where I was going," I said. "But I expect he knows by now."

"Then he will follow."

"Yes, I have thought of that, too." I started the car again. "The first and most important thing is to get rid of that box you are holding."

"Throw it away. Best of all ways, into water," said Jakob shortly, not wasting a word. His breathing was bad.

Everywhere in this part of Russia were lakes and water. I knew I had only to drive on and I would come to one of the canals that cut across this stretch of country.

I passed a peasant cart drawn by a donkey, and then a boy with a flock of geese. Ahead I saw the dull sheen of ice. I drove towards it. At first it seemed close, but although I drove fast, I never seemed to get very much nearer. Distances are deceptive in the snow.

"Not long now," I said reassuringly to Jakob, although heaven knows, I was sick with fear myself.

He didn't answer directly, but presently I heard him mutter: "So it is over at last," and he gave a long, deep sigh.

It may be for you, I thought, keeping my eyes on the road, but for me it is only just beginning.

On these flat roads it was possible to be aware of movement both ahead and behind for some distance. I now became aware that there was a motor car behind me and another in front driving towards me. A little prickle of alarm stirred in me.

Beside me, Jakob was quiet, still clutching his terrible burden. It could go off at any moment, but I had been travelling fast and I was now running parallel with the frozen canal which lay at the bottom of a steep slope so that as I drove I could look down on the frozen surface. There were no houses near, no railway line, and such traffic as might pass on the road at the time of the explosion would surely be protected by the slope? I hoped to be well away myself. It seemed an ideal spot to dump the bomb.

I stopped the motor car and turned to Jakob. He was lying back in his corner with his eyes closed.

"Jakob," I said, "wake up."

He didn't answer. He was quite dead. I had been driving

with a dead man beside me. But I had kept my promise to him. Without being aware of the moment of its happening, I had given him a quiet death.

I took the metal box from his hands, which still held it loosely, and got out of the car. The bank of snow before me had tracks in it, grey furrows in the snow, leading to rugged areas on the ice, where the peasants had broken the ice to fish and where the ice had frozen over again, more irregular and thicker than before, like the crust on a wound. I could have left the explosive in the car and let the whole thing blow up, taking Jakob's body with it, but I felt as though I had a promise to keep to him now as well as to myself.

Skim the box along the ice, like curling at home in Scotland, and run, I advised myself.

I scrambled down the bank towards the canal, the soft fur edging my cloak dragged in the snow, but the snow was dry and floated away like powder. It was very cold, though, and I could feel the chill striking through me.

I looked back at the safety of my motor car behind me and saw another motor stopping a few yards from it. This was the car that had come on the same road from Tsarskoye Selo. Brief as my glance was before I began to run, I knew the shape.

My cloak tripped me and I stumbled, but I managed to right myself before running on. But it had slowed me down.

"Rose," a voice behind me called. Peter's voice.

I ran on, scrambling over the snow to reach the frozen surface of the canal.

"Rose, do stop. I beg you."

But the time for begging me is over, Peter, I thought. He was close behind me now, but I was on the ice, slipping and slithering away from the bank.

I thought I could hear another voice hailing us from the road, and was even conscious of seeing movement there.

Peter caught up with me and seized my arm as I threw the box away from me with all my strength to rest in the centre of the frozen canal.

I was breathless; I could feel my heart banging in my chest. Peter had a firm grip on my arm; I tried to draw free, but my strength was gone. I stood there, taking in the air in great, choking gulps.

"Oh, Rose," said Peter, "in the end, I didn't, I couldn't—"

Whatever he was going to say he could not finish. Perhaps the force of my throw had detonated the explosive, perhaps I had always miscalculated the time I had in hand. There was a blue-white flash and a crack of noise in my ears that deafened them.

Peter threw me to the ice, himself on top of me.

After the whip-crack of sound and the flash came a roar that rumbled on and on in my ears while the world vibrated around me. For a moment I could neither see nor hear anything except the energies that howled around me. I was caught up in the force, whirling in space with it. Then the noise and movement stopped. I could hear a singing in my ears, then this died away, too. I thought: an explosion like this could have brought down the whole palace.

I opened my eyes. I was surprised to see that road, bank and canal were still there. But the ice was tilting, slipping away beneath our feet. A great hole had opened in the ice and it was cracking all around us.

The piece beneath us gave and we were in the water. I felt the deadly cold sucking at me and pulling at my skirt. But there was a hard ridge of ice by Peter's right arm where the peasants had repeatedly cut the ice and it had repeatedly frozen again. He had a grip on this and with the other arm he supported me. Blood was running down his face, and the skin of his cheek was flapping, a bit of metal from the bomb was stuck in it. But even as the blood welled out, it froze.

I could hear the ice whispering and cracking as it reacted to the tension of the explosion. "The ice is breaking up," I said. I think I said it aloud, I don't know. "We shall drown together. And I don't really mind." Aloud or in my heart, does it matter how I said it?

A shout came echoing across the ice: "Hang on!"

The edge of a thick tweed cloak was thrown over the edge of the ice. "Grab it and I'll pull you in towards me."

Another voice was calling behind me, but in the confusion of the moment everything was incoherence and I could make nothing out. Yet I knew it was Patrick holding out the cloak.

In Peter's eyes I read this knowledge, too. He had heard and understood. He supported me while I took hold of the cloak and felt myself slowly, slowly being hauled out of the water, towards the firmer ice.

I turned round to look at Peter. I saw his lips frame one word: "Love," he whispered. "Love."

Then he let his hand slip away and slowly sank back into the water. Horrified, I could only stare. A thick veil of ice was already coating him, blinding him and smoothing out his features. He was turning into an iceman before my eyes.


Patrick and Edward Lacey drove with me to the Denisov house through the dusk. I was wrapped in Edward's travelling cloak. Patrick drove me in Edward's car, in which they had rushed out from St. Petersburg. Peter's car we left by the roadside. I never saw it again. My own car with its dead burden was driven to St. Petersburg by Edward. I remember very little of all this.

Little was said between Patrick and me on that drive. I felt light-headed and sleepy, not really rational. I remember Patrick looking at me with anxiety as he drove. I remember Dolly's face as she received me. Then I remember voices talking over my head as I lay in bed, and a pain in my chest and a mounting fever.

The words "pleurisy" and "pneumonia" floated on a cloud above me. Speechless, I hid gladly in the cocoon of my illness.

But I was strong, and healthy, and very young. I soon recovered. Patrick and Edward had gone from St. Petersburg by then, leaving me letters to read when I was well enough. I kept Patrick's close to me, and read it often.

Owing to the good offices of General Rahl and his long
friendship with the Princess Irene Drutsko, the whole affair
of Peter Alexandrov was hushed up. He had drowned in an
"accident." Nothing was said about Jakob or his death, but I
learnt he had been given a decent funeral in Moscow. I never
heard word of my German servant again, and as far as I
know Dolly never saw her car again either. I dare say there
was much that it suited General Rahl to bury with Peter, too.

Ariadne was sent away; Marisia Lazarev had left Russia.

Two months later, Dolly Denisov and I took our part in the
great commemorative ceremonies for the Tercentenary of
the Romanov dynasty. Our part was a quiet one as we were
both in mourning. We went to none of the glittering receptions and balls in St. Petersburg, but we attended the service
of thanksgiving at the Kazan Cathedral. The Tsar and Tsarina both were present. It was the only function where *She* was
seen.

It had been a gay season in St. Petersburg. Every night
sleigh-bells and music had sounded in the air. By not going
out, Dolly and I had missed a black and white ball, a series of
tableaux at the British Embassy, a Greek mythology ball at
Princess Obolensky's and an endless party at the Orlovs
which lasted, so the gossips said and the host swore, for two
weeks.

Yes, for these two months St. Petersburg had been the gay-
est city in Europe. But I knew what lay behind it.

As we sat together in the Kazan Cathedral, Dolly and I understood each other.

"I had so hoped there might be a child to keep you with
me," murmured Dolly.

I shook my head.

"No, no hope of that, I know. And next week you will be
off. After all, you were only here your promised year." Under the cover of the huge golden Order of Service which she
was holding, she gripped my hand.

"I shall miss you," I said.

"It's right you should go. You have a chance of a happy life with your Patrick.

Edward Lacey had helped to smooth things for Patrick. Of course, Patrick had left the Army, but a new career was opening up for him in the City of London. Edward had friends in high places. From hints Patrick had given me I guessed that I was correct in thinking that Edward Lacey had been sent here as a secret observer of events in Russia. He had always known about Peter Alexandrov. So, too, had the Third Bureau, but they were an incompetent, divided lot.

"And where is Ariadne now?" I asked. Incense was floating over the whole great interior of the cathedral, aglitter with the jewels of the ladies and rich with the colour of the uniforms.

"She has gone to Geneva. She will study to be a doctor. And when you think how she loved clothes and frivolities, such a life will be punishment enough for a girl of her sort. My own marriage was so unhappy, my husband drank and gambled his way to death. I thought he represented all the worst traits of our class and race." Dolly sighed. "Still, she is out of Russia. Which is what I always wanted. I fear what will happen to us here. But I have had to make one concession."

"Oh, what is that?"

"I have had to promise that, in the event of a general war or a civil war, she comes back."

Our eyes met. I suppose we both assessed the situation more shrewdly than most of the people sitting around us.

"And what about you, dear Dolly?"

"Oh, I shall stay," she said quietly. "I always intended that I should." She took up the Order of Service and studied it. "Now, let me see, this must be the procession of the Grand Duke Cyril passing us now."

I had never admired her more.